ciara
geraghty
saving
grace

HODDER

First published in Ireland in 2008 by Hachette Books Ireland
First published in the UK in 2008 by Hodder & Stoughton
An Hachette UK company

First published in paperback in 2009

3

A CIP catalogue record for this title is available from the British Library

B format paperback ISBN 978 0 340 97654 8
A format paperback ISBN 978 0 340 92023 7

Typeset in Plantin Light by Hewer Text UK Ltd, Edinburgh
Printed and bound in the UK by CPI Mackays, Chatham ME5 8TD

Hodder & Stoughton policy is to use papers that are natural, renewable
and recyclable products and made from wood grown in sustainable forests.
The logging and manufacturing processes are expected to conform
to the environmental regulations of the country of origin.

Hodder & Stoughton Ltd
338 Euston Rd
London
NW1 3 BH

www.hodder.co.uk

For my sister Niamh, who told me I could

Praise for *Saving Grace*

'Move over Marian, it's Ciara . . . Impressive and highly
entertaining [with] one of the most authentic female
characters I've read in women's fiction for a long time'
Irish Independent

'So funny and so much fun, it's impossible to believe it's
Geraghty's first . . . Warm, moving and hilarious'
Evening Herald

'Perfect pace and plenty of banter help Geraghty's debut
hit the right balance between hilariously funny and poignant
. . . Accessible and charming.' *Image*

'A touching story of a flawed but loveable heroine'
U magazine

'This novel bubbles along. I loved it . . . Reading the book
in a café, I laughed out loud. I cried, too. This Dublin writer
is a name to watch'
Irish Examiner

Ciara Geraghty lives in north County Dublin with her husband and three children.
Saving Grace is her first novel.

PROLOGUE

Spain, April 2004

The weather has changed.

Still hot but now with a wind that lifts skirts and rattles glasses across tables. The heat bears down as the day gains. Even the wind is hot today. Like air blown from shopfronts. Later, the rains come, falling in straight lines.

It is half past four in the afternoon.

The four of us take to the bar that has become our local since we arrived. Inside, it is dark and smells of the dried meat that hangs from hooks over the counter. We take our beers and bowls of olives outside and sit in the scant shade offered by the awning that sags and gapes. We drink too many beers, one after the other, and quickly grow tired of beating a path to the bar. We switch to bottles of white wine, which we drink in long glasses filled to the top with ice. Dinnertime comes and goes. We graze on nuts and flavourless crisps that we smother with salt.

Closing time is informal. The barman, short and silent, steps outside, locks the door and nods at us as he walks away, whistling a tune I don't recognise.

We walk back along the beach towards the apartment. The wind whips the water like cream and waves crash and bang against sand as yellow as mustard. We sing songs and bump and bang against each other, our laughing drowned in the roar of the ocean. The sea is a wild animal, challenging me.

I am hot and I know the water will be cool. My dress is over my head and thrown on the sand before anyone notices I am gone. I kick my sandals into the sand and run towards the white light of the waves. I can hear them shouting behind me but I am laughing and with the wind rushing around my head, their voices seem far away now, like echoes. I reach the shoreline and let the water rush at my feet, my arms outstretched. It snakes up to my thighs before the first wave comes. It crests in front of me. A dark wall. I can feel the pull and the suck of it, bringing me out to where I can no longer stand. The beach seems far away now. I can't see the others. My shouts drown in the roar of the water.

I swim towards the shore, tiring quickly, making no headway. Panic pushes at me and I open my mouth, water pouring in. I am coughing and choking and gagging on the salt.

Underwater, it is hard to know which way is up.

Then there are arms around me, pushing me up and I re-surface, breathing like it's for the first time.

'It's OK, you're all right, I've got you.' Patrick's voice is near and I reach for it with both hands.

'That way,' he says. 'Swim that way. As hard as you can.' I can make out the words but I can't see him in this watery darkness. His hands under my arms are rough, comforting. His breath is jagged, coming in bursts. I bend my head and pull at the water, my legs rigid and kicking.

I don't remember his hands leaving me. I am nearly there and can make out two shadowy silhoeuttes on the beach. A wave lifts me, spitting me onto the sand where I lie, heaving and coughing. Hands are warm on me. Someone is crying. I lift my head slowly.

Beside me, I see the red canvas shoe. The laces are tied.

'Where is he?' I ask with a voice that is like a whisper. I struggle to my feet.

'He was there. Right beside you. I saw his hand. Just a moment ago.' The three of us wade into the sea but the height of the waves, stronger now, push us back. We shout until we are hoarse.

'Be quiet,' I suddenly shout at them. 'Listen.' We strain towards the sea, three of us now, holding our breaths.

In the gathering dark, the white water near the shore rises and falls like ghosts. Farther out, where the sea blackens towards the horizon, it is still, like a grave.

I

It all started with a bottle of Baileys that was a year out of date but I drank it anyway.

Like most bad ideas, it seemed like a good idea at the time. Now it hurt to open my eyes and I didn't know where I was. I guessed it was an apartment. I could hear voices above and below, although that could have been the hangover roaring at me. I lay face down in a bed I didn't recognise and coaxed my eyes open.

From the looks of the line of clothes on the floor running from the door to the foot of the bed, there was a good chance I was naked. Shielding my eyes from the worst of the daylight, I inched them along the floor:

- Black suede skirt with silver snail trails curling along the bottom: check.
- Much-adored black linen – practically see-through – top: check.
- Black leather jacket: check.

Downhill from there, really …

- Shabby used-to-be-black bra with great thick straps and enough material for ten normal-sized bras and maybe some pants: check.

And yes, there were the dishcloth grey, used-to-be-white knickers that I reserved for periods and Pilates, straddling the bedside lamp. The lamp was on and the light bled through the threadbare gusset. I was in the throes of a laundry crisis brought on by days of neglect, and pickings were slim yesterday morning.

Not even the sight of my beautiful, black knee-high boots with heels like knitting needles comforted me. One of my hold-ups had impaled itself on a heel and a ladder ran down the side of it, ending in a glaring hole in or around the big toe area.

I buried my face into the pillow and tried not to think about Shane.

One year, nine months, three weeks and six days – four weeks tomorrow. What was I thinking? I had no idea what to do in this type of situation. To calm myself, I breathed, Pilates-style, sucking my belly in as tight as it would go until I ran out of breath and had to let it all sag back out again.

A moan followed by a series of pig-like snorts brought me back to the situation at hand. I lifted my head off the pillow, chancing a glance at the other side of the bed.

The shock was like a bucket of cold water. It was the new guy from the IT department. The one Laura called Geek Almighty. The one Norman called the Anti-Versace, on account of his nuclear dress sense. Even Ethan had sniggered. Jennifer was the only one who refused to comment, on account of her being the MD's PA and Sworn to Secrecy on matters of Extreme Importance and Otherwise. I hadn't said anything about him – although it wasn't a refusal as such, it's just that the arrival of single men in the office over the age of twenty didn't excite me as it used to. Because of Shane I suppose. And everything else.

I hadn't really looked at Bernard before now.

Bernard O'Malley from Athlone or Tullamore or Mullingar or somewhere in the midlands. He joined the company a couple of months ago. His arrival had caused quite a stir in the office, but then, the arrival of the water cooler caused a stir in our office. Ditto the coffee machine and even the monthly stationery order, especially when we get away with ordering bright pink paperclips which actually cost more than your common-or-garden metal ones. All this to distract us from the fact that we work in an insurance company. Not by choice, obviously. Insurance seems to be an industry that people sort of fall into without ever meaning to. Ask any of them.

Until last night, I had spoken to Bernard only the once. The conversation had gone a bit like this:

'Eh, my laptop appears to be malfunctioning.'

'Yes, the keypad is indeed quite sticky.'

'I most certainly did not spill a can of Coke on it.' (It was a Club Orange, if you really must know.)

And then: 'How long will it take to fix? I'm expecting a very important email.' (Response from hairdresser to code-red request for urgent attention.)

Bernard O'Malley. He was usually hunched over a computer, peering into the monitor with his teeny-tiny Joycean glasses.

I might have also seen him once in O'Reilly's for the traditional Friday night just-the-one-ah-sure-let's-stay-til-kicking-out-time drink, peering with his teeny-tiny Joycean glasses into the ruby-black depths of his pint of Guinness.

Now, he was lying in a Jesus-on-the-cross type of arrangement, arms akimbo with an enormous erection decorating his nether regions. He was smiling in his sleep – what red-blooded male wouldn't, with a lunch box of that stature down below? And his hair? Roaring red, it was. Even redder than mine. Laura would be furious. It totally contravened Rule No. 35 (hair colour), Subsection D (gingers). As for gingers sleeping with fellow gingers, well, that wasn't even covered in the Rules. That's how wrong it was.

Bernard's hair could not be more different from Shane's. It was that kind of hair that pointed everywhere at the same time. It wasn't long but it could do with a cut. My mother would call it untidy.

His glasses were missing, leaving two deep red indentations on the bridge of a long, narrow nose. I raised my head up a little more, checked he was still asleep and ran my eyes down the length of him. His feet hung over the edge of the bed. I hadn't realised he was so tall, having only really seen him sitting down before (in office, in pub, see above). Oh good Christ, he was wearing SOCKS – brown ones with orange polka dots.

I squeezed my eyes shut and tried not to think about the night before. Even behind the lids the flashbacks came, just out of reach so I couldn't swat them away like flies.

I needed to get some clothes on. First though, I had to cover up Bernard's manhood. It had its own gravitational force: my eyes kept darting south, like magnets to the pole. I eased myself up onto all fours – the car crash in my head developing into a multi-vehicle collision – and leaned over the side of the bed in search of a sheet. Or even a tea towel.

Behind me, I heard him speak.

2

I don't know what he said. I just heard a voice and all the words were lost as I fell off the side of the bed in a tangle of arms, legs and wobbly bits.

'Grace, are you OK?' Bernard leaned over the edge of the bed and looked down at me, then immediately looked away as I pawed at my breasts in an effort to cover them. It would take more than two hands to conceal the girls.

'Sorry, I just thought you might have hurt yourself.' He groped for a sheet and handed it to me, his head turned away. A mark of respect? Maybe he just couldn't bear the sight of me?

Then I noticed his hands. I was a hands woman. Other women were into legs, or buns, or eyes, or length and/or girth of male member. I was into hands. Bernard had what you might call artistic hands, long slender fingers topped with girlishly pink almond-shaped nails. Strong hands with long, fine hairs, lending the requisite manly touch.

I was momentarily silenced as I quickly covered myself with the sheet. My look said, 'your turn now'. He reached down and found a pair of boxers under his bed (white with red roses climbing furiously towards the elasticated waistband on a twisted green stem). I didn't know if they were the ones he had discarded last night or if that was where he kept his stash. I was just relieved that he had covered himself, although his erection strained against the flimsy material, giving the roses a robust, well-tended effect.

The silence that followed was long. Bernard broke it by reaching for his glasses on the bedside table – except they weren't there. He spread his fingers across the top of the locker, tapping his hand up and down against the wooden surface, along the strap of my discarded bra. His fingers slid up the hillock of one of the cups in a way that unsettled me. He obviously couldn't see a thing without his glasses. I hooked my fingers around a strap and reefed it away from him. The clasp cracked against my cheek, stinging.

'Grace, sorry. I really need to find my glasses. Can you see them?' His voice was urgent, the question addressed to an area just above my head.

I eventually found them, folded neatly on a glass shelf in the en-suite bathroom. He must have taken them off before we went to bed. That might explain the deliberate way he moved his hands over my body last night – he had been visually impaired. I shivered, thinking about those hands on me.

Shane's face appeared in my head, like a pop-up picture in a storybook, and I shrank away from the image.

'Are you cold?' Bernard asked. His concern pushed the walls of my guilt farther apart.

'No.' I thrust the glasses towards him. He fumbled for them, brushing his hand against my fingertips. His skin was soft and warm.

With his glasses on, he looked more like himself. In fact, he looked better than he normally did. With no clothes on, I mean. Christ, where had that thought come from? I had to get out of there and act like nothing had happened. I would be lynched in work on Monday if anyone got wind of this, not least because of Shane. Everyone loved Shane. Well, the women did anyway.

Bernard peered at me through the tiny lenses as if noticing me for the first time. I felt out of place, like a sky-high Buddha at a Catholic mass. There was nowhere else to sit so I perched on the edge of the bed.

'Do you mind if I smoke?' he asked.

'God no, not at all.' My voice sounded too hearty in the intimacy of the room. And then I remembered something.

'You didn't smoke last night, did you?'

'No, I only smoke first thing in the morning,' he said, like that was normal.

He pulled slowly on the cigarette, holding it like an old man, between his thumb and forefinger, closing his eyes as he inhaled, emitting vast plumes of smoke from his nose and mouth.

I didn't know whether to be insulted or relieved by his detailed concentration on smoking. I couldn't think of a single thing to say. He handed me the cigarette, his long Inspector Gadget arm reaching across the width of the bed. I removed it from his fingers, trying not to touch him. I didn't want to give him the wrong impression. Although maybe it was a little late for that. The smoking saved us from the burden of conversation. One of us was either smoking or waiting for the other to pass the cigarette. I don't know why we didn't just smoke one each. But the ritual of the shared cigarette calmed me. I made a great show of stubbing the cigarette out in an ashtray on the bedside table.

The silence in the room thickened and throbbed.

'Bernard,' I said with no idea of what I was going to say after that. He sat on the bed, perfectly still. My hands were fidgeting now without the cigarette, my breath loud in the room.

'Grace,' he said finally. At least we both knew each other's names. I comforted myself with this.

'I don't make a habit of this, you know, if that's what you're thinking,' he said.

'A habit of what?'

He looked shy all of a sudden.

'Of, you know, of this type of situation.' (He said 'sitch-ye-ay-shin. Turns out he was from Donegal)

'Oh,' I said. 'Well, neither do I. In fact, I ... ' The phone rang.

'I'll be back in a minute.' He slid out of bed and walked quietly out of the room. His skin was even whiter than mine. A ghostly white.

Like most red-haired women, sallow skin was on my 'must have' list for my ideal world or parallel universe or whatever you wanted to call it. Soft, brown skin with no freckles like mine marring the landscape, just shades of brown and browner. Shane was sallow.

With Bernard gone, I took a good look around the place. If asked, I would swear on Granny Mary's grave (if she were dead) that I'd never been here before.

It was a big room that could have looked bigger were it not for the machines: two hard drives, an oversized monitor, a laptop, a DVD player, a stereo, three speakers. Strangely, only one remote control, a thick brick of a thing that I guessed – correctly – worked on all the gizmos in the room. It could probably pull the blinds, turn down the bed and make a stiff gin and tonic as well. Wires twisted like snakes across the floor and I was surprised I hadn't tripped over one of them last night. Or maybe I had? I checked myself for bruises. A new one on my shin. In the shape of Ireland. It hurt when I pressed on Cork.

Out of place among the technology was a bookshelf that ran the length of one wall. I gathered the sheet about me tightly and swivelled to the side of the bed. Three condom wrappers – empty – littered the floor. Three. I stepped over them, not looking down. The book collection appeared to be divided into genres. The top shelf housed the classics – Charles Dickens, Henry James, Thomas Hardy – which looked as if they had actually been read. In fact, they looked positively loved. I leafed through some of them. There were dog-ears and circles of red wine, dulled brown with age. Below, in varying quanti-

ties, were thrillers, biographies, histories, the obligatory copy
of *Catcher in the Rye*, rubbing shoulders with a Beano annual
from 1978.

I was drawn to the self-help section, mostly because I
couldn't believe there was one. Although, on closer inspection, it was more of a 'how to' section. *How to Play Chess to
Win. The Book of Knots* (I swear to God). One on fashion
called *Dress to Kill* that had to be a present from someone
with a sense of humour. According to the scribbled message inside the front cover, it was from someone called
Edward:

*The title of this book should not be taken literally and you
should stop doing it. Very soon. Happy birthday bro, from
Edward. August 2001*

I looked towards the bed. It was long and wide; a fat finger, pointing an accusation at me. Bernard's discarded clothes
poked out from under the bed, like dismembered bodies. The
arm of a cardigan (he wore cardigans), the leg of a pair of
trousers that might be flannels (he wore trousers that might
be called flannels, ending about an inch above his ankle), the
wrinkled corpse of a T-shirt that I think said 'Ladybirds Rock'
with a picture of two ladybirds squatting on a rock (he wore
T-shirts that said things, with explanatory diagrams).

At work his wardrobe was the subject of coffee-break ob-
servations (mostly – nay, all – negative). I hadn't yet witnessed
his summer wardrobe, but I was willing to bet there was a
pair of leather-strap sandals in there. Laura joked about giving him a charity shag just so she could access his wardrobe
and burn the contents when he wasn't looking.

'Underneath those tank tops and Y-fronts is a fit body, crying out for some Calvin Klein,' she said, more than once.

I closed the book and returned it to its place, letting my

fingers trail along the broken spines until I reached the end of the shelf. A thin book faced the wrong way out. I eased it off the shelf. *Coping With Grief: A Practical Guide.* The cover, creased and torn, pictured an expanse of calm ocean lit by a full moon. Definitely written by an American. There was an inscription: *Bernard, I find this helps. Keep in touch. Love, Cliona. xx*

I shoved the book back on the shelf, my hands hot, as though I had trespassed onto private property.

Bernard was still on the phone. I could hear him if I listened carefully. He said 'aye' a lot.

A photograph in a shell-encrusted wooden frame caught my eye on top of the chest of drawers in the corner. Two young boys in swimming trunks, their arms wrapped around each other, standing in front of a little blow-up dinghy sitting plumply on the sand. They looked identical although one was wearing glasses. He was slightly smaller and skinnier than the other boy. This one had to be Bernard, I decided, picking up the frame. I recognised his hands.

It was exactly sixty seconds later when Bernard returned. That's the thing about IT people. When they say a minute, they really mean, like, sixty seconds. When I say to my boss, for example, I'll be back in a minute, it could be a matter of hours before my return. People seem to know this about me and are never surprised.

'Sorry about that,' he said.

I dropped the frame, the glass rattling across the wood. Bernard reached me in long, slow strides, his arm lengthening to prop the picture up. The inside of his elbow touched my skin through the sheet. He was close. I stopped breathing. He leaned towards me and I knew he was thinking about kissing me. I anticipated the kiss before it happened, tasting it. Then I came to and reefed myself away from him. He rallied well.

'That sheet suits you.' When he smiled, his cheeks dented in dimples, like Patrick's.

'About last night,' I blurted, the guilt forced up out of me, like water through a blow-hole.

Bernard didn't say anything, but he wasn't smiling any more.

'Look,' I whispered. 'I'm sorry. I shouldn't be here, I don't know what I'm at these days.' I paused, hoping he might say something. He did not. I took a deep breath.

'I have a boyfriend,' I said. 'Shane. Shane is my boyfriend. I mean, well, he was and possibly still is . . . It's . . . it's complicated really.' I trailed off, cringing at how pathetic and ridiculous I must sound.

'I'll make some coffee,' was all he said before he left again. I could hear the rattle of crockery from the kitchen and I grabbed my clothes off the floor. I needed to get out of there as soon as possible. Bernard's soft accent had unnerved me.

It seemed I couldn't depend on anything: on Shane to marry me and love me till I was dead, on Bernard to be an IT geek and to have manuals on the programming rituals of Intel chips on his bookshelves. Even the weather was being ridiculous: it was March and the sun was streaming in through slits in the wooden blinds, making everything seem golden and hopeful and new. My world was still in winter: cold and bleak and dark.

3

Walking home from a Friday night in the cold glare of Saturday morning is a sobering experience, which was lucky for me as I was still half-cut from the night before. To stop myself thinking about Shane, I wrote lines in my head, over and over again: 'I will never drink in-or-indeed-out-of-date Baileys again and then sleep with anyone who is not my boyfriend.' *Three times* – no wonder I was exhausted.

It turned out I was in Swords, which meant that Bernard owned the apartment. There's no way anyone would live that far from town unless they *had* to.

I teetered down the Swords Main Street in my impossibly high heels. I had always known why they were called 'killer heels' but maybe the pain was like labour pain: completely forgotten the next day. Take my sister Jane, for example. Three kids under her belt and you ask her to give you a blow-by-blow account on the agonies of childbirth, and she simply cannot. When you complain, she just says she can't remember. Well, it's like that with high heels.

Now my feet shrieked at me, although on the plus side, the car crash in my head had dulled to a tolerable throb.

Bernard had given me Alka-Seltzers, two of them, fizzing furiously in a tall glass of water. Even the fizzing noise made my head throb and it took a while before I could coax the glass to my mouth. He made me coffee (real, mind, none of your instant muck) and even offered me the use of a spare toothbrush (yes, I did wonder at that). No more mention was made of Shane. We also avoided politics and religion. Anything really, that might upset the delicate condition of two people who barely know each other having breakfast together in a place where one of the two needs to ask where the bathroom is.

I wobbled down the street, hazy details of the night before gathering in my memory, yawning and stretching and getting ready to attack.

Yes indeed, the nearly full bottle of Baileys was out of date, discovered by Katya, the Russian cleaning lady, at the back of the drinks cabinet in the office boardroom. Considering that she never raises a duster to my desk, I can't think what she was doing, dusting the inside of the drinks cabinet. Anyway.

'Is olt,' she declared, setting the bottle on my desk with great ceremony, like the true KGB agent we all thought she was.

'Is no goot,' she continued, sending dust motes into the air around my head with a flick of her feather duster.

'Say no more, Katya, I will deal with this,' I responded grandly. I mean, it was alcohol, right? The older, the better, yeah?

All the higher-ups had gone to some meeting or other (emergency board meeting, actually, Bernard told me, to discuss things such as redundancies and whatnot). The point was, we had the place to ourselves, it was Friday afternoon and I was looking for some distraction. I gathered up some paper cups from the kitchen (delivered with the water cooler), sent an email around to a few heads left in the office that sleepy Friday afternoon, inviting them to a 'come as you are' office party, venue: my desk, time: asap. In less than five minutes, a small group of office delinquents was gathered around my 'work area', as I called it, laughing.

'What will we do about Sarah?' Ethan spoke in a theatrical whisper. Sarah was the company receptionist, a tiny woman of indeterminate age and sexual persuasion, but what she lacked in stature she made up for in volume and ferocity. We called her the Bulldog, but only if we knew she wasn't in the building or, preferably, the country, at the time. While she disapproved of any activity where there was an outside chance of people enjoying themselves, she hated being left out.

'Don't worry Ethan,' I soothed. 'I've emailed her, so our arses are covered. On the plus side, she can't leave the reception desk so you're safe enough.'

Ethan was our dote of a marketing manager who also doubled as general all-round skivvy whenever the Boys on the Board needed a stamp licking or some office furniture shifting. He raked a thin hand through thinner hair and smiled his relief at me.

Norman, the office dipso, came to the party armed with two bottles of red wine and a remarkably red face, which led me to believe he'd had more than a ham and cheese sandwich for his lunch. He had a fabulously camp, marbles-in-the-mouth British accent and a full head of thick brown hair cut in a bob like a Trappist monk.

'Daahling,' he winked at me, mincing into a chair and crossing his long, tartan-clad legs. Despite the extreme gaiety of his manner and dress sense, Norman was hard-core heterosexual and, apparently, very good in bed according to Laura, the self-confessed office slapper, also known as the accounts payable clerk when she felt like doing any work. Laura perched on the edge of my desk with her legs crossed, inching her skirt to mid-thigh level so we could all admire her legs, which we duly did – they really were lovely, mind.

So, there's yours truly, feet up on the desk slugging vast quantities of out-of-date Baileys out of a paper cup and waxing lyrical on such topics as whether Julia Roberts's legs are really forty-four inches from hip to ankle, or if Colin Farrell got his Dublin accent from watching re-runs of *Fair City*. Everyone else was drinking Norman's red wine and munching on thin strips of bright orange Easi Singles that Jennifer found at the back of the fridge. The name 'Orla' was scribbled on the front of the packet but she had left the company weeks ago, so no harm done there. Jennifer came too, which was unusual. She took her job as the MD's PA very seriously. She sat on the edge of a chair, ready to leap up and start photocopying at the first sign of a suit. She was a raving beauty: long and thin with shoulder-length black hair that was thick *and* soft (a rare combination I'm sure you'll agree). When she was in a really good mood, she allowed us to touch her hair so long as we didn't take it to the next level (one of our ex-colleagues, Nora, got carried away one day while stroking Jennifer's hair and it all got a bit embarrassing. Nora left the company shortly after The Incident).

'You know, gone-off Baileys isn't actually that bad,' I slurred, draining the dregs of the bottle into my soggy paper cup.

'There's dairy in that, I wouldn't go near it,' Laura chipped in, taking a huge slug of wine out of the bottle in a most suggestive manner.

'Dairy? What are you on about?' I licked the inside of my empty cup.

'Eh, hellooooo! Baileys Irish CREAM. There's milk in cream and milk is a dairy product. You'll probably get worms, drinking that stuff,' Laura continued.

'Sshhh,' Jennifer suddenly hissed. 'What's that?' We all fell silent and listened. It was the unmistakeable hum of the lift in motion. We stared at the dial above the lift doors. We were on the third floor and the lift was heading our way. Now it was on the first floor, now the second. I slid my legs off the desk and threw the empty Baileys bottle towards the bin. It missed and rolled deliberately in front of the lift doors. There was a sharp ping and the doors opened. Sarah stepped out into the office, jangling a glut of keys on a ridiculously large metal ring.

'People,' she barked, rattling her prison-warden keys in our general direction. Then she noticed the bottle on the floor, gave me a look that would wilt weeds and tossed it into the bin I had aimed for earlier. It landed cleanly right in the centre of the bin and Sarah almost smiled.

'It's seventeen hundred hours and I'm locking up, so unless you want to spend the weekend in the office, I suggest you MOVE OUT.' She loved war films.

We didn't need any second bidding as we tripped across the road to O'Reilly's for the traditional Friday night just-the-one-ah-sure-let's-stay-till-kicking-out-time drink. I hadn't actually been to O'Reilly's in ages but the out-of-date Baileys tasted like more and it was Friday night and everyone else was going. If Shane rang I could go outside the pub and talk to him.

By the time we arrived in the pub, the place was awash with suits. There was a bumblebee buzz of conversation as office workers, hysterical at the prospect of two days of freedom, reefed themselves out of straitjackets and pulled noose-like ties from their necks. Laura's expert eye scanned the crowd, her man-monitor charging into top gear. I knew she had found her mark. Her eyes stopped swivelling, her pupils dilated and her mouth assumed its legendary pout. I followed her line of vision and spotted a couple of guys from our IT department hunched over their pints in a dim recess at the back of the pub. One of them was the latest addition on the payroll but I couldn't remember his name. Brendan or something like that.

'This way.' Laura swung her head sharply around, smacking me in the face with a thick blonde plait. I obeyed, mostly because there were a couple of spare stools at that table but also because to resist would be futile. In my wake were Jennifer and Ethan. Norman brought up the rear with his usual attire: two bottles of wine tucked under his armpits, wineglasses dangling by their stems from between his fingers and enough packets of crisps to sink a ship.

'Dinner and drinks,' he declared, scattering the crisps on the table and pouring the wine with his pinkie sticking out, just like a queen. Then he noticed the computer boys.

'Oh, Bernard, Peter, I didn't realise you were joining us.' Bernard and Peter looked at each other, shrugged, and politely scraped their stools around the table to accommodate us. So far, so Friday night.

I had a Baileys buzz and was feeling hot and dizzy, with the throb of the pub pulsing in my head. A man with a brick-red face pushed past me, balancing three pints on a conveniently straining belly, a packet of bacon fries swinging from his mouth. I teetered on the height of my heels and grabbed at Jennifer's arm, which was about as useful as reaching for a reed when you're careering down a cliff face. Her twig-like frame was unable to sustain the pressure and she stumbled. Now I was falling, a mighty oak in a forest of saplings. There was a jolt and then relief as someone caught me from behind and threw their arms about my trunk, their hands clamped indelicately across my chest. Then, I was gently raised onto all-twos again. The hands on my breasts regrouped onto my shoulders and turned me around.

'Are you OK?' It was the new guy. Norman, Laura, Jennifer, Ethan and Peter had all settled themselves around the table and were paying not the least bit of attention to me, being used to my regular brushes with acute embarrassment. Laura bent towards Peter's face while his head made a dent in the wall behind him.

'I'm fine. Hope you didn't put your back out, breaking my fall,' I grinned up at him. He looked at me then and I took an unsteady step backwards.

'Here,' he said, thrusting a full-to-the-brim glass of wine into my hands. 'Drink this down. It's good for the shock.' The corners of his mouth turned up and I realised he was smiling. He reached for his pint of Guinness and clinked my glass gently. I took an almighty slug of wine, then chanced a look-up. He was still there, still smiling, now with a Guinness moustache frothing like milk above his upper lip.

'I'm Bernard, by the way. I've seen you before but we haven't actually been introduced properly.'

'No, we tend not to introduce new people to anyone in the company,' I said, pulling at my skirt to make sure it was still covering my bum.

'Why not?' he said, frowning but still smiling. That was weird.

'The new people. We don't introduce them. We just talk about them and give them marks out of ten under various categories.'

'What kind of categories?'

'Oh you know, the usual kind. Cleanliness, hairiness, funniness, general attitude to work – the worse, the better, obviously.'

You could tell he was wondering how he scored under the different categories, but he said nothing. We talked. I noticed the following things about him:

- When he smiled – which was often – his chocolate brown eyes disappeared into slits beneath dark eyelashes that wouldn't have looked out of place poking out of a spider's body.
- He thought I was funny – I could tell – and not in a funny-weird way either.
- He was attentive to my alcohol levels and obligingly re-filled my wine glass whenever it sank below the halfway mark.
- When it was my turn to buy a round, he insisted on buying it and then bought his own round half an hour later, complete with a selection of crisps, bacon fries and peanuts.

- When I suggested cheese-and-garlicky chips at Kevin's Kebabs (that always made us laugh) after the pub, he took it in his stride and even gave me grounds to believe that it was a great idea. When you're big like me, you sometimes get embarrassed coming up with ideas that involve stuffing your cake-hole with a shocking amount of carbohydrates at 1 a.m. on a Saturday morning.

The redness of the hair and the greyness of the cardigan and the shortness of the trousers became less noticeable as the evening wore on. They were just hair and clothes. As for Shane, I didn't think about him then. There was no need. Bernard and I were just talking. And laughing. I wasn't even surprised that I was having a good time. I was just having a good time and not thinking about it. It felt refreshing, like pink lemonade.

Ethan, Jennifer, Norman, Peter and Laura (locked at that stage in a clinch that only a power hose could rectify) staggered from the pub in search of a nightclub where they could buy drinks for the price of a small island in the Pacific Ocean and slouch around a dancefloor doing vague impressions of Kylie on one of her off-days.

I was just hungry. I mean, I hadn't had any dinner and a girl cannot survive on red wine and fags alone, although you wouldn't think it if you'd seen me on the day of my twenty-fifth birthday – but that's another story.

I ordered milk with my chips and that was my downfall. If I'd ordered a black coffee like any normal grown-up, the situation would not have arisen. I mean, it's not like Kevin's is particularly renowned for its soft lighting and romantic soundtrack, is it? Anyway, I must have had a milk moustache so yer man leans over and rubs his thumb – *oh so gently* – over my top lip. Then, get this, he licks his thumb and looks at me.

'You just had a bit of milk there,' he says in a voice that is suddenly *raging* with lust. I don't even finish my chips – a first for me – and I lean across the table and just kiss him full on the mouth. Suddenly, he's on my side of the table and his hands are in my hair and, luckily, I'd brushed it in the loo of the pub before I left. He touches my face and sucks at my lower lip and it's so unbelievably *pleasurable* and it's been so long, I'm like an eight-year-old in Claire's Accessories – I just want everything, immediately, no questions asked. We touch each other everywhere, hands scratching at clothes that suddenly feel too bulky. He bites my neck. I pull at the soft lobe of his ear with my teeth. If there is a voice in my head screaming at me to stop, reminding me about the existence of a man called Shane, I don't hear it. It seems like the world has stopped and there is only this moment. This hot, wet moment. Nothing else.

'Eh, excuse me . . . Excuse me . . . *EXCUSE ME.*'

We release each other and look up. The pair of us are panting, like dogs in the street separated by a bucket of water. A man – could it be Kevin? – is standing beside our table, looking down on us. He is wearing a cap with a peak like a duck's bill, bright yellow. His name badge says 'Phil'.

'Yis'll hafta lee-af.' His voice is soft and sounds like an apology. People are staring at us and I look down at myself, making sure my clothes are still on. They are. Bernard hands Phil a fiver and curls his hand around my neck and it feels like electricity and I worry that I'm going to come, right there, in the middle of the kebab shop. He steers me out the door, we pulse into a taxi and foreplay our way to his place and, well, you know the rest really.

4

Despite the roar of the Swords traffic, I could hear the mobile ringing from the depths of my handbag – a nearly real Prada that I picked up for a song last summer in New York. I was there for Laura's hen party although the wedding didn't happen in the end – a long story.

I was elbow deep in my sack, squatting on the pavement, when the bus roared up, belching hot, black fumes into my face. With the phone still ringing, I grabbed my purse and yanked at my bag, spilling the contents across the width of the pavement and under the bus. A selection of useless euro coins rolled around the path, glad of the change of scene. They'd probably been there since the euro changeover. I never used change if I could help it. Firstly I was hopeless at maths (and by maths I mean adding and subtracting) and secondly, I just preferred holding crisp banknotes in my paws poised for purchase. Or, better still, one of my variety pack of credit cards.

I nearly cried when I saw my beautiful things lying among the detritus of Friday night: puddles of brightly coloured alcopop vomit, soggy condoms like so many squashed maggots, empty crisp packets. My Clinique lip liner had rolled beside a neat mound of dog turd and not even the hardiest of onlookers could bring themselves to pick it up. I bid it a silent goodbye – it had seen me right on many a night. My matches shed their box and lay scattered about my bulk, every single one of them used. Most of my coins were now under the bus and I clocked a man with long, greasy hair on his hands and knees with his head under the bus counting the booty.

About this time, I realised that one of my hold-ups had ripped and lay in wrinkled folds around my ankle. Burning with familiar humiliation, I reefed my skirt down as far as it would go and removed the torn strips of ultra-sheer 10 Denier from my left leg, shovelling the pathetic flap of nylon into my bag. I drew myself up to my full height – six feet in my heels – and hobbled with as much dignity as I could muster – which wasn't much, to be fair – onto the bus.

'Exact fare, love,' the bus driver mumbled, picking something from his teeth. His head rested across his arms on the huge steering wheel.

'Sorry?' I gushed with a smile, waving my last €20 towards him. I did not take public transport enough to know that smiling and gushing at bus drivers will not enhance your situation in the slightest. You might as well try to pet a rabid dog with a string of sausages tied around your neck.

'Exact fare, love,' he repeated, unmoved.

I glanced into the change section of my purse and saw nothing but dull brown coins nestled in the silky folds of the fabric. Probably about 12 cent in total. I thought briefly about launching into the whole handbag-emptying scenario of a few moments ago. Wisely, I did not.

'I've nothing smaller,' I said in a very small voice.

There was a slight moment of triumph when he was forced to swivel his head towards me to hear what I was saying. He held his hand out, the little finger glistening from its recent foraging in the cracks of his teeth. Then he got chatty.

'I'll take your €20, OK? You get to keep the ticket, yeah? You'll get a refund from head office on O'Connell Street, right?'

His voice was a monotone, and the words tripped off his tongue like a nursery rhyme that he had recited many times before.

Then he smiled, revealing gappy, yellow teeth that could benefit from further investigation with his little finger. I handed my €20 to him taking care not to make any physical contact with the shiny finger. For my money, I received a ticket as long as double chemistry and moved into the body of the bus, allowing the crowd behind me to shuffle forward.

I folded myself into a seat at the very back of the bus and made myself as small as I would go, bending my head and my knees.

The alcohol in my system rolled out its compulsory low. The drama of the incident with Bernard was fading and I saw myself in my mind's eye: a dishevelled woman on a bus weighed down with change totalling 12 cent and a receipt worth €18.60 (but only Monday to Friday, 10 a.m. to 4.30 p.m.). If taxis accepted credit cards, this would never have happened.

Shane's face floated up through the swamp of my mind. I shifted in my seat. Saturday morning in London. What would he be doing now? Shopping in Harvey Nicks for sharp 'salesman recently promoted to sales manager' type suits? Sipping creamy lattes at a fabulous but as-yet-undiscovered streetside café? Working out in the gym, a designer sweat darkening a tight, grey T-shirt?

Was he thinking about me? Had he slept with anyone? I imagined a tiny blonde, all sharp intellect and soft curves, a copy of the *Kama Sutra* tucked into a really real Prada handbag.

And then there was Spain. Shane was there. He knew. I pressed my face, hard, against the window of the bus and squeezed my eyes shut.

'We need a break,' Shane said. A break. That word. The word that people use when they can't bring themselves to say what they really want. But I knew what I wanted. I wanted everything to be the way it was before.

There was no doubt that it was a great career move for him.

'It's just for six months,' he said. He hugged me then and I
let him. He didn't want to see my face. Shane didn't like un-
pleasantness.

He'd been gone two months and it felt like ten.

The bus stopped and I banged my head against the window. I whimpered. I remembered the call on my mobile and
bent my head again into the depths of my bag. The missed
call was from my mother. She hardly ever rang me on my
mobile. 'The numbers are too long, how is anyone supposed
to remember them? And the cost?'

She had left a message and I held my breath and dialled
into voicemail. 'Where are you?' Her voice was high, agitated.
It pushed my hangover to bulge at the edge of my head. 'We're
at the Bridal Boutique, waiting for you. Where are you? Can
you call me back IMMEDIATELY?'

The 'immediately' ended in a crescendo. I could see colour
infusing her face with the word. Fuck, damn and piss. I had
forgotten. Of course I had forgotten. The fitting appointment
for a bridesmaid dress. My sister, Clare, was getting married
– I was a bridesmaid. Chief bridesmaid, as a matter of fact.

'Shite.' Pushing myself back against the harsh upholstery
of the bus seat, I checked my watch. It was 10.10 a.m. If the
bus driver got his finger out (and not just out of his mouth),
I could be at the Bridal Boutique by 10.40 a.m. I tried to
breathe in and out to calm myself but stopped when hyper-
ventilation became a distinct possibility.

Jane was the other bridesmaid. The oldest. The one who
had thoughtfully provided my mother with a selection of
grandchildren so she'd have something to entertain her in her
dotage. The one who always Did The Right Thing. Not that
I have anything against people who Do The Right Thing. It's
just that it makes me look bad in comparison and that's what
I object to. Jane would be at the Bridal Boutique. She would
have arrived on time. She'd be trying on a size ten bridesmaid

dress, berating herself for not being a size eight like Clare. And Clare would say, 'But Jane, you've had three kids, give yourself a break.' And then I would arrive. Late. And over-weight. And hungover. Slightly gawky, slightly awkward. Sent to an expensive middle-class school, an average student of above-average size and height. One of the teachers' report cards read, 'Grace is larger than life and will do well.'

'But at what?' my mother wailed as the Cs fell down along the side of my report card. Now I was twenty-nine years old and I still didn't know the answer to that question. When I left school, I got a summer job in an insurance company as a gen-eral Girl Friday. Ten years later, I was still there, Girl Monday to Friday.

A little old lady got ready to get off the bus. She teetered down the aisle with all the fragility of a duckling waddling to the water's edge for the first time. I watched her, willing her to go to the exit in the middle of the bus.

'Don't go to the front of the bus. Please don't go to the front of the bus,' I begged in my head. Knowing the bus driver, as I did, he would snap the doors together cruelly and announce that it was for incoming passengers only. She didn't and ex-ited without incident.

I rang my mother, my hands slimy against the phone.

'Mam, hi.' I began to speak as soon as she answered the phone with the cheery air of someone in the wrong, winging it.

'I'm on my way, be there in half an hour, OK?' Then I crossed my fingers and waited.

There was no storm. That wasn't my mother's style. Just a sigh. She expressed her disappointment in me with her silence more than her words.

'OK Mam, see you then.' I hung up and looked out the window, watching the world go by, seeing nothing. I felt like a vampire who's just realised he won't make it back to his coffin before daybreak. The bus rattled onto the quays and spilled its passengers onto the footpath.

The Bridal Boutique was up a steep flight of stairs above the Coffee Cave on Grafton Street. The front of the shop was entirely glass, sun splitting onto the mannequins, giving them a startled look, vacant eyes lolling in white hairless heads. My sister stood at the end of the shop in her wedding dress, getting pinned with ferocity by a girl my age with a severe bun that stretched her eyes into slits.

'Howaya,' the girl looked up with a huge smile. I was relieved, having imagined that the Bridal Boutique employees were superior types who could intimidate people into wearing dresses like meringues with matching fabric-covered shoes.

'Grace, how's tricks?' Clare acknowledged me with a wide smile. She turned around, as careful as a person should be with so many pins about their person. Her thick brown hair was swept up in a swollen bun at the back of her head. The biggest thing about her were her eyes: navy blue, slanted in a smile.

'Clare, the dress is fabulous,' I answered. From the front, it looked like her slender frame was wrapped from neck to ankle in fine golden hues of lace and silk. At the back, the dress plunged to the cleft of her buttocks.

'Jesus, don't do too much bending over in that dress, Clare, you'll have builder's bum.' The pair of us fell around the place laughing even though it wasn't all that funny. It's just what we did when we got together.

My little sister was getting married to a modern-day version of a prince wielding his sword: a banker wielding his wad. I thought I'd be engaged by now, but here I was, after nearly two years of my first, serious 'grown-up' relationship, alone and bridesmaid at my younger sister's wedding. I swallowed hard and choked back these thoughts.

'Sorry I'm late.'

'You're just in time,' she said. I never needed to explain anything to Clare.

'What about Mam? She sounded annoyed on the phone.' I whispered that bit.

'I'm just surprised you managed to make it at all, Grace.' The irritation in her voice was familiar now. Clare said I was being overly sensitive, but I knew better.

I turned around and there she was, with pins sticking out of her mouth. She looked like she worked there. In fact, she looked like she owned the place.

'Mam. Hi!' I said, my voice too bright in this sanctuary of wedding dresses. Disappointment was like a dress my mother wore when she saw me these days. She nodded tiredly.

'So,' I said. 'Shall I try on the dress then?'

'Well, that *is* the reason we've been here for the last hour, Grace.' For every step she made towards me, I stepped back, afraid she'd smell the alcohol fumes.

'We've only been here just over a half hour.' Clare. Always the peacemaker.

'Mam,' I said. 'I'm sorry I'm late. It was the . . .' But she had already turned away from me.

'Come on, Grace. Let's not waste any more time. We'll see if we can fit you into this frock.' She strode towards the changing rooms, a great bale of coffee-coloured silk ballooning in her hands. I closed my mouth and followed her. I felt hot and my eyes hurt in the white glare of the room.

In the dressing room, Mam thrust the dress up against me and shook her head with a sigh. She mumbled through the pins.

'This is actually Jane's dress. It'll be miles too small for you. I'll go and get yours.'

I looked at my mother as she carefully hung Jane's dress on a hanger, and I saw myself, thirty years hence. She was obscenely tall for her age, so eyeballing her was a cinch for me, if I could summon up the nerve. Her hair had been like mine, long and raw red – 'I could sit on my hair when I was your age' – but it was now an iron grey, clamped to her head like a helmet in a stiff bob.

'Grace, you're missing a stocking.'

She suddenly stood to attention, looking sharply at my legs. The two shop assistants – or Bridal Consultants, according to their name badges – stared at me, as did Clare and my mother. I blinked against the dazzling whites of the wedding dresses standing shoulder to shoulder in perfect lines around the shop, mocking me. The heat of the room was thick and I suddenly found it hard to breathe.

Opening my handbag, I rummaged for my inhaler which, of course, wasn't there. My breath came in rasps. I struggled to get out of the cubicle but my way was blocked. People were everywhere. I tried to remember to stay calm but I could feel the fear coming, like a hand around my throat. I leaned against the wall of the dressing room, sliding down towards the floor. The brightness dimmed and I closed my eyes against it, afraid.

The next thing I remember, I'm sitting on the floor of the cubicle and Mam is kneeling beside me, holding an inhaler up to my mouth.

'Breathe, Gracie, breathe.' Her voice echoed in my ears and white spots danced around the edge of my vision. I breathed in raggedly, closing my eyes.

She smoothed strands of damp hair across my forehead and called me 'Gracie' again. I could feel her hands on me, anxious. I felt warm all over. I *loved* it when she called me Gracie, which she never did any more. She pressed down on the cylinder poking out from the top of the inhaler and released clouds of merciful vapour into my mouth. I was still breathless but I could feel the panic pulling back. I imagined the Ventolin travelling down my trachea (that's a fancy word for throat, by the way) and into the T-junction of my lungs, just as Dr Evans told me to. When I was ten, he told my mother that I'd grow out of asthma in my teens. Just like giggling, binge drinking and falling over at the slightest provocation, I had not.

Embarrassed in front of my audience, I kept my head down until the wheezing withered to heavy breathing. I sounded like a middle-aged drunk at a swimming pool party for twenty-one-year-olds. I ventured a look up.

'Thanks, Mam.'

'Don't talk, Grace. Just get your breath back.' Her voice was brisk again. Efficient.

'Where did you get the inhaler?' I asked when the world stopped spinning.

'I . . . it's Patrick's. He left it behind.'

Silence followed this. No one knew quite what to say.

'Anyway, it's lucky I had it, isn't it?'

I nodded and looked at her but already she was getting up.

'Sorry,' I croaked to Clare, who was hovering. Colours came back into focus, the pale pink hue of the mannequins' faces, the baby-blueness of the surprisingly clear March sky, the fiery red of my mother's veins throbbing in her white throat. Oh, shit. She was back and had obviously decided that I was no longer in danger of dying.

'Grace, condoms have fallen out of your bag!' She hissed this at me, careful not to let the Bridal Consultants hear her. Her nostrils blew wide and colour ascended into her cheeks from her neck.

The only nice thing about asthma attacks is that the aftermath is a little post-coital. Your breath returns slowly, your sweat evaporates into the space above you. You feel warm, every cell in your body throbbing.

a) Of course there were condoms in my bag. I was a twenty-nine-year-old responsible woman in a world where Bernard O'Malleys lurked. Besides, they had been there since before Shane left and were more than likely out of date.
b) How did she *know* there were condoms in my bag? But then, she knew so much and I told her so little . . .

'Sorry,' I said again, to everyone and to no one in particular. 'Will I try my dress on now?'

The BCs (Bridal Consultants) were relieved that things seemed to be back to normal and busied themselves with bridal boutique-type activities. Pointing with long fingers topped with longer sharp red tentacles to, well, to things within the shop. And smiling. Lots of smiling. Huge, improbable smiles that stretched across perfect peaches-and-cream complexions. If it wasn't for their flat Dublin accents, I would have thought I dreamed them.

After all the drama, getting measured was a walk in the park. Yards of tape were wrapped around my waist (breathe in) and around my breasts (shoulders back) and around my hips (stand tall) and around my thighs (well, you can only do so much).

A mock-up of the dress had been made in a size fourteen. I was truly amazed when it slid over my hips and thighs without undue exertion. Before yelling for Clare to witness the miracle, I glanced in the dressing room mirror. The latté-coloured silk protested against the blotchy whiteness of my skin, but nothing a bucket of foul-smelling fake tan couldn't cure. I undid my hair gingerly. It had a life of its own, you know. It fell in long, full waves to my waist, big and ungainly but glinting gold in places where the light caught it. The dress was cut away at the back like Clare's but most of my back – riddled with freckles – was hidden by endless lengths of thick red hair, like rope. Gratitude slid through me. I *loved* the dress. I had seen many hideous bridesmaid dresses in my time and I had been apprehensive at the thought of wearing one of those contraptions.

'Clare, Clare, the size fourteen fits,' I roared from the confines of the dressing room – the 'boudoir' apparently. Clare pulled the flimsy curtain across the cubicle.

'I knew it would. You've lost weight in the last few months.' She pawed at the material encasing my breasts, pulling it up. 'We may need to make these babies a little more comfortable,' she giggled. My breasts – my pride and joy – were chomping at the bit for oxygen. A size fourteen with massive jugs in latte-coloured silk? I could do this wedding. I could make my sister proud. I bent and hugged her to me. A rip rent the air. The size fourteen did fit, but only if I did not engage in any actual physical movement. I could walk, but only just.

One of the BCs offered to take the dress out a little, but I was having none of it.

'You see, I'll be losing a few more pounds before the wedding,' I assured her. Stress. You can't beat it with a great, fat stick for a spot of totally undeserved weight loss. By the end of Shane's six-month absence, I'd be a stick insect, a bony beauty, all angles and edges. People would say, 'Grace, you've lost so much weight,' in much the same way as they might say, 'Grace, heard about your terminal illness, how tragic.' I would smile down at them and teeter away on my stilt-like legs. I could . . .

'Grace, Grace . . .' My sister's voice seemed to come from far away. I blinked and the room swam back into focus. Clare was tugging at my elbow.

'Sorry Clare, I was just visiting my parallel universe there for a moment.'

'The one where you're famine-riddled skinny and Shane is a commitment addict?' I nodded dreamily, still warm from the glow of my daydream. Then I remembered. 'And Patrick . . .'

'I know, Grace, I know.' Clare leaned over and hugged me. One of the BCs coughed discreetly.

'Ahem, Ms O'Brien, we're expectin' anudder weddin' party here in ten minutes . . .'

Her sentence hung in the air as myself and Clare stared at her. Then realisation dawned.

'Oh, right.' I suddenly understood. 'This is a bit like the way Madonna shops only with time constraints? I was wondering why we were the only people in the shop, thought you'd fallen on hard times. Ha ha.' No response to my little joke.

'Don't worry, I'll be out of here in a jiffy.'

I grabbed hold of the bottom of the dress and extended my arms skyward. A muffled shriek as a pin sank through the tender flesh of my neck. The BC stepped in and tugged at the dress – a little rougher than I thought was necessary, mind – releasing me. Static crackled in the confined space of the boudoir and strands of my hair stood on end. I was exposed again, still in Pilates pants and a monstrous black bra.

'So, eh, Ms O'Brien?' the BC enquired with a slight tilt of a perfectly tended eyebrow.

'Just call me Grace,' I said, reaching for my clothes.

'Do ya tink we could see ya for one more fittin' before de weddin'?' the BC probed. She did not sound convinced of my ability to manage this task.

'Yes, yes, no problem. You can ring me to arrange it,' Clare jumped in.

She took the BC by the elbow and eased her gently out of the cubicle. I was left alone with my thoughts. They settled on me like fog. I pushed my hands against my ears but still they came. Here is a flavour of just some of the things I did not want to think about:

- Shane O'Brien. See? I wouldn't even have to change my name when, *if*, we got married. It was a sign, surely? His initial torrent of emails, phonecalls and texts had slowed to a dribble in the past few weeks. Obviously, thinking about the reasons for this steady decline in communication could send a girl mad, so we move quickly on to . . .

- Bernard O'Malley. A colleague with whom I had exchanged no more than ten sentences since he joined the company a few weeks before. Now, he had seen me naked in unflattering light (AHHHHHHH!), I would have to see him at work on Monday and I had to face the fact that I had been unfaithful to Shane . . .
- Patrick. I just wished he was here.
- My mother. Here's what happened next.

The curtain separating me from the rest of the world was suddenly wrenched back and my mother towered in the architrave. When she's really annoyed, she speaks in a low, controlled voice, which she did now.

'Grace,' she said in a whisper that was nearly a shout. 'Clare is out there paying a hideous sum of money for your dress. You're late, you're hungover, you're missing a stocking. You've got condoms in your bag, you're in such a state you nearly had an asthma attack and *now* you're carrying on like an eejit in here.' Apparently, as well as clamping my hands to my ears, I'd been singing 'Nutbush City Limits', accompanied by the Tina Turner leg-stomp.

My mother counted these sins on her fingers, wrenching each one back in a way that was painful to watch.

'This is Clare's day,' she insisted. 'For God's sake, pull yourself together and let's get out of here.' She left as abruptly as she had arrived. My hands shook as I sucked my belly in to pull up the zip of my skirt. I hated confrontation, especially with my mother. The pressure in the back of my throat built as I tried not to cry. My mother hated people crying in public. I thought about my flat, about being there in the comfort of it. I could cry for the day there if I wanted to. Tomorrow too, if I liked. I felt a little better and ventured back out into the Bridal Boutique. A vibrating beep came from my now mostly empty bag (the condoms were gone) and I dug for the phone, hope surging.

1 message received.

I crossed my fingers and toes and implored the intervention of St Anthony, St Jude, St Thomas, Mary, Joseph, the donkey, Bono. Anyone at all, really. 'Please let this be from Shane,' I prayed. I jabbed at buttons on the handset and felt a short stab of shock. The message was not from anyone in my address book. The message was from a number I didn't recognise.

5

Having sex with almost a stranger on a Friday night is one thing. But giving the guy your mobile telephone number? Had I learned nothing? When had it happened? How?

You left your jacket at my place. Will bring it to work on Monday. Hope you are feeling OK. Bernard

'Who was that email from?' my mother asked, craning her head over my shoulder.

'It's a text, Mam, not an email.' I had arrived at phase two of my hangover: contrariness. My mother was always trying to get to grips with technology and had only recently replaced her ancient wireless with a stereo set incorporating a CD player. DVDs were still a foreign country as far as she was concerned.

'It's from Caroline.'

Caroline was my flatmate and friend. She was also Shane's sister, which had put a strain on our relationship in recent times.

Clare ushered us down the stairs, stress creasing her normally smooth face. She now had to go with our mother to help her choose her mother of the bride outfit. I feebly offered to accompany them – although I would have preferred to have a front tooth extracted without anaesthetic, by an ageing dentist who'd been struck off the register for dubious work practices.

Clare, saint that she is, hugged me and told me to go home, take a shower and go to bed. I didn't need to be told twice.

Before going home, I had to collect my car, which I had abandoned at work yesterday evening. On my last legs, I staggered into the car park. Ciaran, the night and day security guard, was there as usual. Did he *ever* go home?

'Ah, Grace, lass,' he crooned at me in his low, melodious Scottish voice. 'Do ye have no home to go ta?' He smiled at me, his face folding into deep lines, like a freshly ploughed field. He leaned out the window of the security hut. He looked ancient today, like he could use a good hot bath and three days of uninterrupted sleep. In the ten years that I had worked there he hadn't changed a bit and I often imagined that when his mother pushed him out of her womb, he had a quick wash, donned his security guard's cap, got a bus to our car park and never left.

I noticed my boss's car, a brand new BMW convertible, which made a mockery of his regular speeches to us about cutbacks. I quickly waved at Ciaran and hurried to my car, fumbling in my bag for the keys, when I heard the boss's hail-fellow-well-met booming voice. My shoulders slumped in resignation and I turned around. There he was. If I were writing a book and he were in it, nobody would believe the hideousness of him. He had a bald pate which he denied, draping strings of mousy brown hair across the empty space. He wore his trousers hitched up over his ample belly and I often wondered why his wife never told him how wrong this was. Perhaps it was her revenge for a lifetime of misery?

Apart from his ill-advised dress sense (he was one of the last five people in the world who still wore shoulder braces – that's all you need to know to get the picture), he had the people skills of Attila the Hun. He insisted on staff meetings every Monday morning at 8.30 a.m. (Sarah called it 'zero eight thirty, people'). These meetings were never about anything positive or good. They mostly featured monologues about cutbacks, dismal premium rates, increased competition in the marketplace which could be used later to explain our paltry salary reviews. Any Other Business might feature a leak in the ladies' toilets which may take up to four weeks to fix and, in the meantime, could we please pop up to the fifth floor to 'do our business'. In the summer, the air-conditioning always got a mention. Mostly because it never worked.

I wore dark sunglasses during these meetings – citing migraines – and nodded off. One Monday morning, Laura lost it completely and screeched at him.

'For God's sake, it's 8.30 on a Monday morning. We're all hungover and depressed, can we talk about something NICE FOR A CHANGE?' Of course, she had snogged him at the last Christmas party so she felt fairly confident that he wouldn't sack her in case she sued him for sexual harassment and outed him as the sleazy philanderer he really was.

Anyway, there he was in the car park, the stiff breeze raising the few limp hairs on his head. I nailed a smile on my face and walked, very slowly, towards him. He looked nervous.

'Eh, Grace, glad to have bumped into you, actually. There's something I, eh, have to discuss with you on Monday. Can you come and see me in my office at, say, 2 p.m.?' He looked at his feet, apparently admiring the shininess of his black patent leather shoes. He then admired his immaculately manicured nails and smoothed his tie, which had been tossed in front of his face by the wind.

My safe little work world tilted and I felt afraid. Bernard had seemed pretty positive last night that the Boys on the Board were considering an extensive spate of redundancies and, to be fair, he seemed to know what he was talking about. I was one of a gaggle of claims handlers in the liability department and, while I wasn't the most offensive member of staff, I did spend quite a bit of time phoning friends, Googling and occasionally straightening my hair at 4.45 p.m. on a Friday afternoon when I was perfectly well aware that the downing of tools was not supposed to occur until 5 o'clock thank you very much! What would I do if I lost my job? And more importantly, how would I break it to my mother?

'Sure,' I said. 'No problem. Do you want to discuss anything in particular?' I asked the question as casually as I could.

'We'll talk about it on Monday, Grace.' He was already walking away. I was dismissed.

I must have looked upset because Ciaran walked over and invited me into his office for a coffee. I was tempted because in the last year he had become a good friend. It turned out we had a lot in common. He was one of a family of four children, the only one who was unmarried, the only one who never went to university, the only one who lived in rented accommodation. Ciaran, however, was gay, unlike me (unless you count that one time in the Gaeltacht when I was sixteen). He'd discovered his sexuality before being camp, gyms or white singlets became de rigueur. He lived in a flat on Camden Street with his boyfriend Michael, although Ciaran never referred to him as such. He worked as the head chef in a salubrious hotel in town (I'd better not mention the name of the hotel, as Michael has never actually 'come out' as such, being a strict Presbyterian from Armagh, and having an ex-wife and three grown-up heterosexual sons). I had met Michael many times and his warm, companionable understanding with Ciaran made me long for a relationship like that of my own. Someone to play cards with, grow old with, someone who was happy – no, *delighted* – to spend time with me and not want to change me in any way. Someone I could sit in easy silence with, the silence being occasionally broken by the crisp crunch of a choc-ice being demolished – chocolate first, followed by licking – *never* biting – of ice cream.

I often sat in the security hut with Ciaran for my fag breaks. The smoking ban did not apply there, according to Ciaran, who perched on a foot stool, puffing gently on an unlit pipe (he'd quit several years before). He would share his flask of coffee with me, sometimes adding a nip of whiskey if it were really cold or if I were really pissed off. My being pissed off could be triggered by lots of different things: PMT, falling off the dieting bandwagon – again – not having a stitch to wear for an upcoming event, being skint, Shane, my mother, the weather, the boss, a broken nail, the size of my hips, the state of my hair. Ciaran sat and listened. He reminded me of my father. He was on my side. I declined his kind offer of coffee and sympathy and headed for my car. The thoughts in my head had grown wings and were buzzing around the edge of my consciousness, begging for attention: Shane, the impend-ing meeting with my boss on Monday morning, the tautness of the relationship between me and my mother, the Bernard O'Malley situation.

And Patrick. But I couldn't think about him and drive at the same time. In fact, I just couldn't think about him at all.

6

My flat was on Cowper Road in Rathmines, the first floor of a red-brick period house with a stoop at the front and a rambling, overgrown garden at the back. Caroline and I had lived there for two years and the landlord – a dote – hadn't upped the rent since we arrived. In return for this, we kept an eye on his father – old man Jenkins – who lived in the cavernous ground floor of the house. This mostly involved telling him in advance when we were having a party so he felt he couldn't complain about the noise the following day, and calling down when we were skint so he would make us toasted cheese sandwiches smothered in black pepper and pour us vast quantities of the foul-smelling whiskey he favoured. Whenever I had any cash – usually the first couple of days after payday before the overdraft kicked in again – I picked him up a pack of John Player Blues and a copy of the *Racing Post*. He was what used to be called 'a perfect gentleman', a dapper little man, immaculately dressed in a suit that was now too big for him and a fisherman's cap which he doffed at passers-by on the street.

I checked the hall table for letters. My post consisted entirely of flyers and a Visa bill as thick as a bull's leg. I missed getting real letters in the post. Patrick wrote real letters. He loved writing. Loved that connection between pen and paper. Magic, that's what he called it. He wanted to be a writer but was an accountant instead. What was that Oscar Wilde quotation?

One's real life is often the life one does not live.

Patrick was a great writer. He could really express himself on paper. You could see his face and imagine his gestures when you read his letters.

I ignored the post and continued down the hallway, fumbling for my keys as I went.

I had the flat to myself. Caroline was on a blind date set up weeks ago by Clare's husband-to-be, Richard. Richard was one of those types who thought nobody could be happy unless they were one half of a couple that hosted dinner parties and finished each other's sentences. He had set me up with a couple of his cousins. Before I met Shane, I mean. He had stacks of cousins.

Caroline always went on first blind dates in the afternoon, just in case the guy turned out to be a socially challenged psycho. According to Caroline, psycho symptoms did not present themselves till after dark. She was superstitious that way.

I checked my mobile for texts. None. I went into the 'inbox' to make sure none had slipped through while I wasn't looking. Still none. I rang my voice mail. 'You have no messages' I was told in clipped and no uncertain terms.

I thought about ringing Shane and, once the thought was planted, I knew I was going to. I also knew I shouldn't. It was against The Rules (according to Laura). Rule No. 32(b), subsection III clearly states, 'if you have rung your boyfriend and left a message, it is strictly forbidden to ring him again before he has returned your call.' The rule changed slightly if you rang but *hadn't* left a message, but this was a grey area and subject to the call being made to a landline that did *not* have caller ID or any similar identifying technology.

I sat on the couch for ten minutes with the phone in my hand. In my defence, I picked up the receiver and replaced it. Twice. The third time I picked up, dialled and then hung up. The fourth time, I rang, as I knew I would. He picked up on the seventh ring.

'Hello.'

'Hi Shane, it's me.'

'Who?'

'It's me. Grace.'

'Grace, sorry. I wasn't expecting a call from you. How are you?'

I bit my lip – hard – and managed to stop myself asking why he wasn't expecting a call from me. I had called him yesterday morning and left a message. I was his girlfriend of one-year-nine-months-three-weeks-and-six-days. No, seven days – four weeks actually. You'd think, after all that time, I was precisely the person he would expect a call from. Especially since we hadn't spoken since last Wednesday. I had made that call too.

'Grace? Are you there?' I could hear voices in the background. Lots of them. And glasses clinking.

'Are you in the pub?' I sounded like my mother.

'Yes.' Defensive.

'Good,' I said. 'Great. I'd hate to think you were pining for me in your flat all by yourself.' I laughed then, making sure that he knew I was joking.

'Listen Grace, the line is bad and it's hard to hear you. Can I give you a buzz in the morning?'

'Sure. Grand. I'll talk to . . .'

'OK, Grace, goodbye.' The line went dead and the flat was quiet after the noise of the pub on the phone.

I looked at my watch. The call had lasted nineteen seconds.

I ran myself a scalding bath, pouring large dollops of essence of something or other into the steaming water. The bottle promised tranquillity, serenity and calm, which sounded all right with me. I shed my clothes, taking care not to look towards the full-length mirror in the corner of the bedroom. I lowered myself slowly into the bath and lay there for several minutes, sinking below the bubbles, enjoying the sound of the silence underwater. I resurfaced, red-faced and breathless, and thought about Bernard and his text. It was so matter-of-fact, which, for some reason, annoyed me. The fact that I was annoyed, annoyed me further still. Although it wasn't really annoyance, it was something else, but I couldn't quite put my finger on it. It wasn't just the sex. It was more than that. Something real. I had felt something real. It had been a long time since I felt that. It was shocking, like cold water in a hot shower.

The phone rang and I leapt out of the bath and ran, skidding on the tiled floor of the bathroom and banging my knee against the edge of the toilet. It was probably Shane ringing me back. He had gone outside the pub where it was quieter so he could ring me and apologise for being short earlier. Not that he'd been short exactly. I mean, you can't say a lot when you're surrounded by people in a pub, right?

I reached the phone at the fifth ring. It was a wrong number. Somebody looking for Call-A-Cab. Again. It was always happening. Our numbers were almost identical.

'I need a taxi.' Pub noises in the background again.

'Sorry, you've got the wrong number.' I don't know why *I* was apologising. I always did that.

'From Slatterys, in Rathmines. I'll be outside waiting for you.'

'You need to dial a seven at the end, not a six.'

'Just going into town. Dame Street.'

'This is not Call-A-Cab!' I shouted this time, freezing in my pelt with a puddle of water collecting on the floor around my feet.

'Why the fuck didn't you say so before?' He hung up and I was left, again, with a dial tone in my ear.

I hobbled back into the bathroom, my knee throbbing, my teeth chattering with the cold. I comforted myself with the thought of Shane phoning tomorrow. Tomorrow was Sunday.

We could talk for hours. Catch up. I could make him laugh. I loved the way he laughed. Like someone trying not to laugh.

I had met Shane though Caroline, the eldest sister of four lads, one of whom was Shane. I'd met Caroline when she joined our company two years ago and I still remember the look on the boss's face when he told us about her.

'She will be a valuable asset to the department,' he told us, his chest puckering up and his forehead slinky with sweat just thinking about her.

'University educated, buckets of experience, raring to go,' he said, his imagination doing cartwheels thinking about the places he would like her to go, preferably with him, and obviously without his wife's knowledge. Laura had seen Caroline leaving the meeting room after her second interview with Il Duce and reported to us that she was 'quite attractive'.

This obviously meant that Caroline was a stunner, as Laura refused to comment favourably on the physical attributes of other women, whom she called 'The Competition.' We awaited her arrival with interest and not a little trepidation.

She was due into the office at 9 a.m. on a Monday morning. We sat hunched over our monitors, pecking anxiously at keyboards. I was meandering aimlessly along the shelves of eBay, searching for something to buy. I glanced at my watch: 9.30 a.m. and still no sign of Caroline. She hadn't arrived by the time I came back from my first fag break (10 a.m.) and still no show when I returned to my little hen-coop after a quick make-up repair at 10.45 a.m. I was just considering a sneaky second fag break at 11.30 a.m. when she arrived. I immediately sent an email to Ethan, whom I had promised to update with Caroline's vital statistics:

Ethan, she's here – 2 and a half hours late!! I don't know if she's your type, she's very tall, I think you'll just about come up to her

chin, even in your lizard-skin boots. She's very beautiful in a sort of ethereal, blonde kind of way. She's skinny (so obviously I can't be friends with her) and she's wearing a very understated, chic navy suit with a very short skirt (take it easy, cowboy...) and dangerously high heels – I'd better warn her about the grid on the second floor – remember the time I got the heel of The Highest Shoes in Ireland caught in it? God I loved those shoes ... Anyway, I digress. Will keep you posted.
Grace
xx

I got an email back from Ethan almost immediately:

What the flip does 'ethereal' mean???????

Ethan never cursed on email. In fact, he just never cursed. He was old-fashioned that way.

Caroline was walking towards our area, the boss at her side, struggling to keep up with her as she strode towards us rather imperiously. The words 'ice queen' floated up from the murky depths of my mind. The boss brought Caroline to a halt, taking her arm in his clammy pink hand, allowing his stubby fingers to brush against her waist. She stepped away from him with no attempt at discretion and the boss was left with his hand in mid-air, which he slowly lowered.

'Eh, guys, can I have your attention please?' He always called us 'guys' in an effort to simulate a friendly 'team' environment, especially when newcomers arrived.

'Guys, this is Caroline O'Brien, who's joining us today. I've already told you all about her and I'm sure you'll make her very welcome.' He did not look at all sure of this as he said it, his mouth disappearing into a thin line as he eye-balled each of us in turn. Our boss didn't really have too much time for us and it was obvious that he had earmarked Caroline to be his pet, his mole, the one who would make us sit up straighter in our seats and show us how it was really done. And after all his bragging about her qualifications, experience and education, we sort of felt the same way about her.

Then she opened her mouth and spoke. Her voice was that of someone who had been smoking heavily since the age of two: rasping and hoarse. Her Cork accent was thick, uncompromising and when she talked – which was most of the time – the words tumbled out of her mouth in a heap as if there simply wasn't enough time in the world for everything she had to say.

'Ara lads, sorry I'm late. I was just about to explain to the boss-man here that I was out late last night, celebratin' the new job like, and I had such a head on me this mornin', I feckin' missed me train to Dublin, like. I was actually supposed to come up yesterday but sure, ye know yerselves, like, when the session (she pronounced it 'seshoon') starts in the pub at lunchtime, it's impossible to drag yourself away, like.' These three sentences took her approximately two and a half seconds and, while we couldn't really understand everything she was saying, we liked the way she was saying it and the fact that the smug smirk slid off the boss's face like a pancake from a ceiling. She was one of us, and he knew it immediately.

Within three months of starting, Caroline had established herself as one of the brightest employees the company had ever known. She set up a Sports and Social Committee (without the sports bit, obviously), which she cajoled management to fund fifty per cent of, organised a lottery syndicate (so far we've won €3.72 between twenty of us), took over from Brian as the union rep and began a relentless lobbying campaign for flexi-time, more holidays, double-paid overtime and the installation of showers – and possibly a Jacuzzi – in the boardroom.

'Sure, what do we really use that room for anyway?' she quipped at the boss during one of our Monday morning meetings. Caroline liked to jog at lunchtime and was unimpressed with the meagre facilities available to her (i.e. none) to 'quench the stench, like' as she put it.

The boss did not merely dislike her, he *abhorred* her. Meetings were always a lot more entertaining when Caroline was there, which, unfortunately, was not often enough. She was a loss adjuster, which meant that she was out of the office a lot, investigating insurance claims, intimidating witnesses and bullying scangers (that's what she called the claimants) into accepting meagre settlements for their ferociously exaggerated whiplash claims. When she did attend the meetings, the boss kept them as brief as possible – no mean feat when you consider how much he loved the sound of his own voice – and informed us of any Nasty News at the end of the day by email instead before legging it into the sanctuary of his BMW in his attempts to avoid her.

In short, she was the best thing that had ever happened to us at work, and we adored her.

Caroline and I clicked immediately, despite her beauty and brains. We had the same ideas about men (we came from the 'all men are *potential* bastards' school of thought – still idealists really), we both adored clothes, shoes and bags (the more the merrier was our rule of thumb) and we laughed at the same things (like people tripping up in the street when they're on their own; and going into the Information Office on O'Connell Street and asking them what the capital of Nigeria is; and putting on make-up in the mens' toilets of a restaurant, watching through the mirror as the men open the door and then back out with that look men get when they've just had an orgasm or are confused).

At the time, I lived in a basement bedsit in Portobello, riddled with damp and a smell akin to old feet. Caroline shared a four-bedroom house in Blanchardstown with Cork people and, after a month, she admitted that it was just 'too much

Cork, like'. We moved in to Cowper Road shortly after that and we'd been there ever since. While I had heard all about her four brothers – mainly in the derogatory sense – I didn't actually meet Shane until about six months after I met Caroline. Here's how it happened.

Friday, 30 May 2003: 18.00

Caroline and I were heading to Cork for the June bank holiday weekend. We took the train. My car had just failed the NCT, hands-down – again – and was cowering in a garage in Portobello. Caroline didn't have a car and couldn't drive. Why would she, when she mostly jogged everywhere? Apart from us, there were several thousand other people fleeing the city with hysterical haste. I stood under the armpit of an exceptionally tall man with a twitch and a heavy nose cold. Every time he blew his nose – which was often – it sounded like the brass section of an orchestra tuning up. Caroline was bet in against me, trying to read the latest copy of *Heat*. She had to hold the magazine about two inches from her face due to the space constraints. A breeze from a nearby open window blew strands of her hair against my face, which itched terribly. My hands were clamped against my thighs and I was afraid to move them in case people fell out of either end of the train. Instead, I blew at the pale threads of hair, which worked until I ran out of breath, then, like children running home after curfew, they returned to tickle and torment me. I shifted my weight from one foot to the other and stood – again – on the tall guy's sock-clad, sandal-shod foot. He let out a strangled yelp – I was wearing my new silver sandals with a deadly sharp kitten heel – before blowing his reddening nose long and hard into a soggy handkerchief.

'Sorry,' I mumbled – again – against the rough fabric of his shirt. The train stopped at Limerick Junction, screeching

painfully against the tracks. The doors flew open and a torrent
of bank holiday-makers coursed onto the platform clutching
bags, guitars, hurls, hats and small children. One woman, in
wide brown leather sandals and a huge, wrinkled brown dress,
gripped the handle of a cat cage. A pair of bright green eyes
gazed lazily through the bars, ignoring the chaotic scene with
a dismissive flick of her tail. I didn't actually know the sex of
the cat but she looked like a she-cat with her air of haughty
disdain. In fact, she looked a bit like my mother.

Caroline and I sank into two now-vacant seats. The air in
the carriage was thick with hot bodies and stale breath. I exhaled for what seemed like the first time since we left Dublin.

I turned my head towards the window and stared across endless fields that ran to meet an indifferent sky. The fields were
divided by low stone walls, the flat stones piled precariously on
top of each other, their edges jagged and protruding.

'Oh look, there's a cow.' I perked up and pressed my nose
against the window.

'For God's sake, Grace,' Caroline glanced up from her
magazine. 'Surely you've seen a cow before?'

'Yeah, but they seem more interesting when you're on your
holidays in the country.'

'Grace, for the millionth time, we're not going to the country. We're going to Cork, the *real* capital city. Now shut up
about the wildlife and answer this quiz, OK? You've been invited to a fabulous party where you will be rubbing shoulders with the crème de la crème of society, including the guy
you've fancied for the past six months. But you have nothing
to wear and no money to buy anything new. Do you:

a) Wear an outfit you already own: after all, if the guy is
    worthwhile, he won't be all that interested in what you
    look like, right?

Caroline and I exchanged knowing looks at this suggestion.

'My God, who *writes* this stuff?' I threw myself back against my seat in disgust. 'Go on.'

   b) Max out your credit card, beg, borrow and steal if necessary to get yourself a new dress and accoutrements.

'Wait. Would "accoutrements" include hairdo, nails, facial as well as bag, shoes, tights and wrap?' I worried.

'It can mean anything you want it to, it's just a stupid quiz in a magazine.' Caroline's voice was assuming The Tone, which it did when she got impatient with my attention to detail in the fantasy world I liked to visit.

'OK, definitely B then. What's the third one?'

'No point in telling you, you're definitely not going to go for it and anyway, you've already chosen B.' Caroline had turned the page of her magazine and pretended to be absorbed in an article about twin boys, separated from birth, who found each other twenty years later, when it transpired that they were being two-timed by the same woman who was also, incidentally, a twin. I leaned across the table at Caroline.

'Don't make me come over there and . . .' I stopped talking, distracted by the sliding open of the door at the top of the carriage. I glanced up and there he was. He stood at the top of the carriage, tossing floppy, blond hair out of his way to reveal bright blue eyes fringed with long, curling eyelashes. He had everything a romantic hero should have: strong jawline, dark with stubble, a straight nose jutting over dark pink, bee-stung lips. And then he smiled, looking straight at me, revealing two rows of perfectly straight teeth, white as snow against a backdrop of sallow skin. I snatched my head away, pretending to admire my newly painted nails. I painted them in the Dublin colours, just to annoy as many Cork people as possible. For the craic. He bent to pick up his bag and strode towards us, in an immaculately cut suit – dark navy with a blue and white pinstriped shirt.

'Caroline,' I hissed. 'Serious eye candy. Twelve o'clock.' No, *my* twelve o'clock,' I added as she craned her neck down the empty aisle behind me. Caroline's head jerked around and her eyes widened as she took in the Adonis heading our way. Then she grinned and slid out from her seat to face him.

'Hiya,' she said to him in a very ordinary way. He set his bags carefully on the floor before wrapping his arm about her neck and holding her in a rugby-style tackle against his waist, rubbing the top of her head and making her hair crackle with static. I was more than a little alarmed. Caroline's hair was her pride and joy. It was rarely out of place and I shivered to think of her reaction to this manner of greeting. Maybe he was from Belfast or the Faroe Islands and this was their traditional greeting ritual? I'd never been to the Faroe Islands. Or Belfast. Caroline's response to this ill treatment was to hook her foot around the Greek god's leg and shove him backwards. He landed with a thump on the floor of the carriage and began smoothing his hair anxiously. Caroline was smoothing hers too. The pair of them glared at each other and then started to laugh at the same time. Their laughs sounded the same. In fact, they didn't look all that dissimilar. Still, the penny took a while to drop. Caroline extended her hand to him and helped him to his feet.

'Grace, I'd like you to meet my little brother, Shane. Shane, Grace thinks you're gorgeous. She was checking you out when you got on the train.'

At that moment, I hated everything I usually loved about Caroline. I blushed a putrid purple and said in a strangled voice, 'Nice to meet you. Caroline has told me some really dreadful things about you.'

'Oh, so *you're* Grace?' he said. 'Caroline never told me you were quite so beautiful.'

Caroline snorted.

'Leave her alone, Shane. Don't make me hurt you again.' Still reeling from the shock of Shane's casually dropped comment about my beauty – did you hear that? my beauty! – I said nothing at all. Shane sat down beside Caroline, who elbowed him in the ribs. He elbowed her back. I'd say they must have driven their mother crazy when they were kids. Now he was picking up her magazine and reading from the problem page in a pronounced American accent.

'Dear Angie,' he drawled. 'My boyfriend slept with my best friend, but he's, like, rilly, rilly sorry.'

'Give me that.' Caroline pulled the magazine out of his hands, ripping the page. 'Jesus, you're such a child. At least you only have one brother, Grace, and he's normal.'

'Patrick? I wouldn't say normal exactly. I mean, he's the only six-foot redhead I know who plays the violin and likes to go to the ballet of a Friday night.'

'Oh, is he a bit of a nancy boy then?' Shane bent his hand at his wrist and puckered up his lips.

'You should ask Caroline that,' I said, eyeing Caroline with a sly smile. She and Patrick sometimes went out and Caroline didn't always come home from those nights. Caroline returned my look and ignored me.

'What are you doing getting on here?' Caroline asked Shane when she got tired of physically assaulting him.

'Well,' he began in a Cork accent that you could cut with a steak knife. He launched into a tale about a fella called Mossy who gave him a lift from Dublin. The original plan was for both of them to end up in Cork. Shortly after leaving Dublin, Mossy (real name Maurice Fitzgerald, apparently) picked up a hitchhiker called Bridget. Bridget, during the course of the two hours it took to get to where she was going, developed a fondness, shall we say, for the aforementioned Mossy and persuaded him to stay with her for the weekend. It didn't take much to persuade Mossy, who hadn't had much luck with the ladies recently, due mainly to a post-pubescent outbreak of acne that had taken over large tracts of his face and neck. Bridget, it turned out, was a very spiritual person and told Mossy that he had a warm and profound aura: she could tell that he was a good man. Mossy, who fully intended to get the leg over as many times as he could that weekend, had no problem whatsoever in telling his great pal of many years, Shane, to bugger off – in a warm and profound way, of course.

'So here I am,' Shane finished dramatically, flicking his hair again. His telling of the story had involved much gesticulating with his hands, which gave me an opportunity to study the form. The fingers were shorter and stockier than I would have liked, but the nails were well manicured and clean (an absolute must-have). The hands were curiously hairless but smooth and so very brown.

'That Mossy is a venereal disease waiting to happen,' Caroline said with a dismissive flick of her hair. (I later discovered that this was a genetically inherited trait: the whole family did it, even the father, who didn't have a hair on his head. Apparently, he'd had a great mop of blond hair in his youth and, like an amputee who still feels an itch in a long-departed limb, Mr O'Brien still flicked with the best of them).

'You weren't complaining last Hallowe'en, I hear,' Shane said with a grin. He shielded his face with his hands as Caroline's fists rained down on him. The pair of them were off again, pinching and kicking and biting (that was Caroline, mostly) and poking and tickling (Shane). They were like a pair of lion cubs learning how to survive in the wild by beating their siblings senseless. It was quite fascinating to watch and I sat back and wished I had a bucket of popcorn.

Shane was twenty-three then – I know, I know, I was twenty-seven and should have known better. To be honest, I didn't fall in love with him right there and then. It was seven hours later, after The Incident in the pub.

7

Caroline and Shane and I made our way to their family home by taxi after the train finally arrived in Cork at 8 p.m. There were leaves on the track or some such nonsense. Bear in mind that it was spring. Caroline's parents surprised me by being very short. Her mother was about five and a half feet tall and her father came up to his wife's shoulders, where he rested his hairless head at every available opportunity. Dogs and cats had the run of the house, their hairs covering every surface. Shane – the youngest of the litter – had to bend low to give his mother the hug she insisted on. Mrs O'Brien then unzipped the weekend bag he dropped in the hall and removed a large plastic bag full of – dirty – clothes. These were removed to the utility room and divided into three neat bundles (whites, darks, colours). I guessed – correctly – that they would next be seen washed, starched, folded and generally loved-up in Shane's bag for his return to Dublin on Sunday. Irish mammies and their sons. Mam had been like that with Patrick.

'Are you from Dublin originally, Grace?' Mrs O'Brien asked me. She pronounced it 'Aroooooo from Dublin . . .' She looked sad when I told her I was, but rallied quickly and showed me to my room.

'That's a lovely name, Grace, so it is.' Mr O'Brien said at the dinner table. It was the first time he had spoken since I arrived and I was surprised at how deep and serious his voice was, given his shortness. It wasn't that he was shy, just that he couldn't get a word in edgeways, what with Caroline and her mother talking at full tilt.

'Thanks,' I said. 'My mother was going to call me Caitlin but then when I was born, I was really long and skinny, if you can believe that. The skinny bit, I mean.' I laughed there and went on.

'They said I was the longest baby girl born in Holles Street that year and because I was born on a Tuesday, dad insisted I be called Grace.'

'Tuesday's child is full of Grace,' Mr O'Brien quoted softly, his eyes half closed. 'It suits you,' he said, just before I reached for my wineglass and knocked it over. It was an Irish linen tablecloth and even though Mrs O'Brien said it didn't matter, I knew she would curse me later when she ran it under the cold tap and rubbed salt into the blood-red stain. Mr O'Brien made shepherd's pie for dinner and when I found two inexplicably thick dark hairs in the gravy, not dissimilar to the dog's pelt, I moved my fork around the plate, mashing the dinner against the plate in an effort to make it look eaten.

Mrs O'Brien – call me Sheila, like – served lashings of wine with dinner. Considering I'd eaten one Iarnród Éireann super-skinny ham sandwich since breakfast and practically none of the shepherd's pie, I was half-cut by the time myself and Caroline ventured out into the town.

'It's a city, Grace, a city,' Caroline roared at me. Shane had left earlier, his mother trying to comb down the front of his hair with wet fingers. He dodged her and escaped, blowing her a kiss from the safety of the front door. She didn't come away from the porch window until he turned the corner at the end of the drive and she couldn't see him any more.

Despite the fact that I was in the country, I did not tone down my city look and wore enough sequins, sparkles and slashed fabric to sink a ship. Caroline, of the more is more school of make-up, did my face and, while I looked grand under subdued lighting, I would have to be extinguished in more natural surroundings. We stumbled forth to Ryan's bar on Synge Street. Once ensconced in a corner seat with a tall pint in hand, I cast a cold Jackeen-type eye around the pub and noticed the following things:

- Cork people LOVE to talk. They pepper their sentences with 'y'knows' and 'likes' and speak at the speed of light. OK, OK I'm exaggerating slightly, maybe just the speed of sound then. Or just breakneck speed. It was only when someone said 'y'know?' and looked at me that I realised it was my turn to talk, not because of any comprehension I had as to what they were saying.
- Because the Cork accent is so high pitched and sing-songy, you could put the conversation in the pub to music and make a record.
- Cork people love all things Cork. The downside of this is that they seem to hate everything else, especially women from Dublin. I mean, think about it, have you ever met a couple in a *long-term, happy relationship*, one of whom hails from Cork, the other from Dublin? No, I didn't think so.

The Incident didn't happen until nearly closing time. By that stage, myself and Caroline were joined by Mary, Moira and Marie – Caroline's friends from school – as well as Mossy. Things hadn't worked out as well as planned with Bridget. He was now calling her the Hitchhiker from Hell, pulling at an imaginary rope around his neck when he spoke about her. He looked a lot different than I imagined. He was short with a barrel chest and tight leather pants. He was funny though, and charming. After a while in his company, I was beginning to realise why Bridget the Hitchhiker had allowed him into her life, albeit for a brief period. What was very clear to me from the first time I met Mossy was that he was besotted with Caroline. Nothing new there.

Shane stood at the bar for the evening, surrounded by a motley crew of women and men. Mostly women, actually. He had what you might call a *quality*. People listened when he spoke. They laughed with him, not at him, and even when he wasn't talking, people – especially the women – stole glances at him. Glances full of admiration, wistfulness and, as the evening wore on, hope. Shane paid attention to them all. He included everyone in the conversation, bathing them in the light of his smile. Apart from nodding to him on my various trips to and from the bar laden down with ever more complicated drinks as the night wore on, I hadn't spoken to him.

'I'm going outside for a smoke,' I bellowed at Caroline.

'What?' I could see her mouth forming the word but I couldn't hear it. I shook my cigarette box towards her and pointed at the door. She waved and mouthed something I couldn't make out.

I elbowed my way to the back of the pub through the thick fug of noise and sidled past a couple engaged in heavy petting, framed under the arch of the doorway. The smoking area was nearly as packed as the pub and just as hot, with several patio heaters jostling for space and bearing down on me. I moved away, making my way to the side of the building, which was deserted. I leaned against the wall, pleasantly cold against my back. Lighting up, I exhaled, pushing a thick line of smoke out of my mouth before trying to blow smoke rings. I've never really mastered the art and only ever practised on my own. When I heard the crunch of footsteps on gravel, I rearranged my facial features into some semblance of normality and looked up.

A man stood at the top of the alleyway, silhouetted faintly against the slither of moon, lying lazily on her back. He smoked, the end of his cigarette flaring bright orange when he inhaled.

He straightened when he noticed me and began zig-zagging his way towards me, lurching heavily from side to side. He was a big man, bulky with powerful forearms straining against the thin fabric of his T-shirt. A dirty tan lay in a half moon across his thick neck. A dark mat of black curling hairs reached over the top of the shirt. It was quiet down here. Isolated, really. I turned to walk to the other end of the alley leading onto the bright lights of Synge Street, but it was crammed with empty beer kegs, their rounded bellies glinting shreds of silver in the moonlight. They blocked my way.

I stopped walking and concentrated on smoking, fixing my eyes on the wall, gathering my wrap tightly about my shoulders. I could hear his footsteps, stumbling. And then they stopped. I could feel him, inches away, swaying in the small space between us. His breath was hot and damp. I lifted my head and nodded with a smile that was just small enough to discourage him but not too small that it might be construed as rude. I could see then how drunk he was. His eyes, the whites shot through with red threads, focused slowly.

'Howya,' I said. My voice sounded high and breathy. A spotlight on my fear. I'm not usually afraid. I'm a big girl and can handle myself. This felt different.

'I seen you in the pub tonight. You and your mates. Laughin'.' His eyes were slits now.

I laughed one of those laughs you do in an awkward situation.

Encouraged by this, he inched closer. I drew back, the sharp pebbledash of the wall scraping my skin.

'Where are ya goin' later?' He dragged his fingers across my collar bone. They were cold and damp, like fish tails.

'Stop.' I struggled to control my voice. I looked around. There was no one there. We were alone.

'You think you're too good for the likes of me, doncha?' he slurred at me, swaying slightly as he spoke.

'What are you talking about? I don't even know you.' I spoke as lightly as I could, clamping on a smile. 'I'm just here for the weekend. Are you a local yourself?' The words tripped off my tongue as I tried to maintain a semblance of normality.

He bent down towards me, our foreheads almost touching. His breath was hot and I tried not to flinch from him.

'Are you from Dublin?' He spoke in a low voice. My gut instinct was to deny, deny, deny.

'Yes,' I said briefly, then, 'now if you'll excuse me.' I tried to side-step him but there was just too much of him, and he blocked my way. He began jabbing me with the tip of his index finger.

'You bitches are all the same.' He said this slowly, prodding me with his finger on my shoulder after every word. It hurt. Anger pushed past fear in my head.

'Get out of my way.' I tried to push past him, but he was like a slab of concrete. The moon slid behind a blanket of cloud and we were in darkness. I could feel sweat, cold against my skin. My breath caught in my throat, constricted by panic. With his two hands on my shoulders, he pressed me against the wall.

'I'm just trying to talk to you.' He was shouting now, his spittle pricking my face. Instinctively, I thrust my knee between his legs. There was a high-pitched groan and, for a moment, I couldn't tell if it came from him or me. He was bent in two, moaning softly. I ran, but he grabbed the ends of my wrap, yanking me back. I fell against him. He held me by the hair, handfuls of it in his fist. Panic pushed at the pain until I couldn't feel it. I dragged air into my lungs as I struggled against him – I needed my inhaler. My vision was beginning to blur at the edges.

'You fucking cunt.' He whispered the words slowly as he straightened, dragging me against him. Suddenly, there was a shout and the clean crack of a fist connecting with bone. The man slumped to the ground and stayed there, blood running a trail down his face from a gash along his cheekbone. I was on my knees, hysterical for oxygen, the corners of my mouth turning blue.

'Oh Christ.' I heard a man's voice and looked up. It was Shane, breathing heavily, his hand curled into a fist. My breath was a wheeze and I pressed an imaginary inhaler into my mouth, desperate to make him understand. For a second, he stood there. Then he reached down and grabbed the man under each arm, dragging him away from me.

'I'll be back, Grace. Hold on,' he yelled, but the words were lost in the blackness of the night, weighing me down, suffocating me.

The next thing I remembered was my head being lifted and an inhaler clamped between my teeth. It hissed loudly and I strained towards it. My first coherent thought was that I'd had a near-death experience and my life hadn't flashed before my eyes. Nor did I see a dark tunnel with a bright light at the end of it. The second coherent thought was about Shane, who was feeding me my inhaler and holding me in his arms, tight against him. His eyes were wide with anxiety and his breath was warm against my face. He kept repeating himself.

'You'll be all right,' he said. 'You'll be all right.'

And I was all right. That's when I fell in love with him. I mean, what would you do?

8

The sound of the front door banging roused me from my watery depths. The bath water had cooled and daylight leaked from the room.

'Honey, I'm home.' Caroline came straight into the bathroom and pulled the shower curtain across the bath. 'Don't worry, I can't see you,' she said, lowering the toilet seat before sitting on it, sighing. She waited for me to ask.

'How did your date go?' I asked obediently, curling the edge of the curtain around my head so I could see her. Her normally immaculate blonde halo of hair was tousled and there was a rip in her jacket that had definitely not been there yesterday. Her white T-shirt was creased and stained with what looked like muck. The date had either gone extremely well or extremely badly. Now I was curious and wanted details.

'I did a runner,' she answered breathlessly, like she'd just run four miles – I later learned that she had.

'Oh no, not again, Cats.'

'I had to. You have no idea. First, he arrives in a suit with a dickie bow. For coffee! On a Saturday! A dickie bow with tiny Homers all over it, saying "doh", like he was trying to be cool or something. Then, when I suggest Café Java, he's like, "no way, the coffees there are seriously overpriced and they don't support the fair trade lobby".'

'The what?' I struggled to sit up in the bath.

'You know that thing Chris Martin is always banging on about. He wears those wrist bands.'

'Oh, right.' I'd read something about that in *Heat*. 'OK, so
he's politically aware with inappropriate dress sense. That's
hardly the end of the world, is it?'

'There's more.' Caroline fixed me with one of her looks
(narrowed eyes, pursed mouth, furrowed brow).

'So he takes me to this "coffee shop", she spat the words
out, 'which was only a kip with plastic cutlery and one of those
fluorescent blue grid things for electrocuting flies. It was black
with flies, that thing, either dead or dying. Then, when we
order the coffee, he suggests we go *Dutch* because we've only
just met and it wouldn't be fair on either of us to have to foot
the entire bill. THE ENTIRE BILL. Which, by the way, came
to €2.50!'

'€2.50! Jesus. Where did you go on your date? Colombia?
What happened then?' I was in knots trying not to laugh in
the bath. Also, I was turning blue and my body had broken
out into a mass of pointy goose-pimples so I needed her to
finish up quickly so I could get out of the bath.

'So, he finishes his coffee, which, by the way, he nurses for
about half an hour, during which time he lectures me on the
sanctity of the rainforest, the land rights of the Maoris and
the mating habits of the dung beetle. He's then inspired by the
idea of ordering more coffee, so we can *continue to get to know
each other*. I mean, I haven't been able to get a fucking word
in sideways, with his unfeasibly boring monologue. So I say,
yeah, sure, why not, we're having such a blast, it only seems
right. Then I excuse myself, head for the ladies and get up on
the toilet seat and start hoisting myself through this long, narrow window near the ceiling in one of the cubicles. You should
have seen me. I was like Houdini until I got stuck.'

I got a mental image and my body clenched with the effort
of not laughing.

Caroline, unaware of my tense situation, swept on.

'A woman came into the loos and saw me. First, she was

freaked out when she saw me dangling from the window, then she recognised me and knew I'd been sitting out in the caf with yer man. She'd heard him ask about an early bird menu when I was at the loo – it was a greasy spoon, for Christ's sake! – so she helped. Only for her giving me an almighty shove, I'd still be there.' Caroline looked down at herself, noticing the stains on her T-shirt and the rip in her jacket.

'A small price to pay,' she said, almost to herself.

That was it for me. I tried to stop but it was like trying to stop time. The laughing seemed to come out both ears, my nose, my mouth. It was a force; a snorting, guttural, roaring force, like a volcanic eruption. People have likened it to an angry machine gun (is there any other kind?).

Then a dodgy moment when Caroline looked offended, and then the pair of us were off, nearly weeping with the laughing. It felt great.

My mobile rang but neither of us were in any position to answer it. Caroline slid off the toilet seat and was now on all fours, bottom airside, beating the tiles on the bathroom floor with the palms of her hands, tears rolling down her face. I was hysterical. My head slid down the end of the bath and I choked on stagnant bath water. Caroline collected herself first and sat up on the bathroom floor, breathing heavily.

'Seriously though,' she said, 'that's it for me. No more blind dates. I'm done.'

'How are you going to break it to Richard?'

'You mean, Dr Love?'

Underneath his white shirts that were as crisp as brand-new bank notes, Richard was soft as butter. A banker with his heart on his sleeve and a cupid's arrow poised in his hands. If only his aim were better.

'But how are you going to meet men?' This was a serious problem in the city. Not my serious problem – I sent a silent prayer of thanks up to Benevolent Being in Sky – but a problem all the same. Look at my friends: Caroline, Laura, Jennifer. All attractive, funny, bright women, and all single. What was that all about? Where were the men hiding in Dublin? I'm talking about the *single* men, lots of available married ones, of course, just no singletons with only enough baggage to make them interesting. House-trained. Able to stand up straight on two hind legs.

Caroline considered my question carefully.

'Night classes?' she finally came up with.

'What kind?'

'Cookery?'

'No. They'll either be gay or married or both.'

'Art?'

'Gay or elderly or both.'

'Creative writing?' She was reaching now.

'Obsessive. Introverted. Hairy.'

'Well, *what* then?'

'I don't know. A chance meeting. Maybe in a bookshop. Both of you reach for the same book. Fingertips touch. You apologise. He apologises at the same time. You laugh. He insists you take the book. You insist he takes the book. It goes on and on. He asks for your number.'

'Is he handsome?'

'Yes.'

'But not in a bookish kind of way?' (This means thick-lens glasses and a deep crease above the nose from reading in poor light.)

'No.'

'Tell me more.' Caroline settled herself back down on the toilet seat, waiting.

'Turns out he's French. From Bordeaux. He's a poet.'

'No, I'll have to stop you there,' said Caroline. 'Too drippy.'

'OK then, a painter. He's a painter.' Caroline nodded slowly, my cue to continue.

'He's come to Ireland because he's lost his inspiration.'

'Why? What happened to him?'

'Jesus, Cats, I don't know. Why does it matter?'

'Make it up. Please?'

'OK, OK. He's . . . He was . . .' I fished around in my head. 'Oh, I know. He's been disinherited.'

'No, I want him to be wadded.'

'But he still is wadded. With the painting and all. Did I mention that he's a *successful* painter?'

'But I want to visit his family pile in Bordeaux. I don't want him to be disinherited.'

'Anyway,' I said, ignoring her, 'when he sees you, in the bookshop . . .'

'What am I wearing?'

'I was just getting to that. You're wearing your red dress.'

'The short one, with the ribbon under the boobs?'

'Yes, with the matching wedge-heeled mules that make your feet look tiny,' I said quickly before she could ask. Caroline had a thing about her feet. They were long and narrow with toes like fingers. A generous size six and a half.

'Anyway, he sees you and he's completely inspired and he spends the rest of his life painting you and he becomes even more famous than he already is and your portrait replaces the *Mona Lisa* in the Louvre and you live in France, on a vineyard where you lie in a hammock and swing gently in a warm breeze drinking wine and living happily everly after. The end.'

She smiled, believing it just for a moment. Then she came to.

'I'd better come up with something soon. I'm ageing here.'

I sat up and turned on the hot tap in the unlikely event of there being any hot water left. I sang, '*Who let the dogs out?*' with great *woofs* at the end of each line, for no reason that I can come up with here.

'You're in good form for someone with a hangover. You *do* have one, don't you?'

'Yes,' I said, considering it and finding it odd. Not the hangover bit. The good form bit.

'Shane rang, didn't he?'

'I spoke to him just before you came in.' It wasn't a lie exactly, but I was glad of the shower curtain between us.

'Is our-man-in-London going to grace us with a visit any time soon?'

'He's going to call tomorrow. We'll talk about it then.'

I was going to have to ask Shane now. When he was coming over. Even though he hated being pinned down. And he *was* very busy with work and everything. Caroline didn't see it that way.

'He's my brother and I love him, but he'll wreck your head in the end.' She'd said that more than once. I tried to avoid the subject but if Caroline noticed, she didn't say.

Now, she was flossing her teeth, the hands moving backwards and forwards. I could hear her but not see her. I imagined her hands, a blur. She was particular about oral hygiene.

'Where were you last night?' she asked, stopping for a moment. I knew she was inspecting her work, lips curled back, teeth bared.

I stalled for time, unprepared for the question.

'What?' I said, sitting up in the water and pulling the plug. This bought me a minute or so: nobody could speak over the sound of the plumbing in this flat. It was like Niagara Falls after heavy rain. I could hear Caroline saying something but I couldn't hear what. I sat in the bath until most of the water had gone. When I pulled the shower curtain back a little, the bathroom was empty again.

I stood under the trickle of the shower, warming myself.

Back in my bedroom, I checked the missed call on my

mobile. It was from Ciaran – the dote. He'd left a message, wondering if I'd like to meet up with him and Michael for a drink that evening. When you get excited about the prospect of meeting up with two ageing homosexuals in Dublin city on a Saturday night, you need to start asking yourself serious questions about your social life. I threw on jeans and a long – forgiving – dress-like top with appropriate sparkles and spangles. I cursed Bernard for the lack of my all-purpose-all-weather black leather jacket and stepped out of the bedroom – in high heels, of course. They just look uncomfortable, you know. They don't actually hurt.

'So, where did you say you were last night?' Caroline assumed the beached – but skinny – whale position on the couch. The table beside her was strewn with thick orange peel and the skins of plums, black and shiny. She should be in an ad. For yoghurt. Or smoothies. Low-fat ones. Or maybe eternal youth. She had the glow of a woman who's just ingested an orchard in autumn. An alpine orchard on the edge of some far-flung mountain where the ozone layer is still intact.

This time, I was ready for her.

'I stayed round at Clare's.'

'Oh. Good night?'

'Eh, yeah. Look, I'm going to meet Ciaran and Michael for a pint in town. Do you fancy it?' I said.

'No thanks. I'm going to read these again.' There was a sheaf of papers on her lap, creased and worn. Letters. I knew who they were from.

'Grace, this is gas. Listen to what he says here.'

'Sorry Caroline, I've got to leg it. I'm late already . . .' I was halfway down the hall already, running the last few steps. When I closed the door behind me and leaned against it, the wood was cool against the heat of my face.

9

Ciaran and Michael's local pub of choice was the Palace on Fleet Street. It was always full of people who looked like they'd been trekking up the Dublin Mountains for weeks: tall, rangy, bearded men with boots and rainsheeters, women with scarce traces of lipstick and healthy-looking complexions. Lots of foreigners, all drinking pints of Guinness and wishing for dishes of oysters to make it the authentic Oirish experience. It was one of the few pubs left in Dublin that had not succumbed to the lure of the plasma screen, so there was still a hum of conversation about the place, among people sitting comfortably on soft armchairs, simulating a homestead without all the hassles that might entail.

With a brand-new €50 note – borrowed from Caroline against the promise of payday on Monday – I grabbed a taxi at the Swan Centre, getting in the back seat and twisting my neck at a 90 degree angle to deflect any conversation from the taxi driver. He started up anyway.

'Desperate weather love, isn't it?'

March was being honest again, sending rain like sheets down onto dirty streets. I opened my mouth to agree but there was no need. Luckily, he was one of those drivers where silence on the part of the passenger does not indicate disinterest or a wish for peace and quiet. It just means you're a good listener. Every so often, I zoned back in.

'Something, something . . . strikes . . . unions . . . something, blah, blah, ridiculous fares, blah, . . . something, vomiting on seats . . .' It was soothing in its way and we were in town in no time at all.

For being such a good listener, he rewarded me by not complaining about the size of my €50 note so, of course, I gave him a huge tip before remembering that the magic of the ATM machine was suspended till Monday.

I got out at Dame Street. I needed to get a pack of cigarettes before heading into the pub. I was picking myself carefully along the cobbled streets of Temple Bar when I saw him. The sight of him made me stop walking so suddenly, a man behind me bumped into my back before saying something that sounded like 'fuckin' eejit' and continuing on up the path.

He was tall. Even for a man, he was tall. Longer than fashionable red hair tucked behind surprisingly small ears. Duffel coat tightly buttoned over jeans with a tear – a sincere one – in the knee. He felt the cold and liked to dress as if he were still in college where he had wanted to do English literature but did accountancy instead because that's where Dad said the jobs were. But it was the book tucked under his arm that did it. *Dubliners*. Mr Joyce. Jimmy to his friends. His favourite book even when we slagged him and told him he was 'up himself'. 'What's wrong with a bit of Nick Hornby?' I said. 'Or some John Grisham? Tony Parsons, anyone? How about Roddy Doyle? Or just someone who's still alive for a change?'

I was standing there, still, a current of people flowing past me, moving around me. Then he turned and I saw that he was not Patrick. Of course he wasn't. How could he be? But he was Patrick's age. Or at least the age Patrick would be now, and he looked so like him, it was an effort not to move towards him, to put my hand on his shoulder, to say something. The man must have felt my stare because he looked at me then, right at me, with an expression that was almost like understanding.

I turned away slowly and made my way to the pub.

'Eh, Grace lass, what's the matter?' Ciaran looked at me, concerned. I hadn't realised I'd been crying. I told him I'd been arguing with my mother, which was never far from the truth. Although we didn't argue, as such.

'I wish you'd stop fighting with her. She's had a hard time this past year, like the rest of ye.'

'I wish she'd stop fighting with me.' I stabbed at the tears rolling down my face with Ciaran's oversized handkerchief. I was starting to convince myself that I *had* had an argument with my mother and that I was – of course – the wronged party.

Ciaran eyed me with all the wisdom of someone who has been an outlaw all his life (not all that long ago, it was almost legal to go 'gay hunting' on the weekends, no licence required).

'Grace love, talk to your mother,' he whispered to me, rubbing smudges of mascara from under my eyes with his thumbs. He'd been saying different versions of that same sentence for the last year.

Michael came in then and a light in Ciaran's eyes came on like Christmas.

I retreated downstairs to repair my make-up and when I returned they were discussing football results, which I soon put a stop to. We arranged ourselves around a table with a wobbly leg which Michael immediately rectified with some beer mats and an elastic band – he was like MacGyver that way. I told them about Caroline's disastrous date, embellishing wildly, enjoying the way Ciaran threw his head back and shook all over when he laughed. I was surprised to find that I was enjoying myself, the cold beer easing away the last traces of my hangover.

Michael was much quieter than Ciaran, preferring to sit back and listen, occasionally taking huge drags from a Biro he kept in the breast pocket of his shirt, tapping the nib against an imaginary ashtray in the middle of the table. Like Ciaran, he'd given up smoking years ago but sometimes liked to simulate the act, especially when he was having a pint on a Saturday night. The sight of his lips puckering up against the tip of the pen, his eyes creasing in pleasure when he inhaled gave me the gout for a fag so I excused myself and headed out onto Fleet Street. It was raining and I huddled in the porch, smoking quickly and joylessly. A drunken man dropped to his knees in the street, his arms outstretched and his face turned towards the dark vastness of the night sky. Rain streaked down the contours of his face like tears. I turned away and watched empty taxis crawl past, bored drivers drumming their fingers on steering wheels, their doors securely locked against the human condition they would later have to ferry home. Some of them were still talking up a storm. Maybe they were practising for later. Or maybe they were on to 'base'.

A couple walked up the street, linking arms in a curiously old-fashioned way. The man was tall with a powerful body under an unfortunate assembly of clothing (a tatty Salvation Army-esque jacket, a T-shirt that said 'say no to butter substitutes' or something like that, greasy blue jeans that stopped just above bony ankles). He held an umbrella protectively over the woman, who walked with her head down. She looked like she was trying not to step on the cracks in the pavement, oddly vulnerable in the inky gloom of the night. The man looked up then and I saw that he was wearing glasses. Teeny-tiny Joyce-like ones. Oh good Christ, it was Bernard O'Malley. It was too late for me to back into a corner of the porch and paste myself against the wall, unnoticed, which was my immediate reaction. I cursed myself for not touching up my make-up again before coming out for a fag, then cursed myself for cursing myself. I took another long drag from my cigarette, burning my lips on the filter, which had grown hot from my frantic chain-smoking.

'Grace, it *is* you.' He stopped in front of me, shifting awkwardly from one foot to the other. I choked on some speedily
inhaled cigarette smoke and started coughing, great hacking
coughs that sounded wet and diseased. They waited patiently
for me to finish and when I did not, Bernard thumped me on
the back with an outstretched hand – God, he really did have
lovely hands. I was now red in the face with watering eyes. I
took a great gulp of my pint and lit another cigarette, which
helped enormously. I finally managed to say 'hi' in a strangled
sort of voice. There was a silence then, punctured only by the
soft slap of the rain against their umbrella.

'Eh, Grace, this is Cliona. Cliona, this is one of my colleagues,
Grace.' Cliona, who had been doing a detailed study of her feet
during my choking fit, raised her head sharply as soon as she
heard my name. Her tiny face was obscured behind an enormous pair of glasses, à la Deirdre Barlow, and long, dark hair
that hung in curtains down to her shoulders. She reluctantly
proffered her hand, which I shook heartily, making her body
shudder with the ferocity of my bonhomie. Another awkward
silence. Then Bernard and I both said, 'So?' at the same time
and then laughed too hard, not looking at each other. Bernard
rallied first, speaking fast and a little breathlessly, as if he'd just
run up a flight of stairs.

'We're just going in here for a drink, actually. What are you
up to?' What did he think I was up to? Skulking in pub porch-
es, hoping for a kindly word from passers-by?

'I'm having a quick drink with Ciaran from work and his
friend Michael.' I waved my hands dismissively in the air, as
if I was then going someplace fascinating afterwards to do
something extraordinary. Which I was not, by the way. I noticed a patch of bruised skin on Bernard's neck surrounded
by what looked like teeth marks: my teeth marks, if I wasn't
very much mistaken. Cliona's teeth, which were now chattering loudly with the cold, did not look big enough or strong

enough to puncture skin as I had. Bernard, following my line of vision, suddenly reefed the lapel of his (truly terrible) jacket up against his neck and steered Cliona gently into the pub, his hand on the small of her very small back.

'We'll see you inside.' His words were lost in the roar of the crowd as he swung the door open and they were immediately swallowed in the swaying throng of people. The door swung shut and it was quiet again.

The drunk was now on his feet, swaying unsteadily with his head cocked to the side as if he were struggling to hear the voices in his head. He then staggered my way, a wide smile splitting his face. I crushed my cigarette with the pointed toe of my shoe and dived inside the pub. Battling my way through the crowd to our table, I noticed Cliona wedged in between Ciaran and Michael. Ciaran was now puffing contentedly on an empty pipe with his arms crossed comfortably about his ample body while Michael appeared to be putting his Biro out in an empty space in the middle of the table, one hand waving clouds of imaginary smoke away from the table. They should think about going into mime. Professionally. Bernard was bearing down on the table, holding a tray smothered in drinks as he dodged the swaying crowd. He didn't spill a drop. Stopping beside me, he whispered urgently in my ear.

'Sorry, Grace, Ciaran spotted me and insisted we join him for a drink. I hope that's OK with you?' Bernard looked like I felt: awkward and out of place. I waved my hands towards the table.

'No, no, it's fine,' I assured him. He wedged his way in between me and Cliona, placing a pint of Heineken on the table in front of me.

'Ciaran told me that's what you're drinking tonight. I can get you something else if you'd prefer?'

'No, no, it's fine.' God, could I *stop* saying that? I spoke with my head down. We were like two strangers in a lift. Bernard rubbed his hands up and down his thighs, as if trying to warm himself up. A sudden memory erupted in my head: his hands moving slowly along my body with his breath hot in my ear. I looked away from him and clamped my arms across my chest, my body rigidly upright.

'So Cliona, where are you from?' I asked. She looked at me like I'd just asked her if she was a spit or swallow woman.

'I'm from Bernard's hometown.' She staked her claim defiantly, her chin inching up a few inches. Her accent was high pitched and whiny.

'I'm just down for the weekend. I was supposed to arrive last night but I ended up working in the pub. One of my father's staff let him down at the last minute.' She looked at me meaningfully as she said this and I took refuge in my pint, lowering my head to drink from it, like a horse at a desert oasis. When I resurfaced, she was engaged in a lengthy debate with Ciaran and Michael about the filth of Dublin city and how she hated the noise and rush of the place. I became aware of the heat of Bernard's thigh, which was clamped against mine in the confines of the tiny space our little group was crammed into. I excused myself to go to the loo and doused my flushed face with cold water, leaning against the wash-hand basin. I shovelled escaped strands of hair back into my vice-like hair grip and cooled my face down with wet hands. Promising myself that I would leave after the pint, I walked out into the foyer straight into Bernard, who was coming out of the gents.

'Grace.' I loved the way he said my name.

'You're not stalking me, are you?' I peered up at him in a mildly flirtatious manner. What was I *doing*?

'I don't know what I'm at, to be honest.' He inched forward and I inched away until my back was up against the wall.

'I hope this isn't going to be awkward in work? I mean, between us?' I was anxious to get his take on last night.

'I'm really glad you said that,' Bernard sighed with relief, as if he thought I might have lain across his work station on Monday morning and demanded a repeat performance of Friday night.

'I'm only new in the place and I'd hate for there to be any atmosphere between us.' He spoke softly, his breath warm against my face.

'Well, I'm glad we got that sorted.' I spoke too loudly, my hand playing with a newly escaped strand of hair.

'Yeah, me too.' Bernard stood ramrod straight and seemed to have stopped breathing. The space between us suddenly seemed to shrink and all I could think about was this man's tongue on that patch of skin on my neck just underneath my earlobe the night before. I squeezed my eyes shut and tried to think about something else, like a toasted ham and cheese sandwich, with extra mustard and butter.

'Are you OK?' Bernard enquired anxiously.

'Yeah, grand, no bother,' I managed in a strangled sort of voice.

I went to walk away then. My body glanced off his and all good intentions were lost. He sort of grabbed at my face and bent his head to me and we were kissing like lunatics, his teeth crashing against mine, my hands pulling him to me like a drowning woman clinging to a lifebelt. We lurched around the lobby banging against walls and, at one point, the staircase, which left a sharp indentation across my shoulder blades. It was only when someone shouted 'get a room' that we came apart, panting and wild-eyed, staring across the space between us as if we'd never seen each other before. My chest was heaving and I was breathless. Bernard ran a hand through his hair and said, 'Shit,' in a hoarse whisper. With an almighty attempt at discipline, I straightened myself up and rearranged my hair, some of which had been pulled loose in the mêlée.

'Bernard,' I said, trying for a touch of dignity. 'I don't know where that came from. Let's go back to plan A, OK?' He pulled

his hands wearily down his face, looking suddenly exhausted.
Then he steadied himself to look at me.

'You're right. Let's do that.' He paused and I could tell he
wanted to say something. And then he said it. 'But I like you,
Grace O'Brien. You're an interesting woman.' He curled a
strand of hair behind my ear and patted me on the arm in
an almost brotherly fashion. Then he was gone in a flurry of
limbs, taking the stairs two at a time. I stared after him, then
slowly climbed the stairs, holding onto the banisters like an
old woman, heaving my bulk upwards. When I settled myself
back in my seat, Cliona had draped her arms around Bernard's shoulders and was telling Michael and Ciaran a story
about a scone-baking competition that Bernard had won in
second year in school.

'He was always good with his hands.' Cliona stroked his
arm, trying to catch his eye. I took an almighty slug of my
pint, draining it. I felt wronged, somehow. I'd told Bernard
about Shane, why hadn't he said anything about Cliona?

I got to my feet, scraping the legs of my stool against the
wooden floor, and bade them goodnight. I'd had a bellyful for
one day. My bed beckoned.

10

Barcelona, August 2003

Dear Grace,

It's been a week for losing things. First, lost my way to Gaudi park (forgot that 'izquierda' is left and not right). Then lost the key to my hotel room – and I use the word 'hotel' here loosely, although, on the plus side, it's on Las Ramblas (think Grafton Street, with the character of Moore Street, but much bigger and with actual suntanned people). But possibly more importantly, have lost Sinead. Yes, yes I know, to lose one thing is unfortunate but three things . . . fucking careless.

Well, I haven't really lost her, as such. I mean, I know where she is, technically. In bed with a man called Jesus – pronounced Hay-soos. They've been there since last Tuesday. He has a gold-tipped front tooth and one lazy eye but, having said that, I can see how she fell for him. He's got that Latino maleness that I'm told the ladies love.

Anyway, it's not like we were going out or anything but it was nice to have a bit of company. Although, in fairness, two accountants travelling together is not always the best idea. We were so aware of our budget and Sinead could calculate – to within a tenth of a cent – how much over budget we'd gone in any given day. She kept threatening to spreadsheet the cashflow. So it looks like I'm off to France tomorrow, by mine own self, as Clare used to say when she was a baby.

I'm enclosing a postcard: can you please deliver it to my office next Monday morning? It must arrive on Monday for maximum gloating impact. Can't believe I've been gone a month. Even on payday – last Thursday – I didn't miss anything about my old life (apart from my salary, of course). Still, I can get wine, cheese and bread for under a fiver and that basically covers the three food groups.

Am getting exercise – mostly in form of looking for things like Gaudi park (walked about two km out of my way) and key to hotel room (had to retrace my steps and as I was lost in the first place, ended up walking for miles). So can you tell Mam that I am taking care of myself? Also, tell her I'm brushing my teeth cos I know she'll ask. But better than that, I'm writing. Really writing, I mean. Every day. Mostly short stories but there's one I really like that's getting longer and longer so I'm just going to keep going on it and see where it takes me.

How are you doing? Still a 'loved up lunatic'? Liked that expression by the way. Yes, in answer to your question, I do like him. He seems charming and funny and, of course, he's Caroline's brother which can only be an advantage. Got an email from Caroline. She was complaining again about your hair clogging up the bathroom. If you continue like this, you're going to be bald by the time you're forty.

I'd better go. The waiter has arrived with some tapas and a very cold beer. It's hot in the shade and I haven't worn a suit in a month. If this is not heaven, it's pretty fucking close.

Keep in touch.

Love, Patrick

PS: No, will not email you. We may be practically the same age but just accept that some things about me are different to you and allow these letters to fall through the letterbox in your hallway. After all, don't they make a pleasant change from your Visa bills? And your name and address is hand-written, not generated by some half-wit database that always gets it wrong.

I I

Have I told you about my bed? It's up there with the bath on the list of places I love to loll: a monstrosity of a thing that barely fits into my room. As it is, the wardrobe doors can't be opened out fully and I keep a colourful collection of bruises on my lower shins from banging against the bedframe when I'm not careful, which is a lot of the time, really.

It was the only piece of furniture that I actually owned. When we first moved into the flat my room was fitted with a pair of 'Ernie and Bert' beds, as I called them. You know, two narrow single beds made with Victorian waifs or pint-sized puppets in mind, never mind a grand heifer of a woman like myself. Whenever Shane stayed over, I would push the beds together and, in the morning, I'd be wedged in between the thin mattresses where the beds had parted company in the night.

'Goodnight Ernie,' one of them might have said.

'Goodnight Bert,' the other may have replied.

Anyway, the bed I bought was a multi-purpose bed. You could live in this bed and sometimes I did just that, for whole Saturdays at a time. It was very low to the ground, which was handy on nights when I'd had too much to drink. On those nights, I could simply crawl from the bedroom floor to the bed with minimum effort and lucidity, curl up in a foetal position and fall into a drunken stupor. However – and this is important – it wasn't so low to the ground that you couldn't hide things under it. The underside of my bed was home to plates, cups, glasses, books, magazines, an assortment of hair accessories (bobbins, hair bands, bandanas, pretty but useless slides, stern grips, rigid combs, wide-bottomed brushes, straighteners) abandoned shoes – I kept the ones I loved in the wardrobe until I tired of them and then they got relegated to the dark side of the bed – choc-ice sticks, Starburst papers (all those pretty colours!) and Galaxy Caramel wrappers turned inside out with the toffee that sticks to the plastic licked off (by me).

Yes, I know that I am a slob but when I made my bed (or 'dressed' the bed, as my mother would say) and stuffed the clothes on my bedroom floor into the bottom of the wardrobe, my room looked tidy and that was good enough for me. Occasionally – whenever every dish in the flat had vanished – I crawled under the bed, armed with the hoover and a plastic bag to put the world to rights.

Caroline was proud of me on those days.

'Well done, you,' she would beam at me, like a schoolteacher congratulating a junior infant for wiping their bottom properly after depositing a teeny-tiny number two in the school jacks.

Of course, size isn't everything (or so men with small willies maintain). The bed wasn't just enormous. It was beautiful. The headboard was a great slab of curved maple with two candle holders on either side. The duvet was a shocking shade of pink. On top of this I carefully placed a family of throw cushions, painstakingly arranged so that they looked as though they had been flung carelessly at the bed. The cushions varied in colour from bright oranges to dull browns to blood reds. There were so many cushions that, when I wanted to do something practical like actually go to sleep, I had to shovel most of them under the bed, where they lay shivering for the night, rubbing shoulders with a partially eaten banana and honey sandwich and half a bottle of Malibu. Because of the space constraints in the room, I didn't have a bookshelf and had to pile my books precariously on top of each other on the floor beside my bed. I was currently reading the love poems of W.B. Yeats (for the 756th time) and loving them as much as I had when I first read them as a teenager, hiding them between the pages of the *Just 17* magazine. Listen to this bit:

> *Time can but make her beauty over again:*
> *Because of that great nobleness of hers*
> *The fire that stirs about her, when she stirs,*
> *Burns but more clearly. O she had not these ways*
> *When all the wild summer was in her gaze.*
> *O heart! O heart! If she'd but turn her head,*
> *You'd know the folly of being comforted.*

I read those lines over again, imagining myself as the fiery and beautiful Maud Gonne, firearm in one hand, eyelash curler in the other, married to John MacBride, leaving Yeats to his lonely, yet inspired, fate. The extent of his loss and his love still moved me. Did men really feel that depth of passion any more? If so, could they articulate it? The squawking of my mobile scattered these thoughts.

'Hello?' I belted the word out in my chirpiest manner, just in case it was my mother, who might guess that I was still in bed in my pyjamas at 2 p.m. on The Lord's Day. It was only Clare. I tucked ten pillows snugly against my back and settled down for a gossip. Clare sounded uptight.

'What's up?' I sat up straight, scattering cushions across the floor. Their various tassels and beads made a pleasant skittering noise against the yellowing boards. Clare was rarely anything other than good humoured and easy going. If she weren't so kind and good and related to me, I would probably hate her.

'Nothing, nothing,' she said. 'It's just, well, I'm doing up the seating plan for the wedding.' She tapered off.

'Shane *is* coming, if that's what you're worried about,' I answered, too quickly. I didn't know this for sure but I wasn't yet ready to share this doubt with the world at large.

'No, no, it's not that.' Another pause. This was so unlike her. In Clare's world, pregnant pauses and swollen silences did not exist. She could usually talk for Ireland, England, Scotland, Wales and probably a good portion of North America, not to mention the Antipodes.

'Clare, what's the problem?' My voice softened as I tried to assume the wise, older sister role: I was neither comfortable in this role nor particularly good at it.

'It's Mam,' Clare said. 'She wants to bring a friend to the wedding.'

'A friend?' I echoed slowly, my mind racing through various possibilities.

'Well, yes, that's what she said. A friend. A male friend.'

'A *male* friend?' I said.

'Yes, a friend who's a man. A man friend.' Clare stopped when she ran out of adjectives to describe this development.

I suppose if you didn't know my mother you might shrug your shoulders and make a bit of a face and say something like, 'So what?' Or even 'Who cares?' Or perhaps 'Even women over sixty need to get some.' Or something. The fact was that Mam had been in a state of voluntary singledom since dad died over ten years ago. A heart attack, sudden and unexpected.

'Collapsed,' they told us, like he was an unstable building.

To my certain knowledge, from that time to this, she had never dated anyone. She would have laughed even at that word. Dated. Or 'boyfriend'. And especially 'partner', which is one of her most hated 'buzz words'. That's another phrase she hates: 'buzz words'.

And we just took that for granted. Because she had such a strong personality, and because she talked about Dad a lot and remembered him so fondly, it was like she'd always been part of a couple. All these years had passed and we had never really thought of her as being single. It was Just The Way Things Were.

Well, not any more, it seemed.

'His name is Jack Frost.' Clare was still talking. 'She met him at one of her evening classes.'

'No, wait, rewind a minute. His name is Jack Frost? That can't be right. That must be his stage name or something. Nobody is called Jack Frost on purpose. What does he do?'

There was a hesitation. Then, 'he's a magician.'

'A magician?' I knew I was repeating everything she said – a trait that usually drives me to distraction – but I mean, come on. A magician called Jack Frost was walking the streets of the city, befriending vulnerable widows (there was absolutely nothing vulnerable about my mother, but how was Mr Frost to know that just yet?), possibly kissing my mother, maybe even with tongues, maybe even . . . AGHHHHHH.

I threw myself backwards on the bed and banged my head off the headboard. The air should have been blue with the cursing and the room spun in time with my head, which throbbed.

'Are you OK?' This was Clare, who obviously thought I had not taken the whole 'Mam's going out with a magician' scenario very well.

'No, no, I'm fine,' I replied, rubbing my head, the hair regrouping into an enormous knot. I was really more curious than anything else. 'What evening class did she meet him at?'

Our mother was an evening class junkie, the garage of our childhood home strewn with the fruits of her night-class labours. Leaning, thick-edged vases, in depressing shades of brown and grey, from pottery classes. Dog-eared, wrinkled notebooks filled with her large, loopy handwriting from a brief clash with creative writing. A dusty yellow guitar with two strings missing from an attempt at 'music for beginners'.

'They told us everyone is musical at some level,' she wailed when she was sent home after only four of the promised ten sessions for allegedly disrupting the class. She used the word 'allegedly' but I never had any doubt. On a brighter note, there were trophies and medals, now dulled with age, listing on a shelf and shrouded in thick cobwebs from a rather successful spate at line-dancing in the early '90s.

Clare cleared her throat and I turned my attention back to her.

'Car maintenance,' she said in a quiet voice. 'They met at car maintenance class. She thought, you know, with Patrick not . . . well . . . you know what I mean, she should learn how to, you know, change tyres and use a dipstick and things like that.' Clare tapered off.

My eyes stung in my head and I thought about Patrick. He was a mechanical genius: you'd have to be to keep my car roadworthy – and I use the term advisedly – which he did lovingly and without question. Like, for example, why did you put diesel in your car when the sticker beside the petrol tank clearly says 'non-leaded' in capital letters and fluorescent yellow for idiots like me? He never asked me that. He just fixed it. He was much more comfortable with his back resting on a twenty-year-old skateboard under a car than adding and subtracting big numbers which was, as he said, what he was paid to do.

My head was full of questions. Like, what in the name of God was Jack Frost, a grown man – a magician, if you will – of presumably late middle age doing at a car maintenance class?

'Clare, do you mean to say that Mam is going out with this guy and she is bringing him to your wedding?' I finally said in the slow, dull tones of a half-wit.

'Yes,' she answered flatly. 'She just doesn't want to do the whole day on her own. She said it would be too lonely for her. Jack is a good man, you'll like him.'

'You've met him?' I said, sharper than I'd intended. My hands tightened around the phone.

'Grace, it's not like that,' Clare argued. 'He happened to be at the house the other night when myself and Richard called in. They were watching telly and drinking tea. He's good for her, he makes her laugh. Maybe this is her way of moving on. Maybe you should . . .' She stopped there.

'Maybe I should what?'

'Maybe you should think about doing that too.' Clare said this last bit so quietly, I strained to hear her. Then she waited for me to explode. Which I did not do. I hung up instead.

Flinging myself out of bed, I immediately stubbed my toe against one of the legs (low, curved maple with an adorable kitten paw design at the bottom). I spent the next thirty seconds hopping around the edge of the bed – very carefully – holding my red, throbbing toe in one hand and yowling like a tomcat whose girlfriend has been put down.

'Grace, what the hell are you doing in there?' yelled Caroline from the kitchen. 'If you're having phone sex again, could you at least keep the bloody noise down.' I hobbled out of my bedroom.

'If I was having phone sex, do you think I'd be wearing *this?*' I said, pawing at my great tent of a cotton nightdress with a picture of the three bears on the front, standing in front of their wholesome cottage in a pretty little clearing in the wood. The picture was obviously taken before they discovered Goldilocks had stolen their breakfast and totalled the house. Caroline was sitting at the kitchen table eating a banana and drinking carrot juice (organic, of course).

Caroline was wearing her jogging gear and the front of her T-shirt was stained with sweat. Her hair was piled up on top of her head and her cheeks had reddened with the exertion of her daily jog around the park.

She looked beautiful.

I took my Coco Pops out of a press and sat down on the seat opposite her, shovelling large handfuls of them into my mouth.

'OK, what?' Caroline finally asked. I stopped chewing and took a long slug of milk from the carton, forgetting that I wasn't actually allowed to do this when Caroline was in the room. Or at all, in fact.

'You won't believe it,' I said to prolong the suspense, but also because I really *didn't* think she'd believe it. I barely did myself but, because it was Clare who told me, it must be true.

'What?' said Caroline, obligingly.

'My mother has gone and gotten herself a fella. A boyfriend. A partner. An Other Half. A Ball and Chain. A . . .'

'Grace, stop, stop, STOP.' Caroline held her hands in front of her to stop my flow, which it did. But she looked suitably amazed, which pleased me.

I took advantage of the situation by taking a slug of orange juice from an open carton on the table beside me.

'Ughhh,' I screeched. 'What *is* that stuff?'

'It's carrot juice,' she said, removing the carton from my reach and peering down into it. If there were little bits of Coco Pops floating around down there, she didn't say. That's how amazed she was.

'I'll make you a nice cup of coffee,' she offered, as if I'd had a terrible shock or something. Maybe I had. Maybe it just hadn't sunk in yet.

'Real coffee?' I asked. She nodded.

'Fully caffeinated?'

'Yes, and I'll make you a fresh fruit salad as well, OK?'

'Eh, no, just the coffee thanks,' I answered quickly. It was a Sunday, my life was in a spot of crisis, and crisis situations

called for Real Food like bacon and crisp butties smothered in
real butter and great big globs of brown sauce with a touch of
keen mustard and some liberally salted fried potatoes on the
side. As I lived with a health freak and hadn't done any proper
food shopping recently, there was a better chance of George
Bush announcing he was a pacifist than finding rashers, bread,
butter and potatoes in our sparsely populated fridge, so I settled for coffee and Coco Pops. I told Caroline what I knew
about Jack Frost, which wasn't much, but I still stretched it
for a good fifteen minutes. I didn't repeat what Clare had said.
About Mam moving on. I didn't say that.

Caroline, who was a little in awe of my mother, seemed
genuinely impressed with the old girl's ability to snag herself
a man when pickings were so slim in the city.

'Fair dues to her,' she said almost to herself.

'I could end up with a stepfather.' The thought suddenly
occurred to me.

Caroline laughed at me. 'You could all right. He might bring
you to the zoo on Sundays and promise to buy you a pony for
Christmas. It'll be great.'

Caroline's features softened into a smile and she reached
for my hand across the table.

'Seriously though, this is good news. Your mother's getting
on with her life. It's really positive.' She looked at me in that
careful way of hers, as if she could read my mind. When I
didn't say anything, Caroline plunged on.

'And you never know, maybe this guy has a football team of
eligible bachelor sons that we could take turns with?' Caroline
arched her eyebrows at me in a question.

'Well, I'm sorted,' I said. 'With Shane and all,' when she didn't
respond. 'But I'll make discreet enquiries for you, OK?'

'What's his name?' she asked. 'Your Mam's, eh, boyfriend.'
She, too, was having difficulty with the word.

'Jack Frost,' I said, and I waited.

'No way,' she said and we were off. Laughing fit to burst. So long as I was laughing, I didn't have to think about everybody moving on. Leaving him behind. Leaving me behind.

I was still laughing when I went to answer my mobile phone in my bedroom.

'You sound in great form altogether.' It was Shane.

'Shane,' I bellowed, forgetting that I was angry with him for not phoning me for a week. 'I miss you, when are you coming home?' God, where was my self-respect? My poise? Where were my feminine wiles? It appeared that they had all deserted me as I lay on my rumpled bed and pressed the phone tightly against my ear.

'Can I come and see you next weekend? I miss you too, baby.' My insides melted, like chocolate in the sun. I *loved* when he called me 'baby' in his unbelievably-Cork, Cork accent.

'Yes, yes, yes,' I panted in a most suggestive way. 'I'll pick you up from the airport. What time are you getting in at?' I was already wondering what to wear and if I would have time for a haircut, leg, bikini and underarm wax and possibly a bit of botox between now and Friday.

'No, don't bother, I'm getting in on Friday morning. I have to go to a meeting at the office. I'll meet you after work, OK?'

'Oh,' I replied slowly.

'Look, I was going to come over anyway, Grace. Then this meeting came up. Don't be mad with me. I know I've been crap at keeping in touch, but I'll make it up to you, I promise.' Now it was his turn to be suggestive and my stomach – which I had automatically sucked in – did a series of mini-somersaults, leaving me slightly nauseous with excitement.

When he said goodbye, I gathered myself up and stood on my bed, punching the air with my fist. Then I grabbed handfuls of my nightdress, lifting it up to my knees and did a little Irish dance on the bed, the springs creaking in time.

A little bubble of memory – labelled Bernard O'Malley

– floated to the top of my mind and burst loudly. I forced it to the end of the queue for guilty thoughts and told it, in no uncertain terms, to wait until Euphoria had left the building before coming in.

Shane was coming over. He had called me 'baby'. He said he missed me. Things were going to work out. I knew they were.

I2

On Monday morning, I dressed carefully, in anticipation of my 2 p.m. appointment with the boss.

The boss had a tendency to study breasts while talking at female members of staff. To throw him off guard, I wore a very tight but frustratingly high-necked cream top with a tantalising, easily undone ribbon at the neck – just to keep him on his toes. I then shrouded myself in a stern black suit with a skirt that stopped abruptly just past my knees – my worst feature – to reveal lengths of sheer see-through nylon-encased legs down to my ankles (my best feature: uncharacteristically bony). Encouraging my feet into needlepoint stiletto heels ('this won't hurt at all, my darlings'), I rubbed foundation into the pale skin of my face, added some powder and dramatic streaks of blusher before emptying the contents of my dark brown mascara onto my strawberry blonde, stunted eyelashes. I glared at my reflection in the mirror, trying to make myself look as intimidating as possible. Jesus! I rubbed away most of the blusher. The final touch was lipstick – whoreish red – which I slapped on, loving the way it clashed with my hair. I then set about capturing and securing said hair in an almighty long-john of a grip. 'Easy girl, easy,' I coaxed, gathering the hair behind my neck. You had to be gentle with hair like mine: it had a life of its own and could get nasty if attempts to bully it were made. A few dabs of hair-calming serum at the front and I was ready to go. I loved the word 'serum'. It's so relaxing. Up there with 'serenity' and 'botox' for comfort-speak. The language equivalent of bangers and mash. I tiptoed out of the bedroom. Old man Jenkins had begged me recently not to walk with full strength on my high heels. It interfered with his hearing aid and prevented him from fully understanding the evidence presented on *Judge Judy,* which he recorded and watched at odd times of the day and night. He had a thing about *Judge Judy.* It was her hair, I think. He had a thing about women with Big Hair.

Caroline was out for her jog – only four miles on a weekday – and I had the place to myself. Tiring of walking on my toes I slid, ice skating-style, to the fridge. Having had such an odd weekend, I couldn't remember which diet I was currently on. Was it full-fat protein with no carbohydrates? Or low-fat everything with no taste? The fridge door yawned open in a disapproving kind of way. It was nearly empty and seemed bigger than usual. Only the usual suspects remained and I made a note – again – to clear out the crap when I got home from work:

- One solitary egg, forgotten, in the door of the fridge.
- A sliver of cheese wrapped in too much wax paper.
- A family of erroneously purchased strawberry-flavoured actimels. We only like the original flavour but sometimes I forget.
- A packet of cooking chocolate that neither of us can re-member buying (although I suspect it was me, with a craving for chocolate Rice Crispie buns).

And the prize for the longest-standing member of our Fridge Community goes to . . . a can of Ritz. It has towered on the top shelf of the fridge since our flat-warming party. We can't bring ourselves to drink it but neither can we bear to throw it out in case of severe alcohol deprivation one night when we are too weak to resist. It also affords opportunities to play 'who brought the Ritz to the party?' with our friends when we want to pick on somebody.

I shut the fridge door, snatched a browning banana from the fruit bowl and left the flat, my shoes whispering against the floorboards as I did my best Torville and Dean across the hall (which one was the girl? I can never remember). I heard the opening lines of *Judge Judy* barking from downstairs.

'Real people, real cases.'

'Real shite,' I said out loud before noticing Mrs Murphy – the upstairs recluse – gliding like a ghost down the hallway, clutching a thick letter to her chest. She was like a plainclothes nun, although I don't think I've ever seen one of those. I just have an idea of what they might look like without their habit and wimple. I smiled back, as if I hadn't been talking out loud to myself. Maybe she'd think it was just another of the voices in her head.

I stepped outside and walked around the corner to the lane behind the house where my car was parked. My heels click-clacked loudly on the empty pavement. It was early. My breath collected in white clouds in front of my face but my hands felt hot and damp, balled into fists deep inside the pockets of my coat. Last night, buoyed up with pizza (deep pan pepperoni) and two cold beers, I convinced myself that the worst thing that could happen (redundancy) wouldn't be too bad at all. Time off, with pay, to look for a better job, yeah? This morning, I didn't feel quite so sure.

I got to work at 8 a.m. – a first for me – and enjoyed Ciaran's look of shock when he doffed his cap at me. The IT department was mercifully deserted and I almost ran towards my little place in the world, my work station. I touched the soft blueness of its partitions and sank into my black, faux-leather reclining chair, nicked from the office of an ancient director who had died – suddenly, peacefully – two days after his massive retirement party.

I turned on my computer, comforted by its familiar beeps and burps. I knew who I was here. I had a place in the pecking order, no matter how small. I'd been here so long, I'd grown up – to an extent – here in this cubicle. I knew where the paper clips were hidden and where the dead bodies were buried.

I looked at my watch. 8.30 a.m. Five and a half hours to go till the meeting with the boss. Thirty minutes or less till Bernard O'Malley arrived down the hall. With my jacket draped oh-so-casually over his arm. Shane due at the end of the week. I headed to the kitchenette at the end of the hall. I needed coffee.

The little kitchen was conveniently located a mere ten strides from my desk. I counted them one day when I was trying to work out how far I walked in an average work day:

- Ladies' toilets: 10½ strides.
- Ciaran's hut in the car park: 45 strides.
- Vending machine: 14 strides.
- Stationary cupboard: 7 strides.
- Lift: almost 5 strides.

With all this striding around the office (1.1 km in an average day, what with all the smoke breaks, coffee breaks and trips to the vending machine for Maltesers), I convinced myself that this counted as exercise and allowed my gym membership to lapse with a clear conscience.

I poured boiling water over two heaped teaspoons of instant coffee and three level teaspoons of sugar. Good for shock. I stirred the brew with two spoons to make it frothy.

The door to the kitchen opened, startling me. Had I been talking out loud? Or just in my head, like a normal person? I turned round slowly.

Bernard O'Malley stood in the arch of the doorway, still as a statue, watching me in a way that made me feel hot and cold at the same time.

'I didn't realise you were here,' he said. His hand remained on the doorhandle.

He hadn't shaved, the black stubble making his brown eyes darker, almost black. Against the ghostly paleness of his face and the outrageous redness of his hair, his face was like a spare parts counter: a conveyor belt of pieces that didn't quite fit together. He looked tired.

'I'm just making some coffee,' I said and I could feel the colour rising in my face. I mean, what else would I be doing in the kitchen at that time of the day? 'Would you like some?' I bent down to open the fridge door and noticed his shoes. Like schoolboys' shoes with laces thinning and fraying at the ends. They could do with a spit and polish.

'I have these.' He stayed at the door, holding up what looked like sachets of instant cappuccino. 'I even have some chocolate powder to sprinkle over the top.' He smiled now, and I could feel the relief in him. We were having an Ordinary Conversation. About coffee. Next, we might move on to the weather and then perhaps holiday plans. We were like hairdressers.

'That stuff is pure muck,' I said.

Bernard surprised me by laughing out loud. I'd only ever seen him smiling his small smile before. His laugh was like a donkey's bray, guttural and short. When he stopped, the kitchenette seemed too quiet. The silence lengthened.

'Come in, come in,' I said, like we were in a country kitchen and my hands were covered in flour. The teaspoon in my hand pointed at him, like a peace offering.

When he took his hand off the doorhandle, it banged behind him, making us both jump.

He took the spoon from my hand, then surprised me by gently manoeuvring me onto a chair while he busied himself with the coffee preparations. Calm stole across me as I watched him from behind. He made a minimum of noise and moved his long body very sparsely in the small space. Today, his cardigan was navy with orange buttons as big as saucers. He might have gotten away with the faded blue jeans had the waistband not been hoisted up around his waist but hanging off his hips instead, revealing the tops of a pair of designer boxers, as was de rigueur just now. The thick – unfrayed – ends of the trousers stopped just above the bony right-angle of his ankle as if he wanted everyone to see his clean, white socks.

He swivelled towards me with a tall, thin coffee cup in each hand, duly foaming on top. I could tell he was dying to say 'ta daaaaa' in a sing-songy voice. But he didn't. He just sat down at the other side of the table, opposite me, stirring his coffee. He pushed his fingers along his nose even though his glasses were as high up as they could go.

'Aren't the bottoms of your legs cold?' I was genuinely curious.

Bernard smiled and stretched his legs out in front of him, the better to demonstrate the shortcomings of his trousers. He seemed neither embarrassed nor proud. His legs were long.

'My brother Edward used to say that to me.'

Something about the way he said it made me reluctant to continue that line of conversation. Bernard lifted the mug to his mouth with one hand that easily spanned the circumference. The freckles that plagued his arms like dry rot stopped in a line just above his wrist. I tried not to look but I couldn't help it. It had been ages since either of us said anything.

'I think I'm going to be made redundant today.' I couldn't believe I'd said that out loud. I bent and heaped sugar on the froth of my coffee, watching it brown and melt on the thinning foam.

'Well, if you are, there's nothing much you can do about it, so no point worrying.' Bernard's tone was calm and his words washed over me like warm water.

'Thanks,' was all I said. He raised his eyes towards me then to see if I was being sarcastic. I grinned back at him and took an almighty slug of cappuccino.

'Not bad at all,' I said, licking my lips, then stopped suddenly in case he'd think I was flirting with him. We were having a fairly normal, above-board interaction and I wanted to keep it that way.

'So, what's on your agenda for today?' I said.

'I'm going up home. A family thing.' His tone was bland but a muscle twitched on his neck.

'Oh, I see,' I said when it became clear that no further explanations were forthcoming.

'To Donegal, isn't it?' He smiled and nodded very slightly.

'Well, safe trip. I'm sure I'll see you when you get back.'

He lifted himself off the chair and had his cup and spoon washed, dried and put away before I'd even lifted my cup to my lips for a second time.

'See you,' he said. And then he was gone.

'That went better than expected,' I spoke out loud, my voice echoing against the bare walls in the empty kitchen. I drowned out the quiet by singing 'Private Dancer' at the top of my voice and didn't stop until my heart rate slowed to a steady thump.

The impending meeting with my boss didn't seem quite so intimidating after my conversation with Bernard. When I got back to my desk, I discovered a discreetly placed bag (nice stiff paper one with pretty colours and heavy rope handles) under my desk with the neglected black leather jacket I had left in Bernard's on Friday.

'You've come home,' I whispered, burrowing my nose in its soft folds and inhaling deeply.

'Ahem, eh, Grace.'

I lifted my head, banging it off the underside of the desk, and cursed like a docker before recognising the shoes of the voice hovering above me. They were slip-on black patent ones with a silver buckle across the top: so shiny I could see the reflection of a PMT spot forming in the cleft of my chin. These shoes may have last been fashionable in or around the height of the Charlie's Angels era (and I'm talking about the *original* Charlie's Angels here) and could only belong to one man.

'Morning, boss.' I crawled backside first out from under the desk and straightened, nearly poking his eye out with my breasts, which were strapped into a severe bra that narrowed dangerously into points at the nipples. I brushed myself down quickly with my hands before catching a stray strand of hair and tucking it behind my ear. Now I smiled and explained.

'Just checking my network connection. I can't seem to access the main server. The connection seems fine so it might be my USB port.' I said all this very quickly and with great authority. The boss, a luddite, looked suitably baffled but satisfied with my explanation.

'Eh, Grace,' he began again. 'I know our meeting is scheduled for 2 p.m. today but I have a window and I wondered if you are available to meet me now?' He loved all things corporate, especially corporate-speak. Why say 'I'm available' when you can say 'I have a window?' Why say 'from now on' when 'going forward' can be used? He had a whole dictionary of phrases like that:

- Thinking outside the box (using your loaf).
- Off-site (out of the office; usually playing golf).
- Show-stopper (black fly in your chardonnay-type situation which, to be fair, isn't a bit ironic).

'No problem,' I said in what I hoped was a confident manner. I grabbed a notebook and a pen from my work station. I always armed myself thus, even if it was just to play noughts and crosses with myself or to doodle pictures of the boss, with a goat's head and a rat's tail.

Once inside his barn of an office, he quickly put his large, mostly bare desk between us, like a barricade. Then he lowered himself into his seat carefully and made an arc with his fingers on which he rested the folds of flesh where his chin used to be. He picked up a sheaf of papers, shuffled them and then replaced them on his desk, about three centimetres from where they had previously sat. He cleared his throat and sipped water from a plastic cup. I shifted in my seat, folded my arms across my chest and then unfolded them, setting my hands loosely in my lap in an effort to appear relaxed. A crystal clock in the shape of a golf ball ticked on the desk. Then he looked up and smiled at me, which threw me.

'Grace, you probably know by now that we are planning major changes within the company,' he began. I nodded my head slowly and made an effort not to start biting my nails.

'These changes are going to affect you directly, Grace,' he continued, looking at the empty space slightly to the left of my head.

Jesus, he can't even look at me. I sat as straight as I could and ordered myself not to cry, no matter what happened. Whatever he said today, I comforted myself with the knowledge that I would be leaving here with a grand head of hair on my head and he would have to drive home in his BMW with hardly any hair at all. Ridiculous though it may sound, I gleaned some comfort from that, and also from calling him obscene names in my head, waiting for him to continue.

'We're handling fewer claims than we were five years ago, yet we've got more claims handlers than we had then. Obviously that situation cannot continue. I'm sure you can understand that.' He was gaining momentum now, always on surer ground when talking about the business. My mouth was so dry that it was difficult to unstick my tongue from the roof of it. I leaned forward and took a huge slug of water from the cup he had been drinking from, before realising what I was doing.

'Oh God, sorry.' I replaced the cup, too quickly. The water in the cup see-sawed, some of it reaching the lip and spewing onto the gleaming mahogany, where it huddled in a puddle like shame.

'Oh God, sorry,' I said again, using the sleeve of my jacket to mop up the mess. 'Do you want me to get you some more water?'

He was beginning to look impatient and he shook his head, putting his hand up to silence me. I sat back in my chair and took a deep breath, resolving to say no more until he had finished his spiel. He allowed the silence to stretch for a while before continuing.

'Grace, we don't need you as a claims handler any more.' His words slowly fell around me like tired trees in autumn, shedding their leaves. But he was smiling. A sort of evil genius smile, but a smile nonetheless. He exhaled and I could smell strong, hot coffee. Then he was talking again.

'We're getting a new computer system for the liability department. We need someone from our team to represent our interests in the IT department and then to train our team on the new system. You've been here so long, you know the computer system inside out, you've got great interpersonal skills and we think you'd be the perfect candidate for the job. What do you think?'

He sat back in his chair, resting his hands behind his head and, for once, looked right at me. In my head I was lying on the floor with an oxygen bag over my head. In reality, I uncrossed my legs and then crossed them again, then sat on my hands to stop them from shaking. Finally I spoke.

'You're offering me another job?' My voice sounded sluggish.

'Grace, this is not just another job. This is a promotion with great potential. You'll get all the training you need, although we don't really think you'll need much. We're going to be rolling out this new system across the board after the liability department, and if this works out, you could be the person to manage that entire project.' He was beaming at me now and I felt like screaming, 'What have you done with the boss, you evil impostor?' It seemed that delivering good news suited him much better than beleaguering us with the bad stuff. He was still smug and self-satisfied and hideous to look at, but I could have leaned over and hugged him to me at that moment and even possibly lifted my top to afford him a quick glance at The Girls. Don't worry, I didn't do any of that. Nor did I have an asthma attack or fall over or say anything remotely silly. Instead I got business-like and asked intelligent questions like how fat was my raise going to be (obese, as it turned out) and when could I start and could I get some staff to do the farty things like photocopying, faxing and typing.

He seemed relieved that things were back to normal and we spent the next hour discussing the finer details of the job. The Promotion, if you don't mind. I swelled with pride, deflating quickly when I felt intense pressure on the ribbon around my neck, which threatened to snap and ruin my moment of glory.

He said something odd at the end.

'Eh, Grace, I know this last year has been difficult for you, but, well, I just wanted you to know that, um, you're held in high regard by the management team. I hope you know that. Sometimes I think you don't.' He was genuinely uncomfortable with this bald statement and squirmed in his seat like a six-year-old bursting to go to the toilet. To be honest, I felt close to tears and was baffled by his positive comments. Suddenly, I couldn't wait to get out of there.

He cleared his throat and flicked an imaginary piece of fluff from the lapel of his suit jacket, signalling the meeting was at an end. I stood up, unsteady on my feet for a moment. I thrust my hand out and he shook it limply. I backed out of the office, smiling and nodding, making sure he wasn't going to change his mind at the last minute. He didn't and I left in a daze. I didn't know who he thought I was, but it felt good. It felt great.

13

Because it was payday and I'd just been promoted, the obvious thing to do after work was to celebrate in O'Reilly's. Everyone was on for it, except Laura and Peter, who hadn't been seen since the previous Friday, both having rung in 'sick' this morning. Laura hadn't even texted me with Peter's vital statistics – which she normally did with her new conquests – so I worried that she'd broken her golden rule of getting *involved* with someone she was shagging . . . But that was ridiculous, wasn't it?

I gathered the post-weekend shells of Ethan, Norman and Jennifer and marched them across the road at 5 p.m. on the dot. Not even my newfound status of 'IT Liability Consultant' (I made that title up) could encourage me to stay in the office a minute longer than necessary.

'A bottle, nay TWO bottles of your finest champagne,' I declared to Shay the barman, who went quietly about his business, appearing to register no disquiet at my opulence. 'And crisps,' I added grandly. 'Lots of lovely crisps. Nothing is too good for my friends today.' I waited for Shay to enquire about my glorious demeanour and, when he didn't, I filled him in.

His response was disappointing.

'That'll be €69.30 please, Grace, when you're ready.' With thoughts of my grand, fat pay rise, I shelled it out in crisp new banknotes. 'Get yourself a drink too, Shay, I'm celebrating.' He finally agreed to accept a soda water and lime but drew the line at a packet of bacon fries, claiming they gave him wind.

Ethan worried about the new computer system. Ever since the computerised cashiers had been installed at the Tesco downstairs from our offices, he had become obsessed with the notion of computers taking over the world.

'How must the human cashiers feel,' he worried, 'when they see their job being done, perfectly efficiently, may I say, by machines?' I took his cold, narrow hands in mine and rubbed them gently.

'Come on, Ethan, it's not as if they can teach computers to come up with creative marketing plans, now, can they?' He didn't look convinced, comforting himself with a long draught of champagne – we were on our third bottle at that stage.

Norman thought my promotion was hysterical, but then, he thought that everything was pretty much hysterical, especially after a couple of glasses of bubbly.

'Gracie girl,' he drooled at me, 'you're some woman for one woman.'

Jennifer wanted to know what Shane thought about the promotion.

'I left a message for him this afternoon,' I said brightly. 'He'll get back to me later, when he's home from work.'

I emailed and texted him as well, but I didn't share this with Jennifer, who was looking at me with the familiar sympathy that I couldn't bear.

'He's coming home for the weekend. This Friday.' This caught the attention of Ethan and Norman.

'Fatten the calf,' Norman yelled.

'That's great news.' Ethan patted me on the arm.

'Is that the first time he's been home since he left?' asked Jennifer.

'Well, yes,' I said. 'But he's been really busy, with the new job and everything.' I trailed off.

Distraction was provided in the form of Caroline, who had just arrived in the pub following an ecstatic text from me. In the stampede towards her, Shane was forgotten. I was glad about that.

Caroline was matter-of-fact about the news of my promotion.

'It's about time they noticed you in that company, Grace. I hope you didn't accept the first figure they threw at you.' I shook my head. I had accepted the boss's first offer with no thought of further negotiations. 'Next time,' I thought, surprising myself with the notion, 'next time I'll negotiate.' I smiled, unable to help myself, a great wide smile that split my face in two. I raised my glass.

'A toast,' I cried. 'Here's to lovely things happening on a Monday, which make them even lovelier.' Everyone clinked their glasses together and yelled, 'To Grace,' much too loudly. It was a moment.

My phone rang. I recognised my mother's home number and simulated sobriety, a tricky task after several glasses of champagne, especially on a Monday.

'Ma, how are you?' I tried not to slur. 'Great things have happened to me today. I thought the boss was going to sack me, but—'

'Sack you?' My mother interrupted.

'No, no, wait, Ma, I didn't get the sack. I got promoted.' I held my breath and crossed my fingers, an old habit.

'Grace, you're not making any sense.' I could hear her frustration and cursed myself for my glibness. I tried again.

'Ma, I got *promoted* today.' I couldn't wait for her response, but I was also nervous about it.

'Promoted?' She was hesitant now. 'That's nice, dear. I thought you'd been sacked.' She laughed then and I wished, as I often did, that Dad was alive. He would've been so proud of me, much prouder than I ever deserved.

'Are you in the pub again, Grace?' My mother was back on track, her disapproval bristling down the line.

'I'm just leaving now. Had a glass of wine to celebrate, y'know?' I spoke in hushed tones so as not to incur the mirth of Norman. He, however, was preoccupied trying to persuade Caroline to have sex with him if only to convince Harold, our openly gay accountant, that he was heterosexual.

'You'd be doing me a favour Caroline,' Norman was pleading. 'Just think of it as community service.'

'Ma, I'm going to have to go now, were you ringing for something in particular?' I was anxious to get her off the phone.

'Actually, I wondered if you could come over tomorrow for dinner. There's something I want to discuss with you.' My mother sounded nervous and I felt sorry for her. Introducing your twenty-nine-year-old daughter to your sixty-odd-year-old, brand-new boyfriend can't be easy for a mother. I could afford to be generous tonight.

'Grand, Ma. What time?'

'Seven o'clock. Don't be late, Grace,' she said, as she always did. I mumbled my goodbyes and hung up. Today was a day for surprises. I thought about Bernard then, on a plane to Donegal.

'I'm away home,' he'd said quietly. I wondered what was going on there. He seemed down when he said it.

I wondered what Patrick would have said about the promotion. I remembered the funeral mass nearly a year ago. It's almost harder when it's a year down the road and you realise that, despite yourself, time has passed and life has gone on, regardless.

'What are you thinking about, Grace?' Caroline wrestled in on my thoughts.

'Oh, I was just thinking about Shane coming home on Friday,' I rallied, uncomfortable with the lie. I felt apprehensive when I thought about Shane. He was such a beautiful man to look at. He was funny and charming. I sometimes wondered what he saw in me. I sometimes wondered if Patrick had made him stay longer than he'd intended. I confided these thoughts to Clare, who was duty bound, under familial law, to rubbish these fears and tell me I was fabulous.

'More champagne,' Ethan declared in a loud voice, letting us all know he'd had more than enough already. We clapped and cheered when he made his way to the bar, looking anxiously about him as he pulled his wallet from the inside pocket of his jacket, trying to coax a note out from its tight folds.

Norman was boring Caroline by trying to guess the number of sexual partners she'd had.

'I'd say more than seven, less than twenty,' Norman leaned back in his chair, stroking the point of his chin with the tips of his fingers. Caroline ignored him and swivelled her stool towards me and Jennifer.

'I'm damned if I'm telling him that I've only slept with five men,' she whispered, draining the dregs of her champagne flute. Jennifer laughed prettily.

'My God, I'd slept with five men by the time I was twenty. What have you been *doing* in your spare time?'

Caroline laughed humourlessly and dropped her head towards me.

'I've got a blind date on Wednesday night,' she hissed.

'In the night-time?' I was shocked.

'Grace, I'm so pissed off meeting eejits in the afternoon. It's unnatural. It never works out. I just want to meet someone, someone special, someone I can love and who'll love me. No complications.' I was surprised. This admission was so unlike Caroline, who was possibly the most independent woman I had ever met.

'Look at you,' she continued. 'You've got Shane and even though he's an absolute bollix, you love him. I don't think I've ever really *loved* anyone.' She looked at me, trying to lighten the moment by revealing two lines of perfectly straight white teeth.

'He's *not* a bollix. I wish you'd stop saying that.'

'I'm allowed. He's my brother.'

'He's my boyfriend.'

Caroline didn't answer and I was anxious to change the subject.

'What's the story with your blind date?' I asked.

'Well,' she was coquettish. 'He's in computers and he's Richard's cousin. From somewhere that's not Cork or Dublin. I don't know his name or anything about him but I've agreed to meet him under Cleary's clock on Wednesday night at eight. He'll be carrying a copy of *The Catcher in the Rye* so I'll recognise him. Corny, isn't it?' She looked up at me from under long, sturdy eyelashes that were black as night.

'It sounds romantic,' I replied. 'He'll be mad not to be mad about you,' I continued, touching her briefly on the shoulder.

'Don't fill me with shite, Grace,' she warned, shrugging my hand away. 'We both know I'm a tetchy bitch at the best of times.'

'That's true,' I allowed, 'but you look so damn gorgeous, they don't notice until it's too late.'

She laughed and I did too, glad that the conversation had veered back to familiar ground.

14

Paris, September 2003

Dear Grace,
Having a maudlin time here. Been visiting graves. Oscar
Wilde, Jim Morrison, Chopin. All the greats get buried in
Paris. Apparently you haven't lived till you're dead and buried in Paris. The graves are overgrown and some have even
sunk a little. You would think the fans who visit here would
do a spot of 'tending' but they don't. They stop for a moment
and look and take a photograph and then move on. It's like
they want to stay but can't think why. I stopped at Jimmy's
grave (that's Mr Morrison to you) for a while. I went really early last Saturday morning and the place was deserted,
apart from an ancient caretaker sort of man with a gimpy leg
and a runny nose. He kept an eye on me but said nothing. If
he had spoken, the sentence would have had the words 'pesky
kids' in there somewhere, you know what I mean? I brought a
bottle of wine and poured half of it over the grave. Drank the
other half. Otherwise it would have been an awful waste cos
everyone knows that dead men don't drink wine. I must have
been half-cut (half a bottle of wine at 7 o'clock in the morning on an empty stomach. It was way too early for breakfast)
because then, checking the coast was clear, I sang. Out loud I
mean. 'Break on Through to the Other Side.' I suppose Jim's
heard it all but it felt a bit special to me (yeah, yeah, OK,
probably the wine . . .).

As well as that, am drinking lots of dark, strong coffee in tiny little cups. In France, it is strictly forbidden to add milk to your coffee after breakfast time. Only children and half-wits do it, they tell me. As well as my coffee etiquette, my French is improving. When I arrived I could only say 'bonjour' and 'voulez vous coucher avec moi, ce soir.' Now I can ask where things are (the train station, the toilets, the graveyard) and order wine (I mostly just point at the wine I want on the menu for this).

Toilets

You won't believe this but some of the public toilets here are still those hole in the ground arrangements, with the handles on either side of the wall to hold onto, or to grip, if you are 'bound'. (Do you remember? That's what Granny Mary called constipation when we were kids?) Anyway, this S&S method (stand and shit) is not to my liking at all. Especially in the mornings when, as you know, I like to cogitate on the loo for up to thirty minutes with the paper and a cup of tea and a smoke and the radio. None of that carry-on here. Still, they say it's more hygienic so I can always think about that when I'm squatting and gripping.

Meeting people

You get to meet lots of people when you're travelling on your own (Sinead still Barricaded-In-Bed-In-Barcelona, by the way). To date I have met the following individuals:
• *Rory, the Irish expatriate. Except he spells his name something like 'Ruairi'. The fact that he refers to himself as an expatriate is really all you need to know about Rory (using the Sassenach bastard version of his name as is easier to spell and shorter to write and just because I know it would piss him*

off). He works at this bar I go into of an evening, although he is really an artist and is biding his time till he's discovered, blah, blah, blah.

• *Sonia. From England. Also works in the bar. Am I spending a lot of time in this bar? Well, I am since I met Sonia, who is very beautiful in a tiny kind of way as well as being very bright (she's studying European literature at the University of Paris). Sorry Gracie, I know you hate people who are tiny but she really is possibly the smallest fully grown woman I have ever met. Even her fingernails are tiny, like a doll's. And really pink, too. I'd say she drinks lots of milk and eats lots of cheese. We have a lot in common and get on very well, although she calls me 'ginger' (the first 'g' is pronounced like the 'g' in gift) which doesn't strike me as the most complimentary way to describe a person of the red-haired variety. I know for a fact you are nodding your head here.*

• *Have also met a woman called Mme Dupont. She is about seventy years old and sits in a park I like to go to in the afternoons with her dog who is the size of a well-fed rat with a bark like a mouse's squeak. The dog – goes by the name of Henri VIII on account of his penchant for the lady dogs – wears woollen coats about his middle that Mme Dupont knits for him. He has seven. One for every day of the week, all different colours. He wears the white one to mass on Sunday. We don't really talk, Mme Dupont and I. We play chess mostly, in the shade. The chess boards are built into some of the picnic tables and Mme Dupont brings along a chess set that she says her husband hand-carved for her as a wedding present, more than fifty years ago. We eat smelly cheese (that I bring) and drink wine out of paper cups (supplied by my lady friend). Sometimes, we just sit there and watch the people. They're mostly old people who look like they have all the time in the world. Occasionally, Mme Dupont points at one of them and sets off on a monologue that I don't understand. I listen and nod, the language here is like poetry. There's something about drinking red wine in the afternoon heat of a park in Paris. I feel full, with the pleasure of it.*

So, what do these ramblings tell you? Well, it seems that I have stumbled onto the secret of life and it's this: It's the simple things Gracie, the simple things.

More wisdom from your big brother in my next instalment (which should be from Italy, I think).

Lots of love,

Patrick

XX

15

I dressed as I always did when I met my mother: a carnival of colours. Oranges, pinks, reds. As a red-haired child in Ireland in the late '70s / early '80s, these colours were *forbidden*. Instead, Patrick and I were cloaked by my mother in every variant of the colours green and brown there was, and even some there weren't.

People used to smile and pat my head – this was before my growth spurt in 1988 – and call me a real Oirish Cailín. They called Patrick a real Oirish Buachaill and poked their fingers into his dimples when he smiled, which was often.

During this decade and a half of shame, I was on the Most Wanted list of the fashion police and laughed at by my peers, who chanted things like:

- Were ya left out in the rain last night? (due to the rust-ridden colour of my hair).
- Duracell top (never really got this one: if my hair had been the colour of the top of a Duracell battery – sort of golden blonde – I would have been delighted).
- Freckle freak (this from Donal Murphy in fifth class, whose face was blighted by a dark purple birthmark in the shape of Italy that ran from his forehead down to the jut of his jaw. In retaliation I called him The Elephant Man, which I can now acknowledge was cruel but hugely satisfying at the time, especially when I made him cry).

- Redser, ginger, milk bottle top (that was before the Tetra Pak era).

After my Confirmation, things got better. I made £150 (and that's old Irish pounds remember, at a time when you could buy ten fags, a box of matches and packet of Polo mints for under a pound and still have enough left over to splash out on two pink flogs and four fizzy cola bottles). After being ordered to hoard my swag in the post office for two years (my haul made a paltry £2.54 in interest), I was finally allowed into town *without* my mother, where I discovered the joys of the Gap, A-Wear and O'Connor's Jeans and where I also became aware of the glutinous array of colours available in clothes. Anyway, I'm getting side-tracked again.

I drove into Raheny at 6.45 p.m. and, after stopping to pick up a bottle of wine (I knew there'd be none at the house) and some wilting flowers at the local garage, I parked outside my mother's house at 6.57 p.m. My mother hated tardiness and I hated when my mother hated things about me.

I sat in the car for a while, smoking the last cigarette I would have until I left again. Mam hated smoking / smokers / smoke etc. and while she knew I smoked, she had no idea of the extent of my addiction and would have been appalled at my twenty-ish-a-day habit. Through the fug of cigarette smoke, I looked at the house where I had spent the first twenty-two years of my life.

Nothing too extraordinary there. Your average four-bed semi with the requisite attic conversion, conservatory, a garage that had always been the source of great plans but remained a garage and not the playroom / den / study / meditation room / billiards room that my parents talked about over the years. The garden looked neglected. The grass needed a trim, and weeds that never dared to show their faces when Patrick was around now sprouted and spread throughout the lawn, inching their way through the little border that trickled along the edge of the driveway.

Patrick took his role as the man of the family seriously and made himself available every weekend to 'sort things'. That's how he put it. The garden, mostly. And our cars that we lined up outside the house. And sometimes the cars of our friends. He was a man who was *handy*. A man who *got things done*.

The house always looked smaller than I remembered, dwarfed now by a birch tree Dad planted as a sapling in the front garden on the day I was born. In those days, fathers were not expected or indeed welcome in the labour ward, so they had plenty of time for things like tree planting. Other fathers repaired to the pub to wet the baby's head. Our father *gardened*.

The net curtains twitched and my mother's face appeared around the side of them. I pitched my cigarette – half smoked – into the ashtray and sprayed clouds of Happy about my person. There was no time to check my make-up – it was 6.59 p.m. I took a deep breath and stepped out of the car.

'Grace, that's an interesting colour combination you're wearing.' She stood at the hall door, looking me up and down as I teetered up the driveway on new brown suede boots that had not delivered on their promise of comfort when I tried them on in Office.

I'd let it rip when dressing for this evening. I wore a bright orange top with fine spaghetti straps engulfed under an itchy mohair cardigan. Colour? Bright pink. The A-line skirt down to just below my knees was an artist's palette of swirling pinks and oranges. Pink and orange were my current favourite colour combinations, and although they sound like the gastronomic equivalent of chocolate and cheese, they really are more like fish and chips when you try it.

'Hi Mam,' I said too loudly and thrust the wine and flowers at her. She accepted them with a small smile.

'Come in, come in, you'll catch your death in that get-up.' She ushered me in, afraid that the neighbours might spot me. I unfurled my hands from their tight fists and moved into the body of the house, the smell of dinner hitting me like a party. I was a sucker for my mother's cooking. No one did it like her.

'What's for dinner, Ma?' I asked. I couldn't focus on anything else until I knew.

'Nothing special.' She was matter-of-fact. 'Roast chicken with sausage and bread stuffing, roast potatoes and some carrot and parsnip mash. Oh, and an apple charlotte with cream for dessert.' For someone with a fridge as empty and lonely as mine, this was all good. I brightened instantly.

'I need to baste the chicken, Grace.' My mother hurried into the kitchen, closing the door behind her. She discouraged witnesses, said it distracted her. Besides, the heat of the kitchen reddened her cheeks, which she disliked, being vain in her own small way.

I walked into the front room and sat in my father's chair: a yawning, sunken armchair that slumped like a drunk at the fireplace. The armrests were solid wood and could hold a drink, the paper, an ashtray and a pack of fags without straining.

I sat in the chair and fancied I could still feel his presence, still smell that safe smell of him: woody and warm. This was the only stick of furniture in the house that sang of him. The piece he fought to keep when my mother redecorated in the late '80s. I could sense him from here, see his slow smile and hear his soundless laugh. His face split in two with it, his shoulders shaking, but you could still hear a pin drop. It was one of my favourite places in the world to sit.

'Dinner's ready,' my mother called from the kitchen. 'Make sure you wash your hands.' She said this in a sing-songy voice as if I was six and she could still sit on her hair. She had a thing about clean hands. 'Backs, fronts and individuals, she chanted, supervising us in the bathroom. We stood, in age order, single-file at the sink – Jane, Patrick, me and Clare. After a scrub at the sink, it was over to perch on the edge of the bath, holding out our hands for inspection. My mother was the type of mother who should have had a job. A paying job, I mean. She was so bright and so assertive and so interested in the world that went on around her, ignoring her as she struggled to rear four children. If she'd had something else in her life besides us and Dad and the house and the two cats, three goldfish and the rabbit, she might not have been so intense with us. We were her personal project. Any perceived failure on our part was her personal and deeply felt failure. She revelled in our successes, but when you're middle-of-the-road like me, these were infrequent and small.

I went to the upstairs bathroom, where the lighting was kinder to my reflection. The door of Patrick's bedroom was ajar, the light on. This was unusual. The door was always tightly shut. A long line of black bags shuffled inside the door, tied at the top. A floorboard moaned under my weight. I could hear my mother humming over the sound of the extractor in the kitchen. The clock in the hall ticked loudly and I stood there. When I pushed the door wider, it creaked with a terrible sound. I didn't step in but I looked in. The bareness of the room was a shock, like a smack. The shelves without the books. The walls with dark blue squares where posters of Yeats and Beckett and Jim Morrison had protected the paint from the sun's glare. The wardrobe door hung open and the hangers, empty now, clinked quietly in the draught, like wineglasses. The bed was stripped to the mattress. A pillow with no case sagged at the top. But I didn't go in. I never went in.

'Graaaaa-ce.' Mam called me again and I walked down the stairs, gripping the banisters. I made it downstairs without a slip.

'Are you having a clear-out?' I asked. My voice sounded so *ordinary*.

'Oh yes, upstairs you mean? Yes, I think it's about time, don't you?'

She opened the oven door and hot air rushed at me like a noise. I found a corkscrew and pushed it into the spongy cork of the wine bottle. I poured myself a glass and drank deeply from it.

'Grace, you're driving home, don't forget.' She placed a dish of crisp, honey-coloured roast potatoes down in front of me and I held my hands to the sides of the bowl, warming them. I cracked one open, like a hard-boiled egg, allowing a pat of butter to collect on the top like a puddle of gold. I tore a piece of it and placed it on my tongue. The comfort of it. I could feel my hips widening but I didn't care. It was only when I sat down that I realised my legs were shaking. Mam sat at the other end of the table.

'What are you going to do with the black bags?' I asked.

She didn't look at me. She pointed at her mouth and chewed deliberately. I drank more wine, waiting. When she finished, she drank from a tall glass of water. It took for ever.

'Give them to one of those charity shops, I suppose. Oxfam maybe. Or Vincent de Paul.' She dabbed at the corners of her mouth with a linen napkin and then bent her head to her dinner again.

'But what about the books? And the posters?' I set my knife and fork on either side of my plate and leaned forward, willing her to look at me. She still couldn't. Even after all this time. She could clear out his room but she couldn't look at me.

'I haven't decided yet, Grace. Now eat up your dinner. It'll get cold.'

The tapping of knives and forks on plates seemed loud in the silence. It was a relief when Mam turned on the small telly and we watched *Coronation Street*. Now the silence seemed companionable and the kitchen was warm and we cleared our plates.

'Did Clare tell you I'm bringing a friend to the wedding?'

'A friend?' I asked. I wasn't prepared to give her an inch. Not after the black bags. 'A boyfriend?'

'I'm far too old to have a boyfriend.' I might as well have suggested she indulge in a threesome with the next-door neighbours. 'He's a nice man, you'll like him.'

'What's his name?' I managed to ask this without sniggering.

'John,' she offered without embellishing. 'I met him at a night class. He's a good, decent man.'

'Good. I'm delighted for you. It's about time you started going out a bit more,' I said. I meant it.

'Maybe you'll meet a nice fellow for yourself,' Mam said, pouring tea.

'I have a nice fella, remember?'

'Shane?'

'Yes.'

'Oh, is that still all on?'

'Yes, of course. He's just been really busy lately. With work and everything.' I seemed to be saying that a lot lately. 'He's coming over to see me this weekend.'

'Oh, that's nice. You can bring him to dinner on Saturday night.'

'Dinner?'

'Yes, remember?'

I didn't remember. And Shane wouldn't be best pleased. He said he felt awkward now, in the house.

'Oh yes, of course.' I could always make an excuse for Shane at the last minute. Or maybe he'd come this time. I changed the subject.

'Is Ja . . . John coming on Saturday? It'll be nice to meet him.'

'Yes he is. It's no big deal, really. He's just a bit of company for me. That's all.' Her voice was short. 'He helps me. He's a great help. You know, with the house and everything.'

'With the clearing out of the house,' I said suddenly. I hadn't known I was going to say that. I wish I hadn't said that.

She looked at me then, right at me, as if we were two women, not a mother and a daughter. The kitchen was so quiet. I could hear my own breath. Mam's chest rose and fell as if she'd been running. I knew something was going to happen, something horrible. And then it did.

She started to cry. I drew back as if I'd been slapped in the face. My mother never cried. She didn't cry at my father's funeral. She didn't cry when Jane got married or had her babies. She didn't cry when my father's mother – whom she adored – passed away after a long illness. She smiled a brave smile and said it was for the best: a happy release. Had she cried last year? I couldn't remember.

Now she was sitting opposite me, crying openly. Her face was red and contorted with the effort of trying to stop. Tears collected in the creases of her face. They hung off her nose, the top of her lip, the line of her jaw. She looked smaller somehow. I was afraid. Her watch hung off her narrow wrist and I realised with a shock that she had aged in the past year. Her hair, grey for years, was now shot through with threads of white and seemed finer than before, I saw patches of pink scalp in places through the thin curtain of hair.

I handed Mam a tissue and she looked up at me then with a watery smile through her tears. I groped for something to say.

'Mam, it's great about John. Really. I mean it. But remember, you still have us.' I really wanted her to stop crying. I had never wanted anything more. She blew her nose and shook herself. She straightened, like someone pulled her up with strings.

'You all have your own lives and I'm glad about that, don't get me wrong. But I'm entitled to mine as well. I wiped your arses and fed you at four o'clock in the morning for long enough.'

We were back on familiar ground. I'd heard the arse-wiping and night-time feeding stories many times.

'Mam, I said I'm glad about it all.' It was like I had said nothing at all.

'John is a friend, that's all.' She spat the words out. 'I needed some companionship and he was there for me.' The unspoken allegation – that I had not been there for her – might as well have been sung from the rooftops. There was silence for a while as we both pretended to busy ourselves with stirring our coffee.

'John helps me get through it. Isn't that what we all want in the end? Someone to help us through?'

There didn't seem to be anything to say to that so I just nodded.

'This is delicious,' I said.

'Thank you, Grace.' We ate and ate and made a great production of scraping our spoons along the bottom of the bowls. We talked about other things: my new job, Clare's wedding, *Coronation Street*. We did not mention the empty room again.

When I was leaving, Mam patted my arm, like she was patting a hedgehog.

'Grace. About . . .' she nodded towards the stairs.

'Mam, I'm sorry. I shouldn't have said anything.'

'I'm just trying to move on, Grace, you know?' Her eyes were suspiciously bright.

I nodded at her, afraid she was going to say something else. She didn't and hugged me then, in her awkward, stiff way. I could feel her rib bones pressing against me. I pulled away first and practically ran to my car, desperate to be on my own. I turned left at the top of the road and pulled into a cul-de-sac. I killed the engine, turned off the lights and pulled my seat belt off before I let myself go. I cried like a child, loudly and insistently. I made no effort to stem the thick flow of tears that stormed down my face. I cried for my mother. For myself. And for Patrick, whose name we had never mentioned.

16

He died on a Friday but they didn't find him till the next day. Saturday. In a place called the Bay of Angels. That seemed wrong. Everything seemed wrong. That Patrick was lying on a cold slab in such a hot place. When he had been so warm only the day before. When he'd gotten sunburned. His face was slack and could have done with a shave. The sunburn was still red but he felt so cold. The shock of the cold when I put my hands on him. The shock of it. And they were so nice to me. Called me *señorita* and smiled and steered me from room to room. All the rooms looked the same. White and bare. And then the room with the trolleys. There were other people there. Not just Patrick. I could see their outlines under the cold, stiff sheets. I thought of other sisters, mothers, daughters who had to come to this place and nod and say yes, this is my family. I wanted Patrick to wake up. I wanted this to be like my millions of blunders that somehow worked out all right in the end. But he didn't wake up. He lay there as still as I'd ever seen him. I looked at him and people looked at me and I nodded and they led me away, through the endless rooms, into the sunshine as white as the rooms. Now there were three of us. Shane, Caroline and me.

'Is he . . .?' Shane nearly asked.

'Was it . . .?' Caroline whispered.

I nodded without looking at them. My breath was coming in the familiar rasps and I welcomed it, hoped for it. I didn't have my inhaler with me. I didn't have anything with me. Just

my dress that had dried on my body last night. And my sandals that a policeman returned to me on the beach. I didn't
know where my handbag was. I still held the red runner in my
hand, the shoelaces still tied. We never found the other one.

'Your mother and Jane are on their way,' Caroline said, her
voice an apology. I nodded and at that moment, the idea of
my mother was so comforting, like a warm blanket on a cold
night. I felt like I could keep it together until she came and
then allow myself to unravel like a woolly jumper. I don't know
why I ever thought that.

Shane started to cry. The way men cry. Like they're trying
not to cry. The asthma attack that might have taken me away
from myself for a while turned and left. The sun beat down
and the heat pushed against us.

'What about Clare?' I said. My voice was hoarse and my
throat hurt.

'She's in Prague with Richard, remember?' Caroline said.
'Jane said that she'll contact her and tell her . . .' I nodded
again. Jane would tell her. I would let Jane tell her. Jane would
know what to say. Jane always knew what to say.

The day passed although I can't say how. There was an interview with some official-looking people. There was an inter-
preter and a tape recorder and someone with a notebook and
a man who smiled in a gentle way and kept pushing a lock of
hair back from his forehead and didn't notice when it slipped
down again, almost immediately. There was coffee, dark and
bitter, and some class of a sandwich with thin, fleshy meat that
I didn't eat. I can't remember saying anything but I must have
because people nodded their heads at me and wrote things
down and then, finally, clicked off the recorder.

'That is all,' one of them said. 'Zat eees all.' We could have
written it on Patrick's headstone. *That is all.* It wasn't nearly
enough.

There were a thousand arrangements to be made to get Patrick home. You can't just get online and book a ticket. There are forms. Lots of them. There are channels to be gone through. Official Channels. Someone came down from the Irish embassy in Malaga, Brian something-or-other, he was very efficient in a quiet kind of a way. And he was brilliant with Mam. Even now, it hurts to remember her face. White it was. And bare, as if something was missing. Which of course it was. Her son was missing. Patrick was missing.

When I went outside to meet them, Jane moved towards me at once, pulling me into the circle of her arms. She was weeping without making any sound and that's when I knew. That Patrick was really gone and never coming back. And that it was all my fault. My mother never said a word.

17

After dinner at Mam's I looked forward to work the next day. I was busy there and didn't have time to think. Strange things were happening in my head. I kept remembering things about Patrick. Small things, like the way he used to put his toast into the fridge before buttering it because he didn't like the way the butter melted on the bread.

Silly things, like the way he'd dismantle the newspaper and then put it back together again, only in the wrong order, just to annoy Dad. Awful things, like the half-finished manuscript a girl had posted back to us from Sydney.

'He was going to come back, you know,' she wrote. 'When he got his work visa sorted out. He was going to finish the book. I didn't know what to do with it but I read it. I read it and it's brilliant.'

And it was. Funny and tender and so full of Patrick. We didn't know what to do with it either. And now I thought about that too. Where was it now? What had Mam done with it in her clear-out? It was a relief to throw myself into work and shake these thoughts that went around and around my head like a carousel.

Bernard had returned from Donegal but I hardly saw him at all, apart from a brief encounter one afternoon. I got into the lift at the third floor and pressed G for ground floor (fag and coffee break in Ciaran's office). I could hear someone hurrying along the corridor to catch the lift. I jabbed at the 'door close' button because I prefer being in the lift by myself:

there's one of those lovely tinted mirrors there that make my face look tanned. Also you can check yourself, after lunch, say, for signs of spinach snagged between teeth, or after you've been outside, for leaves in your hair (this is more common in the autumn, obviously). If you're going from the sixth floor all the way down, you might have enough time to squeeze a spot and / or apply concealer, but an express run is needed for this, no stopping at any floor in between.

The doors were nearly there, gliding towards each other like skaters when two hands slid through the gap and pushed them back. I recognised the hands. I could have picked them out of any line-up.

'Grace.' (Says he.)

'Bernard.' (Says I.)

And then nothing for a while. And then:

'How was your . . .' (This from me.)

'Are you going . . .' (This from him, at the same time.)

Then we laughed, the way people do when they start talking at the same time.

'You go,' we both said at the same time. This was getting ridiculous, so I pointed at him to indicate that he could talk now.

'I wondered if you were going to that work thingy on Friday night?' Bernard said quickly, as if afraid I might start speaking again.

Was he asking me out? Or just wondering, in an offhand, casual kind of way if I happened to be considering the possibility of going out with the work crowd on Friday night? Second one, right? I thought all this in about one and a half seconds. We were at the second floor now.

'Eh no, I can't. I have . . . plans,' I said, paying great attention to the digital dial above the lift doors. First floor.

'Oh,' he said. Now it was his turn to concentrate on the dial. We were nearly there. Jesus, what was it about him that made me want to lean over and lick him, like he was a choc-ice? It couldn't just be his hands, could it? The feeling was like springtime after a long winter.

'What were you going to ask me?' he said. The lift pinged and the doors slid back. We were on the ground floor.

'How was Donegal?' I stepped out of the lift and turned around to look at him.

'Oh, you know. Family stuff,' he said. I nodded. I knew. I wanted to ask him about Cliona. Had he seen her? Naked? Had he wanted her? Did she squint when she took off her glasses? The doors were moving again and he smiled at me and then he was gone.

Caroline was at home when I got in. I looked at my watch. Jesus, it was after seven. I had distracted myself into working overtime. Without realising it. This was getting out of hand.

'A funny thing happened to me at work today.' Caroline lay on her back on the sitting room floor, her legs stretched back over her body, her feet planted firmly on the ground behind her head. She looked like an S in joined-up writing. She was practising yoga, by the way, in case you're wondering.

I sat at the kitchen table, stirring a bowl of Pot Noodles – cold now – with a spoon. Raindrops zig-zagged their way down the bay window, obscuring my view of the garden, which was a jungle of green, interrupted in places by pockets of bright yellow where daffodils struggled against the wind.

'I met a claimant today,' Caroline continued, oblivious to the excruciating curve of her body. 'She's suing Dublin Zoo for personal injury and emotional torture. She says she was attacked by a cockatoo last summer when she was wheeling her mother around the zoo in her wheelchair. I could barely keep a straight face. Grace? Are you listening to me?'

I looked up and nodded, sucking a particularly long noodle through closed lips.

'It was her hair that did it. It was like a bloody bird's nest. All brown frizz and static. No wonder the cockatoo attacked her. He probably thought he was coming home to roost in it.' She tailed off, looking at me.

'Grace? You haven't heard a word I've said, have you?' Caroline unknotted herself and sat up. The sudden silence in the room and the weight of Caroline's stare brought me back to the present. I had been in the past, excavating the land around Patrick's life with my bare hands.

'Are you OK?' she asked, her head cocked to one side.

'Yeah, I'm grand,' I lied. 'Just got a lot on my mind, with the new job an' all.' I didn't tell her about the empty room. The clear-out. She would have said this was *positive* and that Mam was *moving on.*

'How was your ma last night?' Caroline retreated to her bedroom and shouted from there.

'Grand.' I stood up and wiped a stray blob of Pot Noodley-type sauce from my skirt. I needed to get out. I decided to call round to Clare's house. She lived in Rathgar with Richard. I'd walk there, clear my head.

'Caroline, I'm going out for a while,' I shouted into her bedroom.

'You can't go out, I *need* you,' she whined. I had trouble getting into her room, with all the clothes, bags and shoes lying like a carpet on the floor. Caroline was standing on the bed with her back to the mirror, her head twisted round at an awkward angle to see if her bum looked big in the jeans she was wearing. It didn't.

'Oh, your blind date. I'd forgotten,' I said.

'What do you think? she asked. The jeans were low cut, the waistband clinging to her narrow hips in a very positive way. One foot was encased in a blood-coloured mule, encrusted with ornate stones. You could click your heels together three times in those, say 'there's no place like home' and be back in Kansas with Aunty Em in no time at all.

The other foot was billeted in a stern-looking boot with a narrow heel and a pointed toe. She bent down and picked up a skirt, holding it against her waist. It was very pretty, all swirls and gathers.

'The jeans or the skirt?' she asked with all the seriousness of an American president saying, 'The nukes or the A-bomb?'

'The skirt is very pretty,' I said, 'but more of a third-date outfit.'

'The one where I get some?' she asked, anxious.

'The very one,' I replied with all the wisdom of Solomon. I had to smile – to myself, of course – at people like Caroline. She could have worn a black plastic bin bag and still looked fabulous.

'The jeans then?' she said, throwing the skirt back on the bed.

'Yes, the jeans. With the Dorothy mules and the ridiculously small Cinderella bag.' It could barely hold a Lillet but matched the shoes perfectly. You cannot underestimate the importance of accessories. My work here was done.

'I'll see you later. Enjoy your date and remember to note the position of the emergency exits wherever you're going. You'll kill yourself clambering out toilet windows in those shoes.' I turned to go.

'Wait,' Caroline panicked. 'What about the top?'

I turned back. 'Well, my advice would be to wear one. I mean, it is a *first* date and a modicum of propriety should be established.'

'Grace, pleeeeease.'

'OK, OK,' I conceded. 'The chocolate brown tailored shirt with the three-quarter-length sleeves. It looks great against your hair with the added advantage of buttons down the front. You can have it buttoned up to the neck, or undo a couple, depending on how the date is going.' Caroline looked dubious. I turned to go and fell over a swell of bags gathered about the foot of the bed.

'Jesus, Cats, you're taking this first date thing pretty seriously.' I picked my way carefully towards the door.

'I've decided something,' she said in a way that made me stop and turn back to her.

'What?' I asked.

'I've decided this one is going to be The One,' she said, 'even if he's five foot nothing and spots trains at the weekend. There's only so much dating a girl can do and I'm nearly at the end of my run.' I looked at her, amused. If Caroline had decided this guy would be The One, then that's just what he'd be. I had no doubt about it. Caroline was a woman who got her own way, mostly because she worked hard at it and refused defeat the way some people were able to refuse second helpings of dessert.

'Down or up?' she asked, pawing at her hair.

'Down,' I replied, halfway out the door, 'and go easy on the make-up, for God's sake. Remember if you're doing a "happily ever after" with this guy, there's a possibility he'll see you without make-up at some stage, so you'd better break him in gently.'

I didn't hear her response as I stepped out into the damp of the evening. I took my hair down and wrapped it around my ears and neck to keep me warm. Sparking up a fag, I thought briefly about quitting before clamping my lips around the filter and sucking smoke greedily into my lungs. I walked briskly through the half-light, head down, hands stuffed into the pockets of my coat, fag poking out of the corner of my mouth.

I saw three black cats on my way to Clare's, all of which crossed my path, one of them twice. I couldn't remember if that was good luck or bad luck. Probably the latter.

Clare and Richard lived in a quaint period terrace house

just off the Rathgar Road. It looked small from the outside with its prim little front garden and cobbled path that led to a sturdy wooden door with a zealously polished brass knocker. Inside it was cavernous with gloriously high ceilings fringed with lavishly complicated coving.

Richard – wily and wadded – had bought it for about a fiver back in the mid '80s when people would rather emigrate to Outer Mongolia (where *is* that place?) than buy a property in Ireland. Now it was worth zillions of euro and even though the euro was fairly useless, that was still a lot of money.

Clare answered the door in her dressing gown. She looked so small under the towering architrave of the doorway. Clare was a *homebird* and took her responsibilities in this regard seriously. She loved staying home, preferably in her pyjamas, tending to things. Things like her vast array of potted plants, her cat (George), her hair (she had a thing about crimping), her fiancé (Wadded Willy, or Richard as he preferred). Tonight, her hair was bundled up under a white cotton turban-shaped towel and her toes – painted a bright orange – were splayed uncomfortably, separated from each other by cotton balls.

'Grace,' she beamed at me. 'It's great to see you.' She pulled the door wide, inviting me in. I'd forgotten that I'd hung up on her the last time we'd spoken. I bent down and hugged her gently – she really was *tiny*, I had to be careful with her.

'Sorry for being such a drama queen on the phone the other day,' I said.

'Don't worry about it,' she said, ushering me into the warmth of the sitting room where a fire blazed in the grate.

'Have you had your dinner?' Clare didn't cook as a rule – unless you count toasted sandwiches and baked potatoes – but she was a great source of take-out menus. She had them filed in a colour-coded black folder, in alphabetical order by type with a complicated rating system using gold stars favoured by primary school teachers.

'I'm grand, thanks,' I said, taking off my coat and sinking into the sofa.

'Where's Richard?' I asked. She laughed.

'He had to take his staff on a team-building day out. He's up the Wicklow Mountains. He was playing paintball today.' The pair of us cracked up. I suppose you'd have to know Richard like we do to know that he'd prefer to have his balls severed by a blowtorch than be running for his life, atop a mountain, from armed employees who may not have been entirely satisfied with the salary increases in their last review.

'What's he wearing?' I managed to ask. Richard *always* wore suits. Immaculate ones. With cufflinks.

'He bought a tracksuit.' Clare could barely get the words out and I pictured Richard, running for his life, with a navy pinstriped tracksuit zipped up to his chin and flapping a little around his legs. Even now, the image can still invite hysterics.

'What's up with you?' Clare asked when our raucous laughter had subsided into sighs of pleasure.

'What do you mean?' I said. I wanted to talk to her so much but I didn't know where to start.

'You're chewing the ends of your hair, you're not hungry and you haven't even looked at those chocolates in the bowl on the table,' Clare said, unwrapping the towel from her head.

'No, I did look,' I argued, 'but, in fairness, they *are* Ferrero Rocher.'

'You do have a point,' she allowed. 'But still, something's up. What is it?'

I removed chunks of hair from my mouth and glanced over at her. I decided to go for the jugular.

'Did you know Mam was clearing out Patrick's room?' I looked at her carefully as I asked the question. Apart from a slight flaring of her nostrils, she was very still.

'Yes. She told me,' she finally answered.

'When did she start?' I asked. 'And why?' I curled my hands into tight fists.

'Grace, it's a good thing really. It just means she's . . .'

'Moving on, yeah, I gathered that.' I finished Clare's sentence for her.

Clare ignored me and went on. 'It was two or three weeks ago, I think. I called into Mam's house. She wasn't expecting me.' Clare pulled her sheet of hair behind her ear and chanced a glance up.

'Go on,' I urged. 'Don't worry, I'm not going to throw my toys out of the pram because you didn't tell me before.' I actually felt like throwing acid in the faces of my toys, setting fire to them and jumping up and down on their blackened remains, but I also wanted information. I strained forward.

'Well, Mam was in the house on her own. Her face was puffy and red, like she'd been crying for hours and the place was a mess. And cold too. She was sitting on the couch in her dressing gown. It looked like she'd been there for most of the day. It was dinnertime and she didn't even have any potatoes peeled.'

This was shocking. I couldn't remember Mam *ever* not cooking dinner, apart from the day she brought Clare home from the hospital, which is possibly why I hated her so much for the first six months of her life. I'd always been a girl who loved her grub.

'What did she say?' I asked.

'There'd been a phone call earlier in the day. For Patrick. From his bloody credit card company. She just lost it,' Clare said. 'I think she was in shock or something. When she finally started talking, she couldn't stop. I just caught her at her lowest moment. She needed to talk to someone.' Clare's tone was apologetic as she looked up at me.

'She said she was going to do what she should have done

a long time ago. Close all his bank accounts, cancel his bank cards, his mobile phone account. You know, all that kind of stuff. She showed me a stack of letters in his room, mostly from banks, that she had collected over the last year. She started clearing out his room the next day.'

'Does she still blame me?' I said, looking out the window and holding my breath.

'She *never* blamed you, you know that. It wasn't your fault. It was an accident. How many times am I going to have to say this?' Clare looked as pissed off as it was possible for her to look. I could feel a pulse beat in the back of my throat. Anger rose in me like a tide.

'What about the things she said in Spain?' I asked Clare, trying to keep my voice steady and low.

'She was upset. People say things when they're upset. Things they don't mean.'

'She *did* mean it,' I shouted. 'She meant it because it was true. I *was* selfish and thoughtless and always having to be the centre of attention.' When I stopped talking, my breath was ragged, like I'd run up the stairs. Clare looked at me with her head at an angle. I pitied her. First Mam offloading on her, now me. But what can you do when you have access to someone like Clare, someone who can listen without judging? It's a rare and precious trait.

The phone rang and we both jumped. It was Richard. Clare chatted easily to him and the strained atmosphere over the past half hour dissipated like smoke through an open window. I tried to avoid the one side of their conversation that I could hear. I failed and had to endure it.

'Goodnight, baby. I'll see you tomorrow evening.'

'Me too. The bed's too big.'

'Goodbye. You hang up first.'

'No, you hang up.'

'No, you.'

'I love you too.'

'No, you hang . . .'

I couldn't take it any longer and removed myself from the room. Even a little of someone else's good thing was too much at the moment. I was looking forward to seeing Shane at the weekend but the annoying little man on the right side of my brain (the sensible side) kept poking his head out of my cerebral tissue and reminding me that Shane was really just coming to Dublin for work: I happened to be on the agenda under Any Other Business.

When I reckoned it was safe, I returned to the sitting room. Clare was tightly coiled on the edge of the couch. Her fingers toyed with the ends of her hair, splitting ends like she wasn't getting married in less than two weeks' time. I had done that to her.

'Have you sorted out the seating arrangements?' I asked in an effort to change the subject. It was a rhetorical question really.

'Yes. Ages ago.' Clare stopped playing with her hair and ran to get her wedding folder. You should have seen this thing. It made the Golden Pages look anorexic. A beautifully bound leather folder with multicoloured tabs for the variety of subjects that Clare insisted were important (I mean, come on, there was a section on 'breakfast' with a menu on what the bride and her family were going to eat on the morning of the wedding – way too much fresh fruit for my liking . . .).

'The only thing I was wondering,' she said slowly.

'Yes?' I said.

'Well, it's just that, you know, with you up at the top table, where do you think I should put Shane?' I knew by her tone that she wasn't at all sure of Shane making it to the wedding. To be honest, I wasn't too sure either. He hadn't committed to it. I was determined to pin him down on this point at the weekend. In the meantime, I lived in hope.

'Put him at a table of men. Make sure none of them are gay

or they'll be all over him like a rash. If there have to be wom-
en present, make sure they're deformed or hideously ugly or
about to receive a cheque from the president for managing to
live to be a hundred.' I laughed but we both knew I was half
serious. Clare didn't comment. I loved that about her. She
never asked about my precarious relationship, which compared so dismally to her ecstatic kinship with Richard. She
listened and offered gentle support.

She consulted her list to see if she could accommodate
Shane on the seating plan.

'I have a table of couples, with two empty seats. I could put
Shane in one and Mary in the other?' Clare had her glasses
on and a pencil stuck behind her ear, assuming the persona of
Wedding Planner, with great gravitas.

Mary was my mother's mother. She didn't allow us to call
her 'granny' or 'nana' or anything that smacked of sentimen-
tality or nonsense. We called her Mary. She was tall, like my
mother, but age had stooped her into an R. Her stature, however, was the only thing diminishing about Mary. Her senses
were as sharp as her tongue. She'd be perfect as a wedding
companion for Shane.

'Make it so, Number One,' I said. 'That'll tighten him.'

Clare bent her head to the Wedding Directory and wrote. I
smiled a wicked smile. When I was getting ready to leave, she
mentioned Patrick again.

'You know, Grace, just because Mam is clearing out his
room, it doesn't mean that we're all going to forget about him
or anything. It's just *stuff*.'

I nodded and wished, not for the first time, that I could be
more like Clare.

'Have you been to the graveyard yet? Since the funeral, I mean?'

This was something else that set me apart. Mam went every
other day. Clare told me that. Jane, ever practical, brought the
kids with her every couple of weeks to 'tend' the grave. Clare

went whenever she wanted to tell him something. She said she could sense him there. I couldn't sense him anywhere and a visit to a grave wasn't going to change that.

'No,' I said. 'Not yet.'

Her face was hard to read but she hugged me tight, standing on her tippy-toes.

I wanted to tell her about Bernard but I didn't know why, or how to start. I told her about Shane instead. Coming over at the weekend.

'That'll be nice, Grace. He hasn't see you in ages, has he?' I thought about the question. Clare was right. Shane hadn't seen me in ages. Not for the longest time.

18

Trieste, September 2003

Dear Grace,

Got here yesterday from Venice. The train winds along the coast for a bit and I saw the Adriatic Sea for the first time. You can sail to Greece from here, down the leg of Italy. The idea of following the sun around the world appeals to me, especially when I think about this time next year when I'll be settling into the Irish autumn, just another cold accountant. Yeah, the writing is going well. I can't call it a book yet in case the words dry up. But there are pages now, chapters even. And characters that appear without my knowing about it. I love that about writing. How you don't really know what's in your head, what you're capable of, until you write it down.

After Venice, Trieste seems quiet and more real somehow. There is an aquarium down by the port that you would love. Bright splashes of fish with bloated faces and well-fed sharks that swim overhead and look at you from either side of their heads with black eyes. I met a girl down there yesterday. Chiara. She's been working there for the summer. A marine biology student. She agreed to meet me tonight. I have never been so popular with women since I've been on my travels. Maybe it's because I'm on my own and they're thinking 'would you look at the poor ginger fuck'. And it's not like the sun has tinged me a golden brown or anything. All it's done is given me more freckles and painted me the colour of the salmon of

*fecking knowledge. Whatever it is, I'm not complaining. She's
taking me on the James Joyce trail. He lived here you know,
for about ten years back before World War One. He wrote* Portrait of the Artist as a Young Man. *He finished* Dubliners
here. And started Ulysses *too, they say.*

*I am sitting in the main piazza now, having coffee which is
very small and very strong and very black. It's the afternoon
so no milky coffee allowed. They're even more pedantic about
their coffee than the French. The square is, predictably, magnificent. The mainlanders really know their squares. The sun
is warm on my back and there's a stack of – unread – books
at my table that I picked up for a song in a bookshop along
one of the narrow back streets. There's cobblestones here, and
wooden window shutters. And a winding road up to a walled
castle that overlooks the bay. There's something so appealing
about this nomadic lifestyle. So simple.*

*Got your email by the way. Hope you and Shane have
made up. You shouldn't feel so bad about going to the cinema
on your own. Look on the plus side. You don't have to share
the bucket of popcorn and you can really get comfortable in
one of those seats made for two. Are you raising your eyes to
heaven now and shaking your head? You are, aren't you?
Your latest diet sounds like the craziest one you've been on
so far – and I've witnessed the food beginning with P diet,
remember? You're lovely just the way you are. Dad used to
say that and it's true. Do you remember how he used to bring
us sweets home on a Friday night? In a brown paper bag?
Trigger bars and coconut marshmallows and bags of Tayto
cheese and onion and bottles of TK red lemonade. It's funny,
the things you think about when you've got time.*

Love from Patrick
XX

19

I got back from Clare's at around 10 p.m. Caroline wasn't back but her blind date preparations had sashayed right out of her bedroom and exhausted themselves in the living room. There had obviously been much indecision about the choice of outer garment. Bundles of jackets, coats, throws and cardigans draped themselves over all available pieces of furniture, like spent bodies. She had eventually settled on my black leather jacket, I noted, judging by its glaring absence on the coatstand.

Grabbing the back of the couch, I tipped it forward until the clothes lying on it settled in a soft slump on the floor. I pulled the top off a bottle of beer and lay on the couch, reaching for the remote. Of course, I couldn't find it. Looking for it would involve effort and patience, both of which were out of stock. I threw myself back against the worn leather of the couch, lit up a fag and exhaled soundlessly into the darkness of the room.

I had switched off the lights to trick my mind into thinking the flat did not look like A-Wear at the end of the January sales. It worked. I liked the dark. It soothed me. Sounds eventually broke to the surface of the silence: the creaking of the ancient floorboards, the rattle of water moving through the pipes. Mr Jenkins's cough had worsened, I noticed, listening to his wet hacking as he arrived home from bingo. He played bingo every Wednesday night. He was sweet on the caller, whose name he refused to divulge. 'A slip of a thing,' he offered. 'A real lady.' Judging by the sounds below, it seemed that the old man had once again failed to persuade her back to his pad for a look at his stamp collection (he actually had one). I tipped an impressively lengthy ash into the tiny circle of the beer bottle top. The shrill beep of my mobile cut through the darkness of the room, startling me. It was a text, from Ethan.

> *If you're not too busy and important tomorrow,*
> *how about lunch? 1pm? Usual place?*

I hadn't started my new job but, obviously, this did not prevent my friends and colleagues slagging off my new elevated status. I feigned annoyance but secretly enjoyed it, never having been promoted before. I texted back.

> *I am terribly important but not particularly busy.*
> *See you at 1pm.*

The job started in earnest next Monday, the downside of which meant that I would be working closely with the IT department. That meant Bernard O'Malley and *that* meant a cocktail of feelings that included guilt mixed with tension and something else that felt like butterflies in my stomach which led me straight back to guilt. I had already made up my mind not to tell Shane about my infidelity, but now I wondered if I could manage it.

I took a swig of beer. It had warmed from the heat of my hands around the bottle. If I told Shane, he would never speak to me again. There was absolutely no doubt about that. And it's pretty tricky to sustain a relationship with someone under those circumstances. If I didn't tell him, I would be devoured by guilt and shame. There was no choice. I had made my bed, I had lain in it and had sex – *three times* – in it. Now it was time to get up, change the sheets, fluff the pillows and turn down the duvet in time for Shane's arrival on Friday. This was my chance, maybe my last one. I would *not* fuck it up. I went to bed and dreamed.

I am a pink and yellow unicorn, snatched from the wild and put into the penguin enclosure at Dublin Zoo. A woman with a head of hair like a bird's nest points at me and laughs, an evil genius laugh. Shane passes by with Bernard O'Malley, deep in conversation, both nodding. Neither of them notice me, even though I whinny as loud as I can. The penguins plan to dig themselves to Antarctica and ask me to use my horn that stretches phallus-like from the centre of my forehead. Patrick kisses Caroline under an ancient oak tree. I shake my mane, take a few steps back and stop. Now I am running towards the edge of the enclosure. My mother is there except she is a bat with wings on her hips like hands.

'Typical Grace,' she says. Her voice is high and thin.

'Always has to be the centre of attention.' She raises her wings and beats them slowly, her body lifting away from the ground, a bird of prey now and not a bat after all. I can't see where she is anymore. I run fast and the world looks like a blur, the way it does when you're moving through it too quickly. I fall for a long time, never reaching the ground.

I woke with a start and felt both relief (I was not a suicidal unicorn) and confusion (what the fuck was *that* all about?).

Caroline had already left for the airport. She was catching the red eye to London for a two-day insurance conference. In her new job as Claims Manager for one of our major competitors, she was expected to go to these things, however much she resisted. She had been poached by the competition a few months ago and the boss still hadn't gotten over it, especially when he realised she had taken a small but lucrative group of our clients with her.

She left a note for me on the kitchen table:

Blind date went better than expected last night. In fact, it was better than that! Will reveal all when I see you. Think I might be in love!!! Have no appetite (although in fairness it's 5 o'clock in the sodding morning). Also, am smiling which, as you well know, I don't do much before noon on any given day. I asked to see him again on Saturday night (can you believe that???). Staying an extra night in London (shopping, naturally). Will be home late Saturday afternoon. Cats.

PS: OK, OK, so he's not what you might call classically good looking and his dress sense is clearly a cry for help. But his voice is so soft and you could paddle in his dimples. Wait till you meet him. You'll love him.

I made myself a full Irish (mug of tea and a fag) before sitting down at the kitchen table and rereading the note. No, there was no misunderstanding. Caroline had written the word 'love' on the hastily scribbled note and although there was a 'think' and a 'might' in the same sentence, the word 'love' was there, as stark and glaring as a unicorn in a penguin enclosure.

Since I had met Caroline, she had never had a long-term relationship. She was a serial dater, drifting from dinners to movies to left of centre theatrical productions, in a noncommittal effort to find Mr Right or even Mr All Right.

My theory on this limping line of would-be suitors was the two Bs: beauty and brains. A lethal combination that could make a grown man wet his pants. Caroline had no idea of the devastating effect her physical presence had on these mere mortals. What a bummer. To be beautiful and not even know it. That would be like being a billionaire and thinking you were overdrawn at the bank. If I were beautiful, I would stay home a lot and gaze at myself in mirrors. I would take pictures of myself and send them to death-row prisoners, to cheer them in the face of their impending deaths.

I wondered who the guy was. Maybe Caroline was right. Maybe he was The One. The thought settled uneasily, like a kebab eaten after midnight on a full stomach of gassy beer. Things might change. I hated change. I liked routine. I was like a baby that way. I needed feeding every four hours (at least), occasional winding and the warm weight of soothing hands on me if I couldn't sleep at night. If this guy was Caroline's Significant Other and Shane and I ever got round to planning our future, things would change. I sat at the table, tying tiny knots in strands of my hair. When I glanced at the clock, it said 8.15 a.m. I was going to be late.

'Shit, bugger and damn.' I hauled myself up from the chair and went in search of a top that was both clean and ironed to wear underneath my suit. My tops can usually divided into two categories: (1) clean but not ironed, and (2) dirty and also not ironed. After all, where is the sense in ironing a dirty top? Your time would be better spent ironing a clean one. Or washing a dirty one. Everyone knows that. I found two tops in category 1 and several in category 2. I picked the less wrinkly of the two tops – a close call, it was – and headed to the shower to scald myself awake. As the hot water kneaded my brain, cranking the thought process up to its starting position, I remembered three nice things that were happening today:

1. Meeting Ethan for lunch.
2. Gloating and waving at Ethan when he returned to the office after lunch and I did not (half day from work).
3. Half day from work.
4. Getting spray tanned.

I smiled and did a little dance under the shower, taking great care to keep my feet on the shower mat, remembering what happened the last time . . .

I missed a call while I was prancing about in the shower. Probably Ethan ringing to confirm lunch. He'd send an email as well. I would bet my Tina Turner collection on it.

But the missed call wasn't from Ethan. It was from Shane. He left a message and I dialled into my voicemail, feeling suddenly wary. The message was short.

'Grace, I'm ringing about tomorrow.' Shane spoke in a low voice and I knew he was in his office. He rarely made personal calls from work. I straightened. If I'd had hackles, they'd have been raised.

'Graham is coming to Dublin with me and he's insisting I bring him out on the town tomorrow night.'

Another pause. Then, as if I had objected, he took up again, this time with a sharpness in his voice.

'If I could get out of it, I would. But this is work, you know how important this is to me.' This I did know. Shane was a 'corporate animal' (his words) and prided himself on saying and doing all the right things, preferably within hearing distance of the top cheeses in his company.

'I want to get someplace,' he said, and in fairness to him, he *was* going places. It was the fact that he was going there without me that rankled.

The message ended, softer now: 'I can't wait to see you. Let me get the business out of the way first, then I can concentrate fully on you, gorgeous girl. All right? Grace? Don't be mad, please?'

Then a lot of clunking and banging as if he were hanging up without looking. I sat on the edge of the bed. I was more angry than disappointed. You'd think he could have come up with something better than that. Bringing Graham out for a few drinks? Shane's boss was from bloody Rathfarnham and needed a guide around the city about as badly as Molly Fecking Malone.

I could see him, crouched over his desk, his hands cupped around the mouthpiece of the phone, blond hair flopping across his beautiful face. Could I be overreacting? I mean, the boy *did* have to earn a crust, did he not? I was probably PMT-ish. My two trusty period spots were reddening and preparing to rise and sit in glory on the end of my chin for the next three days. They were almost like old friends, those two, except for the fact that I hated their guts and tried to squeeze the pus out of them as quick as look at them. Another tell-tale sign was the waistband of my skirt, which strained against my belly, leaving wrap-around red welts along my thickened waist.

I suddenly remembered that I hadn't told him about my promotion. I would tell him tomorrow night, when he got in. Or Saturday morning if he was too late. It would be something to talk about.

20

By the time I drove into the car park at work, found a space, parked in the space, reversed back out of the space, parked again only straighter this time and heaved myself out into the day, it was already 9.30 a.m. and I was late, again. Ciaran doffed his cap at me, then hurried out of his hut, looking worried.

'Grace love, are ye all right?' he asked. I was used to this kind of reaction when I presented myself to the world without my Face.

'Don't worry, Ciaran. I'm not sick or anything. Just haven't got my slap on,' I said, reassuring him with my Ad for Toothpaste smile. I felt better and better about my date that afternoon with Tans-R-Us.

'And your hair's wet, Grace. Ye'll catch yer death on a day like this.' Ciaran stamped his feet and breathed into his clasped hands to emphasise how cold it was.

I laughed at him and told him to stop being an old queen, but his quiet concern warmed me. He was better than a bowl of Ready Brek in the morning.

I tried to sneak in the back door of the office, which turned out to be a bad idea. The managing director was striding down the corridor, the sides of his Louis Vuitton suit jacket billowing behind him like a cloak, such was the speed of his gait. I fumbled for my phone and quickly pressed it against my ear.

'Yes, yes, I'm sure,' I barked into the phone, hands gesticulating madly in front of me to add credence to the scenario.

'I've just been talking to his solicitor for the last half an hour and he insists that he won't settle for anything less than

€55,000,' I continued down the phone in my most business-like manner. It would have worked too, if the pesky phone hadn't started to ring. Fuck, bugger and damnation. The MD smiled wryly at me.

'Good morning, Grace. Good of you to join us.' His stride never faltered and in a moment he was gone, leaving a frosty tang of citrus streaking along the corridor.

Here's a funny thing about me: even when there's no one around to witness my mortification (the corridor was now empty), I *still* blush just as furiously as if there was an auditorium of people present to cringe for me.

I walked slowly towards my office, stabbing at the answer button on my phone.

'Hello?' I spoke through gritted teeth.

'Grace, hope I didn't get you at a bad time?' It was Ethan, confirming lunch. However much I wanted to give him a good hiding, I couldn't bring myself to be mean to him. He was just too sweet.

'I've booked the table you like in the restaurant.' When I didn't respond immediately, he continued in a hurry.

'You know the one at the back, where the light is dimmer. You said it's kinder there, remember?' I had no recollection of ever having said that, but if Ethan said it was so, then it just was. He had the memory of a herd of elephants.

I reached the door of my office.

'Ethan, I have to go. I'll see you at lunchtime, OK?'

'One p.m.?' he asked.

'Sure.'

'I'll wait for you downstairs in the lobby.' He waited for my agreement.

'Sure, sure, see you then.'

I flung my phone into my bag and strode along the open-plan office floor trying to look as if I'd already done a full day's work and was just breezing in to check my emails (which is exactly what I intended to do, in fairness). I needn't have worried. Up at the end of the floor, the liability team were reacting to the boss's two-day absence with abandon. He had gone to the same conference as Caroline in London. Put it this way, if there had been a chandelier hanging from the ceiling, they would have been swinging from it. The atmosphere was no less than raucous on the floor.

'Grace, you made it, we were sooooo worried.' This from Norman, who was bet into a pale blue suit with a baby-pink shirt. He should have looked like a low-rent pimp or a nightclub owner but, strangely, he did not. Sashaying towards me, he enveloped me in a bear hug, gushing the words, 'Thank God, thank God,' over and over again, while stroking my hair feverishly. Suddenly, he thrust me an arm's length away and began.

'Don't ever do that again. We were out of our minds with worry.' He ended this sentence in a crescendo, attracting the attention of the cockroaches in the basement.

Everyone's eyes had darted Grace-wards, making me aware of my face, still reddened from the encounter with Mark, the MD, in the corridor. I tried to slink to my desk, but Norman was on a roll. With his arm still wrapped around my shoulder, he turned to His Public. 'Nothing to see here, folks. Go back to what you were doing. We got her back safe and sound. That's the main thing.'

From under my eyelashes, I noticed Bernard O'Malley slotted behind a desk that looked too small for him. He offered me a small smile before swivelling on his chair and assuming The Position (crouched over his desk, peering into his monitor, pushing his teeny-tiny-Joyce like glasses up his nose).

I wrestled myself away from Norman's clutches and half ran to my desk, catching colleagues' eyes as I went, making sure I raised mine to heaven, making clicking noises with my tongue.

Once installed in my little cubicle, I switched on my computer and listened. Yes, there it was. The discreet pinging noise, letting me know I had mail. I *loved* email. Quite honestly, I didn't know what I'd done before the magic of electronic mail. Now, you could, quite possibly, have a substantial life for yourself without ever leaving the comfort of your chair (obviously, you need a computer in the vicinity of this chair, preferably on a desk and connected to the internet). Email was like the confessional, although I hadn't been inside one of those sturdy boxes for years. I had, however, enjoyed the sanctity of it, the telling of your sins in that close dark space, the warm cloying smell, the slick sliding of the panel, the outline of the priest's face silhouetted in the dimness, never looking at you. It felt safe and warm – like I imagined a womb must be for a baby – and I never had a problem confessing my most heinous deeds in that cocoon. 'Bless me Father for I have sinned, it's been a week since my last confession. I pitched a stone at Mrs O'Grady's window and accidentally broke it cos she said we were like tinkers with the screamin' and the play-actin' and she wouldn't let us climb the tree in her front garden any more.' Forgiveness always followed, no matter how shocking the revelations. Absolution. Cleansing. A couple of Hail Marys later and you'd be as good as new, ready to go forth and sin anew so you could go back next week for more of the same.

Anyway, emails were a bit like that for me. It's amazing what you can tell someone when you can't see their face. I had ten new messages, including one from Ethan. Confirming lunch. Settling back, coffee in one hand, mouse in the other, I clicked on the second one. It was from Clare.

It was good to see you last night. Mam rang after you left. She seems a bit worried about you. I said you were fine. You are, aren't you? Fine, I mean? Don't say you are if you're not just cos I'm getting married in nine days' time (ahhhhhhhhh!).

Also, Cate from the Bridal Boutique rang. She wants you to come in for one last fitting on Saturday. I know you said the fourteen fitted you but she was concerned after the ripping incident. Please don't be mad: she's just doing her job in an efficient Germanic kind of a way which I suppose is a good thing. Hope you don't mind although I know it's going to interfere with your weekend with Shane.

Love, Clare
(Bag of Nerves Bride)
XX

Christ. Clare sounded nervous. And why was Mam worried about me? I had enough to worry about without worrying about her worrying about me. I worried at a nail and, after I'd bitten what was left of it, I bent my head to the computer.

Dear Bag O' Nerves,
Yes I'm fine, of course I'm fine, why wouldn't I be fine? Tell Mam not to worry. What time does Cate want me on Saturday? The later the better, of course. Let me know.
See you on Saturday.
Love, Grace (Busty (Chief) Bridesmaid)
PS. No need to be nervous. Just remember to say 'I do' every time the priest asks you a question.

It dawned on me then that I wouldn't get to see a lot of Shane at the weekend. He was flying back to London on Sunday afternoon, so really, we just had Saturday, interrupted by an undoubtedly tight fitting at the Bridal Boutique. This was not what I'd had in mind for our weekend together. In the perfect world in my head – it really was *lovely* in there – our weekend was going to feature long walks in the park against a sound-track of birdsong, lots of hand holding, a fair bit of noisy kiss-ing up against the trunks of ancient oaks (still in the park – stay with me here), and, weather permitting, some laying among tall reeds for a spot of heavy petting. And talking. We would really talk to each other. Really *get* each other. A meeting of minds. A clarity of communication. Now, if I wanted any of that to happen, I'd have to set the alarm to coincide with the dawn bloody chorus on Saturday morning to be in the park on time. Shane might not be too pleased with this idea, given that he may have a head on him like a bag of cats after his session with the boss on Friday night. I sighed and some papers on my desk took off, disappearing over the edge.

I thought about sending Shane a mail to let him know about the fitting on Saturday. He'd be annoyed but more so if he didn't know about it in advance. I bit my lip. Once he heard about the fitting, I could kiss goodbye to my usual rasher sandwich on a Saturday morning. He'd insist on fruit and little else. He was like Caroline that way. Still, maybe I could get up before him and have it cooked and eaten before he got up?

Dear Shane,
Have to go for a final fitting for my (chief) bridesmaid dress some-time on Saturday. Will still try to fit you in – as many times as possible – between Friday and Sunday!!
Love, Grace
(Ardent lover-in-waiting)

The next email was from Tans-R-Us:

Dear Ms O'Brien,
Just confirming your appointment this afternoon at 3 p.m. We have a new system in place in the salon which we look forward to demonstrating to you.
Kind regards,
Zanya

I emailed back immediately, confirming my intention to attend the salon at three and letting them know how much I
was looking forward to trying out the new system. Always
good to keep on the right side of your beauty consultants. I
mean, they can have bad days too, y'know. Only *their* bad days
could mean a seriously disappointing day for you (frizzy hair,
rashes from a potion rubbed onto the delicate skin under eyes
instead of the rough skin on heels, patches of fur left unwaxed
in inappropriate places, roaring red welts of skin where eyebrows used to sit . . .).

I turned my attention back to my inbox. The next one was
from Laura:

Hi Grace,
Just got back into the office this morning (where are you by the
way?). I've been in my 'sick bed' for the last few days with a certain
member of the IT dept. You'll barely recognise me when you see me.
Just watch out for the depleted woman with the John Wayne gait
and the black bin liners under her eyes. Haven't been getting too
much sleep lately. Can't wait to tell you all. But Grace, this one is
different. I know how lame and pathetically girly that sounds but
I think it may be true. I'm scaring myself now. Must go. Talk to
you later.
BTW, what happened with you and Bernard last Friday? Did you
cop off with him? You and he were looking pretty chemical . . .
Laura
XX

My God. What was happening here? Two women that I knew
felled by men in less than a week? And such unlikely women.
Laura and Caroline. Laura who, by her own admission, had
had her heart surgically removed after it was smashed into
smithereens by he-who-will-not-be-named at the tender age
of twenty-six ('Castration's too good for that bastard,' she'd

told me more than once). Caroline, because, well, because she was a serial dater who approached men with the minimum of emotion and the maximum of scathing *froideur*. As men were often intimidated by the mere sight of her, her icy demeanour was usually enough to have them limping away in long, sad processions. (They'd often be limping, you see, because of the scale of the erection in their pants.) I started to email Laura back, then paused. What would I say about Bernard? If Laura had the faintest idea that something had happened, every sparrow in the city would hear about it by lunchtime. It wasn't malicious. It was just that Laura's skin was completely porous when it came to gossip. That stuff just oozed out of her, like sweat out of a sumo wrestler at noon in the Sahara Desert. She was helpless in the face of it. I couldn't let her find out about Bernard unless I wanted it on the company's website by elevenses.

Hi Laura, I'm here you idiot. At my desk. Your sex marathon with himself must have addled your brain. Although in fairness I was a little late this morning. I'm glad to hear everything went well but you're scaring me. He's just a man, remember? With his brain swinging between his legs like a hangman's rope – isn't that what you always say? Don't forget your mantra – All Men Are Potential Human Beings.
Going for lunch with Ethan later. Want to come?
Grace
XX
PS. Bernard who?

As soon as I sent the mail, I knew it was a mistake to tack the PS on the end of it. Laura would know. I don't know how. But she would all the same. The reply came back almost immediately.

Dear Grace,
My senses are on high alert now, by the way. Don't try to fob me off
with your 'Bernard Who' remark. Remember who you're talking
to . . .
Can't come for lunch. Going for 'lunch' with Peter.

Shit. The index finger of my left hand automatically found its
way to my mouth and I sucked on the tip of the nail before
remembering that I was trying to grow them all before the
wedding. No matter. I could always get false ones for the day.
Fingers back in mouth.

I saw Bernard heading to the kitchen, an empty coffee cup
swinging loosely from one of his long fingers. I crouched
low in my seat and looked at him out of the corner of my
eye. He had that sort of awkwardness that some tall people have, trying to fit into a world that's just slightly too
small. His gait was ungainly and he gave passers-by a wide
berth as if afraid he might hit them with one of his long
arms. He didn't look over in my direction and I breathed
out and lowered my shoulders from their clenched position
up around my ears. Incoming mail from Shane. I jumped
slightly. Was this the electronic equivalent of marking your
territory?

Grace,
Disappointed about our interrupted weekend. Can't you switch
the bloody fitting to another day? Surely the closer to the wedding
you get fitted, the more time you'll have to lose that bit of weight
you were talking about?
Shane

Wouldn't it be lovely if we could give men scripts from which
they could read their lines? Wouldn't that make things sim-
pler? Easier? A little less hurtful? I reached for my fags and

headed down to the car park to talk to Ciaran. Actually, wait. Heading back to my desk, I reefed my bag up off the floor. I'd better put some make-up on before I saw Ciaran again. Otherwise, he'd really be up the walls about me.

21

Lunch with Ethan turned out to be more gossip ridden than I'd expected. He had News. About Bernard.

'Jill from accounts knows him. She worked with him last year.' Ethan started the conversation by asking me if I'd had *relations* with Bernard the previous Friday.

'No, I fucking well did not,' I told him. 'Why does everyone think that?'

'Everyone?' His ears pricked up.

'Well, you and Laura anyway.'

'Ah, you wouldn't mind her,' Ethan was dismissive. 'Sure, she thinks everyone's at it or thinking about it or else dead or dying.'

'You're right there,' I nodded slowly before taking an enormous bite of a slice of pizza which left me silent for the next forty-five seconds (olives, sun-dried tomatoes and long elasticated ropes of mozzarella cheese on a crispy slip of a golden brown base).

'So you're sure you weren't at it?' Ethan continued, looking at me carefully from under much bushier eyebrows than his small, slight face suggested.

'What makes you think we might have been at it?' I was curious now.

'I don't know. You just seemed very *comfortable* with each other y'know.'

'Ethan, I'm comfortable with the pizza delivery man,' I shot back. 'That doesn't mean I want to shag him.'

'No, no, it was more than that.' Ethan paused, scratching his lunchtime stubble with nails that, quite frankly, I would have been delighted with. I must remember to ask him where he got them done.

'There was a thing.' He squeezed his eyes shut in concentration.

'A thing?' I was confused now.

'No, I mean, well, like an *atmosphere* between the two of you.' He paused then, like he was on the brink of a sneeze. Then he thumped the table with a tiny fist.

'A charged atmosphere, that's it, that's what I mean.' Ethan nursed his hand gently against the lapel of his suit. He'd thumped the table harder than intended.

A charged atmosphere. I rolled the phrase around in my mind. Jesus, if Ethan thought that was charged, he should have seen the pair of us in the basement of the Palace Bar last Saturday.

'What are you smiling at?' Ethan peered at me, squinting tightly against the sun that was flooding through the stained glass windows, despite our spot at the back of the restaurant. It bounced off the rims of his glasses, which he pushed up the bridge of his nose with the tip of his finger. Then he worried at the tip of his nose with the heel of his hand. It was a habit that I had tried to cure him of on many occasions over the past ten years. For some reason, the gesture irritated me, in a most disproportionate way.

'Ethan, you're doing that weird nose thing again.' I clenched my knife and fork in my hands.

'Was I?' He sat on his hands and cleared his throat. Then he took a long drink of water. A long one. I twitched with impatience.

'Go on, tell me,' I said, leaning towards him.

'It was last March I think. Yeah, Jill said it happened in March.'

'*What* happened?' I pointed my fork in the direction of Ethan's wispy goatee. He smiled, enjoying himself. Then he stopped smiling, straightened in his chair and grabbed my fork from my hand, placing it gently on the table in front of me.

'Actually it's tragic, really. It was his brother.' Ethan stopped suddenly and checked my face. I smiled and nodded at him and he continued, slower now.

'It was his twin, I think. Edward, that's what Jill said his name was. Last March. He left the house on a Friday night. Nobody missed him till the next morning: they just assumed he'd crashed at a friend's house after the pub, or whatever. It was Bernard who found him. In the barn beside the house. He hanged himself. He'd been dead for hours.'

'He *hanged* himself?' I leaned across the table towards Ethan, almost whispering.

'Yeah, hanged himself, in his father's barn. Can you imagine what that would be like? Finding your brother like that?'

We were silent for a few moments.

I thought about Bernard, about the careful way he looked at me, the way he picked up his words and examined them before delivering them in his deliberate, quiet way. There was something so gentle about him, I shivered when I thought of him seeing what he saw that Saturday morning in the barn. He had walked away from that. Gotten on with his life.

Ethan and I sat in silence for a few moments. I thought about the photograph in Bernard's bedroom. The two brothers, their ribs straining against the shiny white skins of their narrow chests. Edward, taller, one foot perched cockily on the edge of the little rubber boat, the captain with the gappy smile. The *waste* of it.

'So you really didn't shag him then, last Friday?' Ethan was back on track, hoping to distract an honest answer from me.

'Ethan, your interest in my sex life is bizarre and, frankly, a little unsettling.'

'Sorry, sorry, sorry. It's just that I can't actually remember the last time I had a meaningful intimate moment with someone. It seems all I can do is live vicariously through the experiences of other people.' Ethan was subdued now, his hands worrying at his hair.

'Ethan, you need to get up off your bony arse and put yourself about a bit.'

'Put myself about a bit?' he said, confused yet hopeful, as if this was something he might manage.

'Look,' I softened my tone. 'All I ever hear from my girlfriends is the shoddy woman-to-man ratio in this city, how there's no good guys left, how every man they meet is either married, gay, divorced with sackfuls of children or just obsessed with himself and his belongings. You're none of those things. Just get the hell out there, join a gym, a night class, get yourself down to your local, hang out, smile at women and try not to be scared of them. You'll surprise yourself. You'll be fine, I know it.' I lifted the last triangle of pizza from my plate, guiding it towards my open nature-abhors-a-vacuum mouth.

'You think I'll be fine?' said Ethan haltingly.

'You'll be magnificent,' I said, smiling a great fat smile at him.

'I don't know.' Ethan was having second, third and maybe even fourth thoughts about it.

'Shall we order dessert?' I asked abruptly. Food was a great distraction. It was my comfort zone of choice and I couldn't recommend it highly enough in this capacity. I mean, I used it often enough and look how I turned out. I was just grand, wasn't I?

I immediately became fixated on dessert. If Ethan said yes, I was going to get the sticky toffee pudding. With bright yellow custard, thick as porridge. And a dollop of cream on the side. If he said no, I would buy a Granny Smith on my way to the tanning studio, thus starting the diet that I pencilled into my diary about four weeks ago.

'Say yes, say yes,' I pleaded with him in my head.

'Sure why not, it's the day before Friday, isn't it?' Ethan beamed at me, aware that he'd answered correctly.

'There's a good boy,' I replied, patting him affectionately on the arm.

We sat and ate in companionable silence and I resisted sticking out my tongue and licking the plate clean.

'There's Bernard now,' said Ethan, peering towards the door. I could feel heat rushing up my face, my blood roaring in my ears.

'Where?'

'No, sorry, it wasn't him. Just some other tall guy.' Ethan sighed when he said this, as if being tall was a club he could never join. Which he never could. Not unless they admit grown men who are five foot six and three quarters.

Ethan turned back to me. 'Oh. My. God,' he said, pointing at me.

'What?'

'You're blushing and you've slid down in your chair to make yourself seem smaller.'

'So?' I hated that Ethan knew me so well.

'You *like* him. You like Bernard.' His tone was triumphant. He was delighted with himself.

I decided to be noncommittal.

'Yeah. I like him. He's a nice bloke. Everyone likes him.'

'No, but you really *like* him. I can tell,' Ethan insisted.

I opened my mouth to say something, but he got in before me.

'I'm delighted, Grace. I really am. It's about time you started going out with someone lovely. Shane definitely wasn't for you.'

It was not for nothing we called him Ethan 'Foot-in-Mouth' McGrath.

'Ethan, what are you talking about? All I said was I like him. I didn't say I had split up with my boyfriend of one year, nine months, three weeks and six days. I mean twelve days. I mean four weeks and,' I counted on my fingers, 'five days.'

'See, you've even stopped counting the days since last Friday. When you met Bernard in the pub,' said Ethan. He was able to work that out without even looking at his fingers. And he was right too. Shit.

'I've got to go, I'll be late.' I threw cash on the table, leaned over and gave Ethan a brief peck on the cheek.

'No, no, I invited you for lunch, I'm paying the bill,' he insisted, shovelling the notes back into the gaping mouth of my oversized handbag.

'But I made you get dessert. You don't usually.'

'You didn't make me. I wanted to. This is the new me. I'm putting myself out there, starting with banoffi pie.' He tapped his concave belly smugly. 'There'll be no stopping me now, Gracie.'

'Oh Jesus, I've created a monster. Lock up your daughters, wha?' I headed towards the door.

'Grace,' Ethan called. 'You're not mad with me, are you?' He looked worried. More worried than usual, I mean. I shook my head, blew him a kiss and teetered out of the restaurant, feeling the familiar cramping in my feet as the pointed toe of my shoes became ever pointier.

I wasn't mad with Ethan. You couldn't be. But I did feel sort of unsettled. I'd liken it to indigestion, if I had to describe it. And I didn't like the feeling. I didn't like it at all.

22

Tans-R-Us was a crude monument of a place, a testament to modern Dublin, all sharp chrome, dramatically polished floors and bright lights. Stepping through the glass doors, there was no getting away from my pale, mottled skin. Reflections of myself mocked me, seeping into mirrors that hung from every available space. If I wasn't careful, a well-meaning passer-by might give me mouth-to-mouth resuscitation, such was my pallor.

The place thronged with people, although half of them appeared to be employees. These were identifiable by their badges, proclaiming perky names like *Tanya!*, *Yazmin!*, *Brit!* and *Zara!* They were also pretty prominent because of their gloriously improbable tans, honey coloured and even. *Tanya!* spotted me and pranced over with a wide smile. Her teeth were white lights against the backdrop of her caramel-coloured face. She looked about fourteen.

'Hi, I'm Tanya,' she announced needlessly. 'What can we do for you today?' she enquired brightly.

'Quite a lot, as it happens,' I began. 'At the moment I look a bit like Brendan Gleeson with long hair. When I leave, I'd like to be like a taller, tanned version of Kate Moss. What can you do for me?'

Tanya giggled prettily and looked me up and down.

'No, not a Brendan Gleeson in sight. More like a curvaceous Nicole Kidman with green eyes. That height. And your hair is magnificent, by the way. We'll have to be very careful with it, you know.' She looked anxious now, pawing at my head and biting her bottom lip.

Inside I was dancing. A curvaceous Nicole Kidman? I knew Tanya was just doing what it said on her job description ('flatter the customers stupid' or was that 'flatter the stupid customers?'). But still, I floated behind Tanya as she led me to the changing rooms.

'Did you get our email about the new system?' Her voice was high-pitched and breathy.

'Yeah, sure. How does it work?' I hadn't started taking off my clothes yet, as Tanya suggested. I would wait until I was alone in the cubicle.

'It's still a spray tan, of course,' Tanya said, 'but it's done by a machine now, not one of us.'

God, Ethan would hate this place. More machines taking over the world.

'High tech, wha?' I was interested now.

'Yeah, it's called the Tanometer.' Tanya spoke quickly now, anxious to get the science bit over with. 'It's easy, really. Come into the studio and I'll show you what to do.'

We stepped into a windowless room just off the changing cubicle. It was dominated by the Tanometer, a slinky, shiny machine laden with buttons, dials and monitors. It wouldn't have looked out of place on the Starship Enterprise. A rigid phallic instrument protruded from the chest of the machine. Tanya stroked the tip of the phallus, making me want to laugh.

'Now, the tan sprays from here,' she explained carefully, rubbing her hand gently along the shaft. Was she doing it on *purpose*? Suddenly, she leapt in front of the machine and began the demonstration. In my mind's eye, the phallus shuddered and went limp. Distracted by this image, I can now look back and identify where it all went wrong. *Grace must pay more attention.*

Tanya assumed a ballerina pose, arms arched over her head, palms together and pointing skywards.

'After you press that button, stand like this directly in front of Thomas. That's what we call this one.' She allowed herself a little smile.

Which button did she mean? The red one? Must be the red one.

'Then, when you hear the beep, turn to the side and do the Charlie's Angels.' With that, Tanya leapt to the side, crouched slightly with bent knees, arms outstretched and bent at the elbows, hands palm to palm, as if in prayer.

Another 90 degree turn. Now she had her back to the machine, giving it Angelina Ballerina again. Another beep and it was off to the other side with her fantastic impersonation of Kelly, Sabrina and Jill.

'See, it's easy, isn't it?' Tanya's breathing was laboured with the effort of the demonstration.

'Um, yeah, should be fine,' I said. The Charlie's Angels was a cinch but the ballerina pose was a different matter altogether. And was there a CCTV camera in the room? I imagined a security guard in some lonely hut watching me thundering around this small room like a baby elephant.

Tanya seemed to read my mind.

'You'll be on your own in here,' she told me with a slow smile, 'but if you need any help, just press that button.' She pointed at a dial on the wall, bright red and big as a saucer. An exclamation mark ran down the middle. You couldn't miss it. Tanya was very good at her job, I decided.

'I'm not too tall, am I?' I asked, pointing to the phallus that came up to my armpit.

'Don't worry,' she said. 'The shaft moves side to side and up and down, once you press the button.'

'The shaft?' I couldn't help myself.

'Yes, this bit here,' she said, pointing to the phallus but not touching it this time.

'Did people lose their jobs?'

'Because of Thomas, you mean? Yeah. Two of us. Michaela and Sam.' We both looked at Thomas, with withering stares.

And then she was gone. I struggled out of my clothes, folding them carefully and placing them on the wooden bench that ran along one of the walls in the tiny changing room. I'm always neater when I'm not in my own environment. The mirrors theme had invaded the cubicle. Even with the towel – the size of a postage stamp – clamped between my armpits, I couldn't get away from my buoyant buns and wobbling thighs. My hair – usually a great distraction – bulged inside an elasticated plastic bag on my head. I looked like one of those old-fashioned aliens. The kind whose brains are too big for their heads.

Closing my eyes, I felt my way into the tanning studio and stood in front of Thomas, studying him, trying to remember which button to press. Thomas beeped, making me jump. I pressed a button – the red one – and took up the ballerina position. Nothing happened. I stayed where I was for a while until my arms, arched over my head, ached. Eventually, I carefully lowered my arms and leaned towards the machine. Spray erupted from Thomas's erect shaft, shocking me with its warm stickiness. I stepped back into position, hoisting my arms above my head. My face itched terribly. I was afraid to move. The machine made a low rumbling sound, like distant thunder.

It was only after the second spray hit that I realised I should have been in the Charlie's Angels position. It rained full frontal down the length of me. Almost immediately the third spurt followed, unreasonably, by the fourth. My mouth was open, lips pulled back in panic. Tan stained my teeth and streaked against my tongue. For those of you who haven't yet had the pleasure, fake tan tastes *vile*. Just as bad as it smells. Even now, I waited for the beep. It never came. I never got to do the Charlie's Angels bit, which I'd been looking forward to.

Where was the beep, for Christ's sake? I was positive that *Tanya!* mentioned a beep in between sprays. I didn't want to press the emergency stop button. It might make a siren-like noise and draw even more attention to me than I would get when people saw me. I was bright orange. The colour of an Easi-Single. An old one.

I retreated into the relative sanctuary of the changing cubicle, leaned on the – smaller, more discreet – call button until I heard Tanya's hesitant knock on the door. I wrapped myself as best I could in the truly tiny towel provided. I opened the door a crack. Tanya's worried face carefully wrapped itself around the door. She took one look at me.

'Oh Christ,' she said in a way that brought no reassurance.

'Malfunction' was all I could manage. It was then I remembered the mirror behind me. No matter how tightly I held the facecloth of a towel against my breasts and belly, Tanya was now getting an eyeful of my perfectly bare behind. There was nothing I could do about it. I closed my eyes. Maybe if I couldn't see anything, neither could she?

My worst fears were confirmed. I had received the might of Thomas's force, all on my front. The colour of an Oompa Loompa there. The rest of me was a ghostly shade of pale. The green of my eyes was reduced to pinpricks in the dramatic sunset of my face. I couldn't cry in case I reddened the white bits: the last outposts of any facial normality.

Tanya suggested a supervised session of Thomas on my sides and back but I couldn't take the risk. I slunk away, clutching a voucher for a free tanning session at Tans-R-Us. To date, this voucher remains in the top drawer of my bedside locker, curling at the edges with age and neglect.

She also gave me a special body scrub to use when I got home. At least, she said it was special.

'I'll call you a taxi so you won't have to walk down the street like that,' she said.

'No, it's OK,' I said. I couldn't wait to get out of the place. There was nowhere to hide in Tans-R-Us. Every corner was flooded with light. And beautiful people. I had to leave.

'Do you want a hat to pull down over your face?' I knew Tanya was only trying to be helpful.

'No,' I said, handing her an almighty tip. It wasn't *her* fault that Thomas was such a vindictive shit.

Dublin bulged with people that afternoon, most of whom seemed to be walking down the street outside the beauty salon. I managed to get as far as Dame Street before it happened.

'Grace? Is that you?' Oh dear, sweet God, I recognised that voice. I kept my head down and kept walking, hoping he would consider himself mistaken. He did not.

'Grace?'

He was directly in front of me, impeding my passage. I had to stop. I saw laced shoes with worn-down heels. I saw the bottom of jeans, flapping loosely above bony ankles. I didn't want to look up but I was running out of choices. I looked up.

'Jesus, Grace. What happened?'

'Oh, hi Bernard,' I said as if we were at the office and I didn't look like a grilled cheese sandwich. *What the hell was he doing here?*

'What happened to you?' he said again.

'Had a run-in with a new member of staff in a tanning studio,' I said with a laugh that I didn't feel.

'Well, you certainly look . . . very . . . eh . . . tanned,' he finally said and I loved him for not laughing at me.

'Nothing a bucket of bleach won't remove,' I said.

'On the plus side,' he said, 'your teeth look unbelievably white against the, eh, tan. You could do an ad for toothpaste. So long as they blacked out the rest of your face, of course.'

We both had a snigger at that.

'So, where are you heading?' he asked.

Getting out of the salon had been a priority. I hadn't thought about a destination. When I didn't answer immediately, Bernard offered me a lift.

'There's no need, really,' I began.

'I insist,' he said, smiling and not shielding his eyes from the tragedy of my face. I admired him for that.

His car was in a garage nearby and Bernard was going to pick it up. There was a coffee shop right in front of us, with one small round table out the front of it, unoccupied.

'Why don't you sit there, have a cigarette and a coffee and I'll go and get the car and bring it around?'

How had he known that my feet were killing me in those heels? And that I would have sold my own grandmother down the river for an espresso? And a cigarette? Before I could agree, he was gone. I sank into the chair. With the sun and the lighting up of the cigarette, the cold steel of the chair under my bum didn't feel as numbing as it should have. I watched Bernard disappear down the street. In the fading light of the afternoon, his red hair seemed softer, less of the raw carrot about it. He walked slowly down the street, picking his way through the crowds, careful not to allow his long arms to swing against any pedestrians.

I had to ask for a second sachet of sugar. The waiter only put the one on the saucer beside the tiny cup. I needed something sweet and two sugars was the only way to make sure I didn't order a chocolate muffin.

I'd only just lit up my second cigarette when Bernard returned. He stopped right outside the café and got out of the car to wave and smile at me. A line of cars formed an orderly queue behind Bernard's car. He didn't seem to notice, even when the horns blared and fists furled through open car windows.

I dropped money on the table and ran to the car.

'How was the coffee?' Bernard appeared set to carry on a conversation across the roof of the car, blind – and deaf – to the danger he was in.

'Eh, I think we should go. Quickly.' A driver in one of the cars behind us was getting out with something in his hand. A baseball bat, maybe? I hurled myself into the car but Bernard took his time, settling himself into the driver's seat that had been pushed back as far as it would go. He was practically in the back seat. His fingers spanned the steering wheel.

'So,' he said as if he wasn't in immediate danger of getting a good hiding from the people in the cars behind.

'We'd better move,' I said. 'We're holding up the traffic.'

It was only then he looked in the rear-view mirror.

'Aye,' he said easily. 'Dublin drivers don't have much patience, do they?' He swung away from the kerb and order was restored. Now we were all stalled, waiting at the red lights while four men in fluorescent yellow jackets picked at the other side of the road with drills.

'So, where are you going?'

Suddenly, I didn't want to go home.

'Somewhere where there are no mirrors,' I said. 'And no small children, either. I don't want to scare them.'

Bernard laughed. 'I know just the place,' he said.

'Don't you have to get back to the office?' I asked when it became clear that we were not heading in that direction.

'Yes and no,' he said. As an answer, it seemed perfectly acceptable. The car was clean but messy. Books and paper coffee cups strewn about the back seat. An empty McDonald's bag rolled on the floor like an old friend.

'Where are we going?' I asked eventually.

'Someplace I love. You'll know it well, but I'm still a tourist in this town, remember?'

It was the Phoenix Park.

'My dad used to take me and my brother and sisters here when we were kids,' I said, sitting up straight. 'I haven't been here for years.'

'I bet you're a middle child,' said Bernard with a bit of a grin at me.

The space in the car suddenly seemed to shrink around me.

'Yeah,' I said then. 'I have one older sister and one younger one, Clare and Jane.'

'What about your brother?' Bernard didn't seem to notice that anything was wrong. He was busy parking the car. We were at a part of the park I had never been to before. Tall trees and long grasses swept along either side of the narrow road where we had stopped.

'He died last year,' I said. That was the first time I'd really had to say that. To explain.

'What was his name?' It was a relief. That he didn't say he was sorry, or try to hug me or shake his head at the unfairness of it all.

'Patrick,' I said and I smiled because Patrick's face swam up in my mind, fully formed and for the first time in a long time, I didn't have to struggle to remember how he looked. I turned towards Bernard and then I saw them. About twenty, or even thirty of them. Deer. And some fawns. In a circle, standing still with their heads cocked as if they were waiting for something to happen.

'Look.' I whispered the word, afraid that they might disappear if I spoke any louder.

We sat there for ages just watching them, not saying anything. In the gloom of the afternoon, they seemed like mythical creatures with slender faces and long ears that twitched at the slightest sound. Their red coats glowed like embers in the half-light. Then they were gone, moving gracefully into the shelter of the trees and disappearing so quickly I thought I had imagined them.

Bernard and I sat in the warmth of his car, not saying anything. It didn't feel awkward though. The hum of the heater and the low rumble of the engine ticking over was like a soft conversation between us. I wanted to tell him about Patrick but I didn't know why or where to start.

'How's Cliona?' I said instead, regretting it immediately. He didn't answer at once and I was suddenly terrified of what he was going to say.

'She's not my girlfriend, you know.'

'Oh,' was all I said.

'She was my brother's girlfriend,' he said eventually and I exhaled, not realising until then that I'd been holding my breath.

'Edward. He died too. Last year. That's why I went home this week. For his anniversary mass.'

'This is kind of weird,' I said. 'Both our brothers are dead. Most people have other things in common, like bands they like or a common hatred of Liquorice Allsorts.'

'I hate Liquorice Allsorts,' he said.

'All of them? Even the pipes?'

'Every single sodding one of them.' He was adamant on this point.

'So do I,' I said and I chanced a look up at him to check he was OK with this conversation. He was smiling and looking at my face in that careful way that people do when they're thinking about kissing you. And I wanted him to – kiss me, I mean. I'd never wanted anything more. I may even have had my eyes closed, I can't remember.

And then he said, 'How's it going with Shane?' and it was like a glass falling on a tiled floor.

'He's coming over tomorrow for the weekend.'

And that was that. The moment was gone, as quickly as the deer, and I was left with the now-familiar guilty feeling and the possibility that I had imagined there had been a moment at all.

'You'd better get back to work,' I said and he nodded and drove slowly out of the park. 'Oh shit.' I suddenly remembered. 'Can I get a lift back to the office with you? I've left my car there.'

'You forgot your car?' he seemed amused at this.

'Yes, but it's a really small one,' I said and he nodded, as if he understood completely.

Bernard drove slowly and gently through the war zone that was Dublin city that afternoon. He didn't beep or raise his voice or make rude hand gestures or get out of his car at any time to accost a fellow driver, all of which would have been acceptable in the gridlock. For some reason, I wondered what kind of dog he'd own if he had one. A labrador, I thought.

'Grace, you're deep in thought there.' Bernard's voice seemed far away and I worried that I might have been talking to myself. Sometimes I do that.

'What were you thinking about?'

'Em, labradors, actually.' He didn't even seem surprised, just nodded and drove into the car park, stopping behind my car.

'Well,' I said, the way people do when they're not quite sure what to say. 'Thanks for the lift and, eh, everything.'

'My pleasure, Grace. I had a lovely time.' He looked like he really meant it too. Again, that heavy sensation in the air between us. Or maybe it was just me imagining things? All I know is it would have been the most natural thing in the world to lean across to him. But I didn't do that. I said goodbye like a normal person and got out of the car without banging my shin against the door or my head against the roof. When I turned to wave, he didn't wave back but mouthed something I couldn't make out. But I knew it wasn't anything derogatory because he was smiling. And then he was gone.

'Jesus, Grace, what happened to you?' It was Ciaran, leaning out the window of his hut with the empty pipe sticking out of the corner of his mouth. I'd forgotten about my orange face. In fact, I hadn't thought about it since the park. I smiled at Ciaran and he blinked in the glare of my teeth.

'Tanning accident,' I told him, stepping into the warmth of the cabin.

'Och, it was-nee that new machine at Tans-R-Us, gurrill, was it?' Jesus, how come everyone knew about Thomas except for me? And why had no one told me? An email should have gone around. From the Health and Safety Department. Ciaran studied my face with deep sympathy.

'Christ, it must look really awful, does it?' I said, trying to catch a glimpse of myself in the sliding window. Luckily, I could see nothing.

'Ach, it is-nee tha' bad,' Ciaran said, backtracking. 'At least you're not as pale as you were this morning.'

Ciaran turned his back on me and poured two steaming mugs of coffee to which he added cream and brown sugar. He even had them in a proper matching jug and bowl. He produced a pack of biscuits: Chocolate Kimberleys, the queen of the biscuit world in my opinion, combining two of my favourite things: chocolate and marshmallow, with that soft hint of ginger. He spent a long time stirring his coffee and I knew he was gearing up to ask me something.

'So, eh,' he finally said. 'Was that young Bernard's car I saw you getting out of?' He thought we were all much younger than we really were, possibly because of that incident last year with the waterguns.

When I smiled, my teeth were all I could see in the reflection in the window. They hadn't been that bright since the milk teeth days.

'Yes, it was,' I agreed. 'I met him in town. We went to the park.'

'The park?' Ciaran leaned forward.

'Yeah. We saw deer. It was . . . nice.'

'He's a nice young gentleman,' was all Ciaran said to that, but I could tell by the way he was turning his cup in his hands that he was thinking things.

'His brother is dead too,' I said suddenly.

If Ciaran was surprised by my mention of Patrick in this roundabout way, he didn't show it.

'Aye,' was all he said, nodding his head. It didn't really surprise me that Ciaran knew things about Bernard. He knew *everything*. I suppose you would, wouldn't you, working down here?

'Shane is coming home tomorrow. Just for the weekend, I mean. But still.' Ciaran took a long drag from his pipe. And then he did something that was completely out of character. He *interfered*. First he cleared his throat with a quiet cough.

'You know, Grace, Bernard asked me about you on Saturday morning. He was collecting his car. Just before you arrived, in fact.' My heart did that funny jump thing when it seems to be beating at the back of your throat instead of in your chest.

'What do you mean?'

'He asked about Shane.'

'But he doesn't even know Shane. He barely even knows *me*, for God's sake.' But my curiosity was bigger than any annoyance I might have felt.

'What did he say?'

'He said he met you last Friday. He knew you had a boyfriend. He wondered if it was serious. Stuff like that, ye know?'

I was pacing now. Three steps to the end of the cabin, three steps back. It was a small space.

'And what did you tell him?'

'Och, nothing really. Just that you hadn't seen Shane in a while. That he'd gone to London.'

'But that he'd be coming back, right? I told you it was only for six months, didn't I?' I stopped pacing and fixed Ciaran with a stare.

'I canny remember, really.' Ciaran was suddenly vague, worrying at a loose button on his waistcoat. I sat back down on the chair and sighed heavily.

'Jesus, Ciaran, this is so unlike you.'

'We've been chatting most mornings for the past month. Just about the weekend, and the weather, and the football. Stuff like that.'

'And me?' I added tartly.

'Only on Saturday. He seemed a bit down and we got to talking. Said he'd met a girl but it turned out she had a boy-friend.'

'Wait, wait, backtrack, backtrack.' I wanted details. 'How did you know he was talking about me?'

'Well, he told me that she was a really tall lassie with long red hair. Funny and . . .' Ciaran scrunched up his forehead the way he did when he concentrated.

'Beautiful,' he said. 'Aye, beautiful. That was the word. Once he told me that she nearly fell in the pub and that's how he met her, I knew for sure it was you.' Ciaran looked suitably abashed when he said this.

'He said all that? He didn't actually say beautiful, did he? And funny?' I was dizzy with the detail.

'And tall with long red hair.' Ciaran nodded, not wanting to leave anything out.

'Why are you telling me all this?'

'I just thought you should know,' was all Ciaran said before standing up and lifting the cups over to the little sink in the corner. This was a clear sign. His work here was done. This conversation was over.

23

I pulled the door of the flat behind me and leaned against it. It felt good to be out of the day.

I walked straight to the fridge, unloaded my shopping bags and stood back to admire it. It was now full of the essentials (beer, wine, champagne, strawberries, smelly cheese, pâté and slabs of pure chocolate – none of your messin' with raisins or nuts), courtesy of a detour to M&S on the way home. I wore a hat pulled down around my face and got away with two stares and a comment, but only from a child of about six or so.

'Mammy, that lady's face is on fire. Look.'

I relieved the fridge of a bottle of beer and a gigantic bar of chocolate and retreated to the couch. Some people can't drink beer and eat chocolate at the same time. I wasn't one of them.

The evening stretched in front of me and I could see it wasting away in a haze of soaps and reality TV if I wasn't careful. I needed a plan. A list. I picked up a Visa bill, blackening out the Total Owed figure with a thick-nibbed blue pen and placed the bill, nasty side down, on the table. The page absorbed a puddle of beer that escaped from the bottle when I pulled the lid off. I pulled up my sleeves and began to write.

To Do List: Thursday: Clean the flat

I leaned back on the couch, sending chocolate crumbs flying from the table to the carpet with the strength of the sigh. They crouched and stared.

'OK, OK, fuck it, I'll clean the bloody flat,' I spoke out loud as I often did when I was home alone and the echo of my voice against the walls startled me. There was no doubt about the fact that it was my 'turn' to clean up. Caroline and I had a theoretical rota of housework but she usually did it all. Not because I didn't take my turn, mind. She just didn't think I did it as it should be done. Me, I could sleep in a skip so long as I had a book and a clean-ish pillow. Shane was as anal as Caroline about bacteria and other household nuisances. His idea of household nuisances included:

1. Strands of hair (long and red) in the bath.
2. Hair (as above) in the shower.
3. Hair (the same) draped across pillows / cushions / backs of armchairs and sofas.
4. Hair (you guessed it) in the spaghetti sauce. That only happened the *once*, I swear to God.

The righting of the flat was going to take half the night, the state it was in. I needed to divide the chores into subheadings to make it seem more manageable. There was also the added advantage of being able to cross out jobs as I completed them, which always made me feel better.

a) My bedroom
 • Pick clothes up off the floor and place in a hanging position (i.e. in wardrobe) or laundry basket or under bed if wardrobe and / or laundry basket are full.
 • Change sheets / duvet cover / pillowcases on bed.
 • Hoover, but only if absolutely necessary.

The flat felt cleaner already. I decided on a quick coffee before continuing. After two fags, a cup of coffee and a bit of a dance around the kitchen (Tom Dunne was playing Kate Bush's 'Wuthering Heights' and I *cannot* let that song pass without doing the arms and hair thing), I set to work. Housework is a bit like having a tooth pulled. The anticipation of it is so much worse than the thing itself. I bleached and polished and hoovered and mopped and dusted and beat the shit out of rugs and mats and then had to hoover and dust again because of all the crap that fell out of the rugs and mats after I'd beaten the shit out of them.

By 9 p.m., the flat was unrecognisable, but in a good way. Clean laundry hung prettily on the clothes horse, the washing machine buckled under the strain of a third load and the hotpress boasted a stack of freshly ironed clothes in two neat bundles: one for Caroline, the other for me. I, on the other hand, was draped across the sofa, a shell of a woman with crazy hair. My hands were cracked and as dry as old dog poo. A smell of bleach wafted from me when I moved and I felt sticky where sweat had dried down my back and collected under my arms. But still. You could eat your dinner off the toilet seat and you could go hungry on the couch with the absence of foodstuffs trapped down the side of the cushions. If I'd had the energy, I would have smiled.

Every item on my list was crossed off, fresh flowers from the garden sang from vases (one chipped and one, in fact, a beer glass) in the two bedrooms, and there was no doubt that there *was* carpet on the sitting room floor and it was a delicate shade of beige. There wasn't one single thing about the flat Shane could complain about. Well, maybe one thing: I caught a glimpse of my orange reflection in the pot-belly of the kettle. My phone rattled on the counter, distracting me from the riot that was my face. It was a text, from Caroline:

All this arse-licking and cock holding has me knackered. Can't wait to get home. Saw your boss today. He still looks miffed when he sees me, like someone piddled in the soup and fessed up after he'd licked the bowl clean. See you Saturday. Cats. XX

I smiled an evil smile. The boss had not been looking forward to the London conference, unlike last year when he had taken Caroline with him. Then, he was like the cat who got a bowl of double cream with an Italian family of mice on the side. Back then, Caroline had been our star adjuster and the boss liked to parade her in front of our most important customers at least once a year. He brought her to last year's conference for the following reasons:

- Caroline wasn't just good at her job. She was brilliant. She was the A to Z of insurance law, her investigative skills made Inspector Morse look like a half-wit and she could value a claim down to the nearest ha'penny.
- Our clients adored Caroline, once they got past their initial terror at the ferocity of her manner.
- Caroline was beautiful and the boss loved to swagger along the streets of London with this magnificent creature at his side. Although usually she would be two paces ahead of him, he struggling to keep up. I imagined his chest swelling with pride as he clocked the envious (incredulous?) glances of the male populace of London town as they walked by.
- Caroline stayed with friends when she went to London so the boss, who was terminally mean, did not have to drain his travel budget on her accommodation expenses. It was a win-win situation for him all round.
- Back then, the boss still harboured vague hopes of winning her affections and thought that if he plied her with enough cheap wine at dinner, he might get to swing his

short leg over her long body. To date, that dream has never been realised.

This year, the boss went to the conference with Damien, a newly recruited senior adjuster and pathological arse-licker. Unfortunately for Damien, he didn't know that flagrant brown-nosing was a trait abhorred by the boss. No doubt he would become aware of this fact during the course of the conference.

I went to bed and dreamed memories, real ones, sepia tinted, curling at the edges. My brain rewound and played snatches of *Shane and Grace, The Movie*. Parts of it were lovely and I must have smiled in my sleep, looking over these reruns. Of course, in my sleep-induced state, I was able to turn up the sun, switch off the rain and take a couple of inches off my waist.

There we are, walking on a beach in west Cork. The sun is setting, pouring itself like honey into a sea as smooth and flat as a glass plate. The sky above is streaked through with slashes of pinks and oranges. The heels of my sandals sink into wet sand with a sucking sound. A wild flower winds through my hair. A gentle breeze touches my skin like warm hands, lifting the ends of my skirt to reveal long, lean, tanned legs – this is a *dream* memory, remember? And there's Shane. The length of him. The blond hair that casually falls across his eyes. The effortless style of him. The smell of him; he smells of sea air and 'eau de Manly Man'. It's the morning after The Incident in Ryan's Bar. Shane is concerned about me, protective. He suggests a walk. I nearly laugh out loud until I realise he is serious. He is a man who walks. I am a woman who will walk beside him in inappropriate footwear for however many miles it takes. I have fallen in love. I'm dizzy with it. The world is at an angle and I am perched on the edge, scrambling to stay upright. Shane is attentive, he bends his head towards me when I speak. He appears fasci-

nated by what I say, laughing out loud at my attempts at humour. Even in my dream, I wonder what he sees in me. We're
about to have our first kiss. Here it comes. I am prattling
away, my brain seeming to have no control over my mouth,
which moves constantly, keeping any awkward silences at
bay. In the silence, he might suggest that we leave this place,
he might tell me about a girlfriend, he might . . .

'Grace.' He stops walking, says my name softly. He presses
a finger against my lips, hushing me.

'Do you ever stop talking?' He is smiling, his face close to
mine. His breath is warm on my mouth.

Even now, I feel that some answer is expected of me. I open
my mouth to respond. What had I been about to say? His
mouth is on mine and his fingers thread through my hair. I
feel delicate, positively girlish. His lips are soft. I don't think
I breathe for the next thirty seconds. His hair tickles my face
but it's not funny. It's *exquisite*. When he pulls away, I realise I
am breathless, like I ran the length and breadth of the beach.

'I've been wanting to do that since I saw you yesterday on
the train.' That's what he says. I swear to God. You can't beat
that. You can't beat it with a long, thorny stick.

I shift, moving to my position of choice, diagonally
sprawled across the bed, feet at bottom right, head at top
left. I fast-forward and the film leaps over those first glorious months, trembling with tactile tenderness, drenched
with delirious desire. I want to get to the meat, the gripping
tension, the cliff-hanger. Our First Fight. Of course it was
my fault. I shouldn't have been on a diet. I'm unreasonable
when I'm on a diet.

I am starving, having had nothing to eat since lunch. I say
'lunch' but it was actually a portion of egg salad, so small it
could only be seen under a powerful microscope (with no
mayo! What is the point?), and a rice cake on the side. Rice
cakes are grand, if you happen to like the taste of ancient

cardboard. The void in me is a hollow cave. We are out in one of those trendy pubs in town with Shane's work crowd. You know the kind. Where the Beautiful People go. Shane has taken his usual pew at the bar where he is surrounded by his congregation. He went to get me a drink ten minutes ago (vodka and slim-line tonic). I am trapped at a tiny table with four of his closest work friends, all female, all trying to figure out how it went so wrong. In my dream, I can see it from their point of view. They worship at the altar of the gym, they haven't had chocolate since the early '80s, they are terribly tanned, toned and taut. In turn, their eyes dart to the bar and feast themselves on the enigma that is my boyfriend. After a particularly heavy gorging by Martha – Shane's assistant – I glance towards him, just to make sure he still has his clothes on him.

'So Grace – it *is* Grace, isn't it?' Martha rounds on me. I nod at her, my mouth watering. I'm twitchy with want. Everything looks like food. Martha's soft cherubic curls are a bed of tagliatelle, her brown eyes are chocolate buttons, soft and sweet, her complexion a bowl of peaches and cream that I want to empty and lick.

'Yes, yes it's Grace.' I smile with my mouth closed, worried about drool.

'So, what do you do?'

'Insurance.' My response is bald, shocking in its banality. There is a series of carefully nodding heads around the table. I'm too hungry to try to sex-up the world of insurance. It's a show-stopper (as the boss would say) in terms of conversation. Pauline, who seems kind (she has allowed black roots to seep a good inch from her skull), struggles through a story that involves her mother, a bag of precious jewels – duly robbed – a claim form – diligently filled in – and an insurance company's refusal to pay on the grounds that the security light in the garden failed to engage.

'The robbers smashed the bloody bulb in the sodding light.' This from an indignant Pauline. There are never any good stories about insurance companies.'

'Where *did* Shane find you?' Chantelle was a haughty blonde who looked as if she wouldn't be surprised if Shane had prised me off the sole of his shoe after walking through a sewage plant.

'Oh, I answered his ad in Meeting Point in *The Star.*' There is a gasp around the table. *Shane reads* The Star*?* I am ever-so-casual, flicking a piece of lint that is not there off the sleeve of my jacket.

'What struck me most about his ad was he said he was look-ing for a *real* woman. There's so much of the faux-female about nowadays, don't you think?' I arch an eyebrow at them and smile. It could have turned nasty then. These girls could have impaled me on their cheekbones. Shane chose that moment to return to the battleground. All the troops rearrange their fea-tures – including me. Our collective jaw-breaking smiles un-settle him momentarily. He divvies out the drinks. I stick my pinkie out with the best of them and soldier on through the night. Eventually I am released out into the street.

I can't wait to get Shane on my own, but I'm thinking about a kebab from Iskander's. I've been thinking about it for the last two hours.

'You're not going to eat a kebab at this hour of the night, are you?' says Chantelle. I mean, when else would you eat a kebab?

'Why wouldn't I?' I say, flapping at the twin peaks of guilt (kebabs weren't on the list of 'Recommended Foods' on my diet *du jour*) and mortification (caught with my yawning need out in public).

'Jesus, Grace, you're never going to lose weight if you keep on like this.' Shane is exasperated. If he'd said it just to me, maybe I could have managed. Maybe I could have accepted his exasperation as concern. But in front of the faux-females, all nodding and twitching and pointing.

'Fuck you.' That's what I say. Out loud. In front of his starving fans. I stagger away from their accusing stares. I head to the kebab shop, on my own. I remember the kebab, plump, with steam curling from it, gently melting the cheese. It tasted like a WeightWatchers manual in my mouth.

We have different variations of this fight many times over the next two years. I wonder why he can't love me the way I am, he tells me he's doing it for my own good. I believe him, mostly, and stumble after the carrot he dangles on a string, the one that promises an increase in love and attention in direct proportion to a decrease in my calorie intake. Being a loyal and fervent fan of the Mars bar, this road has been a difficult one.

When I ask him why he loves me, he always says the same thing. 'You make me laugh.'

And I remember him laughing. And the way he looks at me when he laughs. Like I am thin and sexy: a *keeper*. I think of funny things to say and funny ways to say them. I catch them and keep them till he is in the room. I release them, like kites, and he laughs.

He says, 'You're not like all the other women I've gone out with.' I smile when he says this but I am thinking of league tables. How do I compare? Where do I come on the list? I think about all the other women. How many? I never ask. I'm like an addict, taking it one day at a time.

If I have to sum up our relationship, I would say that I am the question and he is the answer. I think he would agree with that. In fact, I think he would like it.

Here we are, sprawled on the couch in his apartment in Donnybrook, about a week before he heads off to London. Shane feeds me a slim fillet of rainbow trout with a bunch of leaves (mixed salad) on the side. I am hungry.

'Jesus, would you look at the state of Kate Moss,' I say, holding up that week's edition of *Now* magazine. Hunger has made me bitter.

'What's wrong with her?' Shane studies the photograph. 'She looks grand to me.'

'You could turn her sideways and play her ribs like a banjo,' I say. 'You can't possibly find her attractive,' I add. Somewhere inside me, I *know* that men find Kate Moss attractive. I know I shouldn't say otherwise, but hunger has dulled my senses. Especially my common senses.

'She *is* attractive,' Shane insists. 'But so are you. Just in a different way.'

'A fat way, you mean.'

'A bigger way, that's all.' Shane sighs and turns back towards the television. His mood has dipped. I shouldn't have brought Kate Moss into our vulnerable environment. I ease my foot up along his leg, letting it rest in the crotch of his jeans, applying gentle pressure.

He says nothing but I can feel his reaction against the sole of my foot.

'Take me to London with you.' I regret the words the minute they are out of my big, fat mouth. Shane has made it clear to me that he is going alone.

'It's only for six months, Grace . . . It will do us good to have some time apart . . . I need to concentrate on my career.'

These are the things he says. I feel like he is dying to get away. Like every time he looks at me, he is reminded of Patrick.

Patrick is something we don't talk about. There is nothing left to say.

He pushes my foot away and stands up, looking down at me. He is about to say something. Fear pushes at the wall of my chest. I jump up.

'Sorry, Shane. You're right. We're not ready. I'm being stupid.' I kiss him then and I can feel him relaxing, feel the words that I don't want to hear seep out of him in a sigh as we stumble towards the bedroom. Here, we are perfect. We fit. Lock and key. Samson and Delilah. Beauty and the Beast. Our passion keeps us buoyant, protects us from each other. Afterwards I am hungry. I slip out of bed and sit on the edge of the bath, chewing through a king-size Mars bar. The bathroom door is locked. I am safe.

24

A weird thing happened the next morning. I woke up *before* the alarm went off. I was smiling too, but I couldn't think why. Thoughts melted into my mind like syrup on a pancake.

Bernard: I pieced his face together like a jigsaw in my head. I wondered what a group of deer were called. It wasn't a flock, I knew that much. Or a pride. Was it a bunch? A bunch of deer? No, that didn't sound right. A herd? Yes, a herd. Then I thought about chocolate spread. In a jar. A really big one. My smile widened and I burrowed deeper in the bed, warm as toast. And then I remembered. It took a while, but I remembered. Why I had woken up early. Why I was smiling. It was Shane. He was coming home today. For the weekend. I ran to the bathroom and got on the scales, sucking in my belly. I was the same weight as I had been yesterday morning. And the morning before that. And the one before that. I toyed with the idea of pulling a sickie, but my face wasn't as bad as I remembered it from yesterday. A little less Oompah Loompah, more of a jaundice victim now. Anyway, I wanted to go into the office. And I knew why too. But I didn't say it out loud. If I said it out loud, that would make it real and then I might have to deal with it. Saying it in your head didn't count. It didn't count one little bit.

Friday was dress-down day in the office, but really it should have been called dress-up-to-the-nines day because, even though we mostly dressed in jeans, they were our Very Best Jeans. The ones that made us look thinner and longer than the other jeans, with swishy tops and high heels and enough make-up to sink a ship, and bags and bling fit for a king. I tied my hair in a side ponytail, then took it down, then tied it in a bun, then took it down, then put it in plaits. Then I took it down and left it there. Now, I was late. Again. But seriously, my hair takes a very long time to organise and it's so heavy, my arms ached from all the lifting and lowering.

I spent most of the day clearing out my desk. I was moving to the IT section on Monday to start the new job. It was like a house move only worse because there was no removal van on hand to help. Just me and an old tea trolley that listed heavily to one side. I peered over the top of my partition, but the IT department were at some meeting or other for most of the day so I didn't see Bernard at all. I found a file at the bottom of my drawer under an ancient copy of *Heat* magazine. The file was the one we had all searched high up and low down for last summer. Judge Moran adjourned a High Court case because of this file. It cost the company serious cash and here it was, drenched in celebrity gossip, lying on its back at the bottom of my drawer as if nothing had happened. I picked it up, jumping when a shadow fell across the desk.

'Is that The File?' It was Laura and even though she worked in the accounts department, she knew about The File. The search for it had been extensive, spanning many departments at the time.

'No, no, it's just . . . it's another file. We have loads of them down here, you know.' The file – swollen with paper – burst its banks. Without ceremony, I dumped it back into the drawer, closing it. I pressed my foot against the drawer to stop it sliding open. Laura didn't notice. She had an agenda. She wanted to go for a drink after work. I was already shaking my head.

'Half an hour. Tops. That's all I'm asking.'

I looked up, my eyebrows touching my hairline.

'Next you'll be saying it's just for the one,' I said.

'Jesus no, nothing like that.' She was insulted at the notion. 'OK, OK, forty minutes at the outside. We'll have two drinks, I'll tell you about me and Peter and you can tell me about you and Bernard.'

I stopped pretending to key important information into the computer.

'What about him?' I aimed for confused but I could feel heat scorch my face.

'Grace, this is me, remember?' Laura seemed almost apologetic at her near-psychic abilities. She took a notebook out of her bag, flicked expertly through it and stopped at a page, pretending to read from it. At least, I *think* she was pretending.

'You and Bernard were both missing after lunch yesterday. For ninety minutes.' She looked at me over the top of the page, smirking.

'You were seen returning together. In his car. Nice one, by all accounts, a Saab. An old one, granted, but classy all the same.' She bent to her notebook again. 'At approximately 3.30 p.m.'

There was no approximately about it. Her investigative skills were legendary. I aimed for nonchalance.

'I was at Tans-R-Us. I met him on the way back and he gave me a lift. That's all.'

'Come on, Grace.' She leaned down low.

'That. Is. All.' I said it slowly and looked straight at her, amazed at my ability for subterfuge, but it was *vital* that Laura be put off track. If Shane got wind of this, I'd be a three-legged fox at a hounds-on-steroids hunt. Or Caroline. Or Clare – and don't tell me not to be paranoid. This is Dublin, remember? Smaller than a schoolyard in terms of gossip. Rumours skid across this city like they're on tracks. This was important.

'OK, OK then. I'll let that go. For the moment.' Laura threaded the last three words with menace. 'To be honest, I just want to talk about me and Peter. Peter and me. Us. I'm demented. There's a funny feeling niggling at me and I just can't put my finger on it. It's a really strange sensation.'

'Happiness?' I queried gently.

'God, is *that* what it feels like? I thought it would be calmer.'

'It'll get calmer,' I said, like an expert in the field. 'Just takes a while for the lust to subside.'

Laura, sensing that I was flagging, pushed home.

'So, I'll see you at the front door at 5 o'clock then?'

I was tired, what with all the cleaning and the dreaming last night.

'OK, OK, forty minutes and then I *have* to go. I'm expecting . . .'

'I know, I know. Shane the Drain is coming home.' She cut in on me. 'Fatten the calf. Hoist the flag. Lower the draw-bridge. All that jazz.'

I took a swipe at her but she was too quick for me, stepping just outside my range. I threw a pencil at her instead. She had called him Shane the Drain almost from the start.

'He's a drain on your emotional resources,' she said when I asked her about it.

Laura picked up the pencil from where it had landed on the floor, missing her by at least a foot. She left before I had a chance to change my mind. I turned back to the desk, distracted now. The feeling was back. The heavy one with the peculiar tingling sensation. The one that I associated with Bernard O'Malley. It was a curse but I couldn't shake it. He would be there. In the pub. After work. The Social Committee – still going strong despite Caroline's departure – had organised a night out tonight and they were all meeting up in the pub for a pint beforehand. I went into the loos again to check the progress of my face. Definitely not as terracotta as yesterday. I squeezed a tube of cream into my hand and cooled my cheeks with it. My hair was still down and I left it there.

'OK, we need to find a quiet spot,' said Laura when we arrived in the pub at *exactly* 5.02 p.m. She hadn't met me at the front door as promised but rather turned up again at my desk at 4.57 p.m., switched off my computer and frogmarched me over the road.

'A quiet spot?' I said, but my voice couldn't be heard over the roar of the crowd when we stepped into O'Reilly's.

'Oh Jesus, there's Peter,' she said, steering me frantically in the opposite direction. We hightailed it to the snug, squeezing our way to the little bar in the corner.

'Why are you avoiding Peter?' I asked, waving the customary €20 note across the counter at a quietly disinterested Shay. 'I thought you were an "us?" What happened to the Peter and you, you and Peter scenario? Demented with happiness and all that.'

'You were the one who said it was happiness,' she said, glaring at me and at the door in equal measure.

I managed to get the order in and we both drank long and hard from our bottles, resurfacing and licking beer bubbles from our top lips.

'It's just—' Laura began and then stopped as if she didn't quite know what she wanted to say. I said it for her.

'You've spent the last few days shagging him and now that you're back out in the real world, he looks kind of weird with his clothes on and you're not quite sure how to proceed, yeah?'

Laura looked relieved. 'Yes. That's it. Will you go and talk to him?' My beer went down the wrong way and I coughed, my face regressing back to orange. Peter was with Bernard and I didn't want to approach him. For lots of reasons. For starters, I'd told him I wouldn't be out tonight. Because of Shane. Even thinking about him made my face hot and a red face just wasn't a good look for me. It clashed with my hair.

'Aw Laura, I really don't want to. What would I say?'

'It's because of Bernard, isn't it?'

'God, no. Not at all. I just, I don't know why you want *me* to talk to him. *You* should talk to him. I mean, come on, Laura, we're nearly thirty years old. We can talk to boys now, can't we?' She withered me with a look and I couldn't really blame her. I was clutching at straws.

'Look, just start a general chit-chat with him. Ask him what he's up to for the weekend. Or something. Anything.'

She was already pawing at me, pushing me in the direction of the snug door, and I moved away from her, into the swell of the crowd.

'Don't say anything about me,' she yelled just before I rounded the door. I could see them at the other end of the pub, sitting at the counter, bent over pints of porter. Peter with his back to me and Bernard standing beside him, one elbow on the bar. There was a stillness about him, even here, in this zoo. My hastily formed plan had been to just walk slowly past them and hope that one or the other of them would hail me and involve me in their conversation. That didn't happen. Bernard looked up when I was only about halfway there. Then he sort of nodded at me and returned to his conversation with Peter. I felt cold, like I had been dismissed. I soldiered on, remembering Laura's face. I reached them and sort of launched myself into their midst, abandoning my plan altogether.

'Hiya lads.' Peter looked surprised to see me, suddenly there. He scraped his stool back to accommodate me in the narrow space between him and Bernard.

'You must have been here early to get those seats,' I said.

They saw my lips moving although I'm sure they couldn't hear me in the clatter of conversation about the place. Peter nodded, at least.

'I'm just getting a drink for me and Laura,' I yelled at him then. He heard me that time.

'Laura's here?' he asked at once. Using hand gestures and mime, I told him she was in the snug and he was gone, like a greyhound out of a trap. Leaving me and Bernard alone. Together. It was an effort to lift my face towards him.

'Thank God for that,' he said.

'What do you mean?'

'I mean Peter. He's been talking about Laura. A lot. He seems keen.'

'I didn't think boys talked about stuff like that,' I said.

'Peter does,' said Bernard with a sigh and we both seemed to find that much funnier than it was and we laughed.

'Your face looks grand,' said Bernard when we stopped.

'Grand?'

'Well, you know, normal. Back to normal, I mean.' I could feel the familiar red rushing up my neck.

'I'm glad,' I said. 'About Peter. Being keen. I think Laura feels the same and that's pretty unusual for her.'

'Unusual? In what way?' Bernard was trying to attract the barman's attention and wasn't looking at me, which made it easier to talk.

'Like, a three-legged dog kind of unusual,' I said.

'There's a three-legged dog in the estate where I live,' Bernard said.

'Actually, my uncle has a three-legged dog, now that I think about it,' I said.

'Not so unusual then?' Bernard said, handing me a bottle of beer, clinking his glass against it. When he put his glass back down on the counter, he made a great show of rubbing the bottom of it against the beer mat before looking up again.

'I thought you weren't coming out tonight. Isn't Shane coming over?'

And then Peter came back, beaming now, with Laura in tow. She was beaming too, her lipstick smudged.

'Hello!' they yelled at us in the loud voices of very happy people. We smiled at them. It was impossible not to. I studied Peter as he ordered drinks at the bar. He was *so* not Laura's type. Maybe that was why she was suffering from happiness. Maybe the type that she thought was her type hadn't been her type after all. Maybe her type had been a Peter-type all along and she just hadn't known it.

'I'd better go,' I said.

'Stay,' Laura commanded, slipping her hand into the front pocket of Peter's jeans.

'Stay,' said Peter, his arm embedded around Laura's waist. Bernard said nothing.

'No seriously, I'd better head,' I said. 'I'll see you on Monday.'

'Have a good weekend, Grace.' I looked around and Bernard nodded at me, raising his glass in a goodbye.

It was now 8 p.m. and I was waiting for Shane. It seemed like I'd been waiting for him for the longest time. I was fed (a baked potato stuffed with beans and cheese) and clean. I straightened my hair, which ran like pokers down the length of my back. The ends of it tickled the fleshy tops of my buns, which spilled out over the waistband of my most flattering jeans. I resisted the temptation to smoke: Shane didn't approve of this habit of mine and could detect the smell of smoke within a radius of ten miles. I wondered what to do next. I saw my mobile on the mantelpiece where I'd left it that morning. There was a text from Shane.

Am up to my eyes in work.
Will ring you later – much later.

He'd sent that text at lunchtime and not a word from him since. Bernard's face suddenly swam in front of my eyes. 'You're an interesting woman, Grace O'Brien,' he had said, looking straight at me. Shane's conversations were always peppered liberally with 'baby' and 'sweetheart' and 'gorgeous girl' and 'sexy mare'. His hands constantly playing with my hair, his eyes moving over my body.

There were two texts from Clare:

Does 12.30 p.m. suit for the dress fitting?

And, several hours later:

*Did you get my last text? I have to phone
the Bridal Boutique before 6. Can you get back to me asap?*

There were also two missed calls from Clare's mobile. I could smell the hysteria coming off the phone. And who could blame her? I had hardly been the model chief bridesmaid. A text would not suffice. I had to phone her.

Her mobile rang out and her home phone invited me to leave a message after the beep. I did what Clare and I always did when we got each other's answering machine.

'Clare, are you there? Pick up, pick up, pick up, dammit,' like they do in American movies. Why can't they just leave a message like normal people?

'Clare? I'm really sorry, I just got your messages now. I've been really busy all day. Plus I left my phone at home, again. Twelve thirty is no problem, I'll be there on time. I promise.'

I walked around the flat. It was like an army barracks, it was that tidy. Caroline would delight in it. I inspected the fridge again, loving the way the shelves groaned with produce. I was like a caged animal, pacing relentlessly, and it was only 8.06 p.m. God knows when Shane would arrive. I didn't want to text him. He hated being pinned down. There was nothing for it but to wait. Maybe read. And try not to eat.

I must have fallen asleep on the couch because when I woke up, the flat was in darkness and the candles had all burned out. I had a crick in my neck and pins and needles down my left arm where I had trapped it against the couch with the bulk of my body. I was cold. According to my mobile, it was 2.30 a.m. Shane had sent a message two hours earlier:

> *Home sn.*

I headed to my bedroom, discarding the French knickers and sheer vest I'd planned to wear, pulling on a warm pair of cotton pyjamas that would not have looked out of place in the male ward of a nursing home. I sank between the sheets, planning to lie there twitching with annoyance and frustration. I was asleep in seconds.

25

Daylight elbowed its way into the bedroom. Shane lay on the bed beside me, outside the covers, fully clothed. Stubble darkened his face, which seemed thinner than I remembered. His eyelashes were the same, stretching thick and dark towards his cheekbones. His hair was tousled and unkempt and would be given a stern seeing-to as soon as he woke up. I touched his skin lightly with my fingertips: he was cold. He mumbled something and rolled towards me. Jesus, his breath stank. Easing myself out of the bed, I headed for the kitchen. If I had proper breakfast before he woke up, I could munch on an apple later, when he was eating.

I fought the good fight against the urge to have a rasher sandwich smothered in brown sauce. I lost. Slapping two thick rashers on the pan, I paused. The third rasher was in my hand, dangling over the heat of the pan.

Might as well be hung for a pig as a piglet. I loosened my grip and let it fall into a puddle of grease on the pan. The dark flesh pinkened as it sizzled and spat. The smell was fabulous. I was lost in it.

'Good morning, gorgeous. You're never going to eat all that bacon, are you?'

Shane stood at the kitchen door, frowning. He had seen to his hair, which was now flopping carefully over one side of his face. Even with his creased clothes and his sleep-encrusted face, he was a beautiful man. My man. Standing in my kitchen against a backdrop of sizzling rashers. It was as close to perfect as I had been in a while.

'I was making breakfast for you,' I lied, moving towards him until there he was, in my arms, where I had imagined him so many times. Shane expertly undid my robe and slid his hands underneath, stopping when he encountered the deeply practical cotton pyjamas. I moved away from him then, holding him at arm's length.

'Not on an empty stomach,' I laughed. 'You're going to need a lot of calories where you're going.'

'Fair enough,' he smiled at me. I could feel his mood lifting like fog in the heat of summer.

Forgoing a rasher buttie was a small price to pay for sex in a harmonious atmosphere with someone I loved. I bit into a Granny Smith. It was as hard and cold as a stone.

'So, how're things with you?' Shane asked between mouthfuls. Butter dripped down his chin and I longed to lean over and lick it off. My spoon scraped noisily against the bottom of the yoghurt tub, long empty.

'I got a promotion at work.'

'You did not.' His tone was incredulous. 'I'd heard there were redundancies planned in your company. Thought you'd be top of the list, you great dosser.' He smiled at me and wolfed the last of his sandwich, licking his fingers noisily before taking an enormous swallow of tea.

'Well,' I began, 'I would have agreed with you but the boss reckons otherwise. Mad, isn't it?' When I laughed, it made a hollow sound. Shane did not notice.

'Speaking of work, Graham wants me to extend my contract in London. He's really pleased with me and said that a year's experience in the London market could mean a serious promotion when I get back to Dublin.'

'Oh,' was all I could manage.

'Jesus, Grace, can't you at least pretend to be happy for

me?' Shane's exasperation left a deep furrow in his forehead, just above the bridge of his nose.

'No, no, I *am* glad for you,' I insisted. 'It's just that I miss you. I was hoping you'd be back soon, that we could make plans, y'know?'

'Baby, we *will* make plans.' Shane burped discreetly into his cupped hand. 'But right now, I've got plans for you.' He pushed his chair from the table and lunged at me across the crumbs. His kiss was hard, his lips salty and slippy. I let myself get lost in him. We could talk about his plans for us later, couldn't we?

Afterwards, I told him about dinner at my mother's house that night. He didn't look best pleased.

'I wanted to spend some time with you, baby.'

'It's just for an hour, ninety minutes at most.' I sounded like Laura, trying to entice me to the pub last night. 'She wants to introduce us to her new boyfriend. His name is Jack Frost.' I thought that would make him laugh. It didn't.

'Jesus, isn't she a bit old for boyfriends?'

'She's happier than she's been for a long time,' I said.

'You mean since Patrick, don't you?' His face was rigid.

'I just mean that she's happier. She seems to be . . . moving on, I suppose.' I struggled with the words.

'And what? It's OK to emotionally blackmail me just because of Patrick?'

'Shane, for Christ's sake, it's just dinner at my mother's house. I'd love you to come, that's all.'

I didn't want to fight with him. He'd end up in a sulk and mightn't speak to me for the rest of the weekend. Anyway, I couldn't stay annoyed at him for long, what with him being so lovely to look at and to touch and even to smell. Underneath the sharp tang of his aftershave, he smelled of warm soapy water and I loved pushing my nose into the crook of his neck and breathing him in.

I excused myself and went to the bathroom, where I pressed my forehead against the mirror, cooling it. When I got back, he was reading the paper in bed. He had calmed down and I lay beside him, relieved when he put his arm around me.

'Anyway, I can't go to your ma's tonight. I've arranged to meet Pauline for a drink.' His voice was rigid with resolve. When I didn't say anything, he continued. 'I told her we would both meet her. You and me. It's Saturday night, for God's sake. I thought you'd be pleased.'

Fucking Pauline. And the rest. Shane's girl-friends. The hyphen denotes the fact that they were females who happened to be platonic friends of my boyfriend. Now, as far as I'm concerned, Plato was full of shite when he said that men and women can have platonic relationships. I'm more of the *When Harry Met Sally* school of thought. The theory there was that men and women cannot be friends as one party will invariably find the other attractive on some sexual level, especially after a few pints. Shane did not agree. There was Pauline, Charlotte, Brenda, Martha, Chantelle, Colette, Janet, Mya: and they were just his work colleagues. I had met them all at various different times and concluded that, given any encouragement at all, they would stampede towards him, scattering women and children and current girlfriends in their wake, in an effort to get him on the flat of his back. He went for lunch with them, went shopping with them (Shane prided himself on his metrosexuality) and, of course, went for a few drinks with them after work.

'Are there no nice lads in the office you could go out with?' I once asked in a pseudo-casual fashion. That comment resulted in the mother and father of all arguments. Shane hadn't spoken to me for three days, despite my frantic texts and emails. When he eventually forgave me, I was then in the unhappy position of never being able to complain again about his legions of girl-friends, all clamouring for a piece of his pie.

'What?' he barked at me even though I hadn't actually said anything. 'You're not going to go off on one just because I'm meeting Pauline, are you?'

I swallowed hard. 'No, of course not.'

Dinner in Ma's house wasn't brought up again.

By the time I was ready to leave the flat to meet Clare at the Bridal Boutique, Shane was back in bed, snoring like a train. I sat on the bed beside him, scribbling a note which I left on the pillow beside his head:

> *Be back as soon as I can. Remember Cats is due in this afternoon so for God's sake put some clothes on when you get up – you can take them off again when I get home.*
> *Love you.*
> *Grace*
> *xxx*

'How's the lurve god?' Clare greeted me when I arrived at the Bridal Boutique (at 12.27 p.m.). I adopted a John Wayne gait and straddled towards her.

'You dirty-looking eejit,' Clare said in an eerily accurate imitation of our mother. 'Don't worry, she's not here,' she added. 'She's gone off shopping for the day with Jack Frost. Getting him something to wear for the wedding, she said.'

'Jesus, she's dressing him now?' I couldn't get over her. In a *relationship*. Somebody's *girlfriend*. I remembered how she used to cast a discerning eye over Dad before he left the house, straightening his tie, smoothing the lapels of his jacket, tucking his shirt into the waistband of his trousers. She would have smoothed his hair away from his face with licked fingers, if she'd been let. Or if he'd had any hair. He was as bald as an egg when he died.

'I know, it's weird, isn't it?' Clare said, shaking her head at the oddness of it all. She looked sadder than a bride-to-be had a right to look.

'Lurve God is tucked up in bed fast asleep, awaiting my return.'

'Is everything OK with you two?' Clare asked the question softly.

'God yes,' I said, too loudly. 'We've got plans. I'll tell you all about it later.'

'Are you coming to Ma's tonight for dinner?' she asked.

'Yes, of course I'm coming,' I said, clapping my hands loudly together. 'Now, take me to the frock.'

Clare led the way to the changing room, where one of the BCs greeted me nervously.

'Hallo. It's nice to see you again,' I said quietly, in my best-behaved voice, as if nothing untoward had happened the last time. She seemed a little disappointed by my display of normality.

'Grace, you're lovely.' That's what Clare said when the dress had successfully zipped all the way up and I straightened without ripping any of the delicate fabric.

'Don't be daft,' I retorted, giving her a playful push. She half-fell out of the dressing room. Sometimes, I forget my own strength.

'Sorry, Clare, are you OK?' I scanned her anxiously. This tiny bride-to-be. My little sister. She smiled at me as she raised herself to her full 5'2".

'I'm grand, Grace. And you're still beautiful, no matter how you resist it.'

I turned to face myself in the mirror. The fourteen fit perfectly. I had Shane to thank for that. My hair was tumbling down from my head like a waterfall, streaming over my neck and shoulders and arms. Four showers and five loofahs later, my skin had been restored to white goosedown. I suddenly turned to face her.

'I've done something stupid. I can't stop thinking about it.' I spat it out. It left a bad taste in my mouth but I immediately felt better. Clare looked wary.

'Let's get out of here,' she said, 'and we'll talk.'

We sat on the boardwalk, sipping skinny lattes from tall paper cups. Despite the glare of the afternoon sun, our breaths collected in front of us in small clouds. My mouth puckered around the filter of my cigarette and I exhaled long and hard before speaking.

'I slept with a guy from work. I didn't mean to. It just happened. Last weekend.'

The silence stretched between us. I dived into it.

'I was lonely, I suppose. I know that's no excuse. He's such an unlikely person. For me, I mean. Like, he's quiet and considered. Sort of gentle and reserved. He doesn't say much. I've read about guys like that but I'd never actually met one.'

Clare looked straight ahead of her, still holding her counsel. I went for it.

'He told me I was an interesting woman.' I paused for breath and buried my face in my coffee cup, letting the steam snake up my nose, warming me.

'He said you were an interesting woman?' Clare sounded concerned.

'Yeah, but I don't think he meant it like that,' I countered quickly. 'I mean, I think he meant, like, that I was, like, y'know, maybe a bit odd or something.'

Clare looked at me with interest, her pink tongue wedged between her lips, expectant.

'Clare, no, it wasn't like that. It was just sex, really.' I needed Clare to clarify the situation, not to muddy it.

'When was the last time Shane said anything positive to you?'

I opened my mouth to respond.

'I mean outside of the bedroom,' Clare added quickly.

I closed my mouth and considered the amended question. My mind was a blank. I got defensive.

'Clare, we can't all be like you and Richard, y'know. Romeo and bloody Juliet. I'm surprised you haven't built a balcony off your bedroom and he hasn't learned to play the fecking mandolin or something.'

Clare ignored me. 'You said you haven't been able to stop thinking about it.'

I took another deep drag of my cigarette and exhaled for the longest time. We sat in silence, in a slow dance of smoke swirls.

'But I've got Shane. He's got plans.'

'Oh yeah, and what are they?' Clare's scepticism didn't sit well on her, like a pair of runners worn with a cocktail dress. She wrapped her hands about her cup, warming them.

'Well, we haven't discussed them yet.' I looked out over the quays. Seagulls bobbed on tiny waves, their magnificent white and grey chests puffed out, their heads held high. I wanted so little. Why couldn't I get that?

After a long time, Clare said, 'Shane isn't coming to Ma's tonight, is he?'

I said nothing and Clare pressed her hand against my knee. 'Bernard sounds like a dote. I'd love to meet him.'

'That's not going to happen,' I said, stubbing my cigarette out in the ashtray, sparks flying. I decided not to tell her about Shane extending his stay in London. I would wait until I had something positive to tell her. About Shane and I. Me and Shane. Us.

26

Dear Grace,

It's true. The world is round. I am sitting on Circular Quay in the dazzling sunshine that is the southern hemisphere in January. It's hard to believe it's the same sun that hides behind our Irish clouds.

Christmas Day was hilarious; barbequed burgers (turkey ones) on the beach. Shorts and suncream. Cold beers and salsa dips. When I rang home, I could almost hear the cold down the phone and – I have to be honest here – I had a little laugh for myself. I think it's the only time in my life that I could be described as being 'full of glee'.

To my left, the magnificence of the Harbour Bridge. The 'coat hanger' they call it here. Masters of understatement, these Aussies. To my right, the grandeur of the Opera House. The theatre opened in 1973 and was a tram depot before that. In this light, it looks like it might put out to sea. We're due there tonight to see Cinderella. Did I say we? I did, didn't I? OK, then, it's a girl, a woman, if you will. In Australia, the red-haired man is king. I love this place. The woman's name is Mary. I know, I know, I travel to the other side of the world and meet a woman called Mary. She's a born, bred and barbequed Aussie but her great-grandfather was Irish. He milked a cow that wasn't his back in 1850 or something, and was shipped off to this tropical paradise for the rest of his life. Beats the shite out of the Joy any day of the week, wha? She's very tall (nearly as tall as you) and calls me Paaaaatrick, which I love. Wish I could be a girl for a minute and tell you how fantastic she is and how she makes me feel like a purple-heart hero returned from the war. But I'm not so I won't. Suffice to say I like her. And I think she likes me.

The book is going well, in part because of the backdrop of this incredible landscape. I've been doing lots of 'writerish' type things since I got here. I was at a place called the Bridal Veil in the Blue Mountains, for the launch of a book. It's a great mound of pale, grey rock, reaching out of the earth, a sheer spray of veil-white arching down the side of it. The author needed a microphone to be heard over the roar of the water. Our faces were wet from the spray. That's where I met Mary, actually (she's a writer too but in an actual published real-life kind of a way, unlike me).

Anyway, I have to go. Am meeting Mary for dinner in the Rocks, in the hills above the quays, just a short walk from here. I am loathe to lift myself from this spot where I am invisible to the world: just another watcher on a bench, drinking one of them smoothies, sweetened with a baby bottle of Malibu I released from the mini-bar in the hotel room.

Australians shorten all their words. Did you know that? A duvet cover is a 'doona.' (Why do they need duvets here????) The afternoon is the 'arvo' and 'G'day' will suffice for good morning and – in case I don't see you – good afternoon, good evening and goodnight. It's kind of lonely here for the traveller from the Northern Hemisphere. Every time I think about you all, you are fast asleep. It's hard to keep track. I ate kangaroo yesterday. Yes, I did feel bad about it (what's that, Skippy?), but my Aussie boss (I am an official grape picker at the moment) recommended it so roundly, I felt it would be rude to refuse. Especially since he was paying for lunch. Tastes a bit like beef. I closed my eyes when I ate it, if that helps. I thought

about that story Dad used to read you when you were a kid,
about six or so, I don't know if you remember it. It was about
a baby Koala bear called Joey. He wanted to reach to the top
of an apricot tree where the plumpest, juiciest apricot hung.
He couldn't get to it. Don't worry, it has a happy ending. Do
you remember? You hated the dark. You always insisted Dad
stay beside you until you fell asleep.

   It's getting dark now. But don't worry, that means it's
nearly daybreak over there.

   Lots of love,
   Patrick

PS: Yes, visa is up at the end of March so could possibly meet
you and Caroline in Spain in April before the trip to Portu-
gal. Did you have any date in mind? Is Shane going too?

27

It was later than I wanted it to be when I got back to the flat. The March sun dipped towards the horizon, leaving lazy trails of dull orange draped across the sky. Clare begged me to go for a quick drink to discuss the seating plan in detail. There were a couple of loose ends. Clare didn't like loose ends. Like, for example, Uncle Malachy and Aunt Joan. They lived together but hadn't spoken in over ten years, as far as anyone knew. Should she seat them together? We eventually decided to seat them at the same table but not actually side by side, to deflect from their antipathy towards each other.

Then there was Shane. Was he coming? She asked me straight out, no zig-zagging around the issue. That's how I knew she was nervous.

Caroline was home but barricaded in the bathroom, no doubt getting ready for the second date with her blind date. What would you call that now? A *sighted* date? Anyway, you know what I'm trying to say.

I yelled a greeting in at her, hurrying past. I couldn't hang about. A thick fog of steam rose from the crack under the door and reached for my hair, threatening it with a Three Degrees look.

Shane sat on the couch in the sitting room, pecking at the keyboard of his laptop with two fingers. His face discouraged any discussion so I loped on towards the kitchen, pausing only to kiss him briefly on his smooth forehead. He nodded, the *tap-tap-tapping* of his fingers never slowing.

I took a bottle of water out to the unkempt garden at the back of the flat. Mr Jenkins pottered among the pampas grasses strewn across the bottom of the garden. I lit up a fag and headed towards him. He was more stooped than usual tonight. It seemed an effort for him to lift his head.

'Ah, Grace, is it yerself?'

'It is indeed, Mr Jenkins. Isn't it a grand stretch we're getting in the evenings,' I said, echoing half-remembered phrases of my grandmother (on my father's side).

'I see your young man is back.' Mr Jenkins rubbed his nose with the back of his hand as he spoke.

'Yes. Just for the weekend, mind.' Mr Jenkins always saw the good in everyone, so there was no need for me to shine a kind light on Shane and our relationship.

'Well, if it makes you happy Gracie, that's the main thing.' He interrupted himself with a great wracking cough that lasted for several seconds.

'That's grand, Gracie girl, I'm fine now.' Mr Jenkins backed away from my hand patting his back.

'Oh Christ, sorry. Did I hurt you?' In the gloaming, shadows hid the folds of skin that sagged under his eyes and jaw and, for a moment, I saw him: how he must have looked years before. Quite dashing, actually. He straightened.

'Have a happy weekend.' A happy weekend? As an expression, it sounded odd. He shuffled away, looking back once to nod, as if I had disagreed with him. He folded into the darkness. The tip of my cigarette burned devil-red in the dusk and I flicked it away from me, only half smoked. I headed back inside.

'Jesus, you stink.' Shane wrinkled his nose and looked away from me as I leaned over him to kiss his neck.

'Sorry, I'll go brush my teeth.' I backed away, cursing my carelessness. It had been a long time since I'd had to remember to brush my teeth and wash my hands after every cigarette. As

I walked away, Shane pawed at the air dramatically and forced a couple of coughs. I resisted the urge to turn and flick him on the nose (a seemingly playful gesture that actually hurts a lot: perfect in situations where you don't have the time or the inclination for an actual fight). Caroline had vacated the bathroom and I groped my way inside through the swirling mist of steam. I rubbed at the mirror over the sink with a closed fist. Piling my toothbrush with paste, I brushed until my gums bled. Then I flossed. Then I brushed again. I turned the brush upside down and scoured my tongue with the ribbed underside until I lost all sensation in my mouth. I stuck my tongue out and examined it. It was raw red. Blood seeped down between the cracks in my teeth, giving me a well-fed vampire look. I tipped the dregs of the Listerine into my mouth and winced as it stung and sloshed. Then I started on my hands, scrubbing them with a soapy nailbrush, paying particular attention to my smoking fingers – the fore and index finger of my left hand. A cuticle tore and began to bleed. A blood bath. Still, all traces of cigarette smell had been obliterated although my face was now the colour of a tomato, with the steamy heat of the bathroom. I counted to ten, sluiced my face with cold water, counted to ten again, resisted the urge to eat the Star bar at the back of my wardrobe and forced my shoulders down from up around my ears. I walked back into the living room. Shane had abandoned his laptop and was lying on the couch with a bottle of beer. He looked like he was thinking about relaxing. I approached him.

'Are you fumigated?' he sighed.

I nodded, waiting.

'Are you ever going to smoke again?' he continued, lifting his eyebrows skyward.

I shook my head slowly, my fingers crossed behind my back. I *was* going to smoke again, but not until he was safely ensconced on the plane back to London.

He stroked his square jaw slowly but I could see the start of a smile around his mouth. He shuffled over and I leapt onto the couch beside him, wishing I was smaller so I could nestle easily into the crook of his arm. He held his face out to me and I kissed him. His breath smelled of stale coffee. I said nothing. He pulled away and looked at me.

'Grace, seriously, if we're going to have plans, you'll have to ditch those cigarettes. I can't live with them.'

'What are our plans, Shane?' He mentioned them first so I felt safe asking.

The bedroom door banged.

'How do I look?' Caroline vaulted into the room, a blur of colour. She twirled in front of us. I'd never seen her looking so happy. Needless to say, she was a glorious specimen of womanhood. Although she looked different: less stern, more girlish. And – I was shocked to realise – nervous. Caroline was *nervous*. She was wearing a swirling knee-length skirt of baby pink with a leave-nothing-to-the-imagination strapless, pale green top – heavily beaded – that accentuated the delicacy of her perfectly straight, jutting collar bones, set against the smooth tan of her skin. The heels of her sandals were sky-high. Strictly no-alcohol-or-tiled-floor-sandals. Car-to-bar only. There would be no legging home in horror in those things. Unusually for Caroline, her hair was up. She had plaited it and wound it into a knot at the back of her head, lancing it with a pair of those Japanese knitting needles. Her face was a riot of make-up. I had to send her back to the bathroom, twice, to remove a lot of it.

'Do my tits look saggy in this?' she worried, scooping a hand down her top to rearrange herself upwards.

'What tits?' Shane sniggered.

I thumped him in just the right area on his upper arm, deadening it immediately. While he thrashed about on the couch, I turned towards Caroline.

'Your tits look grand,' I reassured her. 'Pert and springy. Why are you worried about them?'

'I'm not wearing a bra,' she admitted.

This was *unheard* of for Caroline. I mean, she didn't really *need* a bra. She could get away with a small training bra, or even a tight vest. But she had been shod since she was about eleven. I sat up straight on the couch, ignoring Shane whimpering beside me.

'My God, Caroline. What is going on? Tell me about this guy. *Immediately.*'

When Caroline started speaking, it was with relief. She had clearly wanted to talk about her blind date since last Wednesday, when she first met him. Her face lit up.

'He's just, I don't know, I just feel, like, so *calm* when I'm with him. He's really tall. He'll look great when I sort out his wardrobe. But apart from all that, he's just got this, this *aura* about him, it's so relaxing, it's like being in a warm bubble bath when I'm talking to him. Although . . .' Caroline looked worried now and went to drag her hand through her hair, forgetting that she had sent it upstairs. 'He doesn't really talk all that much. In fact, when I was thinking about our date, I realised that he'd hardly said a word, really. It was me that did all the talking. And then I got worried that maybe I was boring the shit out of him. Cos, like, he never really gave me any feedback. I didn't *close* him, y'know?'

We both shot a look at Shane, the salesman. He was still nursing his arm. He was the King of Closing, always talking about it, how you had to be *closing* in sales, in life and probably in the afterlife, it was that important. 'Don't leave the room until you *close* them,' he said. 'No matter what business you're in, what situation you're in. Always be *closing.*'

Shane leaned forward on the couch, still rubbing his shoulder.

'You're second dating this guy and you haven't *closed* him?' He seemed incredulous, his eyes popping out on stalks.

Caroline shook her head slowly, mortified. I was intrigued.

'So, what's he like?' I asked. 'What does he do, what does he look like, where does he live?'

Caroline took an enormous breath that threatened to pop the buttons threading up the side of her top when the doorbell rang, making us all jump.

'It's him. Oh fuck, my tits, I'm not ready for him, stall him! stall him!' she shrieked at me, disappearing in a flurry of arms and legs into her bedroom.

I sighed deeply, secretly enjoying all the drama. It was usually me who was unstable. It was lovely to be the sensible one for once. I turned to Shane.

'You get the door, I'll fix drinks.' I was in control of this situation, and *loving* it.

I mixed a large jug of Pimm's in the kitchen. I'd been a convert to this particular drink since being introduced to Jilly Cooper in my mid-teens. I hid the books from my mother, due to the gloriously large tracts of gratuitous sex scenes contained within those thick tomes. I'd learned a lot from those books, not least how to mix a damn good jug of Pimm's. I was in my element, coring apples, slicing oranges and lemons, peeling cucumbers and tearing sprigs of mint from the potted plant on the windowsill I'd bought yesterday, so it was still alive. I could hear voices in the hall. I stopped in mid-peel, my hands suspended over the sink. Shane stopped talking and now I could hear the other voice, clearer now. It sounded familiar. I tried to place it. It was deep and slow, musical almost. The voices got louder, approaching the living room. I stood in the alcove we called the kitchen, listening, my back to the voices. Was it a mid-lands twang? No, wait. It was a northern twang. Like as in the North of Ireland. Lilting with melody. Hesitant and serious. The ice clinked gently against the edge of the glass jug. I turned around, the jug in my hand. My mouth hung open. I could see the back of his head, roaring with red hair.

I could see wide shoulders, straining. Black jeans pulled too high on a narrow waist, puckering against hard thighs, running down long legs, stopping just short of bony ankles. Dreadful shoes, with worn laces that were too long. I walked slowly out of the kitchen, like a sleepwalker. Shane turned to face me, his charming smile brightening his features.

'Grace. Let me introduce you.'

The man had his back to me, hanging his jacket on the coat-stand. He started to turn. It took forever. A drop of Pimm's spilled onto my bare foot. I straightened the jug. The noise of the world shrank away from me. I stood there in bare feet.

'Grace?' Bernard spoke first. The words were choked and strained. Dark colour stained his face. 'What are *you* doing here?' He looked confused, and a little nervous.

I opened my mouth to say something. Shane got in first.

'You two *know* each other?' Shane looked from me to Bernard and back again like a tennis umpire.

It took me a long time to speak. My tongue was stuck to the roof of my mouth.

'We work together,' I said to Shane. 'I live here,' I turned to Bernard. 'What are *you* doing here?' My voice sounded funny to me. High and breathy. Even now, I couldn't let the penny drop.

'Oh great, you've all been introduced. Grace, you've made Pimm's. Lovely.' Caroline's words lanced me as she tottered into the living room. I backed away from Shane and Bernard, turned and walked slowly back to the kitchen. Shane followed me.

'Are you OK?' He looked sharply at me. The weight of the jug suddenly seemed unbearable and I set it on the counter.

'Yeah, I'm grand. Just getting the glasses.' I worked hard to steady my breathing.

'They're here on the counter,' Shane pointed out as I opened a cupboard on the other side of the kitchen.

'Oh yeah. I forgot.' I wanted Shane to be anywhere but here.

'Why don't you go and talk to Caroline and Bernard. I'll come through in a minute. Just going to get some nibbles for us.' I smiled brightly at him and he seemed to relax. The knife in my heart turned a notch. Shane nodded and left. I moved to the other corner of the kitchen, where I couldn't be seen. I leaned against the counter for support. Caroline and Bernard. Bernard was Caroline's blind date. Caroline had chosen him to be Her One. Even if Bernard didn't feel the same way, he didn't stand a chance. I buried my head in my hands, whispering all the curse words I knew.

'Grace, what are you doing?' It was Caroline. I opened a cupboard door and swirled towards her.

'Just getting some nuts and stuff.' I sent her a huge smile.

'So, what do you think?' she whispered theatrically at me, beaming.

'I know that guy,' I admitted weakly. 'I work with him.'

'Really?' Caroline seemed sceptical. 'He never said he worked in your company. How come you never mentioned him? He's so lovely.' She gazed towards the living room as she said this. I followed her line of vision. Bernard sat on the edge of the couch, looking out of place as Shane talked at him.

'Em, we work on different floors. I hardly ever see him. He's just new anyway.'

'With hair dye and a new wardrobe, he could be perfect.' Caroline wasn't listening to me. I turned away and busied myself with bowls.

'Grace.' Caroline sounded concerned as she turned towards me. 'What are you doing? They're popcorn kernels you're putting into that bowl. Do we not have any pre-popped popcorn? I thought we had tortillas? And dips? Let's do that, yeah?'

'Yeah, sorry. Look, you go out there and I'll be with you in a moment, I'll just sort these out, OK?' I needed a moment alone to pick myself up off the floor, where I was lying in my head.

'Couldn't he be beautiful?' Caroline said. She wasn't going to give up until I said something. She waited for me.

I made my head nod up and down. She finally left, brimming over with hope and plans. I followed her with my eyes until she settled herself in beside Bernard on the couch. He shuffled along to accommodate her. He said she was looking well. He laughed when Shane told his IRA joke, even though it wasn't funny. He *was* beautiful. There was no doubt about it.

I opened and closed a few cupboard doors to make it sound like I was doing something constructive in the kitchen.

'Grace, what are you doing in there?' It was Shane, shouting in at me, agitated. I breathed in through my nose and out through my mouth, like a horse in a nosebag. I was nearly thirty years old. I had to face things. I had to face the fact that I would never again get a letter from Patrick. I had to face three people in a living room despite the fact that they'd all seen me naked. Despite the fact that Caroline was in love for maybe the first time in her life. With someone I . . .what? I knew? I was attracted to? I had slept with? I liked? I had to grow up. I moved deliberately into the room, depositing the tray of chips and dips on the floor in front of the couch. I sat on the floor, ignoring the gaping space in between Shane and Bernard on the couch. I smiled up at everyone, like everything was grand and nothing was weird.

'There's sweet and spicy. We cater for all tastes here.' My voice sounded strangely ordinary in the confines of the room.

'Hope you got low-fat ones, Grace,' Shane laughed, cramming his mouth with a fistful of chips.

Caroline reached across Bernard to slap her brother.

'You're such a bollix, Shane. I don't know how Grace puts up with you and your outsize obnoxiousness.'

'Grace knows I'm only joking, don't you baby?' Shane said with his mouth full.

Bernard reached down, picked up the bowl of chips and held them towards me. 'Would you like one, Grace?' I loved the way he said my name: it was like fingertips brushing against skin. I looked at him and he smiled gently at me. I took a chip, although I didn't eat it.

'So Bernard, you're obviously into skinny birds then?' Shane flung himself into the back of the couch, tossing his hair off his face. He looked at Bernard. Bernard looked back. I held my breath. Caroline broke the silence.

'For fuck sake, Shane, would you behave yourself.' She lifted Bernard's limp hand into her own and squeezed it. 'Sorry' Bernard, it's the big brother syndrome. Don't mind him. Do you have any sisters?'

'Aye. Just the one, mind. She's married and I have two nephews.' Bernard was on surer ground now. 'Fionn and Oisin. They're dotes, so they are.' He dug a long hand into shallow pockets and unearthed his wallet. He flipped it open and displayed a worn photograph of two young boys in swimming trunks on a beach, their arms wrapped around each other.

'They're like twins.' I said it before I realised what I'd said. Bernard's face registered nothing.

'Aye, that's what everyone says. But there's eleven months between them.'

'They're gorgeous,' Caroline gushed. 'They both look like you.' She looked at Bernard. He looked away, snapping his wallet shut and shovelling it back into his pocket. The conversation dragged.

'So, I believe you work with Grace?' Caroline said. We both said 'yes' at the same time, then paused to let the other explain. The silence lengthened. Bernard broke it first.

'I'm just new in the company. Grace and I met last week for the first time, really.' He didn't look at me. An image shot through my head of the pair of us in his bath. 'Both of us will never fit into that,' I'd laughed at him when he suggested it after the first time. He ignored me, filling it with warm water, pouring dollops of shower gel under the running taps. 'Sorry, I don't have any bubble bath,' he apologised with a slanting grin. The ends of his hair curled in the steam, making him look younger. Then he smiled at me, really smiled. That smile made me forget about my nakedness, my girth, my height, my freckles, the stark whiteness of my skin. I forgot myself. He went to pick me up then and I collapsed with the laughing. I closed my eyes and curled my hands into fists, hurting myself with the pressure of my nails against my palms.

'Yeah, it was last week,' I agreed, nodding my head. And smiling. God, my face ached with the smiling. When would it end? 'So where are you guys off to tonight, anyway?' I looked up at Caroline and Bernard. Caroline looked at Bernard. He shifted on the couch.

'Maybe the movies?' he offered. Caroline's shoulders slumped. I knew what she was thinking. She wanted to drink cocktails in subdued lighting. She was wearing a fourth-date outfit on a second date. She was clearly hoping for some action. She liked this guy. More than liked him. She *really* liked him. I'd never seen her like this before.

'Maybe we'll go for a drink first?' she leered at him suggestively. 'If we're going to make the seven o'clock, we'd better go directly,' Bernard replied. He was not for turning.

Caroline took it on the chin. 'Sure. Why not? We may as well go now then. Get that Pimm's down your neck.' She got up and went to the hall to get her coat – my coat, actually. Anyway, Bernard and I stood up at the same time. Pins and needles roared up and down my legs. I accepted the pain gladly. It was part of my penance, balm to my guilty conscience. I deserved it. *Welcomed* it. The pain made me sway a little. Bernard caught my shoulders. The want in me was like an avalanche. I stepped backwards, leaving his hands outstretched, I grabbed one of them and shook it, steadying myself. 'Have a nice time tonight. I'll see you on Monday.'

'Yeah, see you Monday.' Bernard smiled his gentle smile. 'See you, Shane.' They didn't shake hands. Bernard turned quickly and left the room. Caroline yelled a hurried goodbye from the hall and then dashed back to utter a discreet 'don't wait up' to us before slamming the door shut behind her. Not looking at Shane, I told him I was going to take a shower. I left the room at a gallop, not turning around.

28

I drove to my mother's house, dropping Shane in town on the way.

'Tell your family I was asking for them,' he said, taking his seat-belt off.

'Yes, of course.' I couldn't wait for him to get out of the car, but he was taking his time. 'What are you going to tell them?' he asked.

'I'll just say you had a long-standing arrangement that you couldn't get out of. They won't mind.' That was true, they wouldn't. Nor would they be surprised.

He had the grace to look sheepish. 'I could come, you know. If you really want me to. I could ring Pauline . . .' He tapered off, waiting for me. I obliged. It was easier this way.

'Not at all. You go and enjoy yourself. Do you want me to pick you up later?'

'No, don't worry. I'll grab a joe and see you back at the flat, OK baby?' He kissed me and got out, the wind whipping his hair about his face. He blew me another kiss, rearranged his hair and was gone. I lit up a cigarette almost immediately, my hands shaking with the cold turkey. I drove slowly, giving myself time to think before I got to Ma's. Caroline and Bernard. The words went round and round like a train on a track. My head ached with it. How did Bernard feel about Caroline? Was he mad about her? How could he not be? Everyone else was. And where did that leave me? And what about Shane?

The driveway at Mam's house was full, which meant there

were two cars in it. I recognised Jane's (booster seats, headless dolls, sawn-off shotguns – the pretend kind – shards of cornflakes, crisps and crackers, and a 'baby on board' sticker fading on the back window). Mam's car was there as well, an immaculately maintained VW Polo, pert and pristine, neatly parked in the driveway, flush against the garden wall. I drove halfway down the street to find a parking spot. When I arrived at the house, I was hot and a little out of breath from the hike up the street – it sloped slightly. I threw my cigarette butt into the long grass of the front garden and watched the red tip burn and fade.

'Grace, what are you doing, just standing there? Come in, come in, child.' My mother stood in the porch, gesturing me forward with her arms outstretched. I was on my guard immediately. Mam looked *delighted*. I'd never seen her so happy. And she was wearing *make-up*. I could tell because there was lipstick smudged on her teeth. Also, her eyelashes were stuck together in wet clumps where she had experimented with mascara. My mother never wore make-up. Not even when Dad was alive. 'She doesn't need it,' Dad would say when we commented on it. 'All the *other* mothers wear make-up.' We were disappointed by her lapse in this regard. 'Your mother is a *natural* beauty,' Dad explained to us.

Mam tugged at my arm, leading me into the house. She wore very dark, very new, greasy blue jeans. A rigid crease down the front of each leg told me exactly when she'd bought them (at 10.32 a.m. that morning, possibly in Liffey Valley). When she walked, the jeans made a low swishing sound, like windscreen wipers. I only mention them because, before today, she only ever wore skirts in sensible colours that fell *exactly* three inches below her knee, with twin-sets – before they became fashionable – and clogs. She was a great woman for the clogs. When questioned about it, she mentioned a Dutch great-grandfather who helped the boy with his finger in the dyke. 'He wasn't the actual one who put the finger in.' She was anxious that we know this, never wanting to seem above herself. 'But he brought him tea and sandwiches and the like.' We were in the hall now, heading down the corridor, when the kitchen door flung open and Ella stood there.

Chocolate – or it might have been dried blood – caked across her cheeks and chin. Her fingernails were black with muck and I guessed – correctly – that she had been foraging in the flower pots in the conservatory for worms. She called them 'wurims'. She loved to pick them up and pull them taut, to see how far they stretched. Not very far, as it turned out. The sandbox in her back garden was strewn with the dismembered bodies of once fleshy, pink worms in the full of their health, now sadly stretched like so much elastic.

'Gwayth,' she lisped, jumping onto my feet, her short, fat arms wrapped around my legs. I did the obligatory shuffle across the kitchen while she squealed with delight.

'What age are you?' I shouted down at her so she could hear me over the din of conversation around the kitchen. 'Four,' she shouted back. She jumped off my feet then, solemnly counting out four fingers, holding them up. No more 'thwee'. She was growing up. Soon she'd be more mature than me. I'd probably be a bridesmaid at her wedding: an ancient, failing bridesmaid, without even the dignity of the matron of honour title.

The kitchen was a sea of bodies. They were all there; Jane and her husband, James. Ella, of course, and her two older brothers, whom she bullied relentlessly, Thomas and Matthew; James was religious: by this I mean he went to mass *every* Sunday and thought that 'Jaysus' and 'damn' were curses. Clare and Richard were sitting at the kitchen table already helping themselves to Greek salad from a glass bowl in the centre of the table.

'Hi, Grace,' Jane smiled up at me from her position at the head of the table. I smiled back but did not approach her. We were not sisters who hugged. An enormous tart oozed over the edges of a pie dish on the table. This thing could have fed Snow White, the seven dwarfs and their wives, with some left over for Prince Charming's hungry hound. The top of the tart was bumpy and thick, the colour of treacle, the sugar on top like a snowfall. My mouth watered. I tried not to let myself get distracted by it. I knew immediately that Jane had baked it. She was a woman who baked things. She also altered clothes (let down hems, sewed on buttons and the like). She called this 'mending'. She spoke in a language I did not fully understand. She ran the local car-pool and the mother and toddler group. She was on the PTA (that's Parent Teacher Association to you and me), the RA (that's the Residents' Association to the likes of us) and made costumes and painted scenery for the local amateur dramatics society. She Had It All. A husband who was not feckless *and* maintained good standards of personal hygiene. Three healthy, beautiful children who could make you laugh as quick as look at you. A roomy family house in Sutton (bought before the property fanaticism of the '90s) with a garden bench that swung slowly beneath an ancient oak that shed proper chestnuts in the autumn. Jane loved to complain about her lot in life but she secretly delighted in the way things had worked out. You could tell by the way she sometimes looked at her husband. A soft look.

I looked around the kitchen but could see no sign of the magician. I took a seat at the table, picking up a square of feta from the salad bowl. I put it in my mouth and let it melt on my tongue.

'Who wants to play Scrabble in the front room?' James yelled around the kitchen. Instantly, he was covered in children, like limpets on a rock. He held the two boys under his arms and made sure that Ella was perched safely on his feet, her short, pudgy arms wrapped around his thighs. 'I'll play too,' said Richard, realising he was in danger of being left alone with the O'Brien women in the kitchen. He followed James, who struggled out of the room. Suddenly, the kitchen was quiet. Us three women sat around the kitchen table. 'So where is Jack?' I asked.

'It's John,' Mam said briskly, taking lasagne out of the oven. 'He's been delayed at work.'

'At an eight-year-old's birthday party,' Clare explained. 'They wouldn't let him go until he'd made each one of them disappear, not just the birthday girl. Apparently, it got ugly for a while.'

'He can make people disappear?' I was impressed with that, having vague memories of magicians with faded black cloaks and cards and jaded cuddly toys in the shape of white bunny rabbits and bits of coloured rope.

'Yes, Grace.' My mother placed the dish on a placemat on the table. 'So you'd better watch out.' I looked quickly up at her, but she was smiling. She had made a joke *and* was wearing make-up. This really was magic.

Crying and bickering could be heard from the front room. Jane got up quickly. 'That's probably James,' she said, moving towards the door. 'The kids pick on him and never let him win.' Jesus, everyone was at it now, joking and the like. At least, I think she was joking.

Mam was at the worktop, her back to us.

'Do you need a hand, Ma?' I asked in my I'm-only-asking-to-be-polite voice.

'No thanks. Just making a salad dressing and then we're ready to eat.' She glanced at the kitchen clock when she said this. Then she bent at the knees to check her reflection in the oven door, patting her hair with the tips of her fingers. She thought no one was looking.

Clare was talking when I turned back to her. '. . . at the wedding. I mean, if the only napkin rings she can get are those manky terracotta ones, we might as well have none at all . . .'

She tapered off and looked at me. 'I'm being pedantic about the arrangements again, amn't I?' She circled her temples with the tips of her fingers.

'Yes, but only because you're nervous,' I said, standing behind her and rubbing her shoulders. 'Christ, you're tense,' I said, kneading at her muscles. I could feel her relax against my hands. 'I could tell you a funny story if you like,' I offered over her shoulder. 'Take your mind off things.'

'OK then.' She sounded sleepy in the warm smells of the kitchen. Mam had left, no doubt to touch up her make-up or iron her jeans again.

'Did I tell you about Caroline's blind date?'

'Yeah, you mentioned it all right. What about it?' Clare tried to twist around to look at me but I held her head between my hands and turned her away from me, the way a hairdresser might.

'It was the guy. The one from work. Bernard O'Malley.' I dropped my hands away from her neck and she turned round again.

'Bernard O'Malley? He's Richard's cousin. From Donegal, I think.' Clare was nonplussed. 'What do you mean, the one from work?'

I sat down in front of her. 'The one I told you about yesterday.'

'The one you slept with?' I had Clare's full attention now and I nodded slowly.

'And Caroline went on a date with him?' The penny was slowly dropping with Clare. Her face was a jigsaw that didn't quite fit.

'And his brother died,' I added. This to me was the strangest bit of all. That something like that had happened to both of us and neither of us knew about the other. That we were there, waiting. If it hadn't been for Shane, and Caroline, and Richard and his sodding blind dates. That was a lot of 'ifs'.

'I remember that. Edward, it was. Richard and I went to his funeral. You were away at the time. In Greece, I think.'

I remembered. It was our first holiday together, Shane and I. It had been perfect. My suitcase never arrived and I wore Shane's clothes for the first two days and they made me look smaller than I really was and as quick as I could button up one of his shirts, he'd have it unbuttoned and thrown on the floor. We didn't see too much of the island, but according to the guide book, it was stunning.

I nodded at Clare. 'Go on.'

'Bernard is Edward's twin brother, isn't he?' Clare asked.

'Yes.'

'I remember him that day,' she said. 'He was great, made all the arrangements, had everyone back to the family home for food. Organised the whole lot. His mother just couldn't cope with any of it.' We both nodded at that and I waited for her to go on, anxious for more details.

'And then, afterwards,' Clare said, frowning to remember. 'Afterwards, he just sort of disappeared.'

'Disappeared?' I leaned towards Clare. 'What do you mean?'

'He left. Went away. For about two months. He left a letter for his mother, Richard's aunt. Under the box of teabags so she'd be sure to find it.'

'Where did he go?' My cup of tea had gone cold in my hand and I set it back on the table.

'I don't know.' Clare shook her head.

'Did you meet him again?'

'Just the once, a few months after the funeral.'

'What did you think?' I leaned so close to her I caught the faint scent of apple drops, Clare's favourites.

'Well, it was just that one time, really, in a pub in Donegal town. Last autumn. There were lots of cousins there, millions of them.'

'But you remember Bernard.'

'Yes, I remember him. It was so sad. He just looked like someone who was lost, you know?' I nodded and touched her hand. We both knew how that felt.

The doorbell rang then, and we jumped at the shrill sound.

'That must be Jack Frost,' I said to Clare in a stage whisper.

'You're to call him John. Otherwise, Ma won't give you any apple tart,' Clare warned.

'But he might be wearing a magician's cloak and a pointy hat. You couldn't call a fella like that John.' I was insistent on this point.

'He'll be wearing slacks and a button-down shirt, possibly with one of those tank tops.' Clare sounded like she knew what she was talking about.

'How do you know?' I asked.

'Because he's middle-aged. Late middle-age. Sixty-some-thing, I think. That's what they wear.' We giggled like school-girls and hunted around the kitchen for something stronger than tea to drink. There was a bottle of sherry in the cup-board under the kitchen sink. It was being used as a gable wall for a spider's web and we backed away from it.

Jack Frost saved the day. He swept into the kitchen holding a bottle of wine in each hand like trophies, his arm draped casually across Mam's shoulders. She was looking down at his face and then I noticed that he was shorter than her – a lot shorter. Another first. And not moving away from the cir-cle of his arm but standing there, looking at him and smiling *all at the same time*. In fact, she was so distracted, she didn't even notice the cupboard door ajar with the aged sherry bot-tle shuffling nervously inside. Clare stood on one leg and gently closed the cupboard door with a foot stretched out behind her. Still nothing from my mother other than the smile that would outshine the sun. Jack took control of the situation and spoke in a voice that was altogether quieter than you would have imagined.

'Hello, Clare. Nice to see you again.' And then, 'You must be Grace.' He set the wine on the counter and walked towards me à la Bill Clinton, arm outstretched, hand splayed, face divided by a wide smile, ready to pump my arm energetically. When the handshake came, I was surprised at its brevity. Just one short shake with his right hand, his left resting gently on my elbow. He stepped back and looked at me.

'Your mother's told me all about you. It's a pleasure to meet you.'

He wore very dark, very new navy blue jeans that were turned up at the bottom. A rigid crease down the front of each leg told me exactly when he'd bought them (at 10.32 a.m. that morning, possibly in Liffey Valley). A cotton shirt – white, riddled with polka dots of every size and colour imaginable and some that were not – was unbuttoned at the top. Thick shoots of greying hair sprouted from his chest, his nose, his ears. Even his toes, strapped in unseasonal leather sandals, were matted with springy, wiry hair. And his head: I'd say he was the envy of all his peers. He could have been in an ad for any number of hair products. He was, quite simply, the hairiest man I had ever seen. I was willing to bet that his back resembled the pelt of a Canadian bear. He was still talking.

'Jack. Or John if you like. I'm a friend of your mother's. I don't want to say boyfriend. Sounds a bit batty when you get to my vintage.' Then he leaned over and kissed Ma. Right on the cake-hole. Making little sucky sounds. In front of us, me and Clare, as if we weren't there. It was Jack who pulled away first and smiled at us as if he hadn't kissed her at all.

It was only when my mother frowned at me that I realised I hadn't spoken.

'Nice to meet you too,' I surprised myself by saying. And it *was*. He was like an open fire on a winter's day.

It was a bit of a squash around the table, but we managed it. Ella insisted on sitting on Jack's knee. 'Because he's magic,' she said when questioned about it. Thomas and Matthew were more reticent than their younger sister but they listened gravely to his stories of magic and adventure, occasionally looking at each other with wide eyes.

'And did you ever see her again?' Thomas asked in a whisper. 'The woman that you made disappear but couldn't get back again?'

'And what did her children say,' asked Matthew, 'when she didn't come back?' His eyes were like saucers in his head and he looked at his mother, afraid she might disappear at any minute. Jack realised he may have gone a little too far with Matthew, who was, after all, the youngest male member of the family and impressionable.

'Oh, I got her back again. The very next day. Had to be flown back from Africa, she did. That's where she ended up.' Everybody was laughing and talking at the same time, and with our shoulders all rubbing up together and the smell of the lasagne and the red wine flowing like ribbons around us and the warmth of the kitchen, it felt like home. The way it used to be. Clare nudged me.

'Grace, Mam's talking to you.'

'Oh. Sorry, Ma, I was miles away. What were you saying?'

'I was wondering where Shane was tonight.' She said his name like there was a bad taste in her mouth. And like a tyre with a puncture, I felt the evening slipping away from me.

My mind went through various scenarios that would place Shane in a kind light and make his absence here seem perfectly acceptable, laudable even. In the end I said, 'He met Pauline, a friend of his, in town for a drink.' There was a collective intake of breath at the honesty of my answer. They knew this was the truth. I could tell by their faces. It was satisfying, actually, and I wondered why I bothered making up elaborate excuses for him before. My mother's mouth was a perfect O of horror.

She had thought the worst of Shane and it turned out she was right all along. It took her ages to collect herself.

'And, and . . . did you tell him you were coming here? For dinner? With your family?'

'Oh yeah, I told him all that. I asked him to come.' I shrugged my shoulders and crunched on a piece of garlic bread like I couldn't care less. I took a huge slug of red wine and smiled around the table. The only person who smiled back was Jack. Everyone else looked either uncomfortable (Richard and James), concerned (Clare and Jane) or thunderous (my mother). Ella, Thomas and Matthew were too busy sucking slabbydabs (a delightful mix of ice cream and fizzy orange, invented by Granny Mary) through skinny straws to pay much attention. Jack broke the atmosphere, standing up and scraping the legs of his chair along the floorboards, something that was strictly forbidden. We looked at Mam, but she was letting it go – this time. He cleared his throat, looking a little uncomfortable. Mam slipped her hand into his and he squeezed it gently.

'I just wanted to say that it's been a pleasure meeting all of you. Your mam's very proud of you all and I can certainly see why.' He looked at me when he said that and smiled.

'So, anyway,' he continued, 'I didn't want to let the opportunity pass without saying something.' He seemed unsure of what to say next, so Jane stepped in, raising her glass. 'Welcome to the family, John,' she said and was about to say something else when Ella piped up.

'Are you going to marry my granny?' She looked at Jack when she said this, her eyes as blue and as clear as a summer sky. We all roared laughing then, lifted our glasses and yelled 'cheers'. Jack leaned over and whispered something to Mam but I couldn't hear what it was over the laughing and the clinking.

After dinner, the menfolk retired to the front room to watch

the end of the golf and the children ran upstairs to the attic
– converted – that my mother had redecorated as a playroom
for them. The women sat around the table, me eyeing up
the apple tart, Clare and Jane talking about the wedding and
Mam making the tea. She hated drinking tea anywhere else
but here. Nobody did it properly any more. No one scalded
the pot – twice – before spooning the leaves in. No one waited
the *absolutely essential* three minutes for the tea to draw. No
one read the leaves that collected in soggy lumps at the bottom of the cups like she could. She hadn't done that for ages,
but she offered to do it tonight, being maybe a little tipsy from
the wine at dinner.

She told Clare that there was much to look forward to and
that she would travel over water (that's the wedding and honeymoon, see?). She told Jane that she would come into money
and, funnily enough, Jane rang the next day to tell her she'd
won €2 on a charity scratch card. I was next and I handed my
drained cup over to her. She peered into the cup, frowning in
concentration. I knew she was putting it on, for effect, but I
was still curious as to what she might say.

'Oh,' she said, 'this is interesting.' We all leaned forward. 'It's
the star symbol.' She looked up at me.

'Go on,' I said. 'What does it mean?'

'It means that there will be change.' And then as if she realised that this sounded a little ominous, she made a great play
of looking back into the cup. 'And you'll come into money
and travel across water,' she added in a way that was unconvincing at best.

There was an awkward silence.

'Who's for tart, girls?' Mam enquired.

We all agreed on a *small* slice, what with the wedding coming up and all. I made sure I got the biggest of the small slices,
which wasn't as big as I'd have liked. Afterwards, Mam cleared
her throat and looked around at us.

'As you know, it's Patrick's anniversary the week after the wedding,' she said. Jane slid her hand over Mam's and held it there.

Clare bit her lip. 'I *did* say I'd postpone the wedding until afterwards, you know.'

'No, no, I never wanted you to do that. You had it all arranged before . . .' She stumbled over the words. 'I still think you and Richard should go on honeymoon directly after the wedding instead of waiting for the anniversary.' Clare said nothing, just shook her head. 'Anyway, it's been nice, having the wedding to look forward to.' She smiled at Clare gently. I sat at the other end of the table, like the elephant in the room that everybody was ignoring.

'So, eh,' I began, not quite sure what I was going to say. Mam looked up quickly, putting her hands back around her tea cup to warm them. 'What do you want to do for the anniversary?' I asked. I didn't have a clue what people normally did, if anything.

'It'll be a low-key affair,' my mother said. 'Just mass, really. Maybe some lunch afterwards. I don't want any dramatics. Not like last time.' She looked straight at me when she said this and I felt her bitterness prick me like needles. It was never too far from the surface.

'I'm sorry, Mam. It was an asthma attack. I couldn't help it.'

'At the graveside,' she went on as if I hadn't spoken. 'Falling in the muck like a drunk.' My hands cupped the mug of tea so tightly, I thought it would shatter. I put it slowly back down on the table and sat on my hands instead.

'Mam, that's not fair,' said Clare in a low voice. 'Grace had an asthma attack, that's all.'

My mother started scraping the leftovers on the dinner plates into the empty lasagne dish. Loudly. 'We were all upset,' she said before moving away from me, towards the sink.

The clatter of dishes made any more conversation impossible, so we all busied ourselves with the clearing up. It was a relief to have something to do.

Jack came bounding into the room, stopping suddenly as if he sensed the atmosphere. 'Is everything OK?' he asked Mam. She had her back to him, pounding at dishes in the sink with a brush.

'Yes,' she said, not turning round. Jack put his hand on the small of her back and eased it up to her shoulder, like a warm iron, resting it there. He left without saying another word and Mam came to join us again at the table after a while. The three of us sat around the table where I had grown up, shovelling apple tart into our cake-holes like it was the Last Supper. The feeling was back, the panicky one that made me want to run as fast and as far away from this house as possible. It was Mam, I suppose. Her grief was like a mirror in which I could see my shame and my guilt as clear as a full moon on a cloudless night. My grief was something I had to hide in front of her. I hadn't earned it. I didn't deserve it. It was a strange feeling, hot and stifling. Like a dress that was too tight. The feeling made my breath labour and my hands curl into fists under the kitchen table. I had to leave but I didn't want to draw attention to myself. I sat there instead and drank more tea and laughed whenever anyone else did and wondered if it would always be like this.

The asthma attack had come on me so suddenly that day. All through the mass, my chest felt tight and my breathing was shallow. I was clammy and hot. I felt full, with tears not yet wept. Mam had barely spoken to me since Spain and the guilt was like a wild animal, clawing at me. It didn't happen until we were at the graveside. They were lowering him down, the dark wood of the coffin banging against the sides of the grave, as though protesting. I remember blue veins straining against the white skin of the gravediggers' arms as the ropes around the coffin lengthened. Someone threw a clod of earth down. It banged against the hard wood. My throat closed with the suddenness of a hand around my neck and I could feel myself falling and not really caring about where I landed. The earth was soft and muddy from the rain earlier. And cold. I remember how cold the ground felt beneath me. And not caring. About anything. The cold, the muck, the not breathing. It was almost a relief to lie there and for a moment I felt peace. It was Clare who found my inhaler in my bag. When the crowd around me dispersed, I saw my mother. She was halfway down the hill, walking, her back to me. I hadn't been back to the grave since then.

Eventually, Jane yawned and said she had better take the kids home. My coat was on me before she'd even finished her sentence.

'I'd better go too,' I said, head down, making a great show of fastening the buttons on my coat.

'I hope you're not picking Shane up,' my mother piped up. 'He couldn't even be bothered to show his face here tonight.'

'No Mam, I'm not,' I said, fumbling for my handbag under the table.

'Hmm,' she said, standing up and smoothing her hands down her hips. She looked down in surprise, forgetting it was jeans she had on and not her usual skirt that she always straightened when she stood up, whether it needed it or not. My hand closed around the strap of my bag and I pulled it from under the table. The strap was caught under the leg of a chair and I crawled under to release it.

'Grace, what on earth are you doing under there?' Mam said. I imagined her shaking her head and raising her eyes to heaven. I banged my head off the underside of the table in my rush to stop annoying her. I stood up unsteadily, making sure I didn't rub the throbbing part of my head. I smiled wide and long, moving towards the kitchen door with the bag clutched around my shoulder.

The feeling was bearing down on me, pushing at me like hands. I flew through the goodbyes and was nearly home and dry, the hall door in my sights, when I could hear Ella running behind me, insisting on a hug. I hunkered down and held her little body close, smelling the warm, soapy smell of her, her curly hair tickling my face. She drew back first, looking up at me.

'When I'm sad, Gwayth, I get my mam to sing me a lickle song. Will I ask her to sing you a lickle song?' I stared down at her, this pint-sized piece of perfection, and my throat was a lump. I ruffled her hair.

'I'm not sad, Ella,' I said, straightening up so my face was in shadow. 'Just a bit tired, that's all. I'll see you at the wedding, yeah?'

She nodded, blew me a kiss and skipped back towards the kitchen. I stood and watched her go and almost didn't see Jack coming out of the downstairs loo.

'Are you off, Grace?' he asked, extending his hand to me. I shook it again, nodding. Dropping my hand, he reached gently behind my ear with warm, dry fingers. He held his hand in front of me then, a euro coin between his fingers gleaming in the shadows of the hall. I laughed, feeling a little foolish.

'You're never too old for a touch of magic, you know,' he said, as if reading my mind. He handed me the coin. 'For luck,' he said, smiling at me. I took the coin and it felt warm in my hand.

'Congratulations, by the way,' he said. 'About the job, I mean,' he added when I looked blankly at him.

'How did you know?' I asked.

'Your mother told me, of course. How else? She's really proud of you.'

'Oh,' was all I could manage. I said goodbye and headed out into the night, the coin clutched in my fist.

29

I hardly noticed the journey home, which was worrying, considering that I was the one driving the car. I sat in the car outside the flat for a long time. The only sound was the hiss of each cigarette burning when I inhaled. I didn't want to go inside in case Shane was there, although that was unlikely given that it wasn't kicking out time yet. A feeling was niggling at me like an itch that I couldn't scratch. I lit up another cigarette, hating it and loving it at the same time. It was something to do, I suppose. Without the cigarette, I was just a crazy woman sitting in the dark staring out the window of a car.

The feeling was a new one. It wasn't grief, or sadness, or guilt, or frustration. It was different. It made me feel hot and itchy. It made me slump in my seat. It made me not want to open the window even a chink but to sit there, marinating in the nauseous fug of smoke. And then it came to me. I was utterly and totally and absolutely *fed up*.

There it was. That simple. I was pissed off. Tired. Sick and tired, in fact, of feeling miserable. Fed up to the back teeth with it. I'd been feeling like this for so long and now I wanted a new feeling. A change of scenery in the landscape of my head. I felt better, now that I'd identified it. I stabbed a half smoked cigarette into the ashtray, enjoying the dance of bright red sparks that soared and fell, the brightness of their light fading all the while.

The flat was empty. This didn't make me feel sad or lonely or frustrated or guilty or grief-ridden, because, you see, I was *fed up* feeling like that. Instead I felt glad and I hatched a plan in my head. The plan involved chocolate, tea, the couch, Scooby Doo slippers and a book. One of my all-time favourite books. I hadn't read it in about a year but, in total, I've read it about twelve times. I'm like that with books. When I find one I like, I *really* like it. I like it to death. This particular book was worn to a frazzle, the spine cracked in a million different places, the pages yellowing and pulpy from reading it in the bath, over and over again. Some books are just like that, aren't they? They call to you, even with their covers closed. Anyway, despite the fact that I hadn't read it in over a year, I knew *exactly* where I would find it; on the floor of my wardrobe, at the back right-hand corner. There it was, wedged between a tambourine (one of those whimsical purchases that makes perfect sense at the time) and an Afro wig borrowed for a '70s party a hundred years ago and never returned. I gathered my comforts around me like a shawl. This was good. In fact, this was better than anything I'd done in ages. Except maybe the Phoenix Park. I shut my eyes tight and forced my mind out of the park, into town, over the river, up Camden Street and back to the flat as quickly as I could manage. Bernard was on a date with Caroline and Caroline was mad about him and thinking about that made me feel sad and I was *fed up* feeling *sad*, so I wasn't going to think that thought.

It was difficult at first to open the book. The pages had stiffened and dampness held clumps of them together. I wanted to get to page 289, which was my favourite bit. I had underlined it, the third time I read it. I had to slide a nail file between pages 288 and 290 to get at it. When I did, something fell out, landing on my lap. A photograph. The picture faced me, right side up so I saw the image immediately and it made me smile and pick it up. I dusted it with the tips of my fingers. It must have been taken about two years ago, in the garden at the back of the flat. Our first attempt at a barbeque, although, as far as

I remember, we ended up ordering out for Chinese food at about midnight. The meat was hard and black on the outside, fleshy and red inside.

Patrick, Caroline and me wincing against the light of the sun. It had been one of those Indian summer nights. Patrick is in the middle, his arms around both of us, more headlock than hug. He is wearing a tall, white chef-type hat with pleats, and an apron that says 'sexy mare' (a present for me from Laura about six years ago). The three of us are in ribbons laughing. I can't remember why now, but I remember the pain in my belly from it. When you really need to stop laughing for health reasons, but you can't. The grass is high and reaches almost to our knees, giving it a meadow look, threaded as it is with all manner of wild flowers whose names I don't remember because I never knew them in the first place. It's a good photograph. A *great* photograph. The sun is setting behind the photographer and the light from it seems engrained in our faces as though they're like that all the time and not just for that one moment before the sun goes down.

I laughed then, and not the kind of laugh that's in danger of turning into a cry. A real laugh, a laugh-out-loud laugh because that's all anyone could do looking at this photograph. And because I was *fed up* with feeling miserable. I knew what I was going to do. I knew where there was a spare frame (in Caroline's room, with a picture of her and her niece in it but I knew Caroline wouldn't mind). In fact, she'd be pleased because this was going to be the first one, you see. The first picture of Patrick on display in the flat. I set it on the mantelpiece beside the lamp and it looked like it had always been there. I got back onto the couch, under the blanket, with my chocolate and tea and slippers and the book that I'd read twelve times and I turned to page 289 and began to read again.

30

Sunday was a funny day. Not funny ha-ha, more funny peculiar, really. I mean, nothing had changed, but something was different. I felt different. But life has a habit of ticking along in the same old way, even when you feel a bit different about it. For a start, Shane was still there. He had come in after I'd gone to bed and, even though I was awake, I closed my eyes when he whispered my name and kept them closed long after he'd fallen asleep.

The first thing I noticed when I got up was that Caroline was not in the flat. I knew this for a fact because I snuck into her room with an excuse all ready in my head if she was there and awake. The room was empty and the bed made. Which meant one of two things: Caroline had risen early, made her bed and gone out. Not beyond the edge of possibility, even though I know it sounds like a weird thing to do before 8 a.m. on a Sunday morning, but this was Caroline, so it was possible. Possibility No. 2: the bed had not been slept in at all, thus retaining its made look from the previous day. I ran out of the room and searched the flat for signs that she had been and gone and not just gone and not come back. Because if she'd gone and not come back, that meant that she was with Bernard O'Malley. And if she was with Bernard O'Malley at 8 a.m. on a Sunday morning, it followed logically that she had been with him since last night. I shot around the flat, eyes darting all around. The coat – my coat – that she wore last night wasn't on the coatstand. The sandals were missing from the rack where she

stacked them in order of season (I'm not making that up). The
bath was dry so she hadn't had a shower, but then, if she was
out for a jog, she'd wait until she came back to shower. She'd
hardly be out for a jog in a long coat and high-heeled sandals,
would she? I gave up and sat heavily down at the kitchen table.
Then I saw it. A note. Lodged in between the salt and pepper
cellars, with my name on it, in Caroline's writing. A note that
had not been there last night. Which meant that Caroline must
have written it this morning. Which meant that she had not
spent the night with Bernard. The relief was like the sun coming out. I reached over and tore the note open. It was short:

Grace, have gone to see Patrick. Back later, Cats. xx

Caroline often went to see Patrick. That's how she put it. She
never said she was going to the grave. Or the graveyard.

'Would you not come with me, Grace?' she asked once. I
shook my head and she didn't ask me again.

I began to worry about the implications of going to see
Patrick the morning after a date with Bernard O'Malley. Was
it a good sign? Or a really bad one? I hated myself for hoping
that it was the latter.

And then Shane arrived in the kitchen and life went back to
feeling a little bit different but being just exactly the same.

Shane and I spent the time we had on Sunday skirting
round each other, filling the spaces between us with sex and
food and beer and two sneaky fags for me, hanging out the
bathroom window and spraying clouds of deodorant around
the small room afterwards. Shane was vague about his attend-
ance at Clare's wedding the following weekend.

'I'll see, I can't make any promises. I'm very busy with work
at the moment.' And then, 'I'm here now, aren't I? For God's
sake, Grace.' I didn't mention it again after that.

He talked a lot about his job.

'I could be in line for a sales manager position in Dublin when I come back from London.'

He spoke about Brazil. Not the country, mind. No. The girl, the woman, in his office who had kindly taken Shane under her wing.

'She's a really amazing woman, Grace.'

I mean, come on. *Who* is called Brazil? If she was a character in *The Bold and the Beautiful* or a famous porn star, I could maybe accept it, but a saleswoman in the IT industry? It was too much. I could imagine what she looked like. I had to, because Shane didn't embellish on this point. She was a Latino beauty, with legs up to her well-waxed armpits, acres of coffee-coloured skin and eyelashes that curled at just the right place. Why couldn't a middle-aged man called Maurice take him under his wing? Why does that never happen?

We talked briefly about my promotion.

'Will you have to work with that geeky guy? What's his name, Brendan?'

'It's Bernard,' I corrected him quietly.

'Yeah, whatever. He's not Caroline's usual type, that's for sure. And did you see the state of his hair?' Shane's hand automatically drifted towards his head. With splayed fingers, he ran his hand across the curtain of hair that fell over one eye, gently moving it to the side. This process took about thirty seconds. I sat in silence and waited for him to finish.

'Did Caroline come home last night?' he asked me over breakfast (a bowl of muesli with Shane and then four slices of white bread and a fat wedge of cheese when he went to take his shower).

'Yeah, she did.' Just saying that made me nearly giddy with relief.

'On her own?'

I looked up slowly. Oh Christ, I hadn't thought of that

possibility. Maybe Bernard slept here last night. With Caroline. But then why did they leave so early? And why would Caroline bring him to see Patrick? Unless he dropped her at the graveyard and then went on home? Shane looked at me as this tyranny of questions crossed my face, tormenting me. I cleared my throat.

'What did you say?'

'Did she bring yer man back, what's his face, Jerard?'

'It's Bernard,' I said, gathering plates and heading to the kitchen sink with them. 'And I don't know. If she brought him back, I mean.' My back was to him and I felt safe for the moment. I could tell he was looking at me though.

'She must have ditched him.' Shane flicked a piece of dust that only he could see off the knee of his jeans.

I said nothing, but I doubted it.

'I'd say he's gay,' Shane continued when every hair on his head was as it should be. I sat back down, resisting the urge to lean across and tousle it with both hands.

Shane was the type of man who assumed that all gay men fancied him. Ciaran and Michael both wanted to ride him, according to Shane.

'Look at them looking at me,' he'd say on the rare occasions that he was in their company. 'Jesus, I'm keeping my back against the wall tonight.' He didn't get that Ciaran and Michael were equal partners in a monogamous relationship that had outlasted many of my friends' relationships. 'Queers don't have relationships, Grace. They have sex.'

There was no changing him on this point and I had stopped trying a long time ago. I was interested in his theory on Bernard's sexuality. I knew he would expand on the subject, so I waited.

'I mean, like, I'd never tell her, obviously, but Caroline was looking top notch last night. But yer man, Brendan, he hardly gave her a second glance. That's just not normal. And his voice! All low and serious and all that eye contact. It's just not natural, y'know?'

Shane looked up when I didn't respond. His eyes hovered around my face and I wondered what he was thinking but knew better than to ask.

'It's Bernard,' I said again, 'and I'm sure Caroline will be able to fill us in on his sexuality when she gets back.' I finished quickly, looking away from him. 'She's gone to visit Patrick. She left a note.'

Shane ignored the reference to Patrick, as he always did. I didn't blame him. He already blamed himself, not that he ever said, but I knew just the same. If he noticed the photograph of Patrick on the mantelpiece, he didn't mention it.

'Speaking about sexuality . . .' Shane reached for me across the table and it felt good to close my eyes and not think about anything at all.

I dropped him off at the airport at four.

'I'll ring you during the week. Let you know if I can make it to the wedding,' he said to me, his eyes scanning the screen to see where he should check in. In his mind, he was already gone as he planted a distracted kiss on the corner of my mouth.

'Shane.' My voice was urgent and high pitched and he turned back immediately.

'What is it, Grace?' He looked at his watch.

'Do you love me?' I almost said it, then stopped myself just in time. Shane hated that question. It was in the same category as 'What are you thinking about?' and 'Can I come to London with you?'

'Nothing. It'll keep.'

He didn't say anything, just raised his hand in a sort of a wave and then turned, disappearing through security. I could still see him through the gap in the smoked glass partition, struggling to get his shoes and belt off and fishing coins out of the depths of his pockets. The machine must have beeped when he strolled through it. A tiny woman with short hair framing a pretty face approached him. She was in uniform: airport security, I guessed. She said something to him, her face set. Shane's face split into a wide smile as he spread his arms and legs wide. I could see him checking her out as she swept her hands up and down both sides of his legs. When she straightened, she came up to his nipples. He bent his head to her and her mouth turned reluctantly upwards in the glimpse of a smile. Shane was working his magic. Her hands slid across his chest and down his sides. When she stepped away from him, she seemed to be blushing. Shane The Charming, I thought as I turned and walked away. My phone vibrated in my pocket and I took it out. It was a text from Caroline:

Am home now. Where are you?

Where was I? I wasn't quite sure, but I did know that I felt different. Not better or worse, but different. Even if life was plodding along in the same old way.

31

Caroline was home when I got home. In the living room. Balancing on her head.

'It's the latest thinking in clear vision.' Her voice was muffled and her face was the colour of a strawberry in season. 'Inversion therapy,' she soldiered on, her breath swallowing her words in sharp bursts.

I took my coat off, trying to ignore her.

'Dan Brown does it.'

Well, that did it for me. I mean, if Dan Brown does it . . . I lowered my head on the floor and let my hands sink into the carpet. It took much more effort than I thought to get my body airborne and upright. I flung my legs against the wall and waited for inspiration. Blood coursed down through my body towards my head.

At first, I panicked and hyperventilated, but then I forced myself to wait and gradually, a calmness came. It was unexpected, like a warm day in February.

I thought about Shane. About us. Old Man Jenkins told me to 'have a happy weekend', but I didn't. We hadn't discussed The Plans. Shane didn't bring it up again and I was afraid to. I knew that wasn't right, but I didn't know how to change it. Why did things have to be so complicated?

My legs were suddenly reefed from the wall and I was falling back towards the earth, a tumble of arms, legs and hair.

'I need to talk to you,' Caroline said.

It took me a moment to come out of my head and I did so reluctantly.

'I want to talk to you about Bernard.' I was immediately guilty, as if I had a 'I slept with Bernard O'Malley and loved it' sticker on my forehead. Had Bernard told her anything about me and him? No, of course not, don't be stupid, why would he?

'What did you say?' asked Caroline, looking at me in her face reserved for lunatics and Dublin football fans. Christ, had I been talking out loud?

'Nothing, nothing,' I said quickly. 'Go on, you wanted to talk about Bernard.' I wanted to talk about him too. I wanted to describe the weight of him on me. To howl about the softness of the skin behind his ear. The way he touched my mouth with the tips of his fingers. The way he looked at me when I was talking like he was listening to me. Really listening.

I lowered myself to a squatting position on the floor, panting. My face was red and my head throbbed from the whole standing-on-the-head business. Caroline headed into the kitchen and returned with two bottles of beer that myself and Shane had overlooked – must have put them in the vegetable compartment. Always plenty of room in there.

Caroline handed me a beer and sighed, sending a sheaf of pages on the coffee table floating gently to the floor, where they settled like lily pads on a still pond.

'I've been really stupid,' she said.

'How?'

'Because I asked Bernard . . .' She stopped there and took a long swig of her beer.

'Asked him what?' My mind was racing.

'Asked him to come to the wedding.'

Jesus. Caroline never asked anyone anywhere: she was always the ask-ee, not the ask-er.

'What did he say?'

'He's going already.'

'He's going already?'

'Bloody, bloody Wadded Willy invited him. He's his fecking third cousin, twice removed or something.'

'No, he's his first cousin, remember? One of a set of twin boys.' I pictured them on the beach that day. Two boys, hair falling across freckled faces. Arms wrapped around each other. 'His mother is Mary, Wadded Willy's father's younger sister,' I explained.

Caroline looked at me like I was pure mental.

'How do you know all that?'

'I asked Clare. Just out of interest, I mean. At dinner. Last night.' I spoke quickly, not looking at her.

'But that's not the shagging point, is it?' she roared at me.

I was confused now.

'I mean, just because he's going anyway doesn't mean he can't go with me. You know. As my, my . . .' her struggle to say the word was crucifying to watch.

'Your boyfriend?' I nudged gently.

'Well, no, I mean, like . . . you know, my partner. Just for the day, I mean. Not like a long-term commitment or anything like that. Just my, like, partner. For the day, like.'

'So what did he say?'

'I *told* you what he said.'

'And what did you say?' This conversation was like pulling back teeth, only harder.

'Nothing. I said absolutely, bloody, sodding nothing at all.'

She looked spent then, slumped on the couch, hair falling about her face, chin in her hands. I was desperate to hear about her date last night with Bernard, but just as desperate not to know. Had he kissed her? Had he taken her to the park? Had he told her she was an interesting woman? Maybe he does that to all the women he meets? Kisses them, takes them to the park and tells them they're interesting? And the worst bit, were they going to see each other again?

'I'd really love to see him again,' Caroline said.

'And are you going to?' I held my breath, waiting for her to answer. This was like a car crash where you don't want to see but you can't look away.

'I don't know. He didn't ask me and after the whole wedding bit, I didn't mention it.'

'Hot chocolate,' I declared to the room, standing up.

'Huh?' Caroline dragged her head up to look at me.

'And a hot water bottle,' I finished dramatically.

'But it's not cold.'

'No matter. It's just what you need. And a Maeve Binchy book.'

'A Maeve Binchy book?' She looked blankly at me.

'Yes, yes, yes. It's the best cure there is for contrariness and angst. Trust me.'

She nodded hopefully at me then, like a six-year-old with the stump of a bloody tooth under her pillow.

Jesus. Men. Had they any idea of the torment we embraced in their name? And Caroline's torment was caused by none other than Bernard O'Malley. This fact sat uneasily in my stomach, like a doughy pizza.

I tucked Caroline into bed like a mother hen, wrapping the duvet around her so tightly she could barely move. Her face was red from the heat of the hot water bottle and an ageing copy of *Circle of Friends* waited, like a soother, on the locker beside her bed.

'I like the photograph, by the way,' she said quietly.

'Oh, yeah, well. It's a good one of him. I thought it would be nice to have it in a frame.' I looked at her and she nodded, smiling.

'I'm glad you did, Grace,' she said. 'I really am.' She lay back against the pillow, looking suddenly exhausted. I turned off the lamp beside her bed.

'Go to sleep now, Cats. Things will seem better in the morning.' I laughed at myself saying that. It was something that my mother used to say to us, when we were younger. Caroline didn't answer and I thought she was already asleep. I moved quietly towards the door, opening it.

'Grace,' Caroline whispered from the bed. I turned back to her. The light from the hall crept over her face, giving her a ghostly look.

'Yeah?' I whispered back.

'I think I love him.' The words cut through the dark like knives.

'I'll see you in the morning,' I managed. I went into my bedroom and closed the door, not turning on the light. I stood in the darkness, cooling the heat of my face against the windowpane. I stood there for a long time.

32

Jane rang first thing in the morning. Which was a good thing really, because I'd forgotten to set my alarm and it was the first day of my New Job and if you're going to be late for work, it's always advisable not to choose the first day of your New Job to do it. Best to wait a week or two before indulging in my customary tardiness.

Jane was her usual brisk and efficient self, greeting me with her customary 'How are you? Good? Good.'

'The reason I'm calling,' she began, 'is to remind you that Granny Mary needs a pick-up from the airport this evening.'

Granny Mary? Airport? No bells rang in my head.

'You haven't forgotten, have you?'

Jane's tone kick-started my brain and I was able to say, 'Of course I haven't forgotten. I'll be there.' Of course I had forgotten. I couldn't even remember where Mary was at the moment. Somewhere in Latin America, I thought. Or maybe South-East Asia? Most other grannies went on organised coach tours or sleepy cruises, played lots of bridge and bingo and shuffled around dance floors to waltzes designed to guide you gently to the grave. Mary didn't do things like that. She *travelled*, with a backpack and a walking stick, to places most decent folk have never heard of, by herself.

'I presume you still have that email I sent you with her flight details and her ETA?' Jane was still talking. She loved abbreviations. 'I sent it to Clare too so if you've lost it, I'm sure Clare will still have it.'

'No, no, I have it.' Brilliant. I could ring Clare later and get the details. She wouldn't have deleted the mail.

'I'd do it myself, of course, but I've got parent-teacher meetings this evening for Thomas and Matthew.' I smiled at that. Jane wouldn't miss a parent-teacher meeting for the world. She loved them: the teachers loved her boys almost as much as she did.

'Don't worry, I'll do it. I don't mind.' And I didn't. Mary always gave me a laugh. Plus, I didn't have anything else on. Or did I? I frowned, trying to remember if Clare had signed me up for any chief bridesmaid-type activities. I didn't think so. She had done everything herself months ago.

'OK so, thanks,' said Jane. 'I'd better go. It's my turn to car-pool and the scones aren't even out of the oven yet. See you soon. Bye. Bye. Bye. Bye. Bye.' Jane never just said goodbye on the phone. She was still saying 'bye, bye, bye' when I hung up. And what was the story with the scones? It was seven o'clock in the sodding morning, for Christ's sake. Oh shit, seven o'clock in the sodding morning and I hadn't showered yet and Caroline was already in the bathroom and there was an outside chance that I might be late for work on this, the first day of my New Job.

As it turned out, I was not late for work. I was early, having sacrificed the lure of breakfast. Three-quarters of an hour early, to be exact. Which would have caused a riot among my colleagues had any of them been in at that time, which, of course, they were not. It was 8.15 a.m. when I arrived at my new desk. Right there beside Bernard's desk, rammed up against it, in fact, like a sign. There was a mug – bright orange – on the desk, wrapped in a pink ribbon and bow, like a car-nival. Lopsided bulging lovehearts in bright pink were splat-tered around the outside of the mug. A yellow stickie was on the handle: *I saw this mug and thought of you. Good luck in the new job. Bernard.* I picked up the mug. The hearts were raised and riotous. What did it mean? Probably nothing. Still, it was lovely. Just what I would have picked. And my favourite colours too. A lucky guess probably. Or just a coincidence. I set the mug back down quickly and glanced around. Still no one about. A good time to revisit the 'to do' list I had compiled in my head on the drive to work that morning:

1. Will try to sort things out with Shane. Not that there was anything to sort, as such. It was just . . .well, the weekend had felt kind of . . . flat, I suppose. And one-year-nine-months-three-weeks-and-four-days is a lot of time to invest in a relationship. Or was it four-weeks-and-three-days? Wasn't sure. Which proved that I needed to concentrate on our relationship more. More than I had been doing, anyway. Since I . . . well, since I slept with Bernard, I suppose. Since I got *drunk* and slept with Bernard. There *is* a difference.

2. Will take my role as chief bridesmaid seriously. Not only that, but will be a shining example to chief bridesmaids everywhere. May even write a 'how to' book on the duties of the chief bridesmaid.

3. Will develop good relationship with my mother. We had one once and we could have one again. Maybe. Can at least try.

4. Will visit Patrick's grave. When? Soon . . .

5. Will remember to pick up Granny Mary at airport tonight.

6. Will forget about Bernard O'Malley. Who? See? It's working already.

I picked up the mug – it seemed churlish not to use it – and headed to the kitchen, where I made physical contact, in an unintentional way, with the boss, who was hovering inside the kitchen door, possibly admiring his reflection in the stainless steel toaster on the counter.

'Ah, Grace.' He always said that when he saw me, as if he were surprised that I managed to make it into work or indeed that I still had a job in the company. 'Big day today, eh?' He grinned at me then, as if he had said something funny.

'Eh, yes. I'm just settling into my new desk,' I said, backing up. 'Wanted to get an early start, you know.'

'Quite, quite,' he said. 'We've set you up beside Bernard O'Malley. Have you met him yet?'

'Yes, I have.' I was impressed at my impassive tone.

'Think you'll work well together,' said the boss, pressing his thick fleshy fingers around the mug of coffee he held in both hands. 'O'Malley has been involved in this type of project before, in the last company he worked for.' The boss always called his male subordinates by their surnames. It could have been a power thing. Or maybe it was because he was from Tipperary and that's how they did things down there.

'I'm sure we will,' I said, edging past his bulk towards the coffee machine that made low spitting noises, filling the kitchen with the thick, heady smell of Monday morning. My stomach growled and my hand tightened around the low-fat yoghurt I had taken from Caroline's stash that morning. I forgot to mention number seven in my to do list:

7. No proper food until after the wedding.

'You and Bernard will be working closely together.' The boss was still talking, holding the kitchen door open with the toe of his . . . oh God, was that an ankle boot? With a heel? It bloody well was. Look away, look away, don't laugh, don't snort, don't grin and for God's sake *don't mention it*. Which brings me to number eight on the to do list:

8. Develop *brilliant* relationship with boss to enhance career prospects.

Laughing at his boots (the *state* of them) would not bring me closer to this goal. I dragged my head up and forced myself to make eye contact with him.

'I want you to debrief him on the liability requirements and then the three of us can meet later in the week to discuss the preliminaries, OK?'

So, I was to debrief Bernard, eh? I know I shouldn't have found this funny, but I did: Monday morning on an empty stomach, that was the problem.

I nodded, not trusting myself to speak, then half turned, edging towards the coffee machine, which was still gurgling in the background.

'OK, Grace, get some coffee and I'll see you later.' He hovered at the door for a moment, then turned and left, leaving me alone with the coffee machine, which is as it should be at – I checked my watch – 8.24 in the morning.

From the kitchen, I detoured to the stationery cupboard, stocking up on paperclips (the pink ones), yellow stickies and a range of gel pens in sparkly blues and greens that had, somehow, made it past the beady eyes of Jennifer, who checked the orders religiously, except when she was riddled with PMT and couldn't care less if we ordered Ferraris and champagne. We tracked her cycle with stealth and knew exactly when to strike.

Thus armed, I headed back to my desk, which immediately felt more like home when I dumped my colourful stash and splashed some coffee on it. Still no one around, so I logged onto the email. As usual, there were lots of them, mostly worky ones and I had to scroll down for ages till I found anything interesting. One from Laura. Subject: Exclusive!! I was just about to read it when she appeared at my desk.

'What the hell are you doing here so early?' she said.

'It's the first day of my New Job.'

'Oh yeah, your new job. I forgot.'

'What's your excuse?' I asked her.

'Couldn't sleep.' She was distracted, her head snatching this way and that.

'He's not in yet,' I put her out of her misery. 'What's the story? I'm just reading your *exclusive* email.'

Laura's smile could have lit up the Christmas tree on O'Connell Street.

'It's me and Peter. We spent the weekend together. Again. We're *going out together*. You know. Exclusive.' The smile was gone and the office dimmed.

'That's good, isn't it? That's what you wanted, right?' My tone was soft, encouraging. This was a delicate time for Laura. She was like a victim of an accident, learning to walk again. Wanting to, but not sure if she could.

'Look at me Grace. Just look at the cut of me.'

And she *did* look different. Fuller, somehow. Shiny and colourful. And tired, like she hadn't slept for days, which she probably hadn't.

'And I can't stop smiling either.' She tried to straighten the upturned corners of her mouth into her usual pout. 'And I'm *twitchy*,' she continued, pointing to an area of her neck where a muscle pulsed.

I patted her hand, smiling at her. 'Laura, your symptoms are normal.'

'Are they?' she asked, looking at me like I was an authority on the subject.

I opened a notebook and took up one of my new gel pens. 'You can't sleep, right?'

'No.'

I bent my head and scribbled on the page. 'How's your appetite?'

'Gone.'

Another scribble. 'What about coherent thoughts, unrelated to the subject matter?'

'None.'

More furious scribbling. 'Work?'

'Haven't done any in over a week.'

'Exercise?'

'You mean apart from . . .'

'Yes, apart from that.' She shook her head sadly. Laura *loved* to exercise.

'How often have you been checking your make-up and hair?' I looked up at her, my pen poised.

'On the hour, every hour.'

'Ok, this is an important one,' I said, doodling very officiously in my notebook. 'When was the last time you wore uncoordinated bra and knickers?' She shook her head slowly.

'It's been over a week now. Oh, God.'

'Yes, Laura, it's official,' I said, adding up the ticks on the page. 'You. Are. In. Love.'

'Oh, Jesus.' She sank into the seat in front of my desk, exhausted. From the look of her, I'd say she'd been up since about six that morning, straightening her hair, waxing her legs, ironing her knickers and possibly even shopping because the dress she was wearing looked suspiciously new.

'Go with it, Laura,' I leaned across the desk to whisper to her.

'Go with it?' She looked at me as if I'd just said 'liver is delicious'. Laura felt strongly about liver: 'It's not a meal. It's an internal organ, for Christ's sake.' She had *views* on liver.

'It's not going to be like last time. Take a chance. Risk it. You're in danger of being happy. Just let it rip.'

Laura sighed long and hard. 'I'd better go up to accounts and do some work. Otherwise nobody's going to get paid this month.'

'OK, then. See you later. What about lunch?'

'Lunch?' Laura looked confused.

'Yeah, you know, the meal between breakfast and dinner.

The one with paninis and smoothies and bagels and chips-but-only-if-it's-payday-or-Friday-or-a-PMT-riddled-day-or-raining?' Using these criteria, I got to have chips most days, but not this week. This week I was going to eat lettuce and love it – how bad could it be, right?

'Oh, lunch, yeah, sure.' Laura wandered away from my desk like a child lost in the zoo.

Back to my emails. Surprisingly, there was one from Shane. He had sent it last night, after midnight:

Hey baby, loved our weekend. Am missing you like crazy already. Have decided to come over next weekend for the wedding. I know you really want me to so don't say I never do anything for you. Will fly in Sat morning and pick you up from the flat. See you then.

It was only when I finished reading the mail that I realised I had straightened five of my one hundred pink paperclips, rendering them useless for anything other than the bin. I found an empty bin under my desk and threw them in there, where they made five tight little pings against the metal bottom. I kicked the bin for good measure. Hard. This made a louder noise and Niall, the IT director, curled his head around his office door and looked at me.

'Everything OK Grace? Settling in all right?'

Niall was what you might call a Family Man. The walls of his office were covered with crooked pictures of his wife, kids (four of them), dog (Mohamed Ali), cats (two; Grant and Phil) and rabbit, even though he had died years before of a broken heart after the girl rabbit next door was put down for shagging people's legs whenever they stepped into the back garden. Especially if they were wearing tall boots. Especially black ones, which was the colour of Ambrose, Niall's rabbit.

Niall brought a packed lunch every day, in a plastic box with his name laminated on the top. Some days he got a fairy cake in the box, along with his usual salami sandwich. Or a piece of fruit. Once he got a bun with his name scrawled in pink icing across the top. It was his birthday that day. He was a man who was much loved and, even though his hair was grey and sparse and his head was too big for his body, he looked lucky.

'Fine, Niall. Grand. Just getting myself organised here.' I smiled at him. It was hard not to. I got up and headed towards the loo. Shane's email had unsettled me. Last week, I would have been grateful for it. Now I felt angry. I burned with it. It was an unfamiliar sensation and I realised that I hadn't felt angry in a long time. I'd forgotten what a positive feeling it can be. How it can channel your energies, help you focus. When I got back to my desk, I pounded at my keyboard in a most unforgiving way until, before I knew it, it was nearly 11 o'clock and I was halfway through the debriefing document for Bernard. I was going to debrief that boy until he begged me to stop. I laid the palm of my hand across the keyboard. It was hot. I looked around. Peter was at his desk, looking exhausted and thinner than I remembered. No sign of Bernard. Where was he? I arranged my face in a bored, offhand expression and sauntered over to Peter's desk.

'Any idea what time Bernard is coming in at?'

Peter looked up and stared at me as if he had never seen me before in his life. Laura had really gone to town on him. He was ghostly pale with at least two days' growth edging up his face. But then he smiled and I knew Laura was going to be OK. Things were going to work out for those two. It was all there, in his smile.

'He's not coming in today,' Peter said. Disappointment hit me like a bucket of cold water. I hadn't realised I'd been waiting for Bernard all morning. To sit down opposite me and smile with those dimples like punches in his cheeks. Despite number six on my spanking new to do list.

'He had to go to the Galway office this morning. Their server is acting up.' Peter was talking again, pecking away on his keyboard at the same time. IT people can do that. He looked up from his screen when I didn't move away. 'He'll be back tomorrow probably. Or maybe Wednesday.'

'Thanks, Peter. How was your weekend, by the way?' I was rewarded with a jerk of his head. Almost a spasm.

'Fine, grand, yeah.' And then he remembered his manners. 'How was yours?'

'Pretty crap to be honest. But in a good way.' I didn't realise that I was going to say that but it didn't matter really. Because Peter wasn't listening. Not really. He was in love, see? With Laura from accounts. Sometimes Monday mornings can be just perfect. I headed out for a smoke.

I hadn't seen Ciaran since our weird conversation last Thursday. He was still there, still in the security hut, still with the unlit pipe and the slow smile. I loved that about Ciaran. There was something so constant about him. He made me feel safe. He was already making the coffee when I stepped into the hut, his back to me. When he turned around, holding out a steaming mug to me, he looked tired. For the first time since I met him, I wondered how old he was. Maybe fifty-five? Possibly sixty?

'How was your weekend with Shane?' Ciaran eased himself into a plastic chair that was bright orange and totally devoid of comfort. He waved a hand towards the other chair and I sat in it, my hands wrapped around the coffee cup. It was cold in there today. Ciaran noticed because he nodded towards the drawer where he kept his whiskey.

'Not today, Ciaran. It's the first day of my New Job. I'm being good.'

He nodded and smiled his slow smile at me, waiting.

'Weekend with Shane was . . .' And then I stopped. What was it? How could I describe it? Suddenly, it seemed important to use the right word.

'Interesting,' was the best I could do.

'Hmm,' Ciaran said, nodding as if he agreed with my choice of word, taking another drag of his pipe, his whole body bending into it.

'He's coming over. Next weekend. For the wedding, I mean.' I set the coffee down and lifted a finger to my mouth, worrying at a nail.

'Aye,' Ciaran said, taking a sip from his mug. The coffee must have gone down the wrong way and he coughed, bending in two with the effort of it. I thumped him on the back. I could do it with full force. Ciaran was a big man and could take it. His cough sounded harsh. Chesty. I glanced around the flimsy hut. The two bar heater was not on and I ran to plug it in.

'Jesus, Ciaran, it's freezing in here. You'll catch your death.' I grabbed his coat from the hanger behind the door and drew it around his shoulders. 'You need to take care of yourself. You're not getting any younger, you know, like the rest of us.' I tried to make it light, smiling at him. He patted my hand, straightening.

'Don't worry, Grace gurrill. I'm not going anywhere.'

I hustled up the usual suspects for lunch and we braved the canteen downstairs, where lettuce was limp and chips were full-fat and served with everything. It was cheap though, subsidised by the company.

'An army marches on its stomach,' the boss was fond of saying, patting his paunch that edged over the belt of his trousers.

Ethan, Norman and Jennifer stared with open mouths at my plate of limp lettuce leaves and tuna salad. The plate looked huge under the forlorn little mound of food. Even Laura came out of her stupor to comment.

'You're not actually going to eat that, are you?'

The truth of it was that I was starving and would have eaten a baby's arse through the bars of a cot if it had been on the menu. Which it wasn't. Company policy, apparently.

'Peter is in love, by the way,' I said, shovelling a forkful of corn into my mouth, washing it down with water.

Laura stiffened, sitting up.

'Don't say that,' she said, her voice a whisper. 'Don't say it unless you know it for a fact.'

I took another slug of water. Jesus, who *makes* this stuff?

'I'm positive,' I said. 'He's displaying all the classic signs.' Heads nodded around the table as if there was a list of *classic signs* pinned to a notice board in reception. Norman set his knife and fork down on either side of his plate.

'What are his symptoms?' he asked, as if Peter were a malaria patient in some hospital tent in a refugee camp.

'Well,' I began and four heads leaned towards me, making it hard to breathe. 'He has done not one iota of work this morning.' More nodding heads. 'In fact, I don't think he's even switched on his computer, but he keeps tapping away at the keyboard like it's on. Like he *thinks* it's on.' I drew back from them, to get some air and to let them digest that little nugget.

'And,' I continued, 'he rang his mother and apologised for not showing up for dinner yesterday. And for not ringing her to tell her he wasn't showing up for dinner yesterday. He must have completely forgotten about it.'

Laura smiled at that. 'We were very busy yesterday afternoon,' she said smugly.

'Shagging on a Sunday afternoon? How passé.' Norman was unimpressed.

'No,' Laura whispered, looking around her to make sure no one else could hear. 'It's worse than that.'

'What?' Jennifer said, her face alive with possibilities. We all leaned towards Laura now. Her face was a curious mix of shame and uneasy happiness.

'We were . . .' She stopped, sucking on her bottom lip with her two top teeth. She looked adorable and I patted her hand.

'Go on,' I coaxed, wondering what the hell she was going to say. My mind had gone blank. I mean, this was *Laura* we were talking about.

'We went for a walk. In some class of a park.' She drew back in her seat and looked around the table, gauging our reaction to this outrage. When no one said anything, she went on.

'We bought rolls. Cuisine de France ones. And fed the ducks. We sat on a bench and he kissed me without asking me to go into the public toilets or the bushes or anything. And we held hands.'

'In public?' Norman could barely get the words out. Laura nodded and then laughed out loud. Her happiness was like another person sitting at the table, it was that present.

'That's it? That's all you did?' Jennifer looked disappointed. This was so un-Laura-like behaviour. Where was the drama? The up-against-the-pebble-dashed-wall-sex? The scandal? The welts/burns/bruises? The embarrassing scene with wild animals and handcuffs and normal people standing around in a circle with their mouths gaping? Laura laughed again and for a moment I saw her face before the heartbreak had set in (Allen broke up with her three weeks before the wedding) and before she had embarked on her chosen path of hardened commitment to never committing. I saw the face that I remembered from years before and then it disappeared as suddenly as the sun on a winter's evening.

'And then we went home and I wouldn't let him go to sleep until we'd christened every room in the house.' She flicked her thick blonde hair over her shoulder and pursed her lips in a 'so there' kind of a way. We were suitably impressed. Laura's dad – a minted hotelier – had bought the house for Laura in Rathmines. It was his wedding present to his only child and even though the wedding never happened, Laura lived there: it was her monument to disappointment and she clung to it like a life belt. It was a modestly sized house, but still, there were at least eight rooms in the place. We were impressed with her stamina – and Peter's, God love him.

Laura sat back and slowly sucked her smoothie through a straw. The conversation was over.

'So, Grace.' Norman turned to me and smirked. 'What's new and improved with you, then?' He made a bridge with his hands and set his pointed chin on it.

'Apart from my fabulous New Job? My promotion, if you will?' I was still a little stunned about that, to be honest. Norman nibbled the icing off the top of his muffin and waved my words away with a flick of his wrist.

'Christ, no. With Shane. And Bernard.' He looked at me from underneath thick black eyebrows with devilish intent. I decided to get stuck straight into number six on my new to do list. No time like the present.

'It's funny you should mention Bernard,' I began, mopping up crumbs of tuna with a chip stolen from Jennifer's gorgeously laden plate. They leaned closer. 'He went on a blind date with Caroline last week.' I sat back, enjoying the communal look of confusion.

'With *Fabulous* Caroline?' Ethan said, finally getting a word in edgeways. He, like most of his male colleagues, was in love with Caroline. He was also a little afraid of her, which added to the tension of his feelings.

'The very one,' I said, taking another chip from Jennifer's plate, then putting it back again.

'I thought you went out with him on Friday?' Norman wasn't going to let it go.

'I just got a lift with him.' I looked pointedly at Laura, who had the grace to look away.

'There's more,' I said, enjoying the way Laura's head snapped back towards me.

'What is it?' said Ethan and I could see he had his fingers crossed below the table, hoping it was something his heart could stand. I hoped it was too.

'Caroline's in love with him.' Nobody spoke for several seconds. I couldn't blame them.

'But . . . but Caroline's never been in love,' Jennifer finally said. And it was true, until now. Their reaction – open mouths and silence – brought it home to me. Caroline was in love with Bernard O'Malley. And who could blame her? The only person I could blame was myself and it was too late even for that.

33

I hated waiting at airports. It reminded me of Spain.

I took the escalator downstairs to arrivals. I always felt like I was in several different movies at once. Some mainstream, some alternative, some just downright weird – or French/Eastern European, if you prefer. I bought a frothy cappuccino from a little kiosk and settled down in a plastic seat to watch.

There he was. The guy with the enormous bunch of flowers. There's *always* a guy with flowers. And if you look very carefully, you'll notice at least one shaving nick, usually along the sensitive neck area. Shaving under pressure, y'see? It simply should not be done. He was handsome enough but had unfortunately disproportionate limbs: his arms were too long for his body and hung down towards his knees, not knowing what to be doing with themselves.

A girl stood as close as she could to the barrier without knocking it over. She looked like she was holding her breath. Her T-shirt – tight and pink – bore the words 'welcome home baby' in CAPITAL LETTERS with lots of exclamation marks!!!!!!!!!!!!!!!!!! Had she forgotten the name of the person she was meeting or was she just hedging her bets in case someone better passed through the doors?

A man who looked like Patrick was stooped low beneath layers of bags draped across both of his shoulders. His breath strained against the weight. He stopped suddenly and a group of Spanish students knocked into his back, nearly toppling him. His eyes ran through the waiting crowd. I lifted myself out of my seat and took two steps towards him before I stopped. A smile of recognition crossed his face and he disappeared into the crowd, leaving a clutch of students in his wake. I craned my neck to see who was meeting him but the crowd was thick. Stepping backwards, I lowered myself back into the seat. Except it was no longer vacant – I was now sitting in the lap of a teenage boy who was busy squeezing the tip of a long, narrow spot on his chin. I yelped and jumped up.

'Jesus, sorry, I didn't see you there. Are you all right?' I asked.

The spot had reddened to a pulsing purple with the pressure of his fingers around it and burst with such simplicity, leaving a tiny string of perfectly white pus stretching along his finger nail. He looked at me with an innocence that could be bottled, it was so potent. His eyes settled on mine and he smiled.

'No worries, missus.'

Jesus, what age did he think I was? Missus? I'm only twenty-nine, thank you very much, young man, I almost said. Instead I turned and headed for the kiosk to get some water (I'd developed a taste for it since my lunchtime experience). Before I reached the shop, I heard it. The whooping, the shrieks, the downright, old-fashioned excitement of reunion. I knew who it was before I turned back to look. Yes, the guy with the flowers. He was swinging an exquisite creature around the lobby, her hair spread out behind her like a carousel. The flowers had been discarded on the ground, their colours now dimmed by the extravagance of the public display of passion. They stopped swinging and kissed in that slow, languorous way, his hands threaded through her hair. I was not the only one looking their way. A happy ending. That's what we were all thinking. We'll have one of those, thank you very much. Plus a bucket of your fattest, whitest, saltiest popcorn, saturated with real butter and a sack of Minstrels that reseal at the top, just so you can laugh and shake your head at such nonsense; resealing a bag of Minstrels . . . who does that?

Granny Mary stepped in front of me and smiled. How did she know where I was and why hadn't I seen her coming through the sliding doors? But that was the mystery of Mary, I suppose. She smiled with her teeth pushed over her lips, not caring that her teeth were long and yellow with a piece of rasher rind caught between the two longest ones at the front. There was something in her hand that she waved at me. A wooden carving. Maybe an elephant? With a very long trunk.

'It's for fertility, Grace,' she bellowed at me.

Being slightly deaf in her right ear, she assumed the rest of us were similarly aurally challenged. People turned to look, as they always did. I took the statue from her outstretched hand and looked at it. It wasn't an elephant. It was a man. With no face and a penis. A long, thick one that I was holding in my hand. I dropped it like a hot stone into my bag and looked at Mary. She would have been as tall as me, were it not for the stoop in her back that grew more pronounced every time I saw her. This was not helped by the rucksack that rose behind her shoulders, strewn with ribbons and flags and shells on rough string, dangling and rustling when she walked.

'I'll get a trolley for you, Mary. Wait here.' I began to walk away when she grabbed my arm. Her hands were like shovels and her grip was strong.

'I'm not dead yet, girl,' she said. 'Come here to me.' She was difficult to hug with the rucksack on her back, but I did it anyway. Her long grey hair fell in a thick rug down her back and smelled of warm apples.

Mary pulled back and held me at arm's length, looking me up and down like I was a horse she was thinking of buying.

'You've gotten thin, Grace,' she said, as if she were addressing the entire arrivals department and not just me, two feet in front of her. More people looked and I squirmed under their scrutiny. Jesus, they must have been thinking I was a right whale before.

'Come on,' I said. 'Let's get out of here. Do you want to go straight home? Or will I take you to Mam's first?'

'Jesus no, girl,' Mary said, bending to pick up a circle of crumpled plastic bags that lay around her feet. More fertility presents, no doubt.

'I want to go to a pub. I want to drink whiskey in a good, heavy, clean glass. And a beer garden where I can have a fag.' She looked at me and I nodded, prising the bags from her hand. This was something I could do. A request I could manage.

'Follow me,' I told her with authority. The pair of us parted the crowds easily, with our height and with Mary's rucksack like a weapon of mass destruction about to detonate.

I took her to her local in Baldoyle, where she was welcomed back with all the excitement of a soldier returning from the war.

'Mary?'

'Is it yourself?'

'You're looking well.'

'Is it true you joined a tribe? Went native, like? Like what's-his-face-in-that-fillum?'

'You'll have a drink on the house, Mary?' This got an immediate response from Granny, who roared at the barman through the barricade of aged fans around her.

'A whiskey for me and one for the girl, Paddy. No ice, no water, no messin'.' Paddy, who had stood behind that counter since I was a slip of a thing with a bottle of TK red lemonade, a straw and a packet of crisps, mouthed, 'The usual?' at me and I smiled at him with a covert nod.

'So,' Mary said when she'd finally escaped from her Dublin fan base. We sat in the beer garden, under the shelter of a patio heater that glowed orange at the top, like embers. Even so, it was cold and I took my hair down and pulled it about my shoulders, like a shawl.

'Tell me what's been going on.' She opened her pouch of tobacco and spilled some along the thin white paper she laid flat on the table. It smelled old and sweet. She pressed the tobacco down gently with two fingers and brought the paper slowly to her lips, savouring the process. She rolled the cigarette carefully between her fingers and accepted a light from me. The whole process took about ten seconds. She'd been doing it since she could sit on her long hair.

She pulled long and hard on her cigarette, worrying at it like a dog with a bone. But then – and here's the crucial bit – she opened her mouth wide, letting the clouds of smoke float out and up, where they hung around her head like a halo. She didn't inhale. Never had. 'Like Bill Clinton, wha?' she always said with her evil genius cackle. I lit up, took a long draught from my glass (gin and tonic, not my usual per se, but the drink I always drank in Granny's local) and looked around me as if checking for eavesdroppers. I was going to enjoy this. Granny watched my performance with studied disinterest.

'Mam's got herself a boyfriend,' I said at last. Granny shot forward in her seat and thumped her knees with the palm of her hands. Hard.

'About bloody time,' she said, whacking her knees with both hands and rocking in her chair with what I can only describe as glee. Her stick, leaning heavily against the table, clattered to the ground.

'What's his name?' she asked when she regained what passed as composure in her world. I went in for the kill.

'Jack Frost,' I said with a straight face.

'You're making that up.'

'It's true.'

'It can't be.'

'It is. Swear on Pop's grave.' Pop was what we called Granny's husband when he was alive. Which he wasn't. Not for years. You could talk about dead people with Mary. She was matter-of-fact about dead people, and death in general. Which was refreshing in one so old.

'I suppose you're going to tell me next that he's a weatherman or some such nonsense.'

'No, God, nothing like that,' I assured her. 'He's a magician.' I said it like you might say 'he's a plumber' and she was off again, slapping her knees and bending over double with her laugh that sounded like a dog barking.

'Christ, but that's great altogether,' she said, draining her whiskey noisily. 'He sounds so *unsuitable*.' Mary beamed at me, delighted that her daughter of around sixty years of age was finally displaying wayward tendencies, even if they weren't as wayward as Mary might have liked.

I told her about Mam clearing out Patrick's room. I could talk to Mary about Patrick. She accepted his death like she accepted everything else. She wasn't happy about it, but that was life and there was nothing to be done about it. If she heard the bitterness in my voice when I told her about the black rubbish bags and the bare walls, she gave no sign of it. She just nodded as I spoke.

'Good, good,' she said. 'She's moving on. It's high time.'

'It's not high time. It's too bloody soon. It's not even a year yet,' I reminded her.

'It'll be a year next Tuesday, won't it?' And in that sentence I caught a glimpse of her grief. She may not have gnashed her teeth and pulled at her hair and wept him a river, but she had counted the days. That seemed almost sadder.

'Anyway,' I said, straightening up in my seat, 'you'll like Jack. But you have to remember to call him John in front of mam.'

Granny went off to get more drinks. She insisted.

'Paddy'll probably give me another round on the house,' she hissed at me as she heaved herself off the chair. 'God help him but he's a desperate auld softie, that fella.'

'Just a tonic for me this time,' I said. 'I'm driving.' I had time to smoke an entire cigarette during her absence and I was just about to head back into the bar when she reappeared, laden down with glasses of whiskey (three: the lads insisted) and a skinny little bottle of slimline tonic for me. I poured it into my glass and took a sip.

'Jesus, it tastes manky without the gin,' I said, my voice straining like I'd just sucked on a lemon.

'I don't know why you can't drink and drive any more,' said Mary, shaking her head with her lips sewn tightly together. She looked like Mam when she did that.

'It's against the law,' I explained, not for the first time.

'It wasn't in my day,' she said, lining her whiskeys in a row in front of her in some kind of order that only she understood. I changed the subject, knowing from experience that this was not an argument I could win, despite having logic and right and the law on my side.

'So,' she said, disappointed that I had given in so easily, 'what's the story with you? Are you still going out with that fella who loves himself?' You might say that my granny didn't mince words. She maintained that when you're on the brink of death like she was, there simply wasn't time.

'Yes,' I said and she waited for me to elaborate. 'Ish,' I finished.

'Ish?' She brightened and leaned towards me, her drink in a grip that whitened her knuckles.

'Well, technically, we are still going out. And he's coming over for Clare's wedding. That's what did it, really.'

'What do you mean?'

'Well, he just announced he was coming. By email. Last night. Well, this morning really. I mean, yes, he was invited and all, but he's been saying for weeks and weeks that he can't come, he's too busy, I'm to stop asking him and then, suddenly, he turns round and he's coming without checking that it's still OK or . . . or anything.' I trailed off. This was not a good enough reason. Another breath in and I was off again.

'And he said in his mail that he'd fly in on Saturday morning and pick me up from the flat. He's just so blasé. And not just about that, about everything. I mean, I'm the chief bridesmaid. I'm going to be busy on Saturday morning. I'm not even going to be at the flat.' I was working myself up into quite a frenzy and absentmindedly took a large swallow from one of Mary's drinks. The whiskey ripped a path down my throat and left me gasping. Mary thumped me on the back. Hard. Christ, she was strong. I scraped my chair back, moving to just beyond her reach.

'I'm fine, I'm fine,' I rasped, holding my hands in front of me, protectively.

'Well, it's a weird reason to break up with someone, but I'm glad you're doing it in any case.' Mary leaned back in her chair and smiled, as if she had just found the solution to world hunger without the help of Sir Geldof or his trusty steed, Bono.

'But I'm not breaking up with him.' Panic pushed against the inside of my head.

'You're not?' Mary was not convinced.

'No. I'm just . . . it's . . . we're just going through an odd period at the moment.'

Mary looked at me like she was studying a map.

'That's grand, Gracie girl. Just don't let this momentary period of oddness turn into the rest of your life. You don't have to tell me that life is short. Look at me. I know.' She cast a disapproving eye down the length of her body, the metal buckle of her most un-granny-like cowboy boots glinting steely in the moonlight.

'Look at Patrick,' she continued. 'If he had known he'd be dead before he was thirty-two, do you think he would have squandered as much time as he did? Studying bloody accountancy? Instead of writing? And travelling? Such a waste.' She shook her head as she said this, as if Patrick had spent his youth strung out on drugs instead of with his head in the financial statements of some blue-chip company or the other.

'Get that down you, Granny.' I stood up and put my hand on her shoulder. 'I'll drive you home.' She didn't even snap at me for calling her Granny. Just nodded without saying anything and finished her drinks, like an obedient child. I realised when she stood up just how drunk she was. As drunk as one of those monkeys she had probably swung through the trees with in the Amazon (that's where she'd been for the last six weeks, by the way).

Pulling up outside her house, I offered to stay with her that night, knowing she'd say no.

'No,' she said, offended. Then she leaned over and patted my head, with her huge hands and her whiskey breath.

'You're a good girl, Grace,' she said, so quietly that I barely heard her. Before I could reply, she was out of the car, gathering her bags and hoisting her rucksack onto her shoulders. I got out of the car but knew better than to offer to help. I leaned over and kissed her, hating the papery softness of her skin that reminded me of her age. Her real age, I mean. Not the age she acted or the age she lied about (I'm only seventy-two, for Christ's sake).

'Off you go, Grace. Don't even think about seeing me in. It's cold out.'

I opened my mouth to speak, but she cut me off with a wave of her hand.

'Yes, yes, of course I've got my keys. I'm not senile yet, you know.' I knew better than to argue with her, especially with four whiskeys under her – wide, sparkly – belt. I got into the car and opened the window.

'I'll see you on Saturday,' I said to the retreating back of my grandmother. She turned around slowly.

'Saturday?'

'Yes. Clare's wedding.'

'Clare?'

'Your granddaughter Clare. She's getting married. It's why you cut your trip to the Amazon short, remember?'

'Oh, yes.' Annoyance flashed across Mary's face as she remembered all the plans she'd had to cancel, just to attend the wedding.

'To Wadded Willy, isn't it?' She was smiling now, her memory clanking into gear like a chain on a bike.

'Yes,' I nodded. 'See you there.' I turned towards the car, in a hurry to get back inside its warmth.

'Grace,' she called, and something about her tone made me stop. I turned around and looked at her. Gone were all traces of inebriation from her worn face. She replaced it with an expression of utmost seriousness. I waited for her to say something.

'I had your fortune read in Bolivia.' Still inebriated then.

'Don't I have to be actually present for someone to tell my fortune?' I pretended to take her seriously. She was my granny, after all. Wacky, I'll grant you, but my granny all the same.

'I brought a token of you. That's all Samuel needed.'

'Samuel?'

'Yes. He's a seer. I heard about him before I went. He's one of the best in the world, they say.' I was curious now.

'What do you mean, you brought a token of me?' She looked a little sheepish now.

'I stole a lock of your hair. From your mother's house.'

'My mother has a lock of my hair?' This was getting weirder.

'Yes, of course.' Granny fixed me with a stare, as if *I* was the mad one. 'She keeps it in her jewellery box along with your milk teeth and your first pair of shoes.' My mother did have a huge jewellery box, so that could be true. But wait, I was getting distracted.

'But why?'

'Why what?'

'Why did you want to get my fortune read or told or whatever this seer did to me?'

'It's Samuel,' she snapped, 'and I did it because I . . .' She stopped and suddenly I didn't want her to go on.

'Because I've been worried about you.'

'*You've* been worried about *me*?' I was angry again although I couldn't say why, exactly. 'What about you? Haring up the bloody Himalayas for weeks on end with—'

'It was the Andes,' Mary interrupted me. 'And I didn't hare up. I walked. With a guide.' She fixed me with a glare, as if that was the most natural thing for an octogenarian to be doing. She set her bags back on the ground and fumbled in the pocket of her jacket for her cigarette pouch. In direct relation to the time it took her to roll a cigarette, I felt my curiosity grow until it got the better of me.

'So what did he say, this . . . Samuel?'

'I won't bore you with all the details,' she said, making me want to be bored to death with every single, solitary detail. 'You just need to know that things are going to be OK.'

'No way, you can't do this. You can't just say things are going to be OK and not give me any juice.' I practically stamped my foot with annoyance.

A gleam came into my grandmother's eyes. 'OK then, I'll tell you something. You're going to meet someone. A man, I mean. A proper one. *The* one.'

'That's it?' I said to her, raising my voice to be heard over the wind that had picked up and laced itself between us. 'You travelled halfway across the world to meet a fortune teller who reckons I'm going to meet a man.' I was smiling now. 'I hope to God you didn't pay him too much money for that little gem. Did he say I was going to come into money? Cross water? Anything like that?'

'Grace.' Mary stepped towards me, her face appearing in front of me like a full moon. 'I know it sounds crazy, but . . .' She paused, as if wondering whether or not to tell me.

'Go on.' I couldn't help myself.

'It's just . . . he *knew* things.' Mary was as insistent as a hen with an egg to lay. 'He knew about Spain and about Patrick. He said he could see Patrick and that he was happy and—'

'Don't.' I hadn't meant to shout. 'Don't say that.'

'He said Patrick has something for you. Something will arrive.'

'What do you mean?' My breath was coming hard in my chest and I could hear my heart thumping in my ears.

'I don't know. He didn't say. But he knew about what happened. In Spain. That's something, isn't it?' Mary was gaining in confidence now, in the face of my doubt. My fear.

'Thank you. Thanks for being concerned about me. For thinking about me. I . . . I appreciate it.'

'I know you don't believe me, but you'll see. It's true. I've heard things about this guy, Samuel. Things you wouldn't believe.' It suddenly struck me that it was Mary who was trying to convince herself of the legitimacy of this Samuel person, because, if it wasn't true, then she was just some crazy old lady raving about a bearded man in the Bolivian hills. I gathered up her bags and handed them to her.

'Go inside, Mary. I'll talk to you during the week, OK?' I was suddenly exhausted.

'You'll see, Grace, you'll see,' she murmured to herself until she reached the front door.

I walked towards my car, hating to leave her like this, hating that our evening had soured, hating my anger that poured through me like lava.

'I know his name.' Mary's shout cut through the dark like a knife; I could feel its tip on my neck. I slowed for an instant, then continued walking towards the car as if I hadn't heard a thing.

In the car, I fumbled with my keys, willing myself not to look back, not to look around, in case she'd be at the window with more crazy talk. I reefed the car away from the pavement and scorched down the street. When I looked in the rearview mirror, I could see her, standing at her garden gate. She was mouthing something, slowly and carefully. I couldn't work out if she was actually shouting his name out loud or just forming the word with her mouth, silently. I could see the name on her lips. I could see it as clear as my hand gripping the steering wheel. I yanked at the rearview mirror, pulling it down, and she was gone.

34

Caroline was in bed when I got home. I stretched my head around her bedroom door and knew by the way she was lying that she was sound asleep. Not resting or relaxing or in that quiet space between sleep and wakefulness that could be disturbed. Her sleeping position was as perfect as she was, on the flat of her back, arms by her sides, legs flush against the sheets, dead straight. She could get out of bed in the morning and the bed would look made, as if no one had slept in it at all. I wanted to shake her awake and ask if she'd heard from Bernard. I really thought about it, skulking just inside the bedroom door, twitching with the want. Her mobile, on the locker beside the bed, vibrated with an incoming message. It lit up the bedroom with its eerie blue light. Caroline didn't stir. I thought briefly of checking the phone, to see if the message was from Bernard. I didn't. I went to bed instead, and dreamed of Patrick.

It is that day. It is always that day. He is standing in the ocean, holding something in his hands. It looks like a letter. The day is hot but dull, the sun hidden behind a thick wall of clouds that persist all afternoon.

'Here,' shouts Patrick, holding his hand out to me. I can't hear him over the roar of the water. I walk towards him but Patrick shakes his head.

'No, Grace. You can't come in.' His voice is an echo.

He is hip-deep in the water. The waves that crash over his head don't wet him. He is smiling.

'Come back, Patrick.' Nobody looks at me and it's as if I'm not there at all. The sand feels warm between my toes.

'Don't worry, Grace. I'll be fine. Everything will be fine.' His voice is fainter now and I run towards the water, but no matter how fast I run, I never get any closer. He is farther away now, the water lapping his shoulders.

'Come back, Patrick.' Even though I shout, the words are like a whisper that is carried away by the wind. It's like I said nothing at all.

'Come back, Patrick.' I am tired now, sitting at the edge of the beach, miles away from the water. I can't see him any more and the dullness of the day pulls me back against the sand and I close my eyes against the harsh heat.

35

'I don't suppose you've ever heard of a . . . seer . . . called Samuel Someone Or Other?' I asked Laura the next day at lunch, picking peas out of my pea soup in a quasi-offhand manner. Laura was into things scientificky and that included palm readings, tarot cards, crystal balls and tea-leaf interpretation.

'Samuel the Seer from Bolivia?' Laura's head jerked up as if it was on a string. She said Bolivia like 'Bo-leave-ee-ya'.

'Eh, yes. I think so. I mean, Bolivia is a big place, I'm sure. There could be loads of Samuels there.'

'No Grace, there's only one.' Laura's tone was reverential and she leaned towards me, whispering, 'Why are you mentioning him?'

'Well, it's Mary, really,' I began.

'Granny Mary?'

'Yes.'

'What about her?'

'She went to see him. Samuel, I mean. In Bolivia.' Laura's eyes widened until it seemed they would burst their banks like a river in springtime. She lowered her head even closer to me, her chin grazing the Formica covering on the canteen table.

'She *found* him?' Laura finally managed.

'Well, yes,' I said. 'Apparently, he's in the book.' I made that bit up and Laura withered me with a look.

'So, what have you heard about this guy?' I asked her, lowering a piece of bread into the soup until it was as green as St Patrick's Day.

'He has The Sight,' Laura said, almost bowing her head when she said *sight*. 'He can see the future as clearly as you and I can remember what we had for lunch yesterday.' We both wrinkled our foreheads, trying to remember. Actually trickier than you'd think. Especially when you eat in a work canteen on a regular basis.

'Anyway,' said Laura, focusing again, 'it's said he's even better than Reggie the Reader in New South Wales.'

'Reggie?' I repeated, unimpressed by the lack of gravitas.

We both bent our heads then and finished our soup quickly. It was bad enough hot, but absolutely manky if allowed to cool. Laura finished first and sat back in her seat.

'What did he tell her? Go on, Grace,' Laura said.

I wondered about the best place to start. I took a breath and told her the whole lot. Even the bit about the lock of hair. Laura nodded through the monologue, looking at my mouth the whole time as if she were lip-reading. When I was finished she threw her spoon into the soup bowl, where it clanged.

'I *knew* it,' she said, slapping her hand against the table.

'Which bit?' I asked curiously.

'The bit about Meeting The One,' Laura hissed at me. 'It's Bernard, isn't it?' I could still see Mary mouthing his name as I drove away. Laura pushed on. 'I mean, it's definitely not Shane. You've barely spoken about him since his trip over at the weekend. In the past, a weekend like that would have seen us right till at least Wednesday.' Laura looked triumphant and I had to admit she was right.

'Bernard's going out with Caroline.'

Laura snorted at this piece of news and tossed her golden mane behind her shoulders with a magnificent flick of her head on both sides.

'What?' I asked. Even with guilt clawing at me like a cat, I was *dying* to talk about him.

'Be honest with yourself, Grace,' Laura said, taking a dainty sip of her fizzy-water-with-the-merest-hint-of-peach. 'I've seen the way you look at him.'

'The way I look at him?' I screeched.

'OK, OK, keep your big hair on. He looks at you like that too. I've seen him at it.'

'Like what?' I needled.

'You know,' she said, smirking.

'No. Tell me.' I held my breath, waiting.

'Like you're the only person in the room,' she said, sighing, bored now with the tedium of the details. I pressed on regardless, unable to stop.

'But Caroline's in love with him.' I whispered this, hating myself.

'I'm not the brightest spanner in the works,' said Laura, 'but I do know one thing.' She looked at me with a smile.

'What?' I asked. 'What's the one thing you know?'

'All's fair in love and war, girl,' she said with a wink.

Then she got bored and started talking about her upcoming auditions for *Big Brother*, not one word of which I heard. I was thinking about Bernard. About him looking at me like I was the only person in the room. Imagine someone looking at me like that. And if Laura said it, then it must be true because her tolerance for 'sick-making lovey-dovey stuff' (her words) was intolerably low.

Still no sign of Bernard when I got back to my desk after lunch. My neck hurt from all the craning I'd been doing over the last two days, keeping an eye out for him. When I wasn't doing that, I was beating a path to the ladies' and back for hourly retouching of make-up, just in case. My eyelashes were coarse and hard from multiple applications of mascara. I'd got up early the last two mornings to iron tops to wear under my suit and this was possibly the most telling aspect of my behaviour. Usually, I put the top I wanted to wear under my mattress the night before, which did the trick quite nicely.

The phone on my desk rang.

'Grace O'Brien. Liability-I-mean-IT Department.' I kept forgetting.

'What did you say?' It was Caroline and fear seized my heart like a closed fist. As if she could read my mind.

'I said, Grace O'Brien. IT Department.'

'No you didn't.'

'Yes I did.'

'You didn't.'

'I did.'

'No you di . . . oh forget it.' Caroline knew I could outlast her. Plus she hated wasting time, priding herself on the brevity of her verbals at work.

I threaded my fingers through the coils of the telephone cable. Caroline rarely rang me at work.

'What's up?' I asked, crossing my fingers and toes, a habit that had persevered since childhood.

'Just, eh, ringing for a chat.' Her tone was unconvincing at best, and I knew that she knew that I knew this was not the case.

'I've hardly seen you at all these past few days,' she began and I loosened my grip on the receiver. 'How's the new job going?' Actually, here was an area of my life that was running smoothly. I had finished the debriefing document for Bernard, met with the liability manager and senior claims handler to discuss their requirements (which I knew anyway, making that part of the job a bit of a doddle) and I'd had a meeting with the boss where he only looked at my chest once when I entered his office, and then seemed to forget about the girls after that. I took special pride in that: those of you who don't have sleazy bosses won't understand, but those of you who do will know exactly what I mean. It was the first meeting I'd ever had with him where I did most of the talking. It felt good.

I was in the middle of telling Caroline all this (it was just after lunch which meant nobody was back from lunch yet) when I realised she wasn't listening to me. I could tell from her perfunctory 'ummms' at the end of various of my sentences. I suddenly stopped talking in the middle of a sentence. She didn't even notice.

'So,' she said, in the cheerful voice of someone who is Up To Something. 'Have you seen Bernard lately?'

I lifted my eyes to where Bernard should have been sitting. 'He hasn't been in all week,' I said.

'Oh,' she said, waiting for more. I knew how she felt.

'He's in the Galway office, fixing something or the other. I haven't seen him since he was at the flat on Saturday.' I sounded so casual, so relaxed.

'Oh,' Caroline said again and her disappointment was like a wind howling. But there was something else. Something like relief. Clearly he hadn't called her. But now there was a pretty good reason for it. Wasn't there?

'Could you . . .?' Caroline began, hesitating.

'Let you know when he gets in?' I finished for her.

'Eh, yes. I mean, if you have time. I know you're busy there, with the new job and everything. How's that going, by the way?'

I told her again. It seemed less cruel. Anyway, I liked talking about it.

'Caroline, I have to go,' I finally said. 'I'm due in a meeting in five minutes.' And it was actually true. Not like the times when my mother rang and I told her I had to go because of a meeting or a conference call – she liked the sound of those – or even a bagel run.

'In my day, we had scones,' she'd say wistfully, casting her mind back like a fishing line, hooking a memory on it. Then she'd tell me about the way she and her colleagues used to backcomb each other's hair in the office on a Friday evening.

'Did I ever tell you about us backcombing each other's hair in the office on a Friday evening?'

Or about Ms O'Riordain, the spinster supervisor who never married and never would and wore her hair in tight curls and stockings as thick as treacle. Mam and her colleagues would line up on the third floor of the GPO at 4.50 p.m. on a Friday (kicking-out time was 5 p.m). Like schoolgirls on a bus tour to Butlins, they were.

'Like schoolgirls on a bus tour to Butlins, we were.' She always laughed when she said that bit, and even though I'd heard it a million times before, I did too. My efforts to divert her, to get her off the phone seemed so small now in the silence that had stretched between us over the last year. Suddenly, I wanted her to ring and get her to tell me about the time she and her friend slipped into the church on a Tuesday evening in November, after benediction, and dared each other to drink from the communion wine bottle (Blue Nun, 1960).

'And the holy Sacrament exposed on the altar,' she'd whisper to me, half delighted with the daring and half afraid she might be struck down by lightning. I always laughed at that bit. Then she'd tell me about the church always being open, back then.

'The church was always open back then,' she said, looking into the middle distance.

'They probably had to start locking it when you young gurriers started nicking the communion wine,' was my – not unreasonable – explanation.

She'd be off then, laughing with tears running down her face. She always cried when she laughed, my mother. Maybe that was why she never cried. Because she cried a river with the laughing we used to do.

My computer beeped, notifying me of an email from Shane, asking for a response to his email from yesterday morning. I typed slowly, thinking about the time I had spent, waiting for him.

Will see you at the church on Saturday. Am [chief] bridesmaid, remember, so will be going to the wedding with Clare, Mam and Jane in Special Car with Fridge and Champagne and Possibly Chocolates.

I deleted the word *chocolates* and replaced it with *strawberries*. Healthier. Less fattening. No need to hand him a stick to beat me with.

Bernard's eventual arrival into the office was quiet and un-assuming. One minute his desk was empty when I looked up to check, the next it wasn't. I felt him first before I saw him and I knew, before I looked up, that he was sitting there, looking across at me with that crooked half-smile and the serious eyes, dark as night. I pecked furiously at my key-board writing lines and lines of 'a;efinrv;nv;aevne'av naerfn e;v ner;ierufhnerfvgebn vre ;' across the screen. It had been nearly an hour since my last make-up maintenance and my hair, beautifully straightened that morning, was now piled on top of my head with a thinning elastic band, a pencil spearing it in place. I thought about ducking under the desk (perhaps to retrieve a fallen stapler?) and releasing my hair, pinching my cheeks and maybe even stabbing a lipstick across my mouth.

'Thanks for that, Grace.' I looked up and there he was, peering into his monitor with the teeny-tiny glasses. But not in his usual IT uniform (T-shirt and jeans). He was wearing a suit. A chocolate brown one. With a cream shirt, buttoned up to the neck. He pulled at the knot on his tie and opened the top button of his shirt with the fingers of one hand. Hair sprang from there, curling around the edges of the fabric like spiders' legs. I drank him in like a glass of cold lemonade on a hot day.

'Thanks for what?' I said.

'For the debriefing document. I got it in Galway but I haven't had a chance to go through it yet.' He picked up an elastic band and wound it around his fingers, testing its elasticity with the body of a pen with which he pulled the band taut.

'No problem,' I said in my fat voice (loud and cheerful). Bernard looked up, a little startled, and disentangled his fingers from the elastic web he had spun around them.

'The boss wants to meet us both tomorrow afternoon,' I went on, gaining momentum, 'so maybe you could look at it this afternoon and we could discuss it tomorrow morning. Say, at . . .' I pretended to consult my Outlook diary, clicking uselessly around my desktop, moving icons around the screen like chess pieces.

'Does eight o'clock suit?' I looked up at him with my official smile (tight and sparse).

'In the morning?' His face was static with shock and my smile softened, relieving the muscles in my face.

'I thought you were an early bird?' I said.

Bernard considered this for a moment. 'I like to get in early so I can have coffee and check my emails. I don't think I could actually discuss anything in any kind of meaningful way much before nine.' He might as well have been talking about me (not that I got in early normally, but the bit about coffee and emails before engaging in worky stuff).

'OK then.' I looked again at my monitor, clicking and clacking across the screen with the mouse. 'Shall we say 9.15?' I said 'nine-fifteen' instead of the usual 'a quarter past nine' in an effort to re-establish the boundaries between us. As a ploy, it wasn't effective. In fact, it seemed to have the opposite effect and, just at that moment, I remembered something lovely.

Lying on the floor in his bedroom, arms and legs threaded through duvets and sheets. My body tingles, alive with possibilities. Bernard is lying on his side looking at me, his face ghostly white in the paleness of dawn's creeping light. He holds strands of my hair between his fingers, plaiting them as carefully as if he is spinning gold . . .

'. . . for coffee. Say around half-eight?' I shook my head as Bernard's voice broke through, and the image fled, hanging its head in shame.

'I'm sorry, Bernard,' I said. 'Could you say that again? I was . . . I was . . .'

He waited for me.

'Miles away,' I finished, the sentence dribbling away like a burst ball.

'If you like,' he repeated, louder than necessary, 'we can discuss it over coffee. Tomorrow morning? Half-eight?' He said half-eight, making my nine-fifteen sound ridiculous.

I opened my mouth to say 'no'. I had to discourage informal meetings between us. There had to be at least one desk between us when we spoke, not to keep me safe from him, but rather to keep him safe from me. Working with him was going to be harder than I imagined: like swimming under water. I'd have to learn to hold my breath for longer. I opened my mouth to say 'no'. I said 'yes'. There was silence then for a while, just the occasional beep of the monitor and the low hum of the printer. I thought about what I would wear for coffee tomorrow morning, hating myself, but not able to stop. Bernard looked around the office. Peter's desk was empty. There was no one around. He cleared his throat.

'Grace, about Saturday night . . .' he began and I knew immediately that he'd been thinking about saying this since he arrived.

'You mean your date with Caroline?' I said, oh-so-casually.

'Well, yeah. Blind date, really. Richard set it up for me ages ago and I'd forgotten about it, to be honest with you. Richard rang to remind me last Wednesday.' Bernard was talking so fast I had to concentrate to keep up with him. 'My cousin's a real stickler for detail. He wouldn't let me cancel.' And then: 'I wanted to.'

I pretended to ignore the last remark, although I knew I would root it out later and pick at it like a scab.

'Good job you didn't,' I said. 'It obviously went well, what with the second date on Saturday.' I struggled to keep my tone light.

Bernard opened his mouth to say something, then closed it again.

'Richard's set me up with a few of his cousins in the past,' I said.

'Which ones?' Bernard tucked his pen behind his ear and leaned forward for the details. It slowly dawned on me that Richard's cousins were Bernard's cousins too.

'Well, first there was Brian.'

'With the ears?'

'The very one.' I giggled, remembering the sticky-out ears, the tips of them red and raw from constant exposure to the elements.

'Then there was Ronan.' I was getting into my stride now. Bernard laughed his donkey-bray laugh.

'Ronan?' he managed between brays. 'Did he say anything?'

I gave this question due consideration.

'He said four things,' I said finally. 'Hello, goodbye, Portishead and Brittany. I think that was all. Other than that, I talked and he nodded, or shook his head. Depending.' I looked at Bernard, loving the way his shoulders shook when he laughed.

'Portishead?' Bernard was confused.

'Yeah, I asked him what music he was into at one – fairly desperate – stage. And where he had been on holidays. It was like being at the hairdressers, really. He paid for dinner though,' I remembered. 'Insisted on it.' Bernard nodded.

'Och, aye, he's fierce generous, so he is. Quiet. But generous.' And the pair of us were off, Bernard's hand thumping the desk in rhythm with the braying.

'So,' Bernard said when his breathing had normalised. 'That was Shane, then?'

'Yeah,' I said, picking my handbag up off the floor and pretending to rummage inside it. 'Maybe the four of us could go out together sometime.'

'The four of us?' Bernard said, taking the pen from his ear and clicking the top of it with his thumb, making the nib appear and disappear, over and over.

'Yeah. You and Caroline. Me and Shane.' I picked a matchbox out of my bag and shook it.

'Oh,' was all he said. I pulled my handbag off the floor and, with the matchbox still in my hand, I moved away from my desk.

'Going for a smoke,' I explained to Bernard's bent head.

'OK. See you later.' He didn't look up and I didn't look back. I knew I had done the right thing. It just felt wrong.

36

It turns out that when you're chief bridesmaid for someone like Clare, there's not a lot to do. Even Clare was restless and distracted when I called over to her later that day.

'You can't possibly have done everything,' I said, appalled at her Germanic efficiency.

'I bloody well have,' she moaned, her head lolling on her neck from sheer boredom. 'And I've taken the sodding week off work,' she went on, 'and it's only Tuesday but it feels like Friday except without the Friday buzz.' She threw herself against the back of the couch with a sigh that could blow petals off a rose at twenty feet.

'And look at the state of the place.' I looked around the pristine sitting room. The cushions were plumped, the floors polished, the fireplace cleared out and washed down. Even the books on the bookcase ran in descending height order, the genres separated by shelves, all spines facing out.

'What are you talking about?' I asked. 'It's perfect.'

'I know.' Clare almost shouted it. 'I can't even clean the sodding house because I already did it on Sunday and even though it's Tuesday, it's still clean and tidy and I can't even bring myself to mess it up even though it would at least give me something to do because I'm just too bloody anal.' Clare's voice rose like a scale during this monologue until, at the end, only the dogs in the street could have deciphered what she was saying. Still, I got the general gist.

Pre-wedding jitters. I'd heard of it but never witnessed it first hand. Laura never got to this stage. Thank God. If it had reduced my mild-mannered sister Clare to this shuddering state, Laura would have been positively demonic. But what to do?

'What about the wedding dress?' I asked. 'Surely that needs to be collected.'

'Done.'

'No last-minute alterations on it?'

'None.'

Then I had a thought. 'How about my dress? When am I supposed to pick it up?'

'I've got it already.'

'The rings?'

'Collected them.'

'What about the photographer and the flowers and the cake? Have you . . .'

'Confirmed them all. I've done it all. Every single fecking thing.' Clare's voice was wobbling now, tears gathering like storm clouds on our horizon. She suddenly leapt from the couch.

'Here, take a look. Here's the checklist.' She yanked a plastic folder off the table and frisbeed it over to me. I caught it with one hand, proudly.

The checklist ran to five pages, every item neatly crossed off. It was hopeless. There was only one thing for it.

'Clare?'

'What?' Her voice returned to monotone.

'Let's go out and get pissed.'

We were in the pub quicker than you could say 'Grace is an alcoholic' and, because it was Rathgar, the barman was able to shake us up two frothy, pink cosmopolitans in wide-rimmed martini glasses without batting an eyelid. Clare was slurring her words by drink No. 2, unaccustomed as she was to mid-week binge drinking. Clare believed that alcoholism was a bit like baldness: once there was one instance of it in your family, the chances of you catching it were pretty high as it front-crawled its way through the gene pool. While there was no baldness in the family to speak of, there were a few relatives who were 'fond of the jar', a phrase which here means 'raging alcoholic'. So Clare observed a strict abstinence between midnight on Sunday nights and 7 p.m. on Friday nights. This lapse was worrying at best, although the alcohol was helping me not to think about it.

'So, where's Richard tonight?' I asked when we came up for air halfway through the second drink.

'Working.' Clare might as well have said 'pimping his granny', such was the venom of her tone.

'He's probably clearing his desk before going on honeymoon,' I offered. Clare was not taking the bait.

'But I need him.'

'What for? You've done everything already,' I argued rea-. sonably. 'All he has to do is show up, say I do, take you on holidays and carry you over the threshold of the home you already own when you get back.' God, when I put it like that, it all sounded so easy. *I* could have managed it. Clare responded by tearing my beer mat up into a thousand tiny pieces, crumbs of paper scattered about the table like a layer of dandruff. When she'd finished she looked around for more but she'd already dealt with hers on arrival. She slumped back against the seat, lifting her drink and draining it. I looked at my glass. Still half full. Or I suppose I should say half empty, in the circumstances.

'I need anuzzer drink,' Clare said with that determined look that drunk people get when they're trying to appear sober. I looked at her. She looked about twelve. No make-up and two St Trinian-like rosy cheeks, high and perfectly circular.

'Are you pretending to be drunk?' I asked her, remember-

ing her efforts after a bottle of West Coast Cooler when we
were teenagers.

'I wasn't pretending that time,' she said, remembering the
incident. 'I wouldn't have fallen off that see-saw on purpose.
I really hurt myself.' Clare had insisted on joining me and
my friends for our traditional Friday night drinking session
in the playground on the edge of the local park. We called it
knacker-drinking then, before you weren't allowed to say the
word 'knacker' any more.

'But you hadn't even finished one bottle. And it was bloody
West Coast bloody Cooler. There aren't enough bottles of that
stuff in the world to get pissed on.'

Clare leaned over and picked up my (half-full) glass, finishing it in a noisy slurp.

'Now,' she said in a 'what the fuck are you going to do
about it?' kind of way. A film of pink froth bubbled on her
upper lip and I'd never felt less intimidated in my life. But
still. I was the chief bridesmaid. It was my duty to do the
bride's bidding. And if she wanted to get pissed on cosmos
in Coman's on a Tuesday night, who was I to deny her? Plus
she looked like a kitten with her huge blue eyes in her little
heart-shaped face. I headed to the bar, where the barman
treated me like royalty, such was the dearth of punters in
the pub on that flaccid Tuesday night. His eyes lit up when
I ordered two more cosmopolitans, they taking about two
minutes longer to prepare than your average gin and tonic
or Bulmers with ice.

'Do you want some nuts with those?' he asked, his arms a
blur of pistons, working the shaker. I nodded and said no at
the same time. He looked up, confused.

'Y'see, I *want* some, which is why I nodded. But I'm on a *diet*
which doesn't include peanuts, crisps or even kebabs. Which is
why I said no.' He set the drinks on the counter in front of me,
understanding completely. He was good at his job.

Halfway through our third drinks, Clare's mood shifted from aggressive (even though it was about as aggressive as a Pomeranian yapping at a milkman) to animated following the receipt of a text message. There was a Problem. A logistical one. With the flowers. The tulips, to be precise, due to be flown in from Holland on Saturday morning, in the same delicate shade of dawn light (read 'cream') as her dress. Except that the baggage handlers in Amsterdam had decided to go on strike. Something to do with the conditions of the men's staff toilets at the airport. This problem would take time to resolve. And time was just the thing Clare had in abundance that week. She was ecstatic but tried hard not to show it.

'Dutch men are so *hygienic*,' Clare complained, bitter as a lemon.

'Well, I could understand if it was about the toilet paper.'

'What?'

'I mean, if they were expected to wipe their bums with that greaseproof paper we used to have in pub toilets. Remember that?' We both clenched, thinking about those little squares, as hard and unforgiving as a cuckold.

'In the olden days,' I went on, 'punters had sheets of newspapers to wipe their whatsits with.' Clare stopped in mid-lift (of her drink to her lips).

'Go on,' she said.

'Well, it was recycling, really. In its truest form. Customers could sit on the pot, read the day's news and then wipe their arses with it.' I sucked my drink through a – pink, curly – straw, my cheeks denting with the effort. I could see Clare's face working, like she was chewing a Werther's Original. I knew she was going to laugh. She couldn't do angst-ridden for long. She just didn't have it in her.

'You're a great bridesmaid,' she said afterwards, her face a warm glow of cosmopolitans.

'Chief bridesmaid,' I corrected her. 'And I'm not. I haven't done a single thing.'

'You have. You do.' Clare waved her hand around the space between us.

'I mean anything practical. I haven't done a single practical thing to help.'

'No,' Clare agreed, 'but I'm practical enough for both of us, amn't I?' I looked up at her, slowly, her words registering in my head. She was right. She *was* practical enough for both of us.

'Clare, I need your advice,' I said very quickly, afraid that I might change my mind. Clare caught the barman's eye and ordered two more drinks using a series of hand gestures and facial expressions. Then she turned back to me.

'Go for it, Grace. I'm all eyes.' Clare's eyes were in fact stretched into slits and I hesitated.

'Don't you mean you're all ears?'

'Whaddever,' she slurred. She arranged herself in a more upright position. 'Is this about you and Bernard?'

'Well, it's more about Bernard and Caroline, I suppose,' I began.

'I thought that was just one of Richard's blind dates?' Clare said, accustomed as she was to the abject failure of Richard's Cupid antics.

'Well, it was. Except that Caroline's in love with him.' I looked around for a beer mat to rip. Nil stock.

'Hmmm,' Clare said.

'What do you mean, hmmm?'

'Does Caroline know about you and Bernard?'

'Jesus, no,' I said, the cold hand of fear curling around my neck at the thought of it.

'Does Shane know anything about you and Bernard?' she asked next.

'No.' I was emphatic about that. 'Although he has been act-ing a bit strange lately. Ringing me. And emailing twice since he got back to London.'

Clare's face stained with pity and I struggled to rephrase.

'No, I don't mean that it's strange for him to ring or email,' – although in fairness, it was – 'it's just, he's been a bit more *concerned* about what I'm up to than normal. That's all.'

'Int-er-rest-ing,' Clare said, stroking her chin and looking into the middle distance like a pro. 'Shane, on some buried level, understands that you're not as interested as you once were.'

'But I *am*,' I insisted, sitting on my hands to stop them reaching over to the next table for a beer mat.

'You've hardly said a word about him since he left.' Clare played her trump card.

'I could hardly get a word in, what with all the talk about the wedding, the flowers, the men's toilet facilities in Amsterdam, Richard's selfish work ethic, the scourge of cleanliness in your house . . .'

Clare held her hands up, laughing. 'OK, OK, you've made your point. I *have* been a bit of a drama queen, haven't I?'

'You're allowed,' I said. 'You're getting married.'

'So,' she said, 'tell me about your weekend.' The weekend suddenly seemed like it had happened a long time ago and I struggled to remember something good.

'Omnibus *Coronation Street*.' I suddenly remembered the glorious hour and a half of lying across the couch, my head warm in his lap, eyes glued to the telly, watching Shelley run the gauntlet with the bauld Charlie and lose, over and over again.

'This renewed contact of Shane's . . .' Clare got ready to deliver her diagnosis. 'It's the male equivalent of pissing on his territory.'

'Charming.'

'No, seriously.' Clare sat up straight to demonstrate how serious she was. 'Animals do it when they feel threatened. Like if they smell another male in the area. Now the thing with Caroline and Bernard.' Clare obviously felt she had solved that particular problem and was ready for her next challenge. She was thorough, if nothing else. And thoroughly drunk as well. Richard would not be pleased with me.

'Is Bernard interested?'

'In Caroline?' I asked, stalling.

'Yes.'

'No.'

'No, he's not, or no, he is?'

'I don't think he is. Interested, I mean. In Caroline.' Even saying it, I was Judas and the bag of thirty coins felt heavy in my hands.

'There you are, then,' Clare concluded, throwing the last of her drink into her mouth. 'Up to now, Caroline could get any man she wanted. Except that she didn't want any of them. Now she's met one who, so far, appears immune to her charms. So, she wants him. Simple as. End of.' Clare looked around, beaming, and I almost expected a round of applause to break out. She leaned over to me and whispered in a way that everyone in the bar could hear her. 'He's her Mount Everest.'

'So what do you advise?' I asked her.

'It's a Hobson's,' she said, and I looked at her like she was speaking Chinese.

'I'm not following.'

'A Hobson's choice,' she explained, talking slowly as if to a six-year-old.

Still clueless.

'It's like this, Grace,' she said, slouching back in her chair. 'You're damned if you do and damned if you don't. A Hobson's, see?'

Clare lifted her glass to her lips again and seemed surprised to find it was empty.

'That's three drinks I've had now,' she said, her words running into each other. 'If I have a fourth, I'll be officially binge drinking.'

Where does she *get* this stuff?

It shocked me to realise that I was hoping she'd call it a night. I had a busy day in work tomorrow, kicking off with my meeting with Bernard (still hadn't decided what to wear).

'But if you can't binge drink on the last Tuesday of your single life, then when can you?' Resigned, I picked up our empties and moved towards the bar.

If I puked later, the carrots would have a pinkish hue. Not that I'd eaten carrots recently. Or in the last decade (mostly because of the horrible, carroty taste).

Even though Clare's house was a five-minute stroll from the pub, we got a joe. Had to, really. Clare's drunkenness had mostly affected her legs, which moved as if independent of her body. I helped her out of the taxi and waved at Richard whose face had appeared like a moon from behind a blind in the bedroom window upstairs. I retreated into the taxi, locked the door and managed to wrap the seatbelt around my girth, all in less than five seconds. Not bad considering my drunkenness, which had mostly affected my eyes (everything had a *pink* hue). Clare slumped against the front door when I looked back, waving and mouthing something. 'Mount Everest', I think. Or it could have been 'Hobson's choice'. My last sighting of her was falling backwards as Richard opened the door. She fell in slow motion, it seemed to me. But I wasn't worried. I knew Richard would catch her.

I snuck into the flat like a thief. I wanted tea and a toasted kebab sandwich but I wanted not to wake Caroline more. I headed straight for my room on tippy-toes, my coat still on, my breath held. I had to walk past Caroline's room to get to mine. Which floorboard creaked there – the third one from the door, or the fourth? No, definitely the third. I raised my foot, cramping now from walking on my toes. Carefully, I set it down on the fourth floorboard. It creaked loudly, a crack of thunder in the silence. The light snapped on in Caroline's room, shooting out from under her door and I stood there, like a moth caught in the rays.

'Grace, what are you doing?' It was not an unreasonable question. It was two o'clock in the morning, I was outside her bedroom door, silhouetted in a shaft of light, balancing on one foot – still on tippy-toes – wearing a winter coat over a summer dress (I do that sometimes when the seasons aren't changing quickly enough). I lowered my left foot to the floor and cleared my throat. Caroline barely registered my unorthodox behaviour, possibly being much too used to it by now.

'Did he come into the office today?'

'Who?' I bought some time and massaged the toes of my right foot with the toes of the left. If toes could talk, mine would have groaned out load with relief.

'Bernard, of course.' And then, almost as if she were thinking aloud, 'Christ, that is *such* a nerdy name.'

I leapt on her comment like a dog on a bone.

'He *is* a bit of a nerd, really. An IT geek. That's what Laura calls him. He can actually speak Java, you know. Like, fluently.'

'Can he?' Caroline's voice lit up like Christmas. 'I bet it sounds gorgeous, in that Derry accent.'

'Donegal,' I said, taking off my coat.

'Whatever,' Caroline sighed, hugging her arms about her like Eliza in *My Fair Lady*. Any minute now, she was going to start dancing around the living room, singing, 'I could have sodding danced all bloody night.' But she didn't. She fixed me with her Mission Impossible look.

'Will he be in the office tomorrow?'

I fished around for something ambiguous to say.

'Yes,' I said.

'Good,' was all she said, walking backwards into her room. She might as well have made a bridge of her hands and laughed an evil genius laugh.

'What are you going to do?' It was a whisper. I was still standing where she'd found me, with my coat – actually, her coat – draped over one arm. Goosebumps rose like speed bumps along the length of my arms.

'What any average red-blooded woman would do,' she said, smiling her Machiavellian smile before saying goodnight and closing the door.

But Caroline was no average red-blooded woman. She'd never been disappointed in love. Why should this be any different?

37

There must be some mistake. I had only just-that-very-minute gotten into bed and wrapped my arms around the pillow when the alarm clock went off. I had forgotten how horrendous a cosmopolitan hangover was. If I had to describe it, I'd liken it to giving birth to an elephant through a tiny hole in the top of your head.

Somehow, I managed to make it into the office by eight o'clock, a feat that did not go unnoticed by Ciaran, who doffed his cap at me as I scorched past the security hut and skidded to an emergency stop at the first parking space I came across.

'Jesus, Grace. Yeer goan-ta burrin yerself ouwt a' this rayte.' I stumbled towards him.

'Do I smell of drink?' I breathed on him and waited for the verdict.

'I can smell peach . . .' he began.

'That'll be the peach schnapps in between the second and third cosmopolitan,' I said, remembering. 'Anything else?'

Ciaran edged closer and sniffed again, like a dog at a lamppost.

'There's definitely an undercurrent of Coco Mademoiselle. I'd bet me year's supply o' haggis on it.'

'Jesus, how gay are you?' I'd have hugged the old git except that it might have embarrassed him.

I sat in the kitchen and waited for Bernard to arrive. Really waited, like people wait in a doctor's surgery. Kept looking at the clock, read a three-month-old copy of *Now* magazine and counted the number of split ends in my hair. I stopped when I got past fifty.

'Oh, you're here. Sorry I'm late.'

I was at the fridge when he arrived, thinking about sticking my head in the icebox to see if that would help – don't worry, I didn't actually do it, just thought about it, and only for the briefest time (about five seconds, maybe less).

It hurt when I smiled, so I stopped.

'Are you all right?' Bernard moved into the kitchen. He was back in his normal gear. Jeans that used to be black, now greying with baggy knees, high of waist and short of ankle. White T-shirt. How white? Oh, very white. Unbelievably white. Staring at the sun white. I had to look away and blink, just to get the sight back in my eyes. Once I turned away from him and busied myself at the counter with the kettle and water and spoons and things, I could talk to him. I decided to come clean.

'Have a hangover, actually.'

'What kind?'

'The four cosmopolitans kind.' I couldn't even mention the peach schnapps. I could feel my stomach reaching for my throat just thinking that. I thought about something else: puppies, in a wicker basket, with a tartan blanket tucked around them. It worked. My stomach returned to me.

'That'll do it all right,' he said. 'Sit down and have your coffee. I'll make some toast.'

'No, I couldn't eat a—'

'It'll make you feel better.' And I did – feel better, I mean. That and the two Alka-Seltzers I'd swallowed earlier.

It was only when I was settled at the table eating toast that I noticed his face. He was pale with dark circles under his eyes that turned his brown eyes black.

'Are you all right? You look tired.'

'Just didn't get much sleep last night, that's all.'

'Oh.' My mind crowded with possibilities. Had he been out? With a woman? Or tossing and turning in bed, wondering what Caroline might look like in a French maid outfit? Or worse, a nurse's uniform? Bernard opened his mouth and then shut it again and busied himself with cutting up his toast. He cut the bread lengthways and then widthways, making four perfect squares on the plate. If you measured them, you'd find they were all exactly the same size. Then he nodded his head as if I'd said something and began to talk.

'It's my mother, I suppose,' he said, as if thinking aloud. 'She hasn't been great since Edward's first anniversary mass. It's like she's grieving for him all over again.' Now he was cutting his toast into eighths and I leaned over and carefully took the knife out of his hand.

'Sorry.' He smiled at me and his eyes lengthened into slits.

'It's OK. I understand.' And I did. About mothers. While my mother guarded her grief jealously, it was always there: a shadow that moved between us.

'So,' I said, shifting in my seat, 'were you out with your mother last night or something?' Please let him have been out with his mother last night.

'No. She rang me and we were on the phone for ages. She wants to put up some kind of memorial for him. Maybe a bench or something. With a plaque, in his memory.' The eight tiny squares of toast sat untouched on Bernard's plate. I remembered what Clare said about Bernard. How he arranged the funeral himself. How his mother went to pieces. Suddenly I got it.

'You're the Jane of the family,' I told him. He looked up, confused. 'You're the one who organises things. The one who gets things done. You're the one people lean on. In our family, that's Jane.' I had envied Jane her control, her calmness. I hadn't considered the downside and I saw the strain of it in Bernard's face. I wanted him to smile again.

'Tell me something about Edward,' I asked.

'Like what?' he said and I could see he was struggling to piece Edward's face together in his mind. I recognised the look.

'Something he liked to do. Tell me that.' There was silence for a while and then Bernard began to talk.

'He loved sailing. The two of us did. We had a boat, you know, when we were younger.' He smiled at the memory.

'What was it called?' I asked.

Bernard started to laugh.

'I'm embarrassed to tell you. We were only sixteen when we christened her.'

'Stop stalling. Just tell me,' but I was laughing too. Bernard's donkey bray was infectious.

'*Babe Magnet.*'

'And was it?'

'Was it what?'

'A babe magnet?'

'Christ, no.' Bernard looked amused at the thought. 'It was a rust bucket really. We spent more time fixing it and painting it than we did sailing it.'

'What happened to it?' I was curious.

'I don't know. Edward discovered a keen interest in girls the following summer and I started displaying worrying IT geek symptoms.' I raised my eyebrows in a question. 'You know, the usual stuff. Dismantling computers and rebuilding them, reading programming manuals, wearing glasses and braces and cords.'

'So no keen interest in girls for you then, no?' The conversation that had been chugging along nicely thank you very much suddenly lurched to one side and I could feel the heat rising on my neck.

'No,' he said, spreading jam on each of the eight freezing squares of toast. He looked up at me. 'Not back then.'

I looked at the clock.

'Jesus, it's nearly nine o'clock and not a child in the house washed.' I got up to go and noticed other people in the kitchen now, microwaving porridge and cutting up strawberries to decorate bowls of Special K. I hadn't noticed them coming in.

'I'll see you back in the office, OK?' Bernard nodded in my direction, still chewing.

I passed Laura in the corridor and stopped to speak to her, but she just sort of floated past, a million miles away. Still in love then.

Love is a great distraction, isn't it? It rescues you from the mundane aspects of life. You no longer notice how long a queue is or if you're in a queue that's two people longer than the one immediately to your left. Getting butter on your roll instead of the mayo you requested isn't a big deal any more. Just a different taste, that's all. And not all that bad. In fact, quite passable if you smother it in salt. Laura was there now. Distracted. I tried to remember what it felt like and was shocked to find that I could not.

'Ouch.' I arrived at my desk sooner than I realised and bumped my hip against the sharp edge of it. Peter was at his desk, still pecking furiously at the keyboard of his computer that was probably turned off. Niall was in his office on the phone, probably to his wife. Something about raspberry Petit Filous, as far as I could make out.

'We didn't actually get around to talking about this afternoon's meeting with the boss.' Bernard stood in front of my desk, his long fingers curled around a mug of steaming coffee. I dragged my eyes away from them and looked up. He sat on the edge of my desk, close enough to touch.

I pushed my chair back.

'Can we do that straight after lunch? I need to finish the spreadsheet for the meeting.' I needed him sitting at his desk, not perched on mine like a distracting paperweight. Bernard stood up immediately.

'Sure. No bother.' And just as quietly as he had arrived, he was gone and, after a while, I was able to get on with my work.

It was about 12.30 p.m. when I heard the clatter of heels on the stairs, the steps assured and steady, falling with intent. I looked up but couldn't see anyone. Just the sound of the steps getting closer and closer. Nobody used the stairs. We were on the third floor, for Christ's sake. There was a perfectly good lift.

The footfalls grew shriller. The only person who had ever used those stairs was Caroline and she didn't work here any more. A shiver snaked up my back and wrapped around my neck. I kept my head trained on the stairwell. I could see the top of a head now. And hair. Blonde and long. The footsteps stopped and the head disappeared from view and then reappeared, just as suddenly, the hair now with a fuller, tousled look. The steps continued, louder now. Out of the head grew a body. A long, taut one. Swathed in a suit barely on the outskirts of Acceptable Office Garb, her skirt as short as it could go without allegations of sexual distraction. The length of the legs, the height of the heels, the flick of the hair. It could only be one woman. And it was. It was Caroline O'Brien. And she looked like she meant business.

38

'Grace, hi.' Her voice was breathy when she got to my desk. 'I was in the neighbourhood and I thought I'd stop by and see if you're free for lunch.'

She was good. She leaned across my desk towards me, giving me, and everyone behind me (Bernard), an eyeful of cleavage, bigger now that she had clamped them into the bra that she liked to call miraculous.

'Oh, Bernard, hi. I didn't see you there.' Caroline looked up, zooming in on her prey. To the undiscerning eye, it looked like she had only just clocked him. I knew better.

'I didn't realise you and Grace worked so close together.' She moved towards him and I knew for a fact that she was wearing stockings and suspenders instead of the usual Wednesday tights that we liked to pull as far up our bellies as they would go, to provide extra warmth and comfort.

Bernard's face was obscured, caught as it was in the shadow thrown by Caroline's toned, thin body.

'Why don't you come for lunch with us?' Caroline was saying, turning to me. 'You don't mind, do you Grace.' It was a statement rather than a question. This was the part where I was supposed to remember an urgent appointment, leaving them to lunch in coupley peace. I said nothing and Caroline turned her back to Bernard and gave me a meaningful look.

Bernard looked from one of us to the other. He hadn't actually said anything yet.

'What about Milanos for pizza and a buidéal of wine?' suggested Caroline, warding me off with her evil eye. I wanted to say yes – and no, it wasn't all about the pizza (although some of it was). Bernard picked himself carefully out from behind his desk and stood up. I noticed that Caroline just about came up to his chest, making her look delicate against his height. I could see them in a photograph together. People would smile at it and say they looked like the perfect couple.

'Grace?' Caroline prompted, waiting.

'Oh, sorry, Caroline. I really can't go. I've to finish this spreadsheet for a meeting this afternoon.' Caroline arranged her face in disappointment and waited for me to go on. I obliged.

'But you two go ahead,' I said. Bernard looked at Caroline and then at me.

'I'd better stay too,' he said. 'We need to do a bit of preparation for that meeting.'

'No, no, there's no need,' I insisted. 'We can do that after lunch. There's plenty of time.' Caroline winked a 'thank you' at me and turned to Bernard, flooding him in the light of her brightest smile. With her hand on his elbow, she eased him away from me.

'See you later, Grace.' Bernard turned his head back to me.

'Goodbye,' was all I said, watching them disappear along the curve of the corridor. I sat down and got back to work. What else could I do?

39

Bernard was late back from lunch. I looked at my watch in a pointed manner when he sat down on the chair beside my desk. He didn't notice my tartness. Instead, he stretched his legs out in front of him – Christ, they were long – and smiled a slow smile with wine-stained lips.

'How was lunch?' I only asked to be polite, having tormented myself with thoughts of the pair of them in a shadowy corner, leaning towards each other over round faces of pizza and crooked little bottles of olive oil.

'Grand,' he said.

I picked up a sheaf of papers on my desk, shuffled them and set them back down again, in exactly the same place. I was turning into the boss.

'Yeah, well, I had work to do here,' I said stiffly.

'This job is important to you, isn't it?' Instead of laughing and thumping him on the arm as I could have done, I considered his question. Although I hadn't done much in the way of work while he'd been out, I conceded that, yes, the job *was* important to me. I wanted to do it well. I squared my shoulders.

'Come on, you. Get yourself into the men's, wash the wine off your cake-hole and hose your hair down. It's sticking up at the front again.'

Bernard grinned but did as he was told, leaving me to stare at him as he walked away. His T-shirt had escaped from the waistband of his jeans and hung down, denying me the pleasure of his bottom. He had one of those real men-in-jeans bottoms, a barely there one.

I imagined them in a clinch, Caroline pulling at his T-shirt, wondering what his back would be like to touch. Very smooth, I remembered. I jumped a little when the phone rang, as if I'd been caught with my hand in Maureen's tips jar. Maureen worked in the canteen and she made a fortune on tips because she stood right beside the jar and jiggled it under your nose.

'Hello.'

'Hey baby, it's me.'

'Shane? Aren't you in work?' It wasn't right to be thinking about another man's buns when your boyfriend rings. I crept closer to the phone. Shane didn't notice anything amiss.

'I got my own office, Grace.' He tried, and failed, to sound blasé. 'I can ring you anytime I like now.' I smiled down the phone: he'd always been a bit infectious that way.

'That's great, Shane. But listen, can I phone you back later? I'm just about to go into a meeting.'

'A meeting? You?'

'Yes. Remember, I told you I started my new job this week.'

'Oh, right.'

Bernard returned, his hair obediently flattened against the top of his head.

'. . . and I need to talk to you.' Shane was still speaking.

'Sorry, what did you say there? What do you want to talk to me about?'

'Is the line bad at your end?' I heard familiar impatience creep into his tone.

'No, no, it's just . . . someone dropped a stack of telephone books and I couldn't hear what you were saying.' Telephone books? Who uses those any more?

Shane sighed down the phone. 'Listen, I'll talk to you later. About our plans. I've worked it out.' Bernard was at my desk now, making drinking gestures with his hands. I nodded and he left to make coffee, I think. I tuned back in to Shane.

'What plans?'

'Jesus, Grace. The ones you've been on at me for ages to make. The ones we were talking about at the weekend?'

I squinted down the phone, trying to remember. We'd hardly seen each other all weekend. There'd been no important conversations. I'd have remembered, wouldn't I?

'But we didn't discuss any plans at the weekend,' I said, confused.

'Well, I'm bloody well discussing them now, amn't I?' Shane's voice was shrill and in my mind I could see his mouth: a thin line. A shadow fell across my desk and I looked up. Bernard placed a mug of coffee carefully on my 'I don't do Mondays. Or Tuesdays, Wednesdays and Thursdays' coaster.

'Thanks, Bernard,' I whispered up at him.

'What did you say?'

'Sorry, Shane. That was Bernard. I was just . . .'

'Jesus, that guy is everywhere all of a sudden. Can't he see you're on the phone? To me?'

I breathed hard: in through my nose and out through my mouth. Then, in a voice that surprised me with its calmness, I told Shane that I had to go and that we could continue this discussion at the weekend.

'I'll see if I can get a flight on Friday night. I could come straight to the flat.'

I told him – again – that I was spending Friday night in Mam's house with Clare and Jane. Maybe the part of his brain responsible for remembering details relating to weddings closed down, like pubs on Christmas Day.

'So, I'll see you after the ceremony then. You know, the bit where they say "I do"?' I couldn't help adding that, just to see what he said. He didn't say anything. Although, to give the man his due, he *had* mentioned plans and, as I returned the receiver to the cradle, I did wonder what he had in mind.

40

It was late when I finally downed tools and left the building. Even the smoked mirror in the lift wasn't doing me any fa-vours. The skin on my face was pinched and pale and my eyes were watery and shot through with tired red veins from an excess of Excel that afternoon. Still, the meeting with the boss went well and I was on track to achieve my objective for the first week of the job: trying not to get found out and fired.

It was still bright when I reached the car park and I stopped for a moment, toying briefly with the idea of going to the graveyard. Whenever I thought about it before, it was dark, which made the decision easy. I mean, who goes to grave-yards after dark? Now it was bright. In fact, it was sunny and I moved my hand along the floor of my bag, feeling for sun-glasses that I couldn't find. The security hut was in darkness, the shutters pulled down, giving it an out-of-season ice cream parlour look. It was the first time Ciaran had left before me. I decided I would send him an email in the morning, asking if he had enjoyed his half-day. Still I stood there, undecided. My car was one of three left in the car park and I tried to work out who the other two belonged to. One was possibly Niall's; the back window was cluttered with toys and empty crisp bags, although the most telling clue was a six-pack of raspberry Petit Filous on the dashboard.

I knew I wasn't going to go to the graveyard, but still I stood there, making up excuses and presenting them to myself as if I were two people: what about if I go after the wedding?

I reached for this thought like a lifebelt. That made sense. This week was busy, wasn't it? I'd have more time next week, wouldn't I? 'I'll go after the wedding.' I said it out loud just to see how it played. It sounded reasonable. Responsible even.

'You'll go where after the wedding?'

I spun around, hurting myself with the speed of it. It was only Caroline. She knew I talked to myself.

'What are you doing here? Again?' It was a logical question.

'Don't look at me like that.'

'Like what?'

'Like I'm a stalker or something.'

'Aren't you?' Out of the corner of my eye, I could see the door opening. The one leading into the office building. We both turned towards it. It was only Niall, struggling out with two Tesco bags, straining with produce. He nodded goodnight to us and got into his car.

'I was at the law library,' Caroline said.

'Oh, so you didn't just happen to be *in the neighbourhood,* like at lunchtime.' My voice was sharper than I'd intended. Caroline was in too good a mood to let me get her down.

'I wanted to take you for a drink and tell you all about my lunch date.'

'Date?' Oh God, stop it, stop it, stop it. Why couldn't I just let it go?

'Well, it was only lunch, but I'm working on it. He's a tricky customer, this Bernard O'Malley. Is everything OK with you?' Her look of concern withered my jealousy and I looked away, ashamed.

'No, I'm fine. Don't mind me. Just had a busy day. A drink would be lovely.' I slipped my arm through hers and we moved off. Usually Caroline wasn't at all tactile, but I knew today she wouldn't mind. Today she looked like the sun had set right where she stood, giving her a radiant, glittery look.

'So, tell me about lunch.' I braced myself.

'Lunch. Was. Fabulous.' She stopped walking when she said this. The voice inside my head was roaring at me 'don't ask her, don't ask her, don't ask her.'

'Did he kiss you?' I asked her.

Caroline tutted at me. 'That's like reading the last page of book before you even start it.' She started to walk again but stopped when she saw that I hadn't moved. I softened my tone.

'Go on. Tell me. Did he kiss you?'

Caroline sighed and fiddled with the strap on her bag and I was weak with relief. And shame.

'No, he didn't,' she said, 'but he wanted to.' I believed her utterly. We both started walking again, heading towards O'Reillys without having to discuss it, giving me time to think. I decided that wanting to kiss someone and not kissing them was in fact worse than wanting to kiss someone and then kissing them. With the first scenario, you've got what I like to call anticipation. You *want* to kiss someone but you don't do it, so you *anticipate* what that kiss might be like, and the anticipation could turn into a bit of an obsession until you simply cannot *wait* for your next meeting with that person that you wanted to kiss but didn't. Then, finally, you can *want* to kiss them and then *actually* kiss them as well – if you get my meaning?

On the way to the pub, Caroline spared no details. Where they went (Milanos), where they sat (in the corner at the back where the light can't penetrate), what they ate (Mexican pizza for him, vegetarian for her, glass of wine each).

'Why didn't you just get a bottle? It's much better value,' I asked, sounding *exactly* like my mother. Caroline didn't notice.

'I know, I wanted to, but Bernard said he had to be sober for that meeting you had this afternoon with the boss.'

This pleased me, although Caroline didn't attach much importance to Bernard's display of moderation.

'Did he talk about work at all?' I reached for nonchalant.

'Not too much.' Caroline gave it due consideration. 'Although he did say that you were very good at your job.' And she was off again, telling me about something the waiter (Mario) said about the sun-dried tomatoes being an especially good aphrodisiac at this time of year. Caroline's face was animated, her mouth barely able to keep up with her brain, words tumbling out. I had to hold my two hands up in a 'halt' gesture when we reached the bar and she looked around, confused, as if wondering where we were.

'What would you like to drink?' I asked.

'No, I'll get these,' she said, taking the slimmest of wallets out of her bag. Caroline's wallets were always slim, being full of €50 notes with not a coin in sight. She didn't believe in coins, especially not euro ones. 'Tat', she called them. She kept them in a biscuit tin at the back of her wardrobe and gave it to a friend of hers who worked for Trócaire at the end of every year. Last year, there was €325.76 in the tin and I resolved to do the same at the start of this year, although, so far I've only managed to buy a tin of biscuits and eat nearly all of them – except the Bourbon Creams, obviously. But still, it was only March. Lots of time left to fulfil New Year resolutions.

Once we were settled with our drinks, Caroline picked up where she left off, showing no signs of tiring. She was like the Duracell bunny on speed.

'Caroline.' I interrupted her. I simply *had* to know. 'What is it about him that you like so much?' I held my breath, desperate to hear but not wanting to know.

Caroline closed her eyes in concentration, giving my question due consideration.

'I honestly don't know,' she finally said, flipping a beer mat with the back of her fingers and catching it, without even looking. She sighed, annoyed with herself for being so vague. 'You think it's weird, don't you. Me being like this.'

'Well,' I said, 'it's just so unlike you. I've never seen you like this before.'

'Maybe it's just my time,' she said after a while.

'Let's make a list,' I said, getting my notebook out of my bag. If I was going to accept this situation, I'd better start embracing it, getting on board and showing a bit of support. Caroline was my friend. She had been there when Patrick died. She knew things without my having to explain. She understood.

'What kind of a list?' Caroline grinned. The organised part of her loved the idea of a list, as I knew it would.

'Things you have in common,' I said. 'We'll start with that.'

'Oh,' was all she said, frowning in concentration. She lifted her glass to her lips although I don't think she drank from it.

'Well, there's you, I suppose,' she began.

'We can't put me on the list,' I said, wanting to.

'Well, we have the same good taste in people. He seems to like you and so do I.' Caroline's argument made sense when she put it like that. I wrote my name at the top of the list slowly, the nib of the pencil straining under the weight of my hand.

'OK,' I looked up at her. 'What else?'

Caroline was fiddling with the strap of her handbag again. 'Well, he loves sailing,' she began.

'Sailing,' I said, drawing a matchbox boat on the page beside my name. 'How lovely.'

'But I don't like sailing,' Caroline quite rightly pointed out.

'No, not the actual getting into the boat bit and the moving across water bit and the bobbing up and down on the waves bit,' I acknowledged fairly. 'But the idea of it. You love that, don't you?' Caroline nodded slowly, looking down at the long sheet of paper in front of me, empty except for the top two lines where I had written:

1. Grace.
2. The idea of sailing.

'This is stupid,' Caroline suddenly said, making a grab for the page with both hands. I slid the page away from her, just out of her reach.

'Hold on,' I said. 'What about pizza? And wine? You both enjoyed lunch today, didn't you?'

'Ah Grace, *everybody* likes pizza and wine. That's like saying we're both partial to inhaling oxygen.'

'Fine,' I said, pushing the paper towards her. I was annoyed now. I mean, what exactly was I *doing?* Encouraging Caroline and her ridiculous pursuit of Bernard O'Malley. I say ridiculous because pursuing men was a brand new sport in Caroline's world. She had never done this before because she'd never needed to. They had nothing in common and Caroline couldn't even come up with one good reason as to why she was interested in him.

'Wait, Grace, you're right.' Caroline suddenly smacked the table with the flat of her palm, making the elderly couple at the table next to us jump in a way that was possibly not the best thing for their hearts.

'What?'

'Food. I'll feed him. I'll stuff him with food. After the wedding. Next week.' Caroline grabbed the pencil from my hand and started to scribble on the page in front of her.

'You're going to invite him over for dinner?' I asked.

'Yes.' Caroline stopped writing and looked up at me. 'You couldn't make yourself scarce, could you?' she asked in a pleading voice. 'I think I'll be able to seduce him once I get him in the confined space of the flat . . . Maybe you could spend the night at Clare and Richard's house. Sure, they'll be on honeymoon anyway. You could water the plants or something. Feed George, maybe.'

'Of course I will,' I said, swallowing back an image of the pair of them spearing delicate strips of organic-corn-fed-free-from-original-sin chicken onto a fork and feeding each other.

'I'll get the food from that place, Dinner-4-2,' she went on, writing it all down. 'You know that place on the corner.' I nodded my head. Of course I knew the place. The same one I used when I first 'cooked' for Shane. They delivered the food, ready made, and all you had to do was transfer it onto one of your own dishes for that authentic home-made look. And it would have worked too. If it hadn't been for the pesky sauce. Turned out there were nuts in it after me telling Shane that there weren't. Turned out he was allergic to nuts. Turned out nuts made his skin blister and peel in a most unsightly way. We laughed about it . . . eventually.

'. . . at least fourteen per cent proof. I'll get him good and jarred and he won't be able to resist me. Three bottles of the stuff. Just to be sure to be sure.'

'Jesus, Cats, it's far from men having to be drunk to want to kiss you you're used to,' I said, shaking my head.

'I know, I know. But Bernard is different. He's harder to read than other guys. Maybe he's shy or something. I just want to be like a Boy Scout, you know. Fully prepared.' Caroline opened a bracket after the word 'wine' and wrote 'at least fourteen per cent proof'. She moved on to the next item. Clothing. She underlined the word three times and chewed the top of the pencil.

There had been nothing shy about the way Bernard unzipped my boots. Or how he removed every single item of clothing I wore that night with a deliberateness that was hellishly sexy. I twitched, as though someone had walked over my grave.

'Cold, Grace?' Caroline asked. I shook my head, not trusting myself to speak. Caroline leaned across the table with a pained expression.

'You will help me, won't you?' she asked. I nodded, forcing a smile. I would help her. Of course I would. It was the least I could do.

My phone beeped and I reached down into my bag to get it. It was a text message. From Clare:

See you soon. Am soooo excited.

And then I remembered.

'Oh, fuck.' I shouted the words and the elderly couple gathered their coats, cardigans, bags, umbrellas, hats and walking sticks, making a beeline for the exit.

'Oh shit, it's the wedding rehearsal, isn't it?' Caroline remembered, too late, where I was supposed to be in exactly – she looked at her watch – twenty minutes. And I knew then that she was in love. Caroline didn't forget things. She was like an elephant in that respect. I was different. Forgetfulness was expected of me.

I sank my face into my hands.

'It's only the rehearsal. Don't worry about it.' Caroline played it down. But I knew how important it was to Clare. And I was the bridesmaid. The *chief* bridesmaid, for fuck sake. I grabbed my coat and bag, shouted a goodbye at Caroline and ran past the elderly couple who were still shuffling towards the exit.

41

Thursday. Last day in work before the wedding. Surprisingly, I was working really hard. So hard, in fact, I took my jacket off and hung it on the back of my chair. So hard, in fact, I forgot to take a lunch break and it was now after two and the canteen would be closing down and Maureen would be counting her tips and asking awkward questions if I went down there, cap and begging bowl in hand. I never missed lunch. Everybody knew that. A figure like this doesn't happen by accident. So what happened today then? Well, I had decided to take Friday off to engage in a wide variety of activities, all of which could be listed under the heading 'body sculpture'. Then, back to my mother's house for a cold buffet with Clare, Jane and some relatives flying over from New York for the wedding. Patrick's anniversary mass was on Wednesday so I had arranged to take Monday, Tuesday and Wednesday of next week off as well. So I was trying to get things in order before I left the office, having acquired some class of a work ethic along with this promotion. It felt strange, like writing with my right hand (I'm a leftie – or a *citeog*, as my primary school teacher called me), but I was getting used to it.

After a particularly loud rumble from my stomach that even Peter noticed, I opened a drawer at my desk and pushed my hand in towards the back of it, groping with my fingers. I found a banana and an Actimel. The banana skin was browning and the Actimel was a day outside its best before date. I demolished them both and got back to work. This was an

area of my life that was running smoothly. Even the boss had
commented on it yesterday at the meeting. *And* he remembered Patrick when I reminded him that I wouldn't be in next
week.

'Oh yes, what day is the mass on?' he said.

'Wednesday.'

'Take Thursday off as well. If you like,' he offered with
a facial grimace that was actually more of a smile than his
characteristic leer. 'You seem to be on top of everything
here. And I'm sure Bernard can manage without you for
a couple of days.' This was unprecedented. He hated annual leave almost as much as he hated sick leave. And maternity leave. And don't get him started on parental leave.
But still. His memory of the anniversary surprised me and
touched me. Bernard caught my eye and smiled with such
understanding, I could feel tears gather behind my eyes like
clouds. Luckily, I created a diversion (dropped the bundle
of papers I was carrying) and by the time we picked them
up, I was grand.

I finished what I was doing and checked my emails. One
from Laura. Subject: EMERGENCY:

*Need to meet asap STOP have nothing to wear to afters on Sat-
urday STOP Ethan bought himself an outfit in Boyers STOP
Unsupervised STOP Norman spent €400 on a pair of trousers
and can't make the rent STOP Emergency summit meeting in
Ciaran's office in five STOP See you then.*

Laura loved to make her emails sound like telegrams to emphasise the urgency of the message. Reading between the
lines, I could tell what she was really concerned about. Peter. She wanted to know if she could bring him to the afters.
They were all coming: Laura, Ethan, Norman and Jennifer.
Clare knew them well by now, having met them several times

in O'Reilly's on our Friday night 'just-the-one-ah-sure-let's-stay-till-kicking-out-time' after-work drinks. I turned towards Bernard's desk. There he was, straining towards the monitor with his teeny-tiny glasses, burning green with the reflection from the computer screen.

'Emergency meeting in Ciaran's office,' I said by way of explanation, getting up from my desk.

'Oh,' said Bernard, standing up. 'That's a strange place for a meeting, Grace O'Brien. Are they often held out there?' He picked up a pen and a notebook and I laughed. I loved the way he gave me my full title. I sounded like a different person, the way he said it.

'Eh, no, Bernard,' I explained. 'It's not a company meeting as such. It's just Laura. Outfit for wedding emergency.' Bernard nodded as if he understood completely.

'I didn't know she was coming.'

'Just to the afters. Her, Ethan, Norman, Jennifer.' I could feel Peter stiffening in his seat. I was right. Laura did want him to come and from his studied air of disinterest, it seemed clear that he wanted to come as well. Things were developing nicely there.

Bernard stepped back towards his desk, setting his pen and paper back down.

'Why don't you come? You look like you could use a break and Ciaran makes great coffee.' I don't know why I asked him, really. Although it meant that the others couldn't ask me any questions about him, in their usual no-holds-barred kind of way. I wondered what we looked like together, walking down the corridor. I had to lengthen my stride to keep up with him. He was lovely to walk beside, being unusually taller than me, and even in the confined space of the lift, I nearly forgot that he had seen me naked in unflattering light (AHHHHHH) and that he was now almost officially the boyfriend of my flatmate and great friend, Caroline.

Ciaran already had the kettle on when we got there, although it was standing room only when everyone arrived. Norman's eyes lit on Bernard, but other than a nod and a wink in my direction, he restrained himself. Jennifer made a beeline for him with some sob story about a problem her computer was having. She was eye-contacting him to death and touching his arm at every possible turn. I turned sideways and pushed through the crowd towards Ciaran.

'Yer lookin' well today, girrull,' he said, a little louder than usual, to be heard over the crowd. I didn't tell Ciaran that I'd been up with the cock (in the farmyard sense) every morning this week to straighten my hair, iron my clothes and carefully apply a subtle (ish) layer of make-up. I was *exhausted* from my efforts but, with Clinique concealer, you could only tell from very close up.

'I call this meeting to order,' Laura announced, looking very official with a clipboard in her hand and a pen tucked behind her ear. She took over the coffee making from Ciaran – he wasn't doing it quickly enough – and divvied out a cup to each of us. There was a pregnant pause while we waited to see if a biscuit or two might be forthcoming. Ciaran snaked his hand towards a packet of Kimberleys (the non-chocolate variety, but still . . .). Laura, with the instincts of a cat, snatched them from his reach and bustled them into a drawer.

'We're all on the Clare Wedding Diet,' she explained, glaring at each of us in turn. We nodded mutely. Not one of us was man enough for her.

'Now,' she began, glancing at the clipboard. 'First up is Ethan.' Ethan nearly fell down. Even though he was amongst friends, he hated being the centre of attention.

'Ethan,' Laura continued, fixing him with a stare, 'it has come to our attention that you have purchased an item or items of clothing in a haberdashery called hereinafter "Boyers" without any, or any adequate, supervision.' She paused to sip from her cup. 'How do you plead?'

'Well, the thing is . . .' Ethan began bravely. There was even the makings of a smile on his face.

'Guilty or not guilty,' Laura insisted. She watched a lot of *Judge Judy* and *People's Court* and loved to shout 'overruled' and 'sustained', even when it made absolutely no sense to do so.

'Not guilty.' Ethan's voice rang out, clear and pure and full of conviction. There was a collective intake of breath. Had Ethan gone shopping with his mother?

'So you *were* supervised?' Laura asked.

'I went with someone,' Ethan corrected.

'Is the bit about Boyers true?' I asked, and in the pause that followed, we bit our lips and held our breaths.

'Yes.' Another gasp from the crowd. 'But I got some lovely clobber,' he insisted. 'You'll see.'

'Omigod, he's saying clobber now,' Laura said, her hand cupped around her mouth in dramatic repulsion. 'Next thing you know he'll be *pressing* his trousers and darning his socks and wearing the darned socks with leather sandals . . .'

'OK, OK, Laura, now it's your turn,' I said, taking control of the meeting. I still had some stuff to do at my desk and I needed to get back to it.

'But we still don't know who supervised Ethan's purchase,' Laura insisted.

'Look,' I said, 'the boy went shopping. Regardless of whatever, eh, clobber he bought, he is to be commended in this.' Laura opened her mouth to argue, but I got in first. 'Do you concur?' I asked.

'Oh, all right.' Laura found a chair and sat down. 'But don't blame me if he arrives at the afters in a tank top and three-quarter-length trousers.'

'I would *never* wear three-quarter-lengths,' Ethan said. He couldn't say the same of tank tops, so wisely, he didn't mention them.

'Now, Laura.' I turned towards her with a bit of a sneer. I couldn't help it. 'Of course Peter can come to the wedding. I texted Clare and she's fine with it.'

Laura's mouth opened and closed and opened again like a fish with a hook in its gums.

'I never said anything about Peter,' she insisted, reddening in Bernard's direction.

'No, you didn't,' I agreed, moving on to the next item on the agenda.

'Norman, you're up.' I rounded on him and he started shaking his head defensively.

'OK, OK, the trousers were €400, but they were *reduced* in the sale from €550, so I actually saved money by buying them.'

'Are you going to be able to eat this month?' I asked.

'Well, I won't be having foie gras or beluga, but yeah, I won't starve.' Norman uncrossed and recrossed his legs, looking delicious in a pair of tight brown cords tethered at his narrow waist with a magnificently oversized belt buckle.

'What about you, Bernard?' Norman turned to Bernard with a sleazy grin.

'What about me?' Bernard took it on the chin, entering into the spirit of our kangaroo court.

'What are you wearing to the wedding? Do tell,' Norman said in his Hugh-Grant-in-*Notting-Hill* voice (his favourite Hugh Grant film to date).

'I hadn't really given it much thought, to be honest,' Bernard said to gasps around the room. He smiled around at us and rubbed the top of his head, making the hair spike in its usual afternoon position.

'What about that suit you wore on Tuesday?' Jennifer piped up.

'Ooh, yes,' Laura said. 'You looked lovely in that.'

'Really matched your eyes, that jacket.' Jennifer again.

'And the trousers made your legs look really long.' Laura said. I wanted to stand in front of Bernard and shield him from their attention. Like cats in heat they were. Instead, I tried to divert them.

'Lovely coffee, Laura.' But she was like an army tank in wartime.

'So, are you bringing a date to the wedding, Bernard?' Everyone suddenly bent their heads to their mugs in the way that people do when they are dying to hear the reply but don't want to appear eager.

'No, not this time,' Bernard said.

'So, what, you might consider bringing a date the next time Richard gets married?' Norman worried at him, not letting up.

'Somehow I don't think there'll be a next time,' Bernard said. 'I'd say Clare's a keeper.' It was the perfect thing to say and I felt strangely proud when everyone nodded in agreement around the hut, accepting him into the Circle of Trust.

42

Friday: Clare's last day as a singleton. Today, there wasn't a single jitter in sight as we traipsed from room to room in the beauty salon, getting ourselves seen to. Just one wobbly moment when I presented my nails to the nail specialist. Well, it was a difficult week and, in spite of being busy, I'd found enough time to bite all ten of my fingernails down to the quick. Karina, the nail specialist, hit a red button on her phone and summoned the supervisor, who, in turn, called for the general manager. Manuals were consulted as the three of them bent their heads over the peeling remains of my nails and discussed how best to attach their false beautiful ones to my real, manky ones.

'We'll have to use the full-strength adhesive,' Marilyn (nail-consultant-turned-general-manager) said, with a grimness in her voice that belied the prettiness of her nails.

'But if it gets onto that broken skin, it'll burn and sting.' So said Madeleine (the supervisor with a degree in political science. I knew this because her degree was framed on the wall beside her diploma in nail technology. The latter was in a larger, more ornate frame, as if to assure customers of her true allegiance).

'And it's going to really hurt if it gets into those broken cuticles,' added Karina, nibbling at the top of one of her own (false?) nails. The three of them worried around me, my hands held out like a bold child.

It was my mother who got them moving in the end.

'Just put the nails on her like good girls. God knows she can't go out in public with those sorry little stumps. And she's got a very high pain threshold, haven't you, Grace?'

This was news to me. I hadn't thought about my pain threshold being high or otherwise, but I had an idea that if I were ever in labour, I'd scream for the epidural in the car park of the maternity hospital.

'How about a local anaesthetic?' I asked. 'Do you do those?'

'Come on, Grace, just get the nails on and let's go. We haven't got all day.' Mam said this with the tightest of smiles towards the three nail women but even they could tell that, really, she wanted to slap me around a little bit.

I closed my eyes and held out my hands, one at a time. Karina was the one who did it in the end. I think they drew straws. Funnily enough, it wasn't that sore after all. Maybe Mam was right and I *did* have an unusually high pain threshold?

We got everything done in the same place. The hair on our head was cut, the hair everywhere else was torn away with strips of wax. Eyebrows tinted and shaped into demure curves, unlike the flatliners I was used to. Lashes tinted and curled. Mine were so short Karina could barely catch them with the curler. She did though, even though they looked like one line of a tight granny perm when she was finished with me. Clare knew I wasn't brave enough for the spray tan – not after Thomas – but I didn't want Mam to know that I was abstaining. She'd think I was making a fuss. Karina took all this in her stride and arranged for me to *appear* to go into one of the tanning booths when the others went into theirs. Then, instead of blasting me with the smelly orange stuff, she sat me down with a copy of *Heat* and a latte and winked at me, in a rather theatrical fashion, before stepping out and pulling the curtains across the cubicle, leaving me with Colin Farrell and his skanger shenanigans inside in Hollywood. Perfect.

Ciara Geraghty

When my mother commented on how pale I still was after the spray tan, Karina rushed in with assurances.

'I used a very light tan on Grace, given the particularly sensitive nature of her skin,' she said. God, she was *such* a pro. Mam looked furious but I think a lot of that was the angry orange of her skin.

'I hope you're not charging her full price for that,' Mam said.

'Don't worry about that, Mam,' said Clare. 'This is my treat.'

'That's not the point, Clare,' Mam pointed out tartly. 'I mean, look at her. She's the colour of raw pastry. It's not right. And she doesn't even smell like the rest of us.' Mam sniffed at the skin on her arm as if she might vomit with the stench of it. Karina said nothing but ushered us into the massage area where a woman called Olga with arms like bridges promised to 'tayk goot cayre ov us'.

After all that, I was falling out of my standing with the tiredness. Seriously. Beauty therapy is *exhausting*. My face was like volcanic rock, with all the open pores. I was vulnerable to infection, my pores were so empty. I was about to suggest a drink (or ten) when Mam marched us all into a taxi and sped us home to prepare for the Pre-Wedding-Cold-Buffet-Supper. I obsessed about smoking a cigarette for the entire journey. The feel of it between my fingers. The pull of my mouth against the filter. The trail of smoke in a thin line from my lips and maybe a couple of smoke rings, if I could manage it. Mam, Clare and Jane didn't notice my watering mouth. They were talking – all at the same time – about the wedding and wedding-related stuff. I wished for Patrick so hard. If he were here, he would soften the edges with his easy laugh and his gentle ribbing. I realised I was the only ginger left in the family. It was really noticeable, between Clare's dark hair, fine and long, and Jane's brunette, sensibly short. And even my mother's iron-grey bob, not one hair daring to move out of place. If he were here, I'd slag him about being an accountant. 'How many accountants does it take to change a light bulb?' I'd tease. 'None. They don't need them. They're all in bed before sundown.' And he'd come back with, 'Was it the glamour of insurance that lured you?' 'As you know perfectly well, Patrick, people who can't do anything else, insure. It was the perfect job for me.'

We'd crack our holes laughing and shake our heads and imagine what we might say on our deathbeds. If only I could have added up a few more numbers (Patrick), if only I could have settled a few more cases (me).

'Grace? Did you hear me?' And I was back in the taxi again, looking at my mother with the blank expression she hates.

'Sorry?'

Mam struggled to contain her annoyance and I sat up straighter and fixed a smile on my face.

'Sorry, Mam. I was just going through the churchy bit tomorrow. Making sure I knew exactly what to do.'

Mam sniffed, a little mollified. She could have mentioned the fact that I had been five minutes late for the rehearsal, but she didn't.

'You'll be grand, Grace.' Clare leaned over and squeezed my arm. 'All you have to do is walk up the aisle with Jane and make sure my dress isn't caught up in my knickers when I reach the altar.'

We all laughed at that, even Mam. It was like Patrick was there, just for a moment.

43

The doorbell rang and in the noise and heat of the kitchen, its normally raucous peal withered to the mew of a newborn kitten. I looked around the table, but no one else seemed to have heard the bell. Mam and Jack were at the kitchen sink, one washing, one drying, their hips swinging in time to an ancient tune playing softly on the radio. Uncle Paul-from-America was telling a loud story, just like a proper American. We always called him that to differentiate him from the other Uncle Paul, who wasn't an uncle at all but a barber and a great friend of Dad's. Everyone else was listening to the story, even the children, who stretched like statues across the Twister board in torturous positions. I walked through the kitchen door and hurried up the hall. Whoever it was made a long silhouette behind the mottled glass of the door. I made out a bag – or a hump – on the person's back. The shadow of a hand patted down hair flying in all directions in the wind. I bent and pulled at the handle. He stood there like a stray dog, wet and shaking himself. It was Shane.

'Where were you?' He struggled into the porch, peeling off his sodden coat.

'What do you mean?' I took the coat he handed to me. 'What are you doing here?'

Shane looked at me, water dripping down his face like tears.

'Jesus, Grace, I emailed you this morning. With my flight details. I texted you when I boarded in London. And when I bloody landed. I thought you'd pick me up from the airport at least.'

By this time, he had removed his shoes and his suit jacket, dropping them into my outstretched arms.

'I wasn't in work today, so I didn't get my emails. I had to switch my phone off in the beauty salon and haven't turned it back on again. I didn't realise you were flying in tonight.'

Shane put his socks on top of the growing bundle in my arms. Even they were wet.

'Did you walk from the airport?' I asked, with a swipe towards humour. Shane didn't find it amusing.

'The taxi driver brought me to the wrong estate. They all look the bloody same in the dark. I've been walking in the rain for the last ten minutes.' Something shifted in me and suddenly I was angry.

'I told you I wouldn't be in work today. You knew I was busy with Clare.'

Shane looked up like he'd been slapped. He looked right at me and I had the strangest sensation. Like we were strangers.

He moved towards me, awkwardly hugging me across the sodden clothes and shoes in my arms.

'I'm sorry, Grace, I forgot that you weren't working today. I just decided this morning to come over tonight. I thought you'd be delighted.' He stepped away from me and looked over my shoulder, past me.

'How did you know I was even here?' I was confused. And cold, with the wet clothes in my arms.

'I rang Caroline when I couldn't get through to you. She told me.' He was still looking around the hall and I realised he hadn't been here, in this house, for a very long time. Maybe not since the funeral.

'You go on through,' I said. 'I'll put your stuff in the hot press.'

'I'll wait for you.' His tone was nervous and I realised he

didn't want to face my mother without me. The door to the kitchen opened and the hallway flooded with light and heat and noise.

'Who was at the door, Grace?' It was my mother, her face pink from two glasses of wine and the heat of the kitchen.

'Mrs O'Brien, it's lovely to see you again. You're looking well.' Shane stepped towards her.

My mother extended her hand towards him and Shane re-arranged himself – he had anticipated a hug – and shook her hand instead. I realised then that they hadn't seen each other since the month's-mind, nearly eleven months ago. There was always some excuse. A cards night she couldn't get out of. A football match he had to see. A migraine pending. An early morning. A late night.

'I'll just go and put these clothes away,' I said, hurrying towards the stairs.

'I'll help you,' said Mam, following me. Shane stood in the hall for a moment before disappearing into the kitchen.

I could feel her behind me. I don't know how, but I ended up in Patrick's room. It was cold in there. When I turned around, she stood there, her hands on her hips, waiting.

'I'm sorry, Mam.' It seemed like that's all I ever said to her any more.

'Grace, I don't mind you having your friends here.' She said 'friends' like you might say 'pet anaconda'. 'I would just like you to let me know, that's all.' We were standing in the dark, in the empty room. The rain battered against the window, like an umpire trying to intervene.

'I'm sorry,' I said again. 'I didn't know he was coming in tonight.'

'Is he coming to the wedding?'

'Clare invited him.' Defensive.

I felt the rush of air as she leaned towards me and took

the clothes and shoes out of my arms. In the touch of her hands on my arms, I thought that maybe we could talk, here, in Patrick's room.

'Mam?'

But she was gone and even though she made no sound, I knew she was standing at the open door of the hot press, folding his clothes and arranging them on the shelves. I left the room and walked past her, down the stairs.

44

The first awful thing happened at 12.40 p.m. I was certain about the time. I stared hard at the hands of the kitchen clock and concentrated on not crying. That's how I knew for sure. We were still at my mother's house, having stayed there the night before. Clare, Jane, Mam and I. Four women under one roof. Never a good idea. The fact that we were closely related made it worse. A bag of cats. Patrick's absence was a presence that we moved around. The space left by Dad had softened with the years, a shadow. Only the women remained. We endured.

It was the knot in Mam's necklace. One of those thin chains that jewellers call 'delicate'. A sliver of a moon hung from it. Dad gave it to her on their wedding day. She had disentangled it from the bottom of her jewellery box and it was strangled in knots. That was when she called his name. Threw her head back, arched her back towards the stairs. Carelessly. Just like she used to do.

'Paaat . . . rick.'

It sounded so natural, so *normal*. For a moment, I expected to hear him on the stairs, taking them two at a time in bare feet, like he always did. He was the knots man in our house. There's always one, isn't there? Someone patient, with long fingers and eyesight as keen as Coleman's Mustard. Patrick was ours. Shoelaces, skipping ropes, elastic bands wound tightly around strands of dolls' hair, hard and matted. I could see him there on the couch, head bent to the task, hair slipping about his face, careful fingers picking at threads of gold until it lay in a perfect line across his lap. Except he wasn't there. Mam's mouth still held the shape of his name. Her face was sore to look at. It had been so long since she had called him. None of us knew what to say. I leapt into the void.

'Here, I'll do it.'

'You won't be able to do it.' Mam rallied well.

'Do you have another chain you can wear?' Jane, always the practical one. My mother looked at Jane like a child might look at a mother.

'I wanted that one.' Her voice was a whisper. Jane nodded, took the chain from her hands and went to work at the kitchen table. The lump in my throat was hard and cold. My eyes smarted.

'Can you go and check on Clare?' Mam rose from the couch, looking pointedly towards me. I swallowed hard.

'Sure, I'll see if she needs a hand.' I didn't look at her, my eyes fixed on the clock. If I looked at her, I wouldn't make it. I stumbled upstairs to Mam's bedroom, where Clare was stepping into her dress.

'You were supposed to call us for this bit,' I said.

'Can you zip me up?' She was standing in front of the full-length mirror. I looked at her reflection from the doorway.

'You're beautiful,' I said. And she was. Even in three-inch heels, she looked tiny, like a doll. You could pop her on the top tier of the wedding cake.

'Don't get soft. What was Mam shouting about downstairs?' If she'd heard his name floating up the stairs, she made no mention of it.

'Nothing. Just sorting out her jewellery.' I moved into the room slowly.

'Can you fix my veil?' It was only when I lifted my hands to her head that I realised they were shaking.

'Are you cold, Grace?' Clare was concerned.

'No, just excited,' I lied. 'I've never been a bridesmaid before, remember?' Somehow I managed to slice the comb of the veil through her hair. 'Wadded Willy is a lucky man.'

'I wish you wouldn't call him that.'

'Why?' I was curious. Clare had never minded this title before.

'I love him, that's why.'

'I know that, what does that have to do with anything? He's loaded, so what?'

'But I just love him. I don't care about the fact that he's loaded.'

'Yeah, but it's still nice that he is. You get to love him in Rathgar instead of a place estate agents call "just off the M50" that is, in fact, Leitrim.'

'Yeah, but I'd still love him in Leitrim. That's what I'm saying.' Clare's voice was shrill.

'It's OK, Clare, I know.' I patted her on the shoulder and she hugged me. The warmth of her calmed me.

Then she straightened and looked worried again.

'Do you think Mam will be OK today? You know, giving me away, I mean.' She was staring at her reflection in the mirror but seemed far away. I knew where she was. In Patrick's favourite restaurant. The Milestone, just off Camden Street. It was his birthday, his last one. He was thirty-one years old. We were all there; Shane and I, Jane and James, Clare and Richard. And Mam, of course, at the head of the table. Clare and Richard were whispering loudly at each other, perhaps thinking none of us could hear them. It sounded like an argument.

'I want to tell them, I can't wait any more.' This from Clare.

'But it's Patrick's night. We should wait.' This from the patient Richard.

'Patrick's a bloke. He doesn't give a toss about stuff like that.'

'Stuff like what?' Patrick cut across them. 'What are you two whispering about?'

Clare looked at Richard and he nodded.

'We have an announcement to make,' she said, looking at all of us and, of course, we all knew immediately what she was talking about.

'What?' Patrick leaned across the table, bushy eyebrows pointing skyward, his face alive with interest.

Clare paused for a moment, making sure she had our full attention. She had.

'I'm getting married.'

'To who?' Patrick asked, winking at Richard.

'To whom, Patrick, to whom.' That was Mam's contribution but she was smiling a smile that reached her eyes.

There was much shrieking and hurling ourselves at Clare. Then we formed a solemn line and took turns to shake Richard's hand – we called him Richard when he was around. He wasn't the kind of man you hugged and kissed. Not that he wasn't lovely or anything, he was. Just in a quiet way. Well, quieter anyway – than us, if you know what I mean.

And then it happened. The conversation. The one we all remembered, especially today.

'I'll give you away, Clare. At the altar, I mean,' Patrick said. 'If you want me to, that is.' He was grinning, but his tone was serious.

'Oh.' Clare was taken aback. 'I hadn't even thought about that part of it.'

'Well, take your time, have a think, there's no rush,' Patrick insisted.

'No, I don't need any time. I'd love you to give me away, I really would.' She put her small hand on top of his.

And then a really strange thing happened. Mam leaned forward and put her hand on top of Clare's – without being asked or told to, I mean. Jane put her hand on top of Mam's and, before I knew what I was doing, my hand was on top of Jane's. An O'Brien family hand tower. It was so unlike us. So *The Waltons*. So *Little House on the Prairie*. But at that moment, I felt connected to these people. This family. Then Patrick said, 'I'll give you away, Grace, when it's your time.' We laughed at that, our hands lifting and moving away from each other, like birds scattering. That was the last time we were all together.

I'll give you away, Grace. That's what he said. But it was me who gave him away in the end.

'She'll be grand,' I said loudly and we both jumped a little at the sound. 'You know, Mam, she's a soldier. She's practically an ox, she's that strong.'

'I wish things were different,' Clare said. Her voice was small and her eyes were bright. I knew we were on the brink of something that wasn't good. Had Clare decided to lose it an hour before her wedding? Ten minutes after the make-up professional left, taking with her all the little pots of magic that could tame a tear-reddened face? Clare had kept it together for so long, kept us together. And now, after a year of composure, poise and strength, she was ready to throw it away, fling it over the edge of a cliff, be done with it. As chief bridesmaid, older sister, and for myself, I could not let this happen. I pulled myself up to my full height in my big knickers, bigger bra and high heels – this was quite high, especially when you consider that my big hair was piled like a crown on the top of my head. I must have been nearly six feet tall, almost as tall as Patrick.

I threw my head back and started to sing at the top of my voice. The first song that came into my head. It was 'Islands in the Stream'. I couldn't believe it. By that fella with the silver hair and the suit. He sang it with Dolly Parton, remember?

It's a curious thing about big girls like me. Most of us can sing – I mean, *really* sing. Maybe it's to do with our biological make-up – big lungs or something. Or maybe it was a gift God bestowed to make up for our unwieldy size. I could sing, and the strange thing about my voice was that it was small and sweet, like it belonged to someone else. I finished the chorus and dragged air back into my lungs to begin it again. I didn't dare look at Clare but I knew she wasn't crying and that was the main thing.

By the time I was half-way through the chorus for the second time – of course I couldn't remember one single line from any of the verses – I started to dance. And then Clare joined in. I chanced a glance at her. She looked resigned. Resigned to her role as the girl who doesn't crack. The girl who doesn't lose it. The Good Girl. That's what our mother called her. I took both her hands in mine and we swung our arms in time with the song, which we were now belting out like Tina Turner at her Really and Truly Final Farewell Gig.

When we started harmonising, I knew we were safe. The door flung open and Mam and Jane stood there, panting and looking concerned. My voice trailed away but Clare continued till the end of the third chorus. God love her, she hadn't a note in her head. But then again, she got to wear size eight dresses and pretty sandals from the kids' section in Monsoon. The pair of us were breathless.

'Clare was a little . . .' I began.

'I just got the wedding jitters,' Clare explained. Mam's face softened and she walked towards Clare with her arm out. For a moment, I thought she was going to hug her, but then she sort of patted her awkwardly on her head before folding her arms again.

'You look lovely, pet.' Then she turned to me.

'Grace, will you for the love of God get yourself dressed.

The car will be here in twenty minutes and Clare doesn't want to be late for the church.' I opened my mouth to say something – I don't know what – but she was gone. Jane took over.

'Here, Grace, I'll help with the buttons.' She was already at the bed, removing acres of baby pink tissue paper lying in folds around my dress.

'Thanks, Jane.' I was grateful to her. Clare settled herself on a stool at the dressing table and repaired her eye make-up. A stray tear traced a track down her cheek, bringing with it a thin line of Midnight Shadow mascara. I caught her eye in the mirror's reflection and she smiled at me. I smiled back, relieved.

'Grace, you'll have to bend over. I can't reach your head to get the dress over it,' Jane said.

'I can't bend over in these pants. They're too tight.'

In the end, Jane stood on a chair and eased the dress over my head.

'Mind my hair.' My voice, edged with panic, was muffled under the rich fabric. A hundred clips – give or take a few – scored through my hair, holding on for dear life. The hairdresser had spent over an hour on my hair that morning and when she was finished, she looked exhausted but proud – like a mother who has just pushed a ten-pound baby out into the world. The thing could blow at any time and my main priority was to make sure it happened after the vows were exchanged and the photographs taken.

'Stand still. Don't move,' Jane commanded. She managed to get the dress over my head without dislodging a single clip. I was impressed but unsurprised. Once the dress negotiated its way past the obstacle of my breasts, it slid down the length of my body, with no recourse to pushing or pulling.

'It fits, it fits!' I punched the air with a fist and got a little Michael Flatley about the legs.

'Of course it fits. Why wouldn't it?' This from nine-stone Jane, who hadn't suffered a diet-related panic attack in her entire skinny life.

'I just, I thought I might have put on a few pounds during the week, what with the eating and the drinking and all,' I said.

'You always think that,' Clare said. 'Anyway, you haven't. You look great.' They were both standing back, looking at me, like I was a new piece in a museum they visited regularly.

Jane's lips were pursed.

'We're going to look like fecking dwarves beside that,' she said, shaking her head slowly. 'Could you not go in your bare feet? Sure, no one would notice, the dress is that long.'

We'd had this discussion before, many times.

'No.' Clare was emphatic. 'She's tall. She's just a tall woman.'

'Yes, but *too* tall.' Jane wasn't going to let it go.

'Eh, hallo, I'm standing right here. I can hear you, even up at this altitude.' We giggled at that, like schoolgirls.

'Grace, are you ready yet?' My mother's voice marched up the stairs, her tone military.

'Yes Mother,' I replied and we were off again, clutching each other.

'I'd better get my shoes on,' I eventually managed.

'You sound a bit wheezy. Don't forget to bring your inhaler,' Jane said, recovering her matronly demeanour.

'No, I'm grand. Just haven't had a fag in the last hour, that's all.' I was on my hands and knees now, looking under the bed for my shoes. 'Jane, where have you hidden them?'

'I didn't hide them. I just put all the shoes into the . . . eh, the spare room.' A silence descended, like fog on a mountain top. The *spare* room. There had never been a spare room in this house. It was a four-bedroomed house and when we all lived there, each of the bedrooms bulged with us and our be-

longings. One for Mam and Dad – we always called it Mam
and Dad's room, even long after he was gone – one for Jane,
one shared by Clare and I and one for Patrick.

'You mean *Patrick's* room.' I spoke in a low, deliberate voice, shocked at the anger pulsing against my skin.
We called Patrick's room 'Patrick's room' long after he
left home, just like we called the den 'the blue room' even
though it had been repainted a cat-sick green five years
ago. This was what people did. Names stuck. Habits of a
lifetime were hard to break. There was nothing spare about
Patrick's room. Nothing spare about Patrick or his life. It
had been a life full to bursting with ideas, plans, actions,
living. He kept stretching it at the edges, making it bigger
and bigger to accommodate more plans and more ideas
that would never now be realised. I did that. I took all that
life and turned it into a spare room. I had to get out. I was
afraid of what I might say or do.

The room *was* beginning to look like a spare room. Un-
cle-Paul-from-America had left his golf bag in a corner. A
box of paper recycling sagged on the floor. The bed was covered in wedding presents, heaped one on top of another like
a Legoland high-rise. And it smelled musty. Like an old person's house. I finally spotted the shoes and grabbed them. I
shut the door behind me and sat on the landing, the bedroom
door firmly closed. I leaned against it and closed my eyes. I
was tired. Shane's arrival last night had unsettled me. And
him, I think. He hadn't stayed long.

'I'll see you tomorrow baby,' he'd said, pecking me with a
chaste kiss on the side of my mouth. I'd felt bad when he left.
I hadn't made enough of a fanfare.

'Grace, what are you doing out here?' Mam said. She must
have tiptoed up the stairs.

'Just getting my shoes,' I said, holding the sandals up by the
straps to prove it.

'I really don't know why you have to put your shoes on out here, Grace, but just remember this, today is—'

'Clare's day. I know. I won't forget.' I kept my head down as I spoke, easing my feet into the sandals that were all heels and straps as thin as spaghetti. The anger in me hadn't gone away. I was afraid of it. I pushed myself upright, my back pressed against the bedroom door. I lifted my eyes to hers, met them, held them. We were the same height, once I was in my heels and she in her flats. I wished for something to say but could think of nothing. She turned away first.

'Come on ladies,' I called in to my sisters. 'Let's do this thing. Let's get Clare good and wed.'

The closed door muffled my sisters' laughing. I headed down the stairs, my toes already straining against the precarious downward slope of the shoes. I moved into the sitting room, my heels making no sound against the carpet. Mam was standing beside the sideboard, very still, her back to me. She was holding a framed photograph in her hands. The one of me and Patrick, in Spain last summer. He was dead before we got that roll of film developed. I hated that picture.

We are on the beach where it happened. The sky is a blameless blue that stretches like a piece of silk over our heads as far as forever. Patrick looks happy, like someone with his life stretching out in front of him, full of possibilities. That's what makes the picture hard to look at. Caroline took the photograph. She must have moved a little just before the shutter came down. It is a little out of focus, blurred around the edges, like time is standing still. Patrick's arm is around my shoulder. A big wave arches towards the beach, its edges frothy, like a milkshake. Mam insisted on framing the photograph for reasons I never asked about. It was my reminder, my guilt, my wish that things were different. Mam traced a finger down his face. It was an unbearably tender gesture – I knew she would hate it if she realised I was there, that I had seen her.

I backed away. This time, I came at her from the kitchen, making sure to open and close the door loudly and clatter with force across the ceramic tiles. By the time I reached the sitting room again, the photograph was back in its usual spot and she was standing with her back to it.

'Ah Grace, you're ready at last. How's the dress? Not too tight I hope?'

'No, I . . .'

'And here she is.' Mam swung round to look at her youngest daughter. 'Clare, you look marvellous, you really do. Not nervous, are you?'

Clare looked over at me and smiled. 'No, I'm fine. Grace sorted me out.'

'Grace, will you take a photograph of Clare and me?' Mam thrust her camera at me. It was one of those big clumsy ones that have been out of production for at least the past twenty years. I held it up to my right eye and focused on them through the viewfinder. Two remarkably similiar-looking women apart from their height. If I wanted to get the ends of Clare's dress, I would have to cut Mam's head out of the picture. No zoom, you see? I backed away as far as I could. I was nearly in the kitchen.

'Hurry up Grace, the car will be here any minute.' Mam scanned the road outside through the nets.

I moved forward, back into the sitting room. I decided I would get conventional and try for *both* heads in the shot, from the waists up. See, I was even calling it a 'shot' now, not a photograph, getting into the swing of the thing.

'Move closer together,' I commanded. Then I realised that I could see the photo of Patrick and me, just on the edge of the viewfinder. I shuffled to the right and it dropped out of sight.

'OK people, say cheese.'

Clare shouted 'cheese' much too loudly and Mam smiled her closed-mouth smile. She never bared her teeth if she could help it – she hated her teeth – but she leant her head towards Clare's and held her hand as a mother bringing a child to school for the first time might.

'Now, your turn, Grace. I'll take one of you and Mam.' Clare walked towards me.

'I'll go and get Jane and we can all get into it,' Mam said walking towards the hall. I turned to Clare.

'Are you ready?'

'For wadded Willy?'

'And his Wadded willy?'

'How do you know it's wadded?'

'Everyone knows that. Rich guys have big dicks. It's as plain as the Barry Manilow nose on their faces.'

We made snorting noises through our noses before Clare stopped, looking me straight in the eye.

'I'm ready,' she said. And she was.

45

In true Clare style, we pulled up at the church ten minutes early.

'Jesus, I can't be *early*. I told him I'd be on time, but I can't be *early*. It seems way too needy. Anyway, his mother might try and make me sign the pre-nup again if I have time before the ceremony.' Clare's shoulders were up around her ears. And her fears about Mrs Ryan – her mother-in-law-to-be-in-ten-minutes – were probably well founded. She was one of those tiny women whose height was in indirect proportion to her ability to intimidate. 'How *naice* to meet you,' she might say in a voice that suggested she had already forgotton your name. She didn't have a job, she ran a foundation, one of those ones that gives money away. She signed cheques for a living. I'd love such a job but, apparently, you need buckets of money for a gig like that. She had been disappointed in love a long time ago. Not one of those disappointments that make you stronger. The other kind. The one that makes you bitter and keeps you that way until you die.

'Once more around the block, Jeeves,' I said in my finest Queen Mother tones while rotating my hand on my wrist and smiling gently at the crowd gathered outside the church. His name wasn't Jeeves, of course. It was Milo, but it's not every day a girl gets a ride in a Bentley. The seats were soft and thick with leather. There was a mini-bar on either side of the cavernous back seat.

'Grace. No,' my mother had said as my hand stretched towards it when we got into the car.

'I was just going to see what was inside,' I said, sulking, but I dropped my hand anyway. Now I would never know.

'Oh, look.' Clare was pointing at a car coming towards us, rattling along at about ten miles an hour. 'It's Aunt Joan and Uncle Malachy.' And indeed it was. The reason we were so sure about that? The ancient Fiat looked empty, that's why. Only Malachy's tell-tale pair of hairy hands – thick and fleshy – gripping the steering wheel were visible. Beside him, in the passenger seat, a straw hat bobbed, laden along the rim with all manner of plastic fruits. The cheap kind, mind: apples, oranges, bananas. None of your cantaloupes or limes or lychees for our Aunt Joan. She had met her match in Malachy and their meaness was legendary. Never mind peeling an orange in your pocket, Malachy would have shovelled the orange down his kacks if he thought it would be better concealed there. We were dying to see what their wedding gift to Clare and Richard would be. Luckily, the windows of the Bentley were tinted so the pair couldn't see us pointing and laughing. Some people say Bentleys are just for show, but really, they do have a practical side as well. Anyway, Malachy and Joan couldn't see above the dashboard so we were safe enough. To pass the time as we sailed around the block for a second time, we took bets on what time our fun-size aunt and uncle would leave the reception.

'When does the bar stop serving the free grog?' I asked.

Clare looked surprised at the question. 'It doesn't.' She was going to be such a *natural* Lady of the Manor, I could tell.

'Jesus H, they'll be there till the bitter end so,' I said. 'On the plus side though, it means they'll be fighting by eight, so that'll be good. Nothing like a good old fisticuffs at a wedding to set the tone.'

'Joan was your father's oldest sister,' my mother sniffed.

'Is that the nicest thing you can think of to say about her?' I asked. Mam thought about it long and hard.

'Yes,' she admitted.

And we were off again, laughing fit to burst. Except Mam, of course. She didn't approve of bitching as a rule. Although I thought I could see a ghost of a smile about her mouth.

The car pulled up again outside the church and we checked our watches. Five minutes to two. Still too early.

'I can't go round again,' Clare said, anxiously. 'If we get the red light on the avenue, I'll be late.'

'Yeah, but only about two minutes late,' I said with a shrug. 'No big deal.'

'But I *promised*.' Clare was adamant.

'*Some* people like to be on time for things, Grace,' said Mam.

'Why don't we just pull into the car park of the school there, just up the road.' Jane always said the right thing at the right time. Milo sighed with relief and looked gratefully at Jane through the rear-view mirror. He could probably sense the cat-fight that was looming between my mother and me and feared for his beautiful upholstery – our nails were long and strong. Milo wasn't to know that mine weren't real.

From the school, we could see snatches of people in the church grounds through a sparse wood separating the two buildings. A taxi pulled up at the church gates, the back door opening before the car came to a stop. Long legs in suit trousers spilled out and I knew who it was long before I saw his face. It was Shane. My stomach bellyflopped and I felt light-headed and hungry at the same time. He always made me feel hungry, as if I knew that whatever he gave me was never going to be enough. He pulled himself to his full height and the sun glinted against the blondness of his hair. All four of us squinted as we took him in.

'He's looking well.' This from Jane in a matter-of-fact tone.

'Those colours are lovely on him.' Clare's contribution. And she was right. He was wearing a dark blue suit with a pale yellow shirt, nearly the same colour as his hair.

He stood there waiting and, sure enough, within seconds, he was surrounded. I think they were cousins from Dad's side of the family. Female, of course.

'At least he's on time,' Mam said after a while, as if that was the nicest thing she could think of to say.

Clare was on a roll.

'And there's Caroline. She looks amazing.' Clare's head craned at an alarming angle as she surveyed her public.

'Who *is* that man she's with? He looks like Robert Redford with messier hair. Omigod, he's *beautiful*.' This from the sensible mother-of-three in the back seat.

'Good lord, he *is* rather dashing.' My mother suddenly sat up straight, unconsciously patting her fingers against her thick, short bob. 'Caroline's boyfriends are always lovely to look at.'

'It's Bernard O'Malley,' I said, without looking. If there was a moon in the sky, I might have howled at it. Luckily, it was sunshine all the way, not a moon in sight. I checked my watch.

'Time to go. It's two o'clock.' I was relieved.

'Wait.' Clare said.

'For what?' Mam said, her hand on the door handle already.

'Just . . . just wait a minute. Someone is supposed to say something. Something important. Something that I'll remember when I think about this day. Something *meaningful*.' Clare looked expectantly at each of us in turn. No one said a word.

'What would *Dad* have said to me?' Clare turned to our mother, in desperation.

My mother spoke slowly.

'He would have said, "When's dinner? I'm feckin' starving."' My mother delivered this line with her deadpan face and we laughed until our bellies ached, all the way to the church.

When the crowds outside the church saw the car pulling up at the gates, they disappeared faster than free samples at a make-up party. All that remained on the melting tarmac were half-smoked cigarettes, smouldering from hurried attempts to extinguish them beneath ill-fitting shoes. It was like we were the only people in the world as we picked our way out of the car. We had to be careful. Clare's veil was long. As long as a summer's day.

'I'll park up by de church door and wait for yis, righ?' Milo's voice seemed very loud in this quiet place. 'Good luck to yis all,' he added in a more reverent tone, suddenly aware of his maleness among us. I held Clare's hand. It was small and cold in mine.

'Remember to walk, don't stride,' my mother hissed at me. And then Jane and I were inching up the aisle, our smiles stretching the width of our faces, our heads nodding at the rows of faces that bent towards us from the pews. We held hands. Tightly, although we hadn't done this at the rehearsal, but it felt right. My eyes scanned the crowd. I saw Bernard bending to Caroline as she whispered something in his ear. He smiled in his small way and then looked up. When he looked at me, I felt six feet tall (well, in fairness, I *was* six feet tall) and, at the same time, vulnerable, like I was walking up the aisle in the nude (a recurring dream I often have after eating taco fries). I looked away first. Shane was on the other side of Caroline, his hand inching through his hair. He winked and blew a kiss at me, his lips pink and puckered, like a spring rose. I kept smiling. I never stopped smiling. This was Clare's day, Clare's day, Clare's day. The altar looked so far away. There was Aunt Joan, counting coins concealed in corners of the smallest purse I'd ever seen. Uncle Malachy must have had a crick in his neck, trying to see inside it. And there was Granny Mary, a reed in the wind, all bent out of shape, but regal with it. She fixed me with a glare and then stuck her tongue out, long and thin, just like her. She grinned and if she hadn't been in a church, I knew she'd cackle, long and loud.

Halfway up and I could see the priest in his cassock. He was a second cousin, or something or other, of my father's. He looked very young and a bit scared, looking at us edging towards him. I smiled at him. Now, he looked terrified. He took a step backwards and tripped over an altar boy who couldn't have been more than nine or ten. They didn't fall over as they should have but sidestepped each other in a bizarre dance that lasted several seconds. I looked away, making a mental note not to eyeball the priest again.

And then we were there. Our hands parted and we sailed to either side, as instructed. Music struck up. The 'Bridal Chorus' – is that what they call it? And all eyes were away from us and down the aisle towards the door. I saw the back of many heads, the men's thinning, the women's groomed and straightened and bound.

It's funny what thoughts go through your head when you're watching your little sister stepping up a long aisle, linking arms with your mother who was only there because everyone else upped and died and left her with the job. She wasn't enjoying it, although probably no one else could tell but me and my sisters. Having said that, I'm not sure Clare noticed. She looked only at Richard and I noticed him for the first time: in a navy suit and a blindingly white shirt. His tie, though, said it all – a joyous gold, strewn with tiny golden cupids, their arrows taut in their curved bows, every one of them pointing at Clare. Not that there was any need. She sailed towards Richard, like a ship into shore. Mam got to him first and kissed his cheek. He hugged her quietly and I could see his mouth forming the words 'thank you'. Mam steered Clare towards him and then stepped back, into her place beside Mary in the front pew. She didn't cry. She smiled: a brave smile. I was proud of her and wished that I could tell her that. I caught her eye and winked instead. I turned then towards the altar, quickly, before I could see her reaction.

Everyone said the service was 'beautiful'. Clare cried when Richard slid the slim golden band over the tiny knot of her knuckle. Richard's voice faltered when he promised to love this girl, to cherish her, for richer, for poorer, in sickness, in health. I listened to their vows and really heard them. They moved me. It was a big task: in health, that was fair enough, but in *sickness* too? And they did it so effortlessly. They meant it. I knew a part of Clare was lost to me then. It was Richard's. Her gift to him. But I couldn't feel sad. For just that moment, I was swimming in a sea of love, an ocean. There was no room for cynicism. Just two people, promising themselves to each other. Forever. It was magic.

And then it was all over and the church bells rang out, their chorus echoing down to Raheny village, annoying all the punters trying to watch the match in The Station House (Tipperary vs. Cork: Tipperary lost by the way, just in case you're interested). We spilled out of the church, a clutch of people in bright colours and shoes that, after that day, would never see the outside world again.

'Mam, you did great,' I said, leaning over and kissing her on the cheek. I was buoyed up with the moment and forgot myself.

'Sure, all I did was walk her up the aisle.' She shook me off like rain. Mary smiled at me, tucking a curl behind my ear. Mam turned to Mrs Ryan.

I ducked and dived through the crowd in my efforts to avoid Caroline and Bernard. I kept catching his face, under arms raised in greetings and through chinks in bodies as the crowd swayed. I moved fast, always in the opposite direction. From Shane I was safe: he was barricaded by a stern group of my cousins who had found him and were determined never to let him go. If he told them he was my boyfriend, they would have broken their chain and sent him back to me, admiring the view of him from behind. But he wouldn't tell them that. It wasn't his style.

I was walking backwards, scanning the crowd, when I bumped into Bernard. I turned, an apology already on my lips, when there he was. He didn't look like Robert Redford, I decided. Even with messier hair. He looked like he always did: the New Boy from the office, tall with dark eyes and those ridiculous eyelashes, like spiders' legs. Freckles and roaring red hair. Dimples and cardigans. His arms were outstretched, as if he thought I might fall and I steadied myself on my heels and moved, just out of his reach.

'Hi.' His hands arranged themselves down by his sides.

'Hi,' I answered, too loudly.

Then silence. Why couldn't he be one of those people who feel the need to fill silences with words, words, words? Instead, I obliged.

'Wasn't the ceremony beautiful?'

'Beautiful.' That's all he said, looking at me all the while.

'Ah, *there* you are.' It was Shane, looking dishevelled. He must have had a tight squeeze, prising himself away from the circle of cousins. And then he sort of descended on me, bending me low from the waist, all arms and tongue, kissing me at that awkward angle, for a long time. I struggled against him but it was no use, bent as I was in a U shape. When he finally brought me up for air, Bernard was still there, still standing, a tight smile fixed on his face.

'You look lovely.' Shane sounded surprised when he said that, his eyes travelling the length and breadth of me, pausing for a moment at my belly, which I sucked in. Then he turned and looked at Bernard.

'I'm sorry, I'm being rude. I'm Shane.' Shane's hand shot out in greeting.

'We've met before. In Grace's flat.' Bernard shook his hand. A firm handshake, I noticed.

'Oh, yes, that's right. Brendan, isn't it?' Shane dropped Bernard's hand, draping his arm around my shoulder.

'It's Bernard,' I said.

'And you're here with my sister, Caroline, isn't that right?' Shane said, pointedly.

Caroline arrived then and I had never been so glad to see her. She did not bring good tidings.

'Your mother's got the hots for Bernard. Did you know that?' she asked, breathlessly.

'I think Bernard's attentions are otherwise engaged, don't you?' said Shane, looking at Bernard with a challenging smile.

All the while, I stood there with a reddening face. I couldn't even ask Caroline for help as I normally would, given the people involved: her brother, her boyfriend.

Bernard spoke first. 'I'll see you later, Grace.' He touched my shoulder briefly with the flat of his hand, warm and dry. 'I've got to go and talk to your mother.' While we laughed, he slipped away silently.

'I can't figure that guy out at all,' said Caroline, gnawing at a nail in a way that was most unlike her. I smacked her hand down from her mouth, like she normally did for me.

'I don't know what you see in him. He's as odd as a cross-eyed dog. And red hair. What were you thinking?' blurted Shane.

'Your girlfriend – who is standing right beside you, by the way – has red hair,' Caroline said.

'It's different on a girl. You know that.'

Shane's comment was not favourably received by Caroline, who flounced away into the throng.

'So,' Shane said, looking at me. 'Are you glad I made it?' Over Shane's shoulder, I could see Bernard's retreating back.

'Grace?'

I looked back at Shane. He was waiting for me to answer.

'Grace?' It was Mam this time, calling me from the other side of the courtyard.

'Shane, I'll be back in a minute. Will you be able to manage on your own?'

Shane looked around him and spotted the cousins, who

were still staring in his direction, some of them with open mouths.

'Yeah, don't worry about me,' said Shane, patting his hair gently. 'I'll be grand. You go do your bridesmaid thing and I'll deal with you later.' He dragged his eyes away from the girl gang, patting me like I was a puppy before walking away.

I approached my mother, who was straightening Jack's tie. He stood still, like an obedient child, loving the attention. For a long-standing bachelor, he conformed brilliantly to Mam's ministrations and to the general noise and chaos of family life. Pleased with the knot she tied, Mam hitched Jack's tie up to his neck and stood back to admire her work while Jack fought for breath and tried not to undo his top button. Any minute now, she'd be licking the backs of her fingers and flattening his fringe with them.

'You wanted me, Mam?' I stepped closer to the pair of them and Jack smiled at me, like he was delighted to see me.

'You sound a bit wheezy,' Mam said. 'Do you have your inhaler?'

'Yes. And I'm fine. Just haven't had a cigarette for ages, that's all.'

'Well, don't bother having one today,' she said. 'You'd probably burn a hole in that beautiful dress, knowing you.'

'You're right,' Jack said. 'Grace really does look beautiful today.' And Mam looked at me, really looked at me for what seemed like the first time in a very long time.

'Yes,' she said. 'She does.' Behind her smile, I knew she was thinking about Patrick and I wished I didn't look so much like him. I was her reminder, just as she was mine.

'Now,' she said, getting all business-like. 'We need to be at the park in half an hour for the photographs, so can you go and find Clare, Richard and Jane and get them into the car?'

Clare was kissing Wadded Willy when I found them. One of those glorious kisses that seem to last forever but are chaste enough for public scrutiny.

'Ahem,' I said, standing beside them. They stopped kissing, but slowly, and turned towards me. They were so loved-up, they could barely focus on me.

'Where's Shane? Did you find him?' Clare's voice was slurred and it wasn't from alcohol – she'd only had one glass of champagne, and that had been drenched with orange juice.

'He's over there, he's grand.' I gestured vaguely into the thicket of people outside the church. In Clare's current condition, she wanted everyone to be paired up and happy, like she was. I'd always presumed that once you were paired up you were happy, but now I knew it didn't always work out like that.

'Everything all right, Grace?' Clare wanted to get back to kissing Richard.

'Eh, yeah, fine.'

'So, did you want me for something?'

'Oh yeah, sorry, Clare.' I stepped into the shade to escape the sun that pushed down on me, making me hot and heavy. 'It's time to go to the park for the photographs.'

'Grand, so. We'll be right there,' Clare said, waiting until I'd walked away before she stepped towards Richard, kissing him again. I didn't care. I had done what I'd been told, so my conscience was clear. I found a shady spot down the side of the church and hiked my dress up, groping my hand along the top of my stockings till I felt the comforting rectangle of my cigarette box. I had – cunningly – put my lighter inside the box so Thunderbirds were go for a sneaky fag. Plus, from my vantage point behind an oversized lilac tree, I had a bird's eye view of the wedding crowd without them being able to see me.

Bernard shook hands with Jack. He stooped a little to hear something Jack was saying and while he was thus distracted, I could see Mam sweep her eyes over him in a way that was not entirely appropriate. Was that his bum she was looking at now?

Bernard had taken Jennifer and Laura's advice and worn the chocolate brown suit, although he had chosen a dark pink shirt to-day. He'd lose points for that colour combination with my mother, but for me, it was ten out of ten. Obviously, Caroline felt that way too as she approached him, slipping her arm around his waist, low down enough to be skirting the top of his buns. Now Bernard was excusing himself, fumbling in his pocket for something. Oh, it was his mobile phone. Caroline's arm hung suspended in the air for the briefest moment, curved in a semi-circle as if he was still there. She lowered it quickly and laughed at something my mother was saying, both of them looking towards Bernard as he walked away with the phone to his ear. Maybe Mam was saying how nice they looked together. What a great couple they made. Caroline's dress was a dark pink, almost exactly the same shade as Bernard's shirt, as if she had known. Maybe she had. Maybe she'd spent last night with him and she'd seen the shirt. Or worse: maybe they'd gone shopping together for matching his 'n' her shirt and dress. That was altogether worse.

I smoked the cigarette down to the filter without noticing. The last drag burned my fingers and I flicked the butt into the flowerbed. Inside the cigarette box I had also secreted a packet of Airwaves and a narrow vial of perfume I got for free with a mascara once. Drenching myself with perfume and popping some chewing gum into my mouth, I patted the hair on top of my head to make sure it was still standing. More Lean-ing Tower of Pisa than Eiffel Tower now, but still standing. I could see Mam and my sisters heading for the car, Mam's head snapping this way and that, looking for me. I took to my – very high – heels, cutting through the crowd in such a way that I made it to the car before any of them. This pleased me more than it should have done.

'*There* you are.' Shane walked up to the car, looking an-noyed. 'I've been looking for you everywhere. I really want to talk to you.'

'Grace, we're leaving,' my mother said pointedly towards us.

'Shane, I have to go. We're going to the park with the photographer.'

'I thought you'd be dying to hear about our plans.' He looked like a sulky three-year-old.

'I've been wanting to hear them for the past two months,' I said, 'so I suppose another two hours won't make any difference.'

'That's unfair, Grace.' Shane lowered his voice, careful not to let my family hear us. 'I wasn't ready to make plans two months ago. I'm ready now. I thought you'd be pleased.'

'Come *on*, Grace.' My mother's voice was shrill and I moved away from Shane.

'I *needed* you two months ago. But you left anyway. I wanted to go with you, remember?'

'We've been through all this, Grace.' Shane couldn't believe I'd said that. To be honest, I couldn't believe it either.

'Look, we can talk later, OK?' I bent to get into the car, sitting beside Jack.

'You can bring Shane if you like.' Mam seemed surprised that I hadn't asked her already.

'No, that's OK, Mam. But thanks.' I smiled and she looked confused.

'Drive on, Jeeves,' I said to Milo and, in fairness to him, he doffed his cap at me and said 'yes ma'am', but in his flat Dublin accent, it didn't sound as grand as it should have done.

I didn't look back as the car pulled away. I wasn't looking forward to the – long overdue – conversation with Shane, but whatever happened, I had a feeling I would be able to cope. I felt strangely strong, curiously coherent.

46

That feeling of strength and coherence fled after two hours with the wedding photographer. The feeling in my feet also fled in that I couldn't feel my toes any more from all the standing. Lockjaw had set in from the smiling. My arms were like dead weights from tripping after Clare's veil, carrying it behind her. Those things don't look heavy, but in fairness, a sack of feathers would feel heavy after two hours with the wedding photographer.

All the other guests got to slink off to the hotel for champagne and strawberries serenaded by the gentle strains of a string quartet. We were driven to the rose garden in St Anne's Park by Milo, who now had a grin on his face to match the brandy on his breath. Now there was only Jane, Mam and me in the car. Jack had got out to accompany Mary on the bus, which she insisted on taking. Since she'd got the free travel pass, she had become a public transport junkie, even at rush-hour when, strictly speaking, she wasn't entitled to her free travel. But what bus driver could deny her? Mam pulled down the car window and looked at her mother and Jack.

'Don't get lost now, will you?' What she was *actually* saying was: 'Mary, please don't bring my boyfriend to a pub and get him pissed and tell him lewd stories about relatives that he might meet later. Oh, and please don't make a pass at him, will you?'

In response, Granny Mary threw her arm around Jack, nearly crowning him, and led him away, as if *she* were the one minding *him* and not the other way around.

Mam and Jane were up to their eyes in an animated conversation about the wedding presents.

'I told her she should have a list,' Mam said thinly. 'I told her that so many times, but she'd have none of it. Now she's got five sets of those John Rocha champagne flutes. That's thirty champagne flutes. Thirty.' This from the woman who had exactly six of everything in her kitchen. Apart from champagne flutes. There were none of those.

'Yeah, but she can always bring them back and get something else.' Jane's logic was hard to argue with, so Mam just sniffed and bristled with annoyance.

I looked out the window while Jane did her best with our mother. She was as taut as a wound clock and I knew that any offering from me would be like fat on her fire.

It's amazing the way sunshine brings out the lovers. The streets were packed with them, draped around each other, arms crossed at the back, hands smugly wedged into each other's bum pockets. Where were they all the other days of the year when it rained? Or on those grey days when you wish it would rain, just to break the deadening dullness? Maybe they're in bed all those other days, feeding each other chunks of fruit and pieces of Terry's Chocolate Orange, hoovering up chocolate crumbs and fruit juice with wet tongues and watching French films that end in the middle of the story. While watching the lovers, it was Bernard I thought about.

The wedding photographer – his name was Conran d'Arcy – had a French accent. Originally from Donnycarney, Richard told us later. He had even grown one of those thin twirly moustaches and wore a black beret, tilted at a rakish angle on top of his head. He was one of those photographers who considered himself an artiste (must be pronounced *ar-teest*) and only did weddings when the starving artist scene became a little dull.

He spoke with a lisp. He could, however, pronounce his Rs, which he rolled at the back of his throat as often as possible. It sounded like he was getting ready to gully.

He didn't know any of our names.

'I want you, you, you and you, here, undair zis tree,' he said, pointing in turn to me, Jane, Clare and Mam. Only for the fact that he came with Mrs Ryan's recommendation ('I've heard he's a *marvellous* little man'), my mother would have taken to him with a wooden spoon.

Not content with getting us right where he wanted us, he then went on to explain his reasons.

'Zis tree represents stability and fertility. Look at ze thickness of ze trunk. Look at ze majesty of ze height.' His arms reached around the trunk, hands stroking up and down as he spoke, as if he were pleasuring an elephant.

'I'll thicken his trunk for him if he doesn't shut up and take the bloody picture.' My mother did not suffer fools gladly. Myself, Jane and Clare had to support each other, we were laughing so hard. It turned out to be the best photograph in the album. Three women, wild and unsteady with laughing. One woman, older, standing sternly at the edge of the picture, but with a trace of a smile about her face. Conran called it his masterpiece, but he never knew how close he came to a good hiding.

The sun beat down. Nobody had thought to bring any sunblock. Or water. We wilted, but Conran was not prepared to release us.

'OK, I need ze moth-air and fath-air of ze bride,' he said, clapping his hands together like a seal.

My mother stepped out and stood in front of the photographer. Now we were at the duck pond (represents ze origin of life).

'Where's your husband?' Conran demanded.

'Dead.' My mother's patience had run out some time ago.

'Oh,' he said, clicking his tongue at the *inconvenience* of it all. He ran his eye along our tattered group.

'You,' he said, pointing at me and clicking the heels of his shoes together with a snap.

'Me?' I said, pointing a finger to my chest in a stupid kind of a way. The heat had dulled my brain.

'Yes, yes,' Conran said impatiently. 'You are zat woman's daughter, no?'

'Yes, but . . .'

He waved me over to Mam with his hands and we stood together stiffly. This did not please Conran. In the end, when he couldn't manipulate our stiff bodies to his satisfaction, he sat us on the grass and commanded that we make daisy chains. We looked at each other but sat on the grass. It was easier than arguing. Because he took so long to set up his equipment, we ended up making a daisy chain. A really, really long one. A companionable silence grew between us. For the first time that day. For the first time in a long time. Later things would deteriorate at an alarming rate. But we didn't know that then, our heads bent to the task, connected by a simple chain of daisies.

'Now I need the moth-air and fath-air of the groom,' Conran commanded.

Mrs Ryan stepped forth. Conran opened his mouth to ask the question.

'He left me. Years ago. For a woman half his age. He's gone native now, somewhere in Africa, I believe.' Mrs Ryan said it with a challenge, daring Conran to comment. Wisely, he did not.

James brought Ella, Thomas and Matthew to the park. Conran threaded wild flowers through Ella's blonde hair. Her brothers made a throne with their hands and scooped their little sister onto it. Ella's smile was gappy and her brothers' faces were solemn but against the backdrop of a bank of blood-red roses, it was perfect.

'Clare, can I wear your wedding dress when I get married?' Ella wanted to know. I adored her innocent conviction: grow up, become a superhero, meet a handsome prince, presume you can fit into a size-eight wedding dress, sit, with grace, on the board of a multinational corporation and, of course, live happily ever after in a pink castle on the edge of a lake. I picked her up and swung her until the trees became a blur.

'Grace, put her down. She'll be sick,' said Mam. She looked tired.

'When am I having my photograph taken?' Mary had just arrived and I could tell by her face that she was gasping for a double brandy. Her feet must have been killing her, in her high-heeled cowboy boots. Her *special occasion* boots, she called them. Today she carried her cane, waving it over her head as she shouted the question, a sure sign that she was losing patience. Conran, wisely sensing that he needed to placate this matriarch, took almost as many shots of Mary as he did of Clare. Mary sighed like a diva, but you could tell that she loved it.

'Now, you can go,' Conran told her, curtly. 'If you like, I mean,' he added when she gave him her filthy look, Grade II.

'No, I want one with all my girls.' Mary fixed Conran with a stare. Obediently, Jane, Clare, Mam and I gathered around the old woman, Mam, Mary and I towering at the back, Jane and Clare – the munchkins – in front. It had always been that way. Mary leaned towards me and put her hand on Mam's shoulder. She smelled of lavender and mothballs.

Then she set off, refusing all offers of lifts, insisting that she would take the bus to the hotel. Jack weakly offered to accompany her, but she snorted and said she'd be visiting him in a nursing home long before they'd see her into one. Everybody believed her. I felt such affection for her then, the oldest of our number, in this family of women.

Jack put his arm around my mother and she leaned briefly against him, closing her eyes for a moment. She looked so unexpectedly vulnerable for that moment, in a way that was hard to watch. I knew that she was inching her way through the day, willing it to be over, wishing for her boy back.

Now, Conran was trying to persuade Clare to climb a tree. Richard was already up the tree, clinging to one of the lower branches. His groomsmen – more cousins – had given him a leg up and were now wiping their hands on the grass.

'Richard, get out of that tree this instant.' Mrs Ryan awoke to the fact that her grown son was climbing trees on his wedding day. 'What about your hayfever? And your fear of heights? And you'll dirty your clothes.' There seemed no end of reasons why Richard should not be up a tree, not least because he was a thirty-six-year-old man with a sensible job and a brand-new bride.

Richard stiffened and it became clear that he needed help. The groomsmen sighed and headed back to the tree.

Back at the hotel, I longed to reef myself out of the dress – growing tighter by the minute – and the shoes that held my feet at a slalom angle.

'Grace, go and talk to Uncle Malachy and Aunt Joan,' my mother ordered, her face pink from too much sun and too much Conran. 'Go on. It's the least you can do.' She steered me in the direction of the garden, where we could see Joan cutting slips from a rose bush, her head snapping left and right, making sure no one was looking.

'Why is it the least *I* can do? Why isn't it the least Jane can do? Or Clare?' I knew I sounded like a petulant child, which wasn't a good idea, as relations between us were more strained than usual. Our pose on the grass making daisy chains had produced a grass stain on the back of her trouser suit. On the left buttock area, to be precise. It was only about the size of a thumbprint, but size didn't matter on this occasion. I don't even know how she noticed it, to be honest. Although maybe she was telling the truth when she told me she had eyes in the back of her head all those years ago. You could never be sure with my mother.

'Grace, that's hardly the point,' she snapped at me when I pointed out that it could only be seen from close up, and then only if you were concentrating hard on her bottom.

Jane happened to have some Stain Devil in her handbag and saved the day.

'Bet you have stamps in there as well,' I said to Jane after she had zapped Mam's trousers with the magic potion. 'And hankies.'

'Yes I do, as a matter of fact. Do you need something?'

And that was why Jane was so wonderful. If she heard the thinly veiled sarcasm in my voice, she gave no indication of it. She avoided testiness as a small mouse might avoid the local cats' home. My mother, of course, did not.

'Just because Jane is organised doesn't mean that you have to make fun of her,' she told me. 'In fact, you could do worse than take a leaf out of her book,' she continued, on a roll now. I knew I was heading for the 'orderliness is next to godliness' speech so I picked Ella up.

'I'd better go change her nappy,' I said, moving away.

'She doesn't wear a nappy any more,' Jane said, proudly.

'She hasn't worn one for more than a year,' my mother added dryly.

'Well, maybe she needs to go to the toilet then,' I said, still clutching Ella, who squirmed against me.

'Yeth,' Ella shouted suddenly. 'I need to do a number two.' She turned to her mother. 'Is a number two a poo, Mammy?'

Crap. Now I'd have to take her *and* wipe her bum.

'Here,' Jane said, handing me a stack of tissues. 'You might need these after all.'

Then Thomas and Matthew decided they needed to go as

well, but thankfully, they were old enough to wipe their own bottoms – or so I thought. In the end I used all the tissues Jane gave me. Every single sodding one of them.

I pretended to head towards the garden, then doubled back into the bar when Mam's eyes stopped boring a hole in my back.

Shane was there, still surrounded by the posse of cousins. I could hardly remember their names. They were offspring of Dad's brothers and sisters. We usually saw them at weddings and funerals and we had seen them at Dad's ten-year anniversary mass. I was twenty-five then. Everybody had spent that occasion shaking their heads and repeating over and over, 'Ten years. I can't believe it's been ten years.' Even I said it after a while. There were no cousins on Mam's side: she was an only child.

I made a beeline for the bar and ordered a packet of hunger buster Tayto cheese and onion. They didn't have the hunger buster pack so I ordered two of the standard bags.

'Are you going to eat both of those?' Shane appeared at my elbow, eyeing the crisps with distaste.

'Yes,' I said deliberately, opening one of the packs and shovelling a fistful of crisps into my mouth. I could see his mouth moving but could not hear what he was saying with the chomping of my jaws thundering in my head. It was nice really, because he was so lovely to look at, even when he was annoyed, which he was now. I could make out some of the words. Diet . . . calories . . . carbohydrates . . . own good . . . weight. Nothing I really wanted to hear, so as soon as I was finished that first enormous mouthful, I dipped my hand again into the bag and crammed another handful into my mouth. When I'd finished the first bag – it took less than three minutes – I opened the second bag and began again. Shane was still talking, now reading from the back of the empty bag of crisps I'd discarded on the counter. When I finished the second bag, I took a long, noisy draught from Shane's pint on the counter in front of me. Then I burped. A real Homer Simpson one. A real cheese-and-onion one. It was vile. Shane recoiled as if I had hit him. I couldn't blame him, I knew I was being disgusting, but the freedom of it. The realisation that I didn't care what he thought any more settled on me like dew at the dawn of a brand-new day. I was giddy with it.

'Excuse me,' I said.

'Grace, that was absolutely . . .' Shane started. I held my hand up towards his face, in a 'talk to the hand' gesture. I didn't say that.

'If you can't think of anything nice to say, don't say anything at all.' My teacher in junior infants used to say that all the time. I knew it would come in handy some day.

'Grace . . .' He began again. 'You're being really strange today. I've come all this way to see you and I've hardly seen you at all and then when I do, you're overeating and . . . and being disgusting.'

'What did you want to tell me earlier?' I interrupted, setting his now half-empty pint on the counter. Behind him, I could see Bernard and Caroline sitting together in a group of wedding guests. Every time Caroline laughed, or even smiled, she leaned into him, making lots of eye contact. She was a pro and no doubt about it. No human man could resist her. Suddenly, Bernard's head turned, as if I had tapped him on the shoulder. It was too late to look away so I smiled back at him with a little wave of one hand that made me feel foolish. Caroline turned around as well, frowning at first, then smiling when she saw that it was only me.

'Grace, I'm trying to talk to you.' Back to Shane.

'Sorry, Shane, I was just waving to Caroline. I haven't seen her all day.'

'You haven't seen *me* all day.' He tried to run his fingers through his hair but they couldn't gain entry, what with all the *product* he had in it.

'OK then,' I said, picking up his drink. 'Let's go out into the garden,' I wanted a smoke, 'and find a shaded spot, away from the madding crowd, where we can talk.'

The garden was hotter than the bar and I could feel my hair curling and fizzing in the humidity. We found a bench partly shaded by the budding branches of a sycamore tree. Shane got there first and sat in the shaded part, leaving me to stew in the sun. Still, it was too late to worry about freckles. I already had a skinful of them and there was simply no more room on my body for any more.

I hitched my dress up and prised the cigarettes out from the stockings. The box had slid half-way down my thigh so it was a bit of a job. Shane looked curious, then excited, then disappointed when he realised what I was at. I lit up and exhaled, turning my head away from him, leaning back into the hard seat of the bench.

'You said you were giving them up a year ago.'

'It's been a hard year,' I said and Shane changed the subject, as I knew he would.

'Ok, do you want to hear the plan?' I straightened up and looked at him. I *did* want to hear the plan. I nodded, waiting.

'All right then. You jack in your job and come and spend the summer with me in London. If that works out, you could always stay until I finish my contract and then we can head back to Dublin next year and we'll see where we go from there.' Shane leaned back, lacing his hands behind his head and waited. When he realised I had made no sound, he turned to me.

'What?'

'What about my job?' My voice was quiet.

'What about it? You'll get another one, won't you? Claims handlers are ten-a-penny in London. There's loads of work.'

'I'm not a claims handler. I'm a . . . a . . . I got a promotion, remember?' Shane smiled, indulging me.

'Whatever you do, Grace, you can do it in London.'

'But I like my job. I'm good at it.'

'Yeah, but you like me better. You're good at me. Anyway, you've wanted to come to London for ages. So now here's your chance.'

'So let's see if I have this right.' My anger was contained and Shane didn't notice it. 'I'm supposed to give up my new job, my promotion, and live with you on a trial basis for the summer. Then, if I'm a good girl, I get to stay for another little while. Is that it?'

A muscle in Shane's face twitched. 'Grace, come on, I thought this was what you wanted.'

'I wanted it two months ago when you left, remember?'

'I wasn't ready then.'

The fact that all of these plans revolved solely around Shane didn't seem to have occured to him at all. I dropped my cigarette on the grass and crushed it with the heel of my sandal. My body was like a dead weight in the heavy heat of the afternoon.

'I can't believe you're not over the moon about this,' he said. And he really couldn't. Believe it, I mean. He looked lost. I could feel my anger dissipating and, with it, my resolve. It was the hotel intercom that saved me.

'Could the guests of Mr and Mrs Richard Ryan make their way to the ballroom, where dinner will be served shortly.'

'Shane, I've got to go in. I'm at the top table. I'll see you later. We can talk then, OK?' I was already hurrying away, talking to him over my shoulder.

'But, but where am I sitting? Who have you put me beside?' Shane asked in a voice that was a tinny whine.

'You're at table three.' I decided not to mention that his next-door-neighbour at the table was my grandmother, Mary. He wasn't all that fond of Mary and she'd disliked all my boy-friends over the years, and Shane more than most.

I didn't wait to hear his response and fairly jogged to the dining room, which was some feat, considering my footwear.

Of course, the room was empty when I arrived. I knew that nobody pays the slightest bit of attention to the first dinner announcement at weddings, especially when there's a free bar. I also knew that I had to get away from that conversation on the bench.

On the plus side, full bottles of wine were set on the tables, the whites bobbing in ice-ridden silver buckets, the reds standing alone, obediently breathing at room temperature. I lifted a bottle of red and filled a large wine glass with it, ignoring the line on the side of the glass that tells you when to stop pouring. I only stopped pouring when the wine threatened to overflow onto the crisp, white linen tablecloth. I wondered where Clare had sat Bernard. Probably among the legions of Richard's cousins. I checked the list at the entrance of the ballroom. There he was, at table six. Caroline was seated at table two, unofficially known as the singles table. Table six was just inside the door and I walked around it, admiring the place cards penned by Clare. The names were beautifully scripted on pieces of linen, hanging from miniature silver pegs that bobbed on tiny trees Clare made, months before, from papier mâché. The trees were bare – leaves had proved a step too far, even for Clare – but the sparkly silver spray that covered them made them magical. One of the tiny pieces of paper had slipped from its peg and fallen to the table. I bent to replace it: the name on the place card was not one of the names on the list outside the door. It said 'Caroline O'Brien' and smacked of subterfuge. I thought – briefly – about returning the card to where it belonged before replacing it on the tree beside Bernard's and moving away.

A balcony ran the length of the room and I slunk out there to hide for a while.

After a powerful gulp of wine, I lit a fag and settled myself on the ground, which was warm under my bum. I felt the buzz of the alcohol flowing through me and settling on me like a smile. I drank in the view from the balcony. To my right, Ireland's Eye and the dribble of her tear. And Howth Head. On the left, Lambay Island with its tiny line of yellow beach and the purples of the heathers running up to the top of the island like carpet. I knew I was hiding, but it felt more like retreating. Just for a moment. Just till I gathered myself a little.

'Where is Grace? I *told* her to be on time for the meal.' I heard my mother's voice inside and I stiffened. I couldn't let her see me out here, drinking and smoking and neglecting my bridesmaid duties.

'Can I go out to the balcony, Nanny?' It was Ella. I stubbed my cigarette out against the ground, sending sparks far too close to my dress for comfort. Draining my glass – to get rid of the evidence – I hauled myself to my feet and slipped down the balcony, away from the voices that gained on me. At the end of the balcony, a door led back inside the ballroom. Feeling like Ethan Hunt in *Mission Impossible*, I plastered myself against the wall and waited for the voices to materialise onto the balcony.

'Are you all right, Madam?' A tiny waitress, perhaps Japanese, had suddenly appeared by my elbow and I nearly threw myself off the balcony with the fright.

'I'm fine,' I whispered, never taking my eyes off the other end of the balcony. She nodded and left as quietly as she appeared, nonplussed by the encounter. She'd probably seen it all before.

When Mam and Ella emerged into the light, I eased myself back into the ballroom like a pro and ran back up to the top of the room, taking care to rub away any fangs of red wine from the edges of my mouth. I bit down on two tabs of chewing gum.

'Isn't the view gorgeous from here?' I said lightly, stepping back out onto the balcony. My mother looked confused to see me, and not altogether pleased, but I was so used to that, I barely noticed.

'Gwathie.' Ella ran to me and threw her arms around my knees. Well, it had been about half an hour since she last saw me, you must remember. What is it about four-year-olds that can make you feel so cherished? So loved? So special? I lifted her and buried my head in her hair. She smelled like summertime, with a hint of chocolate.

When I set her down again, she looked up at me, her eyes squinting against the sun.

'Uncle Mal said that you look just like Uncle Patrick,' she said, looking curiously at me. 'How can you look like Uncle Patrick, when he's in heaven?' The day dimmed and the space between me and my mother shrank. Ella stood patiently, looking up at me, waiting for an answer. It was Mam who finally spoke. Her voice was steady.

'They were like twins, Ella. Grace and Patrick. Everyone said they were like twins.' I looked at Ella, not able to lift my head, not able to look at her. We never spoke about Patrick, me and Mam, not on our own, not since it happened. Sometimes, Clare and Jane talked about him when we were there, but we never discussed him otherwise.

'But why did he go to heaven?' Ella was persistent as she struggled to understand. 'Did he not want to come to the wedding?'

'He'd love to be here, Ella,' Mam said slowly. 'But God needed him in heaven, so he had to go.'

'Maybe God was lonely,' Ella reasoned in her four-year-old way.

'Oh, look Ella, a ship,' I shouted suddenly, pointing out to sea and making us all jump.

We turned to look at the ship. It didn't seem to be moving on the horizon, but disappeared from view all the same, the sky swallowing it up.

'Where did it go?' Ella wanted to know. I took her small hand in mine and guided her back inside.

'It's gone to America, twice through a hole,' I said. That's what Dad used to say when I asked him where the sun went when it set. Or where the moon went in the daytime. Or where the rainbow went after the rain. The answer was always the same. 'Gone to America twice through a hole.' I know why he said it now. Ella was satisfied with the answer and questioned me no more on the subject. I turned my head to look at Mam, but her back was to me as she stared out at the sea.

The speeches happened before dinner. *Before* dinner, I say: has the world gone mad? Five speeches I sat through, all on an empty stomach, if you discount the two packets of Tayto earlier. Richard's mother conducted a lengthy mother-of-the-groom speech in which she mentioned her disappearing act of a husband only in passing ('Richard was a pleasure to rear, in spite of the fact that his father left us when Richard was only two'). She said this with her usual calm grace, only the thinning of her lips giving voice to that old war wound. My mother, who had previously rejected all requests to speak, stood up suddenly after Mrs Ryan sat down. Maybe she was comforted by the fact that her husband had *died* rather than left her. Maybe she didn't want to let Clare down. Maybe she'd had a glass of wine on an empty stomach. Who knows? She stood up and then seemed to falter, as all eyes fell on her, waiting. I held my breath, egging her on.

'Em . . .' she began, probably cursing herself for not subscribing to the local Toastmasters' club. She joined everything else, why not that?

'Eh . . .' she started again and colour bled into her neck and moved up into her face. My hands were clenched in fists and my nails dug trenches in my palms as I willed her to get a grip. And then she did.

She welcomed Richard into the family. She spoke of the happiness she felt for Clare at the beginning of her new life of love. That's what she called it. A life of love. She spoke of her hope of more grandchildren and fondly mentioned Ella, Thomas and Matthew. Her little people, she called them.

'So that's two down, one to go,' she said then, with a smile. Everybody laughed and looked at me and I squirmed in my dress that felt hot and tight.

She spoke of absent friends and family and we raised a glass and toasted the ghosts: Dad, Patrick. Even Pearce, Richard's father – although Mrs Ryan lowered her glass at the mention of his name.

Mam spoke slowly, carefully, her eyes trained on the far wall, and I knew how much she hated all that attention, all those eyes on her. She did it for Clare, and for Patrick, who would have spoken beautifully and made everyone laugh and cry at the same time. She did it for Dad. She did it because she was a mother and that's what mothers do. They do things they don't want to do. For their children. With love. She stopped as suddenly as she'd started and sat down. Everybody clapped and cheered and took huge slugs of wine from wide-bellied glasses after clinking them with every single person at their table. The room sounded like a bell tower gearing up for Sunday mass.

Clare spoke – tearfully, emotionally – making everybody cry with the sweetness of her love.

Richard spoke – briefly, solemnly – but with Clare's tiny hand tucked gently into his all the while.

I nearly lost my reason when the best man stood up shuffling a stack of paper in his hands, as thick as a telephone directory. 'Oh, please dear God, don't let that be his speech,' I prayed.

But it *was* his speech. Not only that, it was typed, in tiny font, single-line spacing, on *both* sides of each of the millions of pages. He read from the pages, his finger moving carefully underneath each word. After every paragraph, he paused and stared at his – very captive – audience for *exactly* 2.5 seconds (I timed him) before returning to the pages. Buried in the monologue delivered in the monotone was a story that stopped me – momentarily – from re-arranging the names in my phone into *groups*. A story about the cousins, on holidays in County Clare years ago, playing football against the uncles and fathers. The punchline involved one of the uncles falling down a mine shaft and breaking his leg in four different places, but embedded in the story was a list of the cousins who played that day. Bernard and Edward were on the list. He said 'God rest his soul' after Edward's name but didn't elaborate further. My eyes sliced through the crowd and found Bernard, who sat perfectly still and straight. His hands were the giveaway. They were on his knees, curled tightly into fists, his knuckles white, straining against his skin.

Caroline leaned towards Bernard and asked him something. He nodded and turned back towards the top table, looking for all the world like he was listening to the speech. Which of course he could not have been. Unless he'd had time to have a frontal lobotomy between the churchy bit and the speechy bit.

As I turned away, I caught a glimpse of Shane beside Granny Mary. He sat as far back in the chair as he could, but still she came, leaning further and further into his private space, her hand clamped around his wrist so that running was not an option. She smiled at him for some reason – I suspected a generous dose of brandy. When she smiled, her eyes disappeared into a series of wrinkles and loose folds of skin and she revealed teeth, long and yellow, like a donkey's. I quickly looked away before Shane's eye caught mine and begged me to rescue him.

At the end of the speeches, the crackle of crisp notes changing hands filled the room as the length of each speech was announced, argued about, and then confirmed authoritatively by Caroline, who had timed them on her Blackberry (forty-seven minutes: sixteen for Clare, Richard, Mam and Mrs Ryan, thirty-one for the best man. The longest thirty-one minutes of my life, even including the time that I will never get back watching a play called *The Bog of Kite* which should have been called *The Bog of Shite* really).

Dinner took forever, mostly because we were all quite drunk, what with all the toasts during the speeches, the long lulls between the many courses and all the different wines served at each course, encouraging you to drain your glass in readiness for the next one. Even Jane started slurring her words, calling me 'Grashie' and pinching my cheek in a way that was most unlike her.

The top table is a funny place to sit at a wedding. You can see everything, almost as if you're looking down from an elevated position. Nobody really looks up at the top table, or if they do, it's just to check the bride and groom are still there, still feeding each other bits of lobster bisque (they were) and had not snuck away for a quick after-dinner consummation (they had not). I was sitting in between the priest, Fr Rafferty (Please, call me Ray), and Mrs Ryan (Mrs Ryan). Pretending to listen to a desperately dull conversation about the decline of young men joining the priesthood, I watched Bernard's table out of the corner of my eye.

Caroline was pulling out all the stops. She wore hardly anything except make-up, her eyelashes bowed under the weight of at least three layers of Black Seductress. There was nothing discreet about her body language. She should have a sticker across her forehead with the words 'shag me till I pass out'. Instead, she leaned ever forward, giving Bernard an eyeful of cleavage. She enlarged her breasts by pressing them together with her elbows, the oldest trick in the book. She laughed a lot and touched his arm when she spoke. When I saw Bernard laughing at something she'd said, lowering his head towards her, it felt like a cold hand around my heart.

'Grace? What do you think?' My attention snapped back to our table like an elastic band.

'Oh, they should be allowed to have sex. That might encourage more of them to sign up,' I said. 'People need to have sex. In fact, not only should it be permissible, it should be *compulsory*,' I finished.

Fr Rafferty – I mean, Ray – looked delighted and edged his chair closer to mine.

'Well,' replied Mrs Ryan stiffly. 'I haven't had sex in thirty-five years and there's not a bother on me.'

I didn't agree, to be honest. A good shag might have taken some of the stiffness from her features and relaxed the ramrod straightness of her back. However, now was not the time to share these reflections. Shane was headed my way, twitching and out of breath. He looked over his shoulder and I followed his line of vision. It led straight to my grandmother who was mouthing the word 'brandy', a large one I'd say, if her hand gestures were anything to go by.

People were missing from Bernard's table. Bernard and Caroline were gone, their empty seats mocking me. I scanned the room but I couldn't see them and I slumped in my chair, defeated. Caroline had got him. Bernard never stood a chance once she had set her sights on him. No mortal did. I felt a hot sting just behind my nose. I imagined them kissing. If they got married, Caroline might ask me to be her bridesmaid. If they had a baby, I might be the godmother. I would always be close, but not close enough.

47

'Grace, have you listened to a single word I've said?' Shane had arrived at the table. He was tugging at my hand, a pleading look in his eye.

Pushing my chair back, I rose on unsteady legs, took his hand and allowed myself to be led from the dining room.

'Where are we going?' I asked when he stopped outside the lift, jabbing at the call button with the heel of his hand.

'Upstairs. To your room. I need to have sex. Your grandmother totally freaked me out. You would not *believe* some of the stuff she was saying to me.' He spoke quickly, as if he was out of breath, snapping his head in all directions.

I was curious. 'But what's that got to do with having sex with me?' I asked.

'I'm all stressed out. It'll calm me down.' His eyes were glued to the indicator above the lift doors. It was on the third floor and heading our way. He jabbed at the button with his fingers.

'Shane, I'm not a sedative, you know.' I stepped away from him.

'Jesus, Grace, I know that. I was just . . . I thought you'd want to as well. It's just been a really weird day. One of your cousins can roll her eyes into the back of her head and it really messed with my head. Then your granny . . .' He dragged his hand through his hair although his heart wasn't really in it.

'Why did you come today?' Suddenly I really wanted to know.

A sharp ping rent the air and the lift doors slid open. Caroline and Bernard were inside and Shane and I fell away from each other to allow them out.

'We were just looking for the piano bar,' Bernard explained to no one in particular.

Caroline caught my eye and winked. Her normally pale face was flushed a pretty pink and strands of hair escaped the bun at the back of her head.

'Ah yes, the good old piano bar,' said Shane, leading me into the body of the lift, his hands on me. 'That's just where we're heading ourselves.'

I looked at Bernard and he looked back at me. Caroline waved at us as the lift doors closed.

Immediately, Shane was on me, pushing me against the wall, his fingers feeling for a zip. I couldn't tell him that there *was* no zip, just millions of tiny buttons: a row of pinheads, hidden under a seam that ran the length of the dress. I couldn't tell him – mostly because of his tongue in my mouth – but I couldn't tell him anyway because I was *thinking*. You know the way people say that just before you die, snatches of your life flash in front of your eyes? At that moment, with my bum flattened against a metal handrail and my back freezing against a cold, clear mirror, I could see, with my eyes closed. Snatches of us. It was like watching a film on fast-forward. Not the highs and lows, strangely. Just bits and pieces, small things really. Him straightening my hair one Saturday night, mostly because I took too long to do it. He knew his way around a GHD. Me waiting for his train at Heuston Station, shivering in the wind that cut down the platform. Him pouring champagne into my well of a belly button and then drinking it with such loud slurping noises, I fell out of the bed with the laughing. He laughed too, after a while. The pashmina he bought me for my birthday. Bright orange, like sunset. His hair, wet from the shower, with that smell of his, like cut limes. The whiteness of the sun in Spain. The height of the waves.

Him crying outside the morgue, his hands bunched into fists, pressing against his eyes, trying to stop.

Through this stream of thought, Shane still hadn't found the trail of buttons on my dress. I put my hands on his shoulders and eased him away from me.

'Shane, you didn't answer my question.'

'Umm?' His hands were still moving around me. He couldn't *believe* he hadn't found the entry point. Frankly, neither could I.

'Shane?' I moved sideways, just out of his reach.

'What?' He focused on me now, realising that I wasn't where I was supposed to be.

'Why did you come today?'

'That's a weird question. The answer is obvious, isn't it?'

'Just . . . tell me.' I looked over his head at the dial over the lift doors. We were on the second floor now, rising.

'To see you, of course. And to discuss the plans. You *know* why.' He looked confused. I wanted to be anywhere but there. But I pressed on. It was time.

'Yes, but why didn't you want to do any of that before now? See me? And discuss plans? What's changed?' I waited. Third floor now.

'Nothing baby, nothing's changed.' Shane's voice was soft and persuasive and, for a moment, I let it soothe me. It was always warm on the sunny side of this man.

We stopped with a jolt at the fourth floor and the doors slid open. Uncle Malachy stood there, swaying. He smiled when he saw us and made his way inside. He came up to Shane's elbow.

'Graysh wedding,' he said by way of conversation. I suddenly felt sorry for him, married to Aunt Joan. He had to take his pleasure where he could find it and if that was at the bottom of a bottle of whiskey, then so be it. And if that bottle of whiskey was free, all the better.

'I waa-sh at the piano bar,' he continued. I was surprised. There really *was* a piano bar?

For some reason, he stumbled out at the third floor and we were alone again. The lift was going down now.

'Why are you being so weird with me, Grace?' With the big eyes and the hair flopping across his face, he looked like a junior infant on his first day at school. He was delicious. If he were food, he'd be lobster: exotic, impressive, tricky to handle.

But the answer was in his confusion: he really didn't know what was wrong with me, and now was not the time to enlighten him. Today was Clare's day – Christ, even I was saying it now. I took a breath, not knowing what I was going to say. The sharp ping of the lift saved me. We were on the ground floor and the raucous sounds of the band tuning up hit us in the face.

'Shane, listen, I'm sorry. I have to go. I'm supposed to dance with the best man in a few minutes.' Shane's mouth hung open, his face slack. He'd hate to see the folds of skin that gathered around his jawline when he looked shocked. I backed out of the lift, apologising.

'I'll be free in five minutes. I'll catch up with you then, OK?'

'What am I supposed to do with *this*?' He pointed at the crotch of his pants as the lift doors slid closed. The zip buckled against the strain.

For some reason I felt like laughing, but laughing out loud in public when one is by oneself is unacceptable in our culture. So I didn't. I felt itchy.

The stage was abandoned when I reached the ballroom.

'Where's the band?' I asked Richard, who was trying to find his dinner jacket. He'd have had a better chance of finding a laying hen in a fox's lair. The back of every chair in the room was draped with dinner jackets – all identical.

'Gone for a break,' Richard said, replacing yet another jacket on a chair as carefully as if it were his.

'A break? But they've only just started tuning up,' I said, not unreasonably.

'Union rules, or something.' Richard dreaded the first dance (Clare had forced him to learn a samba). He'd probably paid them to disappear.

The evening guests began to arrive. Through the window in the ballroom, I saw a taxi pull up and my work crowd spill out of it, like wine from an overturned bottle. Laura, Peter, Norman, Ethan and Jennifer. Ciaran and Michael couldn't make it. They were at the Elton John concert in London. Caroline ran out to meet them and there was much air-kissing and slapping of hands on backs as if they hadn't seen each other for months. Laura and Peter were inseparable: it was hard to see where one ended and the other one began. Ethan, despite sporting an outfit from Boyers, looked perfectly acceptable and almost happy as he was swept towards the bar by Norman and Jennifer.

I felt like a bee in a jam jar with the lid on. I lowered myself onto a windowsill. My feet were killing me. Maybe if I could just sit there for a moment. Then I could go and *attend* to things. I knew there was something I was supposed to be doing. Something Mam had asked me, or maybe Clare?

I wondered where Bernard was. When I thought about him, he was back in his shabby brown cardigan and his ancient grey, used-to-be-black jeans that were too short for him and those loafers with the frayed laces, worn down to a wafer at the heel.

'Grace, what are you doing sitting here, smiling to yourself like the village idiot?' It was Caroline, pulling at my arm.

'I wasn't smiling.' Guilt had me defensive as a cat.

'You were so. You were like a Billy Barry kid.'

'Have you seen Mam?' I asked. 'Or Clare?'

'No. Why?'

'I think one of them asked me to do something and I can't remember what.'

'Ah, don't worry about it,' said Caroline with the confidence of one who has been lowering champagne for the best part of an afternoon.

'I saw Shane, though,' she said. 'He was heading for the men's toilets. Looked a bit agitated, to be honest.'

'I think he has wind,' I said. No idea why I said that. Caroline either didn't hear me or wasn't interested. She sat beside me, her skinny bottom slotted between me and the wall, and assumed a conspiratorial tone:

'Did you check out Bernard in his suit? Talk about the ugly duckling turning into a swan.'

'Oh,' I said, stung. 'Did you think he was ugly?'

'Well, not ugly exactly. But definitely in need of a refurb. The guy was a nerd.'

'Yeah, but he'll probably be a nerd again. Tomorrow, I mean. When the wedding's over.'

'Not if I have anything to do with it,' said Caroline. She looked like she was going to do her evil genius laugh. I stopped her before she could get going.

'Look Caroline, I'd better go and attend to my duties.'

'Grand so. Come into the bar and join us then for a drink. Laura and the others have arrived. If I'm kissing Bernard when you arrive, don't disturb me, OK?' She left, laughing.

My fingers shook a little and longed for the comfort of a cigarette. I felt the top of my leg through my dress, my hand closing around the bent rectangle of the cigarette box. Breathing again, I headed outside.

48

The incident that led to the argument that led to everything else was an insignificant one, as they often are.

If I hadn't been hiding on a bench behind a wall in a far-flung corner of the garden, smoking, it would never have happened. It was just easier – smoking in secret, with Mam around. Anyway, I wanted to be on my own for a while. The bench was warm against my back and I leaned against it, closing my eyes.

The air was thick with the promise of summer. Buds pinked and swelled and some early clematis tumbled down a trellis that had seen it all before. The smell was sweet and full. The evening sun was hot and I could feel freckles spreading and darkening on my face.

A conversation prickled at the edge of my consciousness. At first, I couldn't make it out. I heard two voices, a man and a woman, heading my way. Their voices became clearer as they neared.

'. . . the only thing I asked her to do . . .typical . . . careless.' It was my mother. I knew immediately that she was talking about me and, even now, I couldn't remember what the hell it was she had asked me to do. I pitched my cigarette into the dry earth and impaled it with a heartless heel. I pressed myself into the back of the bench. There was nowhere to hide, so I stayed put and waited. Jack's voice came from in front of the bush I was hiding behind.

'. . . a great day . . . probably with her friends . . . young people . . .'

He was such a dote.

They were close now. Kissing sounds.

'Stop it Jack, someone'll see.' She called him Jack! I *knew* it.

More kissing. Sucky kissing. I was like a beetle on its back, wriggling, not able to move. If I moved, they might hear me. If I moved, I might not hear what they said next.

And then the conversation. The one I deserved. The one I hoped never to hear.

'What is it, love?'

'I miss Patrick. He should be here today. I miss him so much.' My mother's voice was like a prayer. She knew it did no good to say it, but she said it anyway.

Jack's response was muffled and I guessed he was holding her tight. She said something then, but I couldn't make it out.

'There's no point in saying that, love. Grace blames herself. That's enough blame for anybody,' Jack said.

The words hit me in the stomach like a punch. I had to get away. I would have, too, if it hadn't been for the hem of my dress tucked around the edge of the bench. The filmy material tore with a shriek. Panicking now, I unhooked the dress from the corner of the bench and walked as fast as I could. I couldn't run because of my heels that sank cleanly into the earth at every step.

'Grace?' It was Mam, her face red from circumnavigating the bush that had separated us moments before. I turned to face her and I've never felt so afraid. Everything I feared was true. She blamed me for Patrick. It was one thing to blame myself, but before, I only presumed she blamed me. Now I knew that she did.

'Hi, Mam. I was just going to do the party bags for the evening guests.' Suddenly, I remembered what she had asked me to do earlier.

'It's a bit late for that, don't you think?' Her surliness wasn't quite as sure of itself as usual. Did she suspect I'd overheard her conversation with Jack?

'No,' I said, pulling the torn bit of my dress behind my back. 'They're only arriving now and the cake hasn't been cut yet. I was waiting for that.' I remembered that Clare wanted the guests to have a party bag with a piece of wedding cake in it, taxi vouchers and a disposable camera. I was In Charge of the project. I was giddy with relief, remembering.

'That's great, Grace. It seems you have it all under control,' said Jack, smiling. Mam was having none of it.

'What are you doing here? Your dress is torn. Where's Shane?'

I was exhausted. If you're going to be a disappointment to your mother, you might as well just *be* one and stop sidestepping it, like I'd been doing for a year.

'I don't know,' I said. And then, a little louder, 'I think we're going to break up.' I was as shocked by this as Mam seemed to be. Jack said something – I didn't hear what – and moved away from the pair of us. Mam recovered quicker than I did.

'Typical Grace. Today, of all days.'

'It's not *happening* today. I didn't mean for it to happen at all.'

'No, of course not. You never mean for anything to happen.' Her tone was bitter as lemon.

'What's that supposed to mean?' Even though I knew – of course I knew – but I wanted her to say it out loud.

'It doesn't matter, Grace.' She looked around, realising that Jack had gone.

'No, tell me.' I wanted her to say it. Finally. To get it out there. Between us. Where it had always been. Silent. Waiting.

'OK, then,' she said and I could see her mentally throwing away her cover.

'Why did you have to choose today to do it? It's Clare's day, it's got nothing to do with you. You have to take centre stage, every time.' Colour rose in her cheeks until her whole face was flooded with it.

I stepped towards her and spoke in a low voice.

'I *know* it's Clare's day. I know it in spite of the number of times you've told me. No one knows about me and Shane except you, and I only said it to you now because you were asking about him. And because you're my mother. I thought you'd want to know.' I was breathing hard, like I'd been running for a long time.

She sighed and went to turn away. My hand shot out, pressing into the bones of her shoulder.

'No, wait. What do you mean, I have to take centre stage?'

Mam looked at me like I was a stranger.

'I'm not going to have this conversation with you today. Not today.' Her tone was tight.

'When are we going to have it? We've been not having this conversation since it happened.' My breath, shallow now, was coming in spurts. She stopped in the turn she had been making. We stood, inches apart, staring at each other.

'Since what happened?' she said. It was a challenge and I reached for it.

'Since Patrick died. Since he drowned.' There. I'd said it. Out loud.

Mam flinched like I'd slapped her. 'Don't you dare . . .' she began.

'Stop saying that, stop telling me not to talk about him. I loved him too. He was my brother.' I was terrified of what she might say, so I said it first:

'I know it's my fault. I live with that. If we hadn't been drinking, if there hadn't been a high tide, if I hadn't gone for a swim, if we'd never gone to Spain. I go over and over it, it's still the same. He's still dead and I can't change that.' I was crying now, my face puckered and red.

My mother didn't move. She spoke, barely moving her lips.

'I gave birth to him. I carried him for nine months. I named him. I reared him. And he's gone. And I'm still here. And that's not right. That's not the way it should be. It's *nothing* to do with you.' She spat this last bit and her look cut me in two.

'Yes, but I'm still here. You carried me too. I'm still here.' She turned then and walked slowly away from me. She looked out of place walking back through the trees, her back stiff, the evening light glinting off the silvery grey of her dress.

'I'm still here!' I shouted it, my voice echoing back at me in the forest that seemed darker now. She didn't look back. She never looked back as she moved away from me.

There was a trail from the wood to the beach, over the sand dunes, scratchy with grasses. I took it, running. The pain in my feet forgotten with the adrenalin pumping through my body. Fight or flight. Isn't that what they say? And I took the flight option, every time. It felt like I'd been running for so long now. I didn't stop until I was far enough away from the hotel. I sank into a scooped-out section of a sand dune and let the tears fall. They surprised me, storming down my face, oozing between my fingers. I could taste them in my mouth, salty and warm. Then past my mouth, down to my chin, where they hung, like stalactites. I didn't make a sound.

I don't know how long I spent there before he arrived. Quietly. Without ceremony. I wasn't even surprised that he was there. He crouched in front of me, holding a man-size tissue in one of his man-size hands. A white flag. I held the tissue to my face. It was sodden in seconds. He handed me another one. I blew my nose noisily, head down.

'I saw you running,' said Bernard. His voice was soft, a caress.

I knew if I said anything, I would cry again. I shook my head. He waited for me.

'I . . . I was arguing with my mother. We talked about Patrick, for the first time since . . . the first time in ages.'

'It's not your fault, Grace. It's nobody's fault. Just an accident. A tragic accident.' He shook his head and I raised my eyes to his.

'I . . .' I tried to say something, but my body heaved from the strain of the crying.

I tried again.

'How do you know – about what happened, I mean?'

'Caroline. I asked her why you were sad and she told me.'

'You think I'm sad?'

'Yes, I do. You are, aren't you?' He was matter of fact.

'Well, yes, but I thought I was doing OK, getting through, getting on with things,' I said.

'Look Grace, I understand. I know how you feel. My brother died. I told you that, but I didn't tell you that he killed himself. I found him. I was supposed to go out with him that night, but Cliona wanted to talk to me about him. She was worried about him. So was I. I left him on his own. I shouldn't have. And he killed himself.' Bernard's voice caught in his throat and he stopped talking.

'Do you blame yourself for Edward's death?' I asked.

Bernard looked at me. He struggled with the answer.

'I did. For a long time. But then I didn't. He was dead and I was alive. I had to come to terms with that. To get on with things, as my mother would say.'

'That's what I keep thinking,' I said. 'I'm alive and Patrick's dead and it's just not right. It doesn't feel right and it's like nothing will ever feel right again.' I was crying again. It felt strange to talk about the guilt that was strangling me, but there was relief too.

'Come here.' He knelt down beside me. He held me close and rocked me, like I was a baby. It was soothing. The smell of him. And the warmth. I was safe and I felt myself relax. I cried, but slower now. I could hear waves, and stars popping out of the fabric of the sky. I don't know how long we stayed like that.

And then something shifted and I wasn't relaxed any more. I became aware of the hammering of his heart in his chest, the skin on his neck. I could see the fleshy lobe of his ear. The throb in my body, like a drum in Drumcree on the twelfth of July. I pulled away and looked up just the tiniest bit. He was looking at me, so *carefully*. I touched his face, I couldn't not. And then he kissed me. Not like the other times. A tender kiss, soft and sweet. Neither of us moved.

Bernard pulled away first. He seemed about to say something and then he didn't. He kissed me again, his hands about my face, his breath coming faster now.

The voice took us both by surprise.

'What are you doing?'

It was Caroline. The red stone hanging around her neck glinted furiously. Otherwise, she was pale. She stood there, looking at us.

Bernard and I leapt apart, like scalded cats.

'Caroline . . .' Bernard got to his feet and stepped towards her. Her silence held him back.

'Caroline, I . . .' My voice was hoarse from crying. I scrambled to my feet and moved towards her, not knowing what to say.

Caroline shook her head slowly and backed away from us. She didn't seem angry. That was the worst thing. If she had screamed at me or, better still, hit me, my guilt, roaring like a football crowd inside my head, might have been more bearable. But she did none of those things. She just walked away, without saying a word.

We stared after her.

'I'd better go and talk to her,' I finally said.

'Grace . . .'

'I'd better go,' I said again and he nodded and turned towards the beach.

When I caught up with Caroline, she was nearly back at the hotel. I had to jog to catch her before she disappeared inside.

'Caroline,' I touched her arm. She shook me off like an infectious disease, but she stopped and turned around. The tip of her nose was white, which happened when she was furious, but she didn't look furious. She looked sad. Disappointed. Let down. I could barely look at her.

'Caroline, I . . .'

'How long?' she said, the words snapping like dry wood.

I knew exactly what she meant. It's the first question I would have asked too. I opened my mouth but wasn't quick enough for her.

'HOW LONG, GRACE? HOW LONG?'

'It was the weekend before your blind date. I was drunk, I was pissed off with Shane. I didn't plan it, it just happened.'

'The night you told me you stayed at Clare's?' Caroline had the memory of an *elephant*.

'Yes.'

'You mean you *stayed* with Bernard that night. You *slept* with him.'

'Yes.' It was almost a whisper.

'You *knew* how I felt about him.'

'It happened before you met him. I didn't know he was a cousin of Richard's. I didn't know he was your blind date until he came to the flat that night.'

'And you never said a word.'

'What could I say? I was guilty about Shane. I was worried you'd hate me.'

'Well, it's a bit too late for that now.'

'Caroline, listen to me. Since that weekend, we agreed to forget about it.'

'So what was that back in the sand dunes? Mouth-to-mouth fucking resuscitation?'

'No, that was . . . that wasn't supposed to happen . . . I was upset . . . I'd had a fight with Mam and he just . . .'

'Stop. Just fucking stop. I don't want to hear any more of your pathetic excuses.'

People were starting to look over at us and Caroline stopped shouting, breathless. Without another word, she turned and disappeared into the foyer. I stood there on my own for a moment, the stares of onlookers weighing me down like bags. I thought about a cigarette, but that would mean hiking my dress up and pulling them out of the tight band of my stocking.

'Grace, what are you doing, standing here all by yourself?' It was Clare, happiness spilling from her like warm light. I pulled my sunglasses down off my head and hid my swollen eyes behind them.

'I was talking to Shane earlier and he told me about his plans for you to come and live with him in London. It's perfect, isn't it?'

'Well, I . . .'

'So that's you and him sorted. And Laura and Peter look like the perfect couple, don't they?'

'Yes, they . . .'

'Everything's working out, isn't it?'

I nodded. What else could I do?

Back inside the hotel, I floated like a ghost, slipping in and out of crowds that called my name and swayed like sailors in the soft light of dusk. In a dark corner of the bar, I saw Laura and the others and I ran towards them, seeking refuge. They all took turns to hug and kiss me and didn't notice my puffy eyes and tear-stained face in the dullness of the room. In fact, they all seemed pretty drunk. Laura filled me in.

'There's a tab at the bar for the wedding guests.'

'We got double cosmos,' Norman purred, his long hand clenched around a long-stemmed, wide-rimmed glass with three umbrellas floating on pieces of lemon at the top of the cloudy pink drink.

'Have one, Grace. They are simply *delicious*,' slurred Jennifer, who'd already had two and was half-cut.

'I'll get you one,' said Ethan, leaping up and nearly knocking the drinks off the table.

'So?' said Laura, looking at me with raised eyebrows.

'What?' I answered warily.

'Where's the bould Shane?'

'What's wrong with Peter?' I was desperate to distract her. We both looked over at him.

He sat in the corner, not speaking. He was busy smoothing Vaseline on his lips that looked bee-stung and sore.

'They're all dry and swollen,' Laura explained to me in a whisper, 'from all the kissing we've been doing.'

'Yours look OK,' I said, squinting at her perfectly peach pouted lips.

'Yes, but I'm *used* to it. Peter, God love him, was seriously out of practice, although, I must say, he shows promise.' Laura gazed at her protégé fondly.

'So when is he due to graduate?' I asked. Laura prided herself on taking a man, training him and releasing him back into society, well versed in the art of lovemaking. Her training included such tricky topics as:

- How to prevent premature ejaculation (think of your mammy giving head to your daddy, the pair of them buck naked in the middle of O'Connell Street).
- Cunnilingus, the proper way.
- How to tell a fake orgasm from a genuine one.

- Pain-free anal sex (Laura *loved* anal sex).
- S&M for beginners.
- S&M for improvers (for graduates of the beginner course).
- S&M, advanced module (to my knowledge, no one has ever been deemed good enough by Laura to graduate onto this course).

Laura saw this as her contribution to society. It made her feel good about herself, knowing that her band of graduates would go forth and spread the love. Laura's School of Love, we called it.

She was still gazing at Peter, so I asked her again.

'When is Peter graduating?'

She withered me with a look.

'Not any time soon. He's going to need a lot more work before I'm finished with him,' she said, licking her lips and moving towards him with intent. Peter shuffled along the bench to accommodate her. He looked tired but happy, I thought.

Ethan came back with my drink, beaming.

'What's up with you?' I asked him.

'I met a girl,' he said, his chest swelling with pride.

'Just now?' I asked, looking around me.

'No, last week at my evening course,' he explained. 'I took your advice, got out there, joined a class and there she was. Her name's Lily and she's *perfect*.' I'd never seen him so happy and relaxed and I smiled at him, delighted.

'What class did you join?' I was curious.

'Parenting skills,' he said, without skipping a beat. 'I thought it would be full of put-upon, under-appreciated women. And I was right.' His eyes shone with his find.

'You mean full of *married* women,' I said, appalled at the monster I had created.

'Lily's a single mother. I would never go out with a married woman.' Ethan drew himself up to his full height and crossed his arms tightly.

'Well, good luck with that,' I said. 'Let me know how it all works out for you.'

'Aren't you happy for me, Grace?' Ethan looked at me with his huge, worried eyes and my heart melted.

'Of course I am. Lily is a lucky woman. And her baby. What age is the baby?'

'He's going to be seventeen next month.'

'They're so cute at that age.'

'He's not cute, exactly. To be honest, teenagers rarely are.'

'You mean he's seventeen YEARS old?'

'Eighteen next month, actually. I'm taking him fishing.'

Before I could hit the roof, I noticed Caroline walking towards us and I bolted like a greyhound at the races. I know, I know, but I just couldn't face her.

Back in the ballroom, I skulked near the walls, in dark corners. Clare and Richard were dancing. Well, I say dancing, but really, they were standing on the dance floor, arms locked about each other, gently swaying to a very fast, noisy song the band were belting out. Seems I missed the dance with the best man but he didn't look too put out, bet as he was into one of my girl cousins from Offaly (not the one who could roll her eyes into the back of her head). It looked like she would do enough putting out for the pair of them.

My mother and Mrs Ryan were deep in a conversation that involved lots of shaking of heads and wringing of hands. Probably discussing Pearce. I looked around for Bernard but saw no sign of him. Shane was at the bar, chatting up a leggy blonde with gravity-defying breasts and very short, spiked hair that would look ridiculous on most people but looked *fabulous* on her. I bet her name was Mercedes. Or Portia.

Escaping to the ladies', I splashed cold water on my hot

face. I did my best with my hair, pinning up thick strands that
had escaped during the course of the day. I wondered about
Bernard, hating myself. I knew one thing for sure. I wanted
him. For keeps. It was that simple.

Back in the ballroom, the band had returned (from their
third break) and made up for their absences with a Queen
tribute, the lead singer a dead ringer for Freddie Mercury
with his taut body and his acrobatics with the microphone
stand.

'Come and dance.' Laura pulled at my hand. When she
turned away from Peter, he looked like a diver without an
oxygen tank. Ethan was doing his best James Dean and Norman was trying to shake two of Richard's gay cousins. Still,
Norman was *asking* for it with those pink drainpipes and that
batwing top. Besides, he loved the attention.

I slunk around the edge of the group, pretending to dance,
running my eyes along the walls of the room. Eventually I
spotted her.

She was in a dark corner with Shane, their heads together, his
arm around her shoulders which were heaving up and down.
I could see she was crying and the knife in my heart twisted.
Shane must have felt the weight of my stare. He looked up
and caught my eye, making me shiver with the coldness of his
face. A movement to my left. I looked towards the door. Bernard walked into the room. Shane's head jerked towards him
and then he was up on his feet, first walking and then sort of
jogging towards Bernard. Shane's normally refined features
were taut, his face dark with anger. Bernard saw him coming
and he stopped walking. He watched, resigned. Shane's hands
curled into fists. The distance between them narrowed. Bernard didn't move, took his glasses off, waiting.

'Shane,' I shouted. I started to run. Shane didn't stop or
even look over at me. He reached Bernard, his fist connecting
with Bernard's face in one fluid movement. The sound of it

was shocking: a sharp crack. Bernard was still standing but swaying, holding his face in his hands. Shane swung his fist again, this time connecting with Bernard's eye. There was a thick wet sound before Bernard lost his balance and fell back. Shane moved towards him again, his breath laboured.

'Stop!' I shouted. I stood in front of Shane, my arms outstretched. The room had gone quiet. Nobody moved. The band had stopped mid-song, the drummer's hands suspended in the air. Shane seemed completely unaware of his surroundings. I had never seen him so angry.

'You bitch,' he screamed at me and I flinched away from him. 'All your whingeing about me not phoning and not coming over. And all the time you were shagging your best friend's boyfriend behind her back, and mine.'

There was a collective intake of breath from the guests. The drummer lowered his arms and leaned forward. I could see my mother and Clare at the top table, frozen with shock.

'Shane, can we talk about this somewhere a bit more private?' I whispered urgently.

'No we fucking well can *not*,' he spat at me. 'I'm not going to waste one more breath on you, you fat slag.' He pushed me then, both hands on my shoulders, and I stumbled back, cracking my hip on the edge of a table before tripping over a chair and landing on my side on the floor. A bloody tooth stained the carpet beside me. It was Bernard's.

There was noise in the room now: people were moving. Bernard struggled to sit up, his face bloody, his eye swelling like a bun in an oven.

Mary arrived at my side and knelt down beside me, ruffling my hair.

'Get up,' she said, but her tone was soft. She helped me to my feet and led me from the room, her arms around me. Without saying a word, she brought me through the foyer and out into the car park, where she hailed a taxi and put me carefully in the back seat. I let her. I didn't know what else to do. She got into the front seat and barked her address at the driver.

'But I haven't done the party bags yet.' I sat bolt upright in the seat, thinking about my mother.

'Don't worry, pet. Jane and I did them.' Granny Mary never called me 'pet'. Things were serious.

I sank back into the softness of the seat and closed my eyes. Mary didn't say a word to me. To be honest, she was too busy bullying the driver.

'Take a left here onto St Anne's Road and go straight onto the Strand Road. That's the quickest way and I know *exactly* how much it costs so no funny business, all right?'

The poor unfortunate driver wasn't given a chance to answer because Mary started to sing then, 'Consider Yourself' from *Oliver*: in fairness to her she knew all the words, too. She never stopped until the taxi pulled up outside her house in Baldoyle when she dug into a tiny little purse and counted out the exact fare in what looked like one, two and five cent coins.

Mary's house was the most grannyish thing about her. A sweet little whitewashed cottage with two tiny sash windows on either side of a horseshoe-shaped front door with a riot of roses climbing up the walls. A crooked gate creaked and opened onto a narrow cobbled path that wound its way through the garden between the sweet smells of lavender, honeysuckle and jasmine. Inside, the house creaked with rocking chairs, a grandfather clock and a great big wooden table that groaned under the weight of a sewing machine, travel books, exotic plants that might come under the heading 'contraband' and two enormous bottles of brandy, both at the halfway mark. The house could have done with a good going over with a hoover and a duster, but it was comfortable and warm and seemed to wrap its arms around me as I lowered myself onto a chair.

Everything hurt. I pulled up my dress to examine my hip – dully throbbing. A dark purple bruise gathered on my skin around the hip bone, which jutted, surprising me. A blue one sat in a perfect circle on my lower thigh where it had banged against the side of a chair, and my bum hurt from its crash-landing on the floor.

But these injuries were as nothing compared to the mortification, the shame, and the humiliation. I closed my eyes but the scene kept playing in my mind, worse each time. Images returned to me. Clare's face, her mouth a perfect circle of shock . . . little Ella, nestled in her father's arms, looking on with interest as the adults beat two shades of shite out of each other. And my mother. Oh God, my mother. I groaned and dug my nails into the bruises on my legs.

'You'll have a brandy,' Mary told me in no uncertain terms.

I took the glass from her and drained it in one gulp. Then coughed and spluttered while she banged me – hard – on the back.

'Go easy, Grace, go easy,' she told me, filling my glass up again.

'Granny, what am I going to do?' I asked quietly when I got my breath back.

'You'll stay here with me,' she said, her voice so gentle and soft, I started to cry. She sat beside me, patting my hand.

'I can't stay here forever, Granny. What about after that? What'll I do then?'

'Life goes on, Grace,' she sighed wearily. 'It always does, whether we want it to or not.'

We were quiet then, both of us, for a while.

'I miss Patrick,' I said quietly.

'So do I, girl, so do I,' said the old woman and we sat side by side for a long time, her hand occasionally patting mine, our breath disappearing into the darkness of the room where we had lit no lights.

49

I woke up the next morning with no idea where I was or how I had got there. The bed was a high, narrow one with layers of sheets and blankets instead of a quilt. The bedclothes were tucked around me so tightly I could barely breathe. But I was warm and safe in those few magic moments before memory kicked in and the events of the previous night replayed in slow motion on the big plasma screen in my head. In those first few moments, I noticed the slanting tongue-and-groove ceiling and the tiny window beside my bed that looked out over Mary's vegetable garden, where rosemary and garlic grew wild and thick. I remembered summers spent in this house with my siblings when we tore across the road and swam in the sea before breakfast. I thought about the potato cakes that Mary cooked on a heavy skillet and the way they melted on your tongue, the salt crackling on top. I remembered nights by the fire with Mary's husband, Joe – we called him Pop – telling stories of Fionn MacCumhaill and the Fianna and the fiery Queen Madhbh and the beautiful Sadhbh. His skin like old paper, yellow in the glow of the fire. His eyes a faded blue, watering from the heat of the flames and the maudlin yarns he spun like gold for us. He had been dead for so long I'd almost forgotten he existed. Mary seemed like a woman destined to be alone, independent and brave.

Then I remembered. I pulled the stiff white sheets over my head and rolled myself into a tight ball, my eyes clamped shut, as if that might help. It did not.

The smell of rashers and fried bread climbing up the stairs did help a little, though. I pulled the sheets down just past my nose and inhaled, my mouth watering.

The bedroom door flew open and Mary appeared. She had to bend, with the slant in the ceiling.

'Breakfast in two minutes, girl,' she said before leaving as quickly as she had arrived. She was already dressed. A grand-dad shirt that fell over her – bootleg – jeans.

'Mary,' I called after her. My voice was a wail.

The footsteps on the stairs stopped.

'What?' she roared up to me.

Then silence as I tried to work out what it was I wanted to say.

'I can't face it. Any of it.' I flung myself back against my pillow, banging the back of my head on the stone wall where a headboard should have been.

'Can you face breakfast?' she called up.

My stomach rumbled. The smell of the rashers roared in through the open bedroom door.

'Eh, maybe,' I said, cursing my appetite for being so healthy.

'Well, come on down so, and we'll start from there.' Mary continued her trek down the stairs, her stout – cowboy – boots thudding against the bare boards.

We ate in silence. The only sounds were those of chewing and occasional sucking as Mary slowly pulled rinds of rasher from her closed mouth. Also gulping, as we both drank huge amounts of tea from chipped mugs as thick as walls.

'Why do I call you Mary?' I asked finally, when I could eat and drink no more. She didn't answer immediately.

'I don't know, girl,' she said finally. 'Your mother always called me Mary and I suppose you kids heard her and did the same.' She started clearing away the plates and cups from the table.

'But why did she call you Mary?' I persisted. 'I mean, why didn't she call you Mammy? Or Mother? Or Mam?'

'I don't know, girl,' she said again. 'Joe always called me Mary. I never let him call me Mammy, like most of the fellas did back then. I couldn't have gone to bed with a man who called me Mammy.' She looked at me with a glint in her eye and I nodded quickly, not wanting her to elaborate.

'Granny,' I said, waiting for her to correct me. She did not. 'What am I going to do?'

'Nothing,' she said simply, looking at me. 'At least, not today.' And that seemed to be the end of that.

She gave me chores that kept me busy for much of the day. Granddaughterly things. I collected carrots in the garden and washed them. That takes a lot longer than you might think.

I cut fat swathes of lilac from the tree in the front garden and arranged them in several vases about the house.

I banished spiders' webs, thick as wool, from the five rooms in the house with a long-handled broom. 'I can't see them so well any more,' Mary said.

I polished a silver tea set which sat behind smoked glass on a sagging shelf in the 'good room' until I could see my face in the pot belly of the teapot. I had to stop then.

Mary sat during most of this, listening to a radio that she called a wireless and beating her stick in time to any music that played. In spite of everything, I felt myself relax. Mary had taken my mobile from my handbag: it felt like we were removed from everything – on a different planet – and that was just fine with me. I knew I couldn't hide out forever, but maybe just for a day or so. Just till the dust settled. Just till I sorted out what I was going to do.

I heard Mary on the phone to my mother on that first day.

'She's all right, she just needs time. There's plenty of that here.'

'No, there's no need to come over. I think she could do with a bit of space, as the Americans say.' She laughed at that, delighted with her pop psychology.

'Don't worry about her. I'll mind her.'

And she did.

Sometimes I thought I'd write everything down. Make a list and go from there. But somehow, there was always something to be done, something easy and relaxing and methodical, like pulling fat stalks of rhubarb for a pie or running to the corner shop for a bottle of brandy (for medicinal purposes, Mary insisted).

In the end, I wrote letters I'd never send: one to Clare, one to Mam, one to Caroline, one to Shane and one to Bernard. In the dark warmth of Mary's kitchen, listening to the stubborn ticking of the clock that seemed slower there, it was possible to write down what I wanted to say, without any drama, without any bitterness, without any fear of consequences.

Clare's one was easy enough. 'I'm sorry,' I wrote and really, what else could I say, although it ended up being four pages of 'I'm sorry,' but I was. Really sorry. It was an unfortunate series of events and some of them were beyond my control. I didn't write that bit, but I realised it as I wrote the letter. 'I'm sorry,' I wrote, and I meant it – sorry for everything.

'Dear Mam,' I wrote and then chewed the top of my pen for an hour until it frayed.

I put the page to one side and went on to Shane's letter. That was easier.

You were kind to me when Patrick died. You took pity on me: I was in such a state. But that's not enough. Not for me and not for you. Let's be honest with each other. If it hadn't been for Patrick, this would have ended a long time ago. You were too nice to say it's over and I was too scared to.

We never talked about it. About Patrick, I mean. What happened to him. It was like a barrier we couldn't fit through.

The thing with Bernard? Well, it's not something I'm proud of although I'm not sorry it happened. It forced me to realise things. Important stuff. Like about you and me. You weren't happy with me. How could you have been? I wasn't happy with me. Not for a long time. I want to change that. I want to be happy. I want you to be happy. I know there's a lot of 'I wants' in this letter but I'm trying to be as honest as I can. There's one thing I really want. I want us to be friends. Maybe we can't now, maybe not ever, but that is my wish and this is my letter so I can wish for anything I bloody well like.

Shane's letter was a single page and some of the ink blurred with my tears, but I had written it and felt the better for it. I shoved it into an envelope and sealed it, not reading it back. I wrote his name on it and set it aside.

Bernard's letter began on a factual note:

Funnily enough, I didn't fall in love with you immediately as one might be tempted to think, given the dramatic events of recent times. I was caught up in myself and my crappy life and my shoddy relationship with Shane that was as much my fault as it was his. But I did fall in love with you. I just didn't realise it until it was too late. I fell in love with you for lots of different reasons. Here are a few of them:

1. You really look at me when you're talking to me, as if you can see me. I mean really see me. Right down to my big, fat bones.

2. And when I'm with you I don't feel fat (see (1) above). I feel dainty and petite, like I've got really thin bones and a high bottom and tiny feet and a narrow waist. This is how you make me feel and I've tasted it now and it tastes great, like a chocolate milkshake.

3. *You only say something when you've got something to say. Do you know how refreshing that is? And how unusual?*

4. *You said Patrick's death wasn't my fault.*

5. *I feel different since meeting you. In a good way. I'm moving on. I'm changing things. Thank you.*

6. *On a more base note: you're sexy. Really sexy. I remember having sex with you that night, and how good that felt, and how we slept afterwards, like crescent moons tucked around one another. I remember the warmth and your arms around me.*

7. *Your hands (I'm a hands girl).*

8. *Your brown eyes. (With the red hair? How did that happen? And the long eyelashes, you lucky bastard.)*

9. *The way you laugh . . . And don't get me started on the dimples . . .*

I can write all this stuff because I'm never going to send you this letter. This letter is just for me and, to be honest, it's making me smile when I thought I never would again, after the fiasco of Clare's wedding. I won't say that I hope you get back together with Caroline because that would be a lie, and this letter is only about the truth, but I do hope you have a happy life. I think I'll be happier, because of you. That is your gift to me, whether you know it or not. Thank you. Thank you so much.

Love, Grace

I wanted to keep on writing so I moved on to Caroline.

Dear Caroline,
I fell in love with Bernard before you ever met him. This is not my defence. This is simply a fact. I was confused and should have done things differently. I wish things were different but I can't change what's happened. I can only wish that we can be friends. Your friendship has meant a lot to me. I think

you know that. The thing is, I don't think Bernard was the man for you. He just isn't your type and I think, deep down, you know that. You were lonely (and I know how that feels). I stayed with Shane for that reason. You need someone dynamic, someone like Bill Gates or Bill Clinton (weird the way they're both called Bill?). And that type of person is difficult (although not impossible) to find. It's not Bernard and I know that – and so do you. What I did was wrong. I acknowledge that and I'm sorry. Sorry for hurting you. Sorry for not being the kind of friend that I want to be. Just sorry.

Love, Grace

I tried many times to write the letter to Mam. In the end, I sat at the table, surrounded by balls of crushed paper, chewing my pen. I didn't know how to say what I wanted to say.

I cried a lot in those days with Mary. She sat beside me and handed me tissues and tea. At night we sat at the fire and drank her burning brand of brandy and she told me stories about me and Clare and Patrick and Jane that I'd forgotten. She showed me photographs, old yellowing photographs that curled at the edges, of Mam in a long black evening gown, laughing, with her head thrown back, her hair in a beehive. She looked like I do now – without the beehive.

Of Patrick and me, with scabby knees and fishing nets, holding hands on a beach, blue with cold.

Of Clare, sitting high on my father's shoulders, eating an ice cream cone that's bigger than her face, ice cream dripping off the sharp edge of her elbow.

Of Jane, sitting at the window seat in Mary's front room, reading furiously.

I had been in Mary's house for two days when I started to come to. The first thing I demanded was my mobile.

'No,' said Mary flatly.

'I have to face facts, Granny,' I said. 'I can't stay here and wash bloody carrots for the rest of my life.'

'Why not?' she said simply. 'That's what I'm going to do.'

There didn't seem to be a reasonable response to that so I ignored it.

'Granny, I need to get back to my life. These days, you can't have a life unless you have a mobile phone. It's that simple. No mobile phone, no life.'

And then I realised that the letters I had written were gone from the table. Even the one to my mother that just said 'Dear Mam' with nothing else on the page.

'Where are the letters?' I asked quietly.

'What?' she said in the very loud voice she reserves for door-to-door salesmen and beggars.

'The letters,' I repeated, trying to keep calm. 'Where are they?'

'What letters?'

'The ones on the table. I wrote them and put them in envelopes on the table. Five of them. Where are they?' My voice was rising now.

'Were there any stamps on the envelopes?' she said suddenly, remembering.

'No, no. Just names and addresses?' I was hopeful now. Maybe she'd shovelled them into a drawer. God knows there were enough places to squirrel them in this house.

'Oh, *those* ones,' she said. 'I posted them and you owe me €2.05 for the stamps. And that's not including the time I took to go to the post office and back, mind.' She went to turn away, as if the conversation was over.

'No!' I yelled. 'They weren't meant to be posted. I just wrote them because I . . . because it . . .'

'Because you had something to say and you said it?' she said with a smirk.

'Yes!' I shouted. 'I mean, no. I was just . . . just . . . I was . . .' I ran out of steam, and breath.

'Grace.' Mary's voice was suddenly soft. 'Life is too bloody short to pussyfoot around. You have to say what you want to say even if you think the other person won't like it.'

'Why are you saying that?' I asked, my hands up around my head.

'Remember you asked me what you were going to do?' she said. 'The night of the wedding.'

'Yes,' I snapped, annoyed now.

'Well, this is what you are going to do. What you have done. Talk to people. Tell them how you feel. If you had done that in the first place, this situation would never have happened.'

Oh Jesus, the old biddy was right. And she knew it.

'But I didn't write anything to Mam. I just said "Dear Mam" and that was it,' I remembered.

'I know, Grace,' she mumbled.

'How do you know?' Realisation dawned. 'You read the bloody letters, didn't you?'

'Yes. Although I had to steam Shane's one, you sealed that one.'

Seeing my look, she thumped her walking stick on the ground. 'Sometimes I get bored washing carrots. What can I say?'

And then I started to laugh, hysterically at first, then a real belly laugh. Mary looked at me for a moment and then joined in, her filthy cackle raising the roof.

'What's Mam going to think?' I said finally when I stopped laughing. 'A letter with nothing written on it, just "dear Mam".'

'Sometimes, saying nothing says it all,' said my granny sagely and then we were off again, howling with the laughing till our bellies ached and our throats were hoarse. After that, I knew it was time to go home.

50

Like a recovering addict leaving a rehabilitation centre, Granny handed me my mobile phone and my wallet with due ceremony. They were like long-lost friends and I held them carefully. I didn't turn the phone on. I wasn't ready for that. I checked the wallet. The contents appeared untouched but I still gave Mary a suspicious look as I rifled through it.

And then it hit me.

'What the hell am I going to wear?' For the past two days, I'd been wearing clothes from the eclectic selection in Mary's ancient wardrobe. But I hadn't been anywhere or seen anyone (I knew) so it hadn't mattered.

'What's wrong with what you've got on you?' Mary looked me up and down, shrugging her shoulders.

I was wearing a pair of black leather trousers tied at the top with a nappy pin (the zip was broken and possibly had been for the last twenty years). A black polo neck with an unfortunate mosaic on the front featuring the cover of one of Led Zeppelin's albums. A bright orange cowboy jacket with long thin tassels that flowed like kite tails when I moved. With my high-heeled gold sandals that I'd worn to the wedding, I looked like the worst kind of fashion victim, stuck in 1972 or thereabouts.

There was nothing to be done. I couldn't trust Mary to buy clothes – God knows what she'd have come back with.

Mary shuffled about at the front door.

'I suppose I won't see you till Christmas,' she said sullenly.

'I'll see you at Patrick's anniversary mass,' I said quietly. 'It's tomorrow, remember?'

'Of course I remember,' she snorted. 'That was a joke. About Christmas.'

I leaned towards her and gathered her in my arms. She held me tightly and kissed me wetly, just below my ear. I kissed her cheek and shut my eyes tight, not wanting to let her go.

'Don't start saying you love me or anything farty like that,' she warned, her stick raised.

'See you at Christmas, Granny," I said, backing away from the door, smiling at her. She ruffled my hair, her whole face creased with her smile. She turned back into the house and closed the door.

The outside world felt strange. Brighter than I remembered. Noisier. Dirtier. More alive, somehow. Mary's house had been like a refuge for the past few days and apart from daily forays down to the corner shop, I hadn't been out in the real world at all. It was good to be back. Nobody knew where I was or what I was doing at that particular moment. It felt like freedom. The fact that I was just sitting in McDonald's having the breakfast special on O'Connell Street didn't matter a jot. I decided I would go and give a pint of blood on d'Olier Street and then go to Eason and wander for an hour. It was raining, so I bought one of those ridiculously cheerful umbrellas: a pink one with tiny purple elephants clinging onto tails of white balloons. It was gorgeous. Of course, by the time the rain stopped, one of the spokes had snapped.

I dreaded going home. Facing Caroline. Had she got the letter?

I sat in a café for hours, maybe the one where Caroline had sat with her horrendous blind date. A fly-killing machine hung from a wall, shedding lines of bright blue light across the table. I drank cup after cup of black coffee and read from one of the books I'd bought. It was one of my favourite poems. 'Digging' by Seamus Heaney. I'd just finished the second verse of it:

Under my window, a clean rasping sound,
When the spade sinks into gravely ground,
My father, digging. I look down.

The thought came, like a worm threading through earth. Once it was there, I couldn't get rid of it. Even when I left the café and set off along the canal and walked for hours – first up one side, then down the other – it was still there, still wriggling, like a fish on a hook.

Eventually, I hailed a taxi, not surprised when the very first one I flagged down stopped immediately. The taxi driver leaned across and opened the passenger door for me. He smiled, like he'd been expecting me.

51

It was dark when I got there. The car pulled up at the gates and the driver killed the engine, as if he was getting out as well. I paid him, adding a bigger tip than usual. He'd been kind and hadn't asked any questions when I'd told him where I wanted to go.

'Thanks,' I said.

'Good luck,' was all he said.

The gates were shut but I could see people moving around inside. There seemed to be a lot of people, dark shapes bent at the upright stones, silvery in the moonlight. It was a weekday night. Cold and dark and damp and yet there were people here. It was comforting in its way and I didn't feel afraid. I thought I would feel afraid – maybe that's why I'd never come back.

I walked towards the gates, my heels loud against the path. People turned from their dead to look at me, then looked away again. Just another mourner, only in unsuitable shoes. One woman sat on a folding chair, knitting by the light of a kerosene lamp glowing beside her. She was talking but I couldn't hear what she said. She might have been in a living room, she looked so at home. A man knelt on a mat with rosary beads threaded through his fingers, his lips moving, making no sound. Two people perched on a low wall around one of the graves. Talking. Like they were in the pub on a Friday night. People nodded at me but said nothing. Perhaps they were regulars here? People who knew the graveyard etiquette. Nod but don't talk. Smile but don't laugh. Pray with no sound.

I couldn't remember where Patrick was. Were the graves in alphabetical order? No, of course not. People don't die in alphabetical order. Otherwise people with surnames beginning with 'A' would be fucked. I walked and walked and what with the clacking of the heels and the chattering of my teeth, I was like a one-woman band. The moon slipped behind a cloud and an owl hooted, the sound floating from the shadows of trees. I felt like I was in a dream, where you keep on walking but stay in the same place, getting nowhere. And then I saw it. Patrick James O'Brien. Born 1972. Died 2004. The inscription was lines from a poem Patrick loved:

> *I will arise and go now, and go to Innishfree*
> *And a small cabin build there, of clay and wattles made:*
> *Nine bean-rows will I have there, a hive for the honey-bee,*
> *And live alone in the bee-loud glade.*
> *And I shall have some peace there, for peace comes dropping*
> *   slow,*

Dad's name was at the top of the headstone. Patrick Tomas O'Brien. I stood and looked at the grave. Now that I was here, I didn't know what to say, or if I should say anything.

'Hello, Patrick,' I whispered. I reached into the depths of my bag and pulled out a mini bottle of Bell's.

'Cheers' I said before pouring the amber liquid onto the soil near the head of the grave. 'Sorry I didn't come sooner. Since the funeral, I mean.' I pressed my hand into the soil where I had poured the whiskey. It was warm and wet. A gigantic black *creature* with more legs than any creature had a right to have slithered between my splayed fingers. I yelped and hauled myself to my feet before dancing the Dance of the Creepy Crawlie. You know this one. You shake your hands till they appear only as blurs at the end of your arms. *Both* your hands, mind, regardless of which one, heretofore, had been touched by The Creature. You also run on the spot and shake your head just in case The Creature decided that your head might be a nice place to bed down. After a while, you cease all movement and carefully check yourself, and the immediate vicinity, to see if there's any sign of him (it's always a him). There never is. You feel terribly itchy – all over. Not just on the part of the skin on the finger of the hand where he creeped and crawled.

It was only when I'd calmed down that I remembered the other people in the graveyard. But they must have become used to all sorts of antics because they didn't pay a blind bit of notice.

I was knackered after all that, and in the silence that followed, I smiled. Imagine if Patrick could really see me. Jaysus, he'd get such a laugh. Imagine if there really was a heaven and it really was the way I thought it was when I was younger. Full of gingerbread houses (everyone had their own) and little cobbled paths through leafy forests where no wolves lurked. And pancakes. Every morning for breakfast. And as many books as you could imagine. And a swimming pool in your garden. And a lilo in the pool that was just for you and not for sharing with brothers or sisters.

All around me was a low hum of people whispering and talking to their dead. I couldn't talk to Patrick. What would I say? I edged a bit closer and hunkered down, searching for a cigarette in my bag. I wondered if you were allowed to smoke in a graveyard? Then I told myself to stop being stupid and struck a match. In the flickering snatch of light, I saw the grave, beautifully tended with a cluster of rose bushes in the centre, buds dark and swollen, hanging heavy on the stems. A vase of lilies stood at the base of the headstone. It could be a garden, this grave. It could be entered into a garden competition it was so well tended. I lowered myself onto the marble lip that circled the grave and waited for something to occur to me. I knew I wasn't going to cry or pray or talk. In the end I decided to picture him in my mind, but it took a long time to pull the features of his face together. They kept getting away from me, dissolving like rain on a lake. And then there he was. Smiling. With the deep wells of dimples in his cheeks. The red hair tickling his collar. A couple of inches taller than me.

'Stop smiling, Patrick,' I used to say. 'Grumpy people age much better, you know.' My big brother who should have been thirty-two this year. Patrick James O'Brien. Born 1972. Died 2004. He used to wink at me and touch me briefly on my shoulder. That was his goodbye. I'd never said goodbye to him. I felt that now. That touch.

The memory comes slowly at first, like dawn on a cloudy day. It's Spain, but for the first time, it's not *that* day, it's the first day.

We are at the airport. Arrivals is a sea of bodies. The heat is like a wet shirt against my skin and the air is hot in my mouth. The three of us stand there, waiting. Shane slips his hand down the collar of his shirt, coaxing air down his neck. He lowers his hand then, slips it into mine. Our palms are wet and hot and make sucking noises when they part. I smile at him, still not quite able to believe that he is mine. I want to remember everything.

The scream is Caroline's and it seems to part the crowd.

'There he is,' she roars, her finger pointing towards the sliding doors. And there he is. He looks taller than I remember. The sun has painted even more freckles across his wide face, but his eyes are the same. Maybe bluer, but smiley and surprised with the wonder of the world in them. He is still Patrick and I am running, my bags dropped and forgotton. He swings me. He is the only man I know who can swing me. I come up to his jawline, even in my heels.

'Hello, Grace,' he says and his voice is even and low and sounds like he knows the answers to all my questions. I can see inside the bag he has slung around his shoulder. The zip is broken. There are pages inside and I recognise the sloping curl of the writing on them. He shakes Shane's hand and hugs Caroline at the same time.

'It's great to be home,' he says then.

'You're not home, you big eejit,' Caroline says.

'It feels like home,' he says and he looks at me in that way he has and we move towards the exit.

52

The taxi driver dropped me outside the flat but I didn't go in straight away. Instead, I walked to the top of the road and stood there, stalling. The sky was clear and I could see my breath gathering in front of my face. My hand burrowed around the bottom of my bag, reaching for cigarettes. The box, when I finally found it, was empty. I must have smoked them all in the graveyard.

The shop across the road was preparing to close, the shutters rattling in the silence. I ran.

'Ah, Grace, is it yourself?' It was Ray, the owner, counting the takings at the till. He always greeted me thus, like he was a seventy-five-year-old from Kerry. He was actually forty-something from Ranelagh.

''Tis,' said I, as I always did. I waited for him.

'And will ye be wantin' an aul' pack of fags? And maybe a coconut snowball to have with the cup of tay?'

'I will, Ray, thanks.'

We'd been having this same conversation for years, and tonight I took comfort from its familiarity.

Old man Jenkins shuffled into the shop after me and treated me to one of his wide gummy smiles. It felt like ages since I'd last seen him.

'Where have you been, Grace? The house hasn't been the same without you.'

'I was staying with Mary for a couple of days.'

'Oh,' was all he said. He'd met Mary once and let's just say once was enough.

'Is Caroline in?' I asked, holding my breath.

'She is. Her and her brother. That young man of yours.' Jesus. What was Shane still doing in the country? In my flat? He was like the bloody 15B. Never there when you need one and then lines of them taking up the road when you're stuck in the car.

We walked back to the house together. I walked slowly, partly because of Mr Jenkins's laboured gait, but mostly because I didn't want to get there. But I had to get supplies (the outfit I needed for the mass tomorrow) before heading to Laura's house: she'd sent me a text, *'mi casa es su casa'*, that I'd interpreted literally.

I had to go in.

'You're very quiet, Grace.' Mr Jenkins stopped at the gate for a rest before braving the driveway.

'I had a bit of a falling out with Caroline and Shane,' I explained with severe understatement. I sat up on the wall, finishing my cigarette.

'That's not like you,' he said. And he was right. I *never* fought with Caroline. There'd never been any need. Shane criticised and disapproved but because I always felt under an obligation to him – for being my boyfriend – I rarely fought with him.

'What happened?'

How to sum up?

'I slept with Caroline's boyfriend. Well, he wasn't her boyfriend at the time, but then I kissed him after they got together and Caroline saw me and told Shane, who beat up the boyfriend – Caroline's one – black and blue in the middle of Clare's wedding reception.' I ran out of breath, but in fairness, Mr Jenkins got the general gist.

'Do you fancy coming down for a whiskey and a toasted cheese sandwich?' Tempting though the offer was (the sandwich part), I declined.

'I'd better go and face the music upstairs,' I said, laughing. And, oddly, it wasn't a fake laugh at all. Granted, it was a quiet one. But real.

'If I hear knives rattling, I'll come up. Pretend I'm borrowing a cup of sugar, OK?'

'Thanks, Mr J.' I bent and kissed him briefly on the cheek, catching that faint smell of his, like fresh hay, dry and sweet.

The hall table was empty and already, that seemed ominous. No flyers, no Visa bills, no postcards from Laura. She was *always* going on holidays. Off to conquer Sweden this weekend, she'd say. Or Austria. Or Latvia. The letter I'd written to Caroline wasn't there. Maybe she'd read it? With nothing to distract me further, I continued towards the front door. It opened before I could turn the key in the lock.

'I heard you outside,' Shane said. 'Laughing.' The last word was like an accusation and I stood there, saying nothing, not sure how to plead. 'Are you coming in?'

'Is Caroline here?' I asked, looking over his shoulder.

'She's in the bath.' Relief washed through me like a spring tide. I wouldn't have to face her. Not tonight, anyway.

Shane stepped aside to let me in.

'I'm just getting something. I'm not staying.' I was anxious that he know that. He closed the door quietly. He looked tired. Still beautiful, of course, but tired.

'I didn't think you'd still be here,' I said.

'Yeah, I took a few days off work after the wedding,' he said. 'I'd planned to. Before everything . . . I was going to take you away. Take your mind off the anniversary, y'know?' The conversation with Shane was not what I was expecting. It was like a foreign country.

'Christ, Shane, I'm so sorry.' And I was.

'Do you want a drink?' The last time I'd seen him, he'd

been so angry. Now here was the calm after the storm, unsettling me.

'Eh, no thanks, I'm just . . .'

'Look Grace, I think we need to talk, don't you?'

The bathroom door was closed and I could hear the second song on Alison Moyet's greatest hits album. Caroline would stay in the bath until the end of the album, which gave me about twenty minutes.

'OK,' I said, nodding. I sat down on the edge of the couch. The flat was cleaner and tidier than usual, a monument to my absence. Shane handed me a bottle of beer and sat on the other end of the couch. He broke the silence first.

'Where have you been? And more seriously, what the hell are you wearing?' There was a ghost of a smile in his voice.

'They're Mary's clothes.' I was anxious to have that understood. 'I've been staying with her.' He nodded.

I put the beer bottle on the floor and straightened, taking a breath.

'Shane, I'm sorry.'

'I'm sorry too.'

'Why?' I asked. I hadn't been expecting that.

'Caroline told me that I've been neglecting you since I went to London. Since before that, really.'

Caroline had said that?

'Since Patrick died, I suppose.' He said it slowly, groping his way along the sentence.

'It wasn't your fault,' I said.

'I should have tried to help him. I should have been the one to go in after you. I was the strongest swimmer.'

'Patrick saved me,' I said. It was like noticing the stars for the first time. 'I was drowning and Patrick saved me.' I said it again, louder now, looking at the photograph on the mantelpiece. It might sound strange, but I'd never seen the incident from that angle before. My memories had sagged under the weight of my guilt. Gratitude. That's what it was. Lighter than air. Making me smile.

I was alive. Patrick had saved me.

Water belched through the pipes in the flat. Caroline must have pulled the plug.

'I'd better go,' I said, standing up. Shane stood up too and looked at me.

'You don't have to go. I don't want you to go. Maybe it doesn't have to be over,' he said. 'Maybe I could forgive you, for, you know, Brendan.'

'It's Bernard,' I said quietly.

'Whatever,' he said. 'We could get over that. People do it all the time.' There was an echo of panic in his voice and I recognised it. He was thinking about being alone. I'd had time to get used to the idea.

Just for a moment, I allowed myself to see us in his flat in London, sitting on the balcony sipping Pimm's and watching the sun sinking across the city, setting fire to London Bridge. But then I'd be wondering what he was thinking. If he regretted me. If my bum looked big in this skirt or that. I shook my head, and we were gone.

'It's not just that,' I said. 'It's not all about Bernard. Or even Patrick. It's you and me. You weren't happy. Not with me, anyway.'

'Why are you saying that? I don't know what you mean.'

'My weight, my hair, what I ate, the car I drove, the job I had, my clothes. You were never happy with any of it.' I was shocked, remembering all these things. And disgusted, remembering how I had accepted them all.

'That's not true. Not at all. Anything I said was for your own good. You know that.' I wasn't even going to dignify that with a response. Suddenly, I wanted this conversation to be over. I wanted to get on with the rest of my life. And I wanted the rest of my life to start as soon as possible.

'Listen to me, Shane.' I wanted him to understand. 'When you left, I was gutted.' He nodded. He could understand that bit. 'Then I got used to you being away, and not staying in contact.'

He opened his mouth to say something, already shaking his head.

'And the thing is, I realised that I liked it. I mean, I like you – being away. No, no, I don't mean it like that. What I mean is that I quite like *me* when you're not around. I prefer being around me when you're away. When you're here, I don't like myself. I don't like what you see. It's not me.' I stopped then, my tongue tangled in the words.

Silence hung between us like heavy curtains.

'I need more than that.' And then, 'I *deserve* more,' surprising myself.

'We wouldn't even be having this conversation if it weren't for that fucker Brendan.'

'It's *Bernard*,' I said, the only time I raised my voice.

He knew then that it was over. He turned and walked away, disappearing into the tiny room off the kitchen we called the computer room, closing the door. He was not expecting me to follow him.

I walked into my room and stuffed what I needed into a bag. There was a click and the bathroom door groaned open. Caroline stepped out into the hall, shrouded in white mist. I could smell lavender. I stepped out into the hall. She walked past me into the sitting room and at first I thought she wasn't going to say anything. She made for the mantelpiece, her hand reaching up, behind the photograph. When she turned back again, she was holding it in her hands. An envelope.

'Caroline, I . . .' She ignored me.

'This arrived,' was all she said.

'What is it?'

'It's for you.' She pushed it into my hands. For a moment,

we stood there, her hand in mine. She waited until I looked at her. Then she nodded, briefly, before going into her room, but the memory of her hand was warm. I looked down.

It was a letter. A proper letter, I mean. With a proper stamp and my name and address handwritten across the front of the envelope. The envelope was creased all over and torn at one corner. It was littered with postmarks. I recognised the hand-writing immediately and I stood there for a long time looking at it, afraid to open it, afraid not to. I looked at the postmarks: Thailand, Australia, Papua New Guinea, Mexico, Mauritius, England and finally here, where it belonged.

The oldest postmark was Thailand, the date 11 March 2004. The letter had taken over a year to get here. My hands shook as I fingered the envelope. The paper felt pulpy and damp in my fingers. I turned it around, knowing before I saw the name written on the back who it was from. According to the address scribbled on the back, it had been sent from the Haven Hostel, Queenstown, New Zealand. I opened it gently. Inside was a single page, covered in his familiar writing. '*Dear Grace,*' it began.

53

The church bulged with people, despite the rain. An ancient smell of incense mixed with steam rose from raincoats in the pews. Most of the congregation were Patrick's age. The age he should have been. He was always going to be thirty-one to us. I wore an outfit Patrick had commented on favourably, long ago. A dress, actually – bright orange – that clashed outrageously with my hair. Pink linen roses climbed the fabric that clung to my breasts and fell to just below my knees. The bright colours were a far cry from the funeral mass last year when we had dressed in shades of black. Who knew there were so many shades of black?

I was nervous. I recognised so many people. Friends of Patrick's from work, from school, from college, from the old neighbourhood, from everywhere, really. So many of them. I was proud: of them for remembering him, of him, for being remembered. What would he be doing now if he were alive? Something unexpected. Could he see us? I hoped he could. I inched up the side aisle of the church and spied my family in the pew at the front. Mam, Jack, Mary, Clare, Richard, Jane, James, Ella, Matthew and Thomas. They were bunched together like sausages in an egg pan. I crept into the third aisle from the front and rummaged in my bag again, closing my hand around the letter. It was still there.

The priest glided onto the altar as smoothly as if he were on wheels. Two small boys in white robes accompanied him. They held bells and walked to either side of the altar.

They knelt down, their heads bowed. The bells rang. The mass began.

I was surprised to find that this wasn't just Patrick's anniversary mass. He shared it with a woman called Eileen O'Rourke and a gentleman by the name of Hugh McLoughlin. Eileen had been dead for five years and poor old Hugh had left the world before I'd even been born. This was Patrick's first time. I hoped he would approve of what I was going to do.

I didn't hear much of the mass. I was distracted by the light pouring, like gold, through the stained glass behind the altar. I was distracted by the gonging of the bell when the church became as quiet as a grave and everyone bowed their heads. I was distracted by my mother, who held Ella tight to her for the duration, like a lifebelt. I was distracted by Mary, who spotted me and kept turning round and smiling at me with those great long teeth. I was distracted by Patrick, who should have been there and was not. I could feel him around me, like an arm around my shoulders.

And then it was nearly over and the priest began to speak. My heart rampaged about my chest like a bull.

'We are here today to mark the first anniversary of Patrick O'Brien's death,' he began in a routine-enough type of way. Then he looked up and coughed gently into a curled hand. The congregation seemed to lean forward in their pews.

'Patrick's sister, Grace, would like to say a few words to us today.' He looked up again, his eyes scanning the front row where my family sat. I could sense their shock, even from behind. Their bodies remained stationary but their heads rotated furiously as their whispers carried around the church. There was that rustling sound everywhere: that sound that people make when they expect something to happen. My legs felt heavy, like lead, as I reached into my bag and wrapped my hand again around the letter. I stood up. Heads swivelled towards me and I moved towards the altar. I'm not sure how

I got there, but I did. Up onto the altar and behind a lectern where the priest lifted the microphone as high as it would go to reach my mouth. When I opened my lips to speak, no sound came and I swallowed hard, longing for the communion wine, inches away from me, barely touched by the priest.

I cleared my throat. The sound was dry and rasping. It startled me and most of the congregation who stared at me. There was nothing else for it. I started to speak.

'I got a letter yesterday,' I began. 'It's come a long way. Sent more than a year ago. From Thailand originally. It got to as many countries as it could before it arrived at my flat. A bit like its sender: it was from Patrick. It reminded me that you don't have to be dead to still make sense, to still be here with us in some way, to still matter, to still be loved. I thought you might like to hear it.' I stopped but didn't look up. 'Anyway, this is what he says.'

Dear Grace,

It's so hot here. I can hardly feel myself breathe. Even my nasal hairs are bleached blond in this white heat. The clothes I have are all wrong: too much fabric. My landlady is called French Fry and is very beautiful in a long, dark, Thai way. She used to be a boy, she tells me, but she always knew she was a girl. Her body betrayed her, she says. It looks fine to me, to be honest. At first, I didn't know what to call her. She likes me to call her Chips. Says it reminds her of her Oirish roots (her great-great-great-grandfather was sent to Australia for looking sideways at a mayor's daughter and leapt off the boat near the southern Thai coastline).

Anyway. Where was I? I am in Chang Mai. The markets here are incredible. The smells hit you like a fist. Even if you're not hungry, your stomach rumbles. Here, they eat spiders and beetles and lizards and snakes and all manner of creepy crawlies. It would be your idea of the Anti-McDon-

ald's. I can't decide whether you would love it or hate it. It's noisy. I can see you itching your hair away from your face and clenching your mouth shut so you don't swallow any of the flies that blacken the space in front of you. Still, the people are lovely and the monkeys eat from your hands, if you let them.

A place like this makes you think about life. What is it for? A lot of these people are Buddhists. They lay altars at dawn for their gods. Beautiful flowers and the freshest foods are set out in heavy trays in front of gold statues. The flowers wither in the sun. The food dries and shrinks. Still the people come the next day at dawn. They collect the wilted flowers, they pick up the food that hasn't been eaten by monkeys – hard and curling – and set the altar again. Their Buddhas are magnificent, some of them 100 feet high, gleaming in their gold, with smiles as wide as the world. Our god is nailed to a cross: bloodied and beaten. No wonder these people smile. Their god smiles. There will be a happy ever after.

After travelling so much and seeing so many different people's gods, I can wonder at it all. We can't all be right, right? Our god is all about repentance, while here, it's about well-being. To be honest, Grace, I don't believe in any of it. We go down the mossy bank, as Dad used to say, and that's an end to it. Make the most of it while we're here. Anyway, enough philosophy.

Really looking forward to Spain next month. Looking forward to swimming in water that is cold and blue. Looking forward to seeing you and your big hair.

It's seems funny now, my travels are nearly at an end. I have seen the world and am none the wiser. But I have seen some beautiful things. Seals on warm rocks at sunset. Dolphins jumping out of water in slow semi-circles. Snow-white water rushing through a blow hole. A volcanic lake, the colour of cornflowers. Towering pyramids. A bear, standing on his back legs with a grin – yes, a grin – about his mouth. It still doesn't mean anything. We are born. We die. It's what we do in between that counts. I really believe that. And I have decided that I am going to do everything in between.

Love from Patrick

54

I reached the grave before everyone else. I made sure of that. I settled myself on the edge of the plot, balancing my bum on the thin marble lip, as before. There was no sign of The Creature. The grave looked different in the daylight.

I could hear voices now, breaths straining as they came slowly up the hill. I pulled myself up, gripping the headstone. The stone was warm beneath my hand.

They stopped in a knot, just a few feet from the grave. Caroline was there too, although she stood a little apart from the main group. Clare caught my eye and smiled gently at me. Ella and the boys chased around the headstones. Jane tried to stop them with fierce movements of her eyebrows, to which they paid no attention.

My mother and grandmother stood tight together and when Mam looked up, her face was wet with tears that she didn't try to brush away. I stepped towards her.

'Mam, I'm sorry. I'm so sorry,' I whispered.

She looked at me and smiled through her tears.

'That was brave, Grace. What you did in the church. I was proud of you.'

'I'm sorry, Mam,' I said again, my voice hoarse from holding back tears.

'I know, Gracie,' she said, shaking her head. 'I'm sorry too, love.' She reached her hand out to me and I took it and we stood there, holding hands and crying and then laughing when Mary took the opportunity to let rip one of her outlandishly loud – but never smelly – farts that rent the peaceful air of the graveyard with a roar. If Mary was put out by the hilarity caused by the breaking of wind in the graveyard, she didn't show it. Instead she reached into her bag and extracted a bottle of brandy and several paper cups, which she doled out very efficiently to everyone, considering her great age. When she had poured a finger of brandy into each of the cups, she raised hers and waited for silence.

'A toast,' she said, with an authoritative air.

We waited for her to continue. I could tell Mam was anxious, wondering what Mary might say. Her fingers curled around mine and I tightened my grip, so she knew I understood.

'To Patrick,' said Granny at last. 'May he go in peace.' We all drank to that and Granny poured the rest of the bottle of brandy on top of the grave. No wonder the rose bush was doing so well.

The walk back from the graveyard was much easier than the walk up. For starters, it was downhill, which is always good. The warm breeze dried my tears, Jane hugged me and Ella told me she wanted to be just like me when she grew up. I caught up with Caroline at her car.

'Caroline, I . . .'

'Stop, Grace.' Caroline cut me off. She fixed me with one of her looks before continuing. 'Just tell me one thing. Do you love him?'

'Jesus, Caroline, I can't just . . .'

'Just answer the question, Grace. You can only answer yes or no.' Caroline waited, looking straight at me. I took a deep breath.

'Yes,' I said.

'Good,' she said, turning to get into her car.

'What do you mean?' I asked.

'Well, I'd hate to think you did it just because you liked him. Or to get back at Shane.'

'No, no, Caroline. I really do love him and I think that he . . .' I stopped there, biting my lip.

'Go on,' said Caroline.

'I think he loves me.'

'I think he does too,' Caroline said.

'Why?'

'You're hard not to love, Grace.'

'Am I?'

'You are. Now, go on with you. I've had enough of being selfless and understanding for one day, thank you very much. I'll see you later, back at the flat.' She drove away without looking back. I stood for a while, watching her go, and for the first time in a long time, I felt something good inside me and I wondered what it was. Then I knew and I smiled. It was hope.

My mobile squawked inside my bag and I rummaged for it. It was a text. From Bernard.

Would love to see you. Are you free?

I'm on my way, I texted back.

And I was.

EPILOGUE

March 2006

Richard and Clare have been married now for nearly a year and are as happy as ever. Clare's belly is swollen like a basketball, but that's OK, because she's about to give birth to Richard the Second any day now. They know it's a boy and have decorated the nursery in shades of blue and white. It looks like a pin-striped suit. In fact, it looks like a welcoming committee from Richard's company. Clare weighs more than I do and even though I'm not pregnant, it still feels nice.

Jane is the chairman of the board of the local primary school and gets to tell people where they can and can't park, which makes her happier than I can tell you. Herself and James have recently returned from their very first weekend away without the children. Well, they lasted for one night and came home because James was bitten by a dog (at least, that's what they said).

Mam got married again. To a man we call Jack Frost – but only if we know Mam is not in the building, or preferably the country, at the time. She smiles and seems younger than before. Jack moved in with her and they've spent the last year redecorating. Jane's old room is now the spare room and Patrick's room is still Patrick's room.

Laura and Peter have Moved In Together. Laura maintains that Peter is still her Work In Progress and that she will release him back into the wild any day now. But we know better, don't we?

Caroline is going out with a guy called Bill Gately (I swear to God). He's an entrepreneur. A millionaire. Or a billionaire. She's moved into his castle (not pink, more of a mint green) on Killiney Hill and has learned to cook moussaka (his mother is one-quarter Greek). But there's always Baked Alaska on the menu when we go there for dinner. She knows it's my favourite. Sometimes Shane is there with Brazil. The girlfriend. Not the country. He moved back to Ireland six months ago. He's still beautiful, of course, just not *my* brand of beautiful, if you know what I mean.

And me? Check me out. I am lying on a beach on some island in the Caribbean. I can't remember the name of it just now. He is sucking my toes and, with the heat of the sun, the warmth of the margarita in my belly and the softness of the sand through the towel under my back, I can't think straight. Toe jobs: Don't knock them till you've tried them. That's all I can say on the subject. For the moment, anyway.

And then he stops. But wait, he's working up my legs, licking and kissing. He stops when he gets to the edge of my bikini. A certain modicum of propriety has to be maintained on the beach, I suppose.

'Grace,' he says, and I love it. I love the way he says my name. Like fingertips on skin.

'Yes?' I push my elbows into the warm sand and raise my head, slightly breathless. And there he is. The pale length of him, his skin shrouded in factor 50 in this melting sun. And he smiles at me. And I smile at him.

'I think we should get one of those patio heaters for the back garden,' he says.

'Why?'

'So we can do this at home.'

'Maybe we should get an awning too. Just in case it rains.' In my new world, rain in Ireland is only a possibility.

'Brilliant,' he says, looking at me like I'm the only person in the room. Or on the beach.

Then he lowers his face to mine. And when he kisses me, it feels like chocolate, melting in my mouth.

ACKNOWLEDGEMENTS

It was my mother really. She was the one who introduced me to them: Anne Shirley of *Green Gables*, Jo, my favourite of the Little Women, Mary Lennox from *The Secret Garden*; all the greats that I read and re-read and read again until I knew them off by heart. To be a writer, you have to be a reader, and my mother gave me the gift of reading at an early age. My father's role was more logistical, as father's roles often are. He drove me to the library every week; that was our time together and I remember it with great affection. For this, and for everything else, I thank them both.

I started writing 3½ years ago when I signed up for a creative writing course in Whitehall College, mostly to get out of the house of an evening and occupy my brain with something other than child-rearing and dirty dishes. Emma Sweeney taught the class and under her gentle persuasion, guidance and encouragement, I started to really write. People like Emma should be cloned and given to everyone who ever had a dream; thank you, thank you, thank you.

I would like to thank my writing group who read the first, shaky-legged drafts of *Saving Grace* and provided fantastic feedback, suggestions and advice. Their enthusiasm for the project was an invaluable source of encouragement and motivation. Thank you Pauline, Mark, Noreen, Aisling, Bernadette and Maeve.

Thanks also to my agent, Ger Nichol. Her enthusiasm, support and guidance has been fantastic.

Thanks to everyone at Hachette Books Ireland who have made me feel so welcome. A special thank you to my editor,

Ciara Doorley whose commitment and professionalism are hugely appreciated.

Thanks to Colm Toibin who, at a public talk in Baldoyle Library, advised a roomful of aspiring writers to 'let the house go to wrack and ruin'. I took his advice literally and wrote, ignoring the crumbs on the dining-room table and the stains on the kitchen floor. There is great freedom in being able to do this and I would advise all aspiring writers to follow suit. Also, think on this; if you mop the floors today, they'll only have to be done again next week . . . and the week after. My house may be in disarray but my book is published and that beats clean floors any day of the week.

Thank you to Lynda Laffan for reading parts of this book and taking the time to give me her insightful feedback and advice.

Thank you to Gerard Donovan and Denise Deegan, who read parts of this book and offered invaluable advice and encouragement.

A big thank you to my sister, Niamh who read this book from the beginning, who encouraged me when I didn't know what to write next, who cheered me all the way to the finishing line, who is always there for me. Everyone should have a sister like you.

During the writing of this book, my children, Sadhbh and Neil, were endlessly patient with me and did not kick up too much of a stink if I took them to the chip shop for their dinner instead of ladling up home-made soups and wild mushroom risottos. Thank you for that. I must also mention our brand new baby, Grace who, at the time of writing, is two weeks old today. She sleeps through the night which is the reason that I can write this without falling asleep across the keyboard. Thank you Grace.

And finally, an almighty thank you to my husband and best friend, chief bottle washer and doer of laundry, and maker of shepherd's pies, Frank MacLochlainn. This book would not have been written without your constant support, love and kindness. Thank you for giving me the space and time to write.